THE ANGLESEY MURDERS...

UNHOLY ISLAND

CONRAD JONES

The Anglesey Murders
Unholy Island
A Visit from the Devil
Nearly Dead
A Child for the Devil
Dark Angel
What Happened to Rachel?

The Journey (May 2018)
DI Braddick Series
Brick
Shadows
Guilty
Deliver us from Evil
Alec Ramsay Series
Nearly Dead
The Child Taker
Slow Burn
Criminally Insane
Frozen Betrayal
Desolate Sands
Concrete Evidence
Thr3e
Soft Target Series
Soft Target
Tank
Jerusalem
Blister
18th Brigade

PROLOGUE

Liam stepped over the low wall onto the clifftop. It was too dark to see the surf crashing onto the jagged rocks hundreds of feet below. Out to sea, the South Stack lighthouse stood stoic in the foaming sea; its powerful beam penetrated the darkness for miles. He sipped from the whisky bottle and felt the liquid burning his throat. It was an expensive single malt he'd saved for a special occasion. What could be more special than finding out his wife had been cheating with his brother? That was pretty special. Being made redundant the following day was special too, especially as the firm had gone bust and he wouldn't be paid his salary or any redundancy pay. If there was ever a more special time, he couldn't think of it.

Earlier, as his wife, Carla, walked out of the front door with his son and daughter and their suitcases, he'd made his mind up that he was going to kill himself. What was there to live for? Everything he loved had gone to live with the only family he had left. Wife, son, daughter, and brother gone in one breath, followed by the threat of financial ruin; he didn't have many options. The thought of unemployment and being alone, without his kids, was devastating. He couldn't go on. As he teetered on the edge of the cliff, his future played out before him. Divorce, repossession, bankruptcy, heartbreak, and despair.

He gulped the whisky and took a handful of tramadol from his pocket, swallowing them greedily. Better to numb his body as much as possible. He was a coward, Carla said. She was right. He wanted to die but he didn't want to feel the pain of impact on the rocks, nor did he want to feel the bitter cold of the sea or suffer the dreadful panic of drowning if he survived the fall. Numbness was the answer. He filled his mouth with tablets again and washed them down with whisky. He heard the sound of a car on the wind. The headlights pierced the night and he heard a door open and slam closed. Then he heard footsteps on the gravel path. Someone was coming towards him.

Suddenly, he felt frightened. Frightened of falling over the edge, frightened of dying. Something inside him told him he had to pull up his big-boy pants and get on with it. Life was worth living. Was he the first man to feel the sting of betrayal? No, of course not. The wind rocked him and he could feel the fog of the drugs descending in his mind. He edged back from the abyss and held onto the low wall. The silhouette of a man appeared on the path. He walked towards him quickly. The car's headlights picked him out against the dark sky. It was a common place for desperate people to contemplate life and death. Some walked away, others didn't.

'Are you okay?' a voice asked from the darkness. Liam blinked against the lights.

'Not really,' Liam said. He swigged from the bottle again, almost draining it.

'Are you thinking of stepping off the edge?' the man asked.

'Thinking about it, yes,' Liam said. 'At least, that was the plan. I can't even do that right.'

'You shouldn't be too hard on yourself,' the man said. 'Life can be difficult sometimes. Death is a way out.'

'I thought it was,' Liam agreed.

'You should embrace it,' the man said approaching. He raised his right hand.

'Embrace what?' Liam asked, confused. The whisky was slowing him down. He tried to grasp the man's hand.

'Close your eyes and enjoy the ride,' the man said. He shoved Liam hard in the chest.

Liam staggered backwards. He opened his mouth to scream but the wind took it away. His arms grabbed at thin air as he toppled over the edge. It seemed like an eternity before he hit the rocks.

The man waited and watched as the lighthouse illuminated the cliffs for a few seconds before it was plunged into darkness again. A wave swept the body from the rocks and sucked him beneath the surface. It was the first time he'd killed and it felt good.

CHAPTER 1

Detective Inspector Alan Williams parked near the top of the slipway at Trearddur Bay. The tide was high, and the rain was pelting down. He glanced at his passenger. Kim, his detective sergeant, was staring at the rain through the windscreen; her view was warped and blurred, like looking through melted plastic. Alan shook his head as the wind rocked his BMW. The storm was intense. Neither of them wanted to climb out of the vehicle. The wind was driving the sea against the rocks, pounding the shore, and sending huge waves across the promenade with awesome force. A wall of water hit the windows of the Black Seal, threatening to shatter them and swamp the drinkers and diners inside.

'It's packed in there,' Alan said, wishing he was in the bar.

'It's always packed in there. It's the best view on the island, especially with a large gin in your hand,' Kim said. 'There's Barry with the lifeboat.'

The orange clad lifeboat crew were gathered in the car park to Alan's right and he recognised some of the men as the senior members of the station. One of them spotted his car and jogged over, holding the hood of his floatation suit over his head to stop the rain seeping in. Alan didn't want to open the window to talk to him but did so anyway. The wind whistled through the small gap.

'Jump in the back,' Alan said, closing the window as quickly as possible.

'Thanks for coming out,' Barry shouted over the wind. The back door opened and he climbed in, accompanied by the gale. He slammed the door closed and shook the rain from his grey hair. Retirement from the service wasn't far off. 'We weren't sure what we had at first but we are now.'

'The call was a bit vague,' Alan said. He had been at home, less than a mile away when the call came through. 'What is it you think you have?' The wipers struggled to clear the windscreen as the deluge continued.

'It's a double fatality,' Barry said.

'Double?' Kim said. Barry nodded.

'Are they fishermen?' Alan asked, assuming anglers had been swept from the rocks again. He couldn't imagine anyone had launched a boat in such weather.

'We don't think so. A wave watcher spotted something off the rocks at Craig-y-Mor this morning. We launched but couldn't find anything.' Barry pointed to a place beyond the dark rocks at the mouth of the bay. 'The tide has brought them around the headland into the bay. One of them is wearing red waterproof trousers, so he's quite visible. We spotted them from the lookout platform about half an hour ago but we can't get to them until the tide turns.'

'It's rough out there,' Kim said. She turned in her seat. Her wavy blond hair was tied back in a ponytail. 'You sound certain they're not fishermen.'

'Yes. That's why I phoned you. This isn't an accident. They're tied together at the feet,' Barry said. 'It'll be a while before we can get them away from the rocks but it's clearly a suspicious death.'

'Tied together at the feet?' Alan said to himself. He turned to face Barry. 'That's a first for me. Have you seen anything like that before?'

'Similar but not quite like this,' Barry said. 'The way they're dressed is bizarre. I'm not a hundred per cent sure but they appear to be naked from the waist up and we think they're missing some limbs. They both have wellington boots on.' He shook his head and frowned. 'The waterproofs made us think they might be seamen involved in a boating accident until we saw they were bound together. It's odd to say the least.'

'They wouldn't lose their clothes in the water?' Kim said.

'Not like that. I remember we pulled two men out from near Rhoscolyn, about ten years ago. They'd been tied together, just like them. We couldn't find out where they came from. The coast guard investigated a couple of big foreign tankers that had sailed through our waters but they were both from south east Asia with Asian crew. The men we pulled out were European; DNA said they were probably Iberian.'

'What happened?' Kim asked. Fine lines creased the corners of her green eyes despite the gallons of creams she'd applied. 'Did they turn anything up?'

'Nope. It was a dead end.'

'Where do you think they were from?' Kim asked.

'I've got no idea,' Barry said. 'My best guess is they were from Spain or Portugal sailing a small craft, carrying something they shouldn't have been carrying, probably from Morocco.' He tapped his nose with his index finger. 'Cannabis is a huge business and most of it comes in by boat. They were probably double-crossed by their buyers somewhere down the coast, tied up, and thrown overboard and their boat scuppered. No one knew they were here so nobody reported them missing. We'll never know where they were from.'

'Drug smugglers, eh? Makes sense,' Kim said.

'There's nine-hundred miles of Welsh coastline, most of it is remote and unwatched,' Alan said. 'There's all kinds of shenanigans going on out there that we'll never know about.'

'True,' Kim said.

'One thing I do know for sure is no one gets half naked, puts on a pair of wellington boots, ties himself to his mate, and jumps into the sea in a storm,' Alan said, nodding his head.

'You should be a detective,' Kim said. Alan looked at her and smiled. She had an acidic sense of humour that he loved. 'I'll get a CSI team on standby.'

'Yes please,' Alan said.

A knock on the driver's window interrupted them. One of the lifeboatmen gestured to Alan to wind the window down. Reluctantly, he did.

'There's a call for you in the station, Inspector,' the man said. 'They've been trying to reach you on your phone.' Alan checked his mobile, but the screen was blank.

'Bloody phone signals. It's like being on the moon here,' Alan moaned. 'I'll be retired by the time they sort out the signal in the bay. Or chief inspector.'

'Or dead,' Kim said. 'In the meantime, you'd better go and take that call.' Alan frowned and shook his head. 'Are you pulling rank on me?' she asked.

'I'm afraid so. Your legs are younger, and my knee is giving me gip again. I'd better stay here and keep a look out just in case.'

'Just in case of what?'

'In case something happens.'

Kim shook her head and opened the door. She was greeted by an icy blast and a deluge of rainfall. Alan could hear her swearing beneath her breath as she ran towards the lifeboat station. He chuckled as he watched her. She stooped and ran against the wind.

'What time does the tide change?' Alan asked, looking at his watch.

'She's on the turn now,' Barry said. 'We'll have to wait a little longer to recover them. They're too close to the rocks. The wind will drop on the wane. We'll be able to grab them in about half an hour.'

'I don't suppose it's going to make much difference to them,' Alan said. Barry's radio crackled into life. The bodies had been caught by a riptide and taken out to open water. One of the smaller lifeboat ribs had secured the bodies to the boat and was dragging them across the bay towards the ramp.

'They're bringing them to the ramp now,' Barry said. 'Ten minutes at the most.'

'Let's go and have a look,' Alan said. He opened the door and climbed out into the wind. Barry was right, it had dropped and changed direction. He fastened his zip to the neck and pulled up the hood, tucking his hands deep into his pockets. They walked to the ramp where all leisure crafts were launched from and waited for the lifeboat to return. A crowd of onlookers had gathered near the station, filming the recovery on their smartphones. The rib navigated the rocks with well-practised ease; the bodies left in the water, supported on floatable cradles to stop them breaking up. Alan could see they weren't bloated yet.

'They don't look like they've been in very long?' Alan said. He studied the bindings around the ankles. It was orange rope, the type used by trawlermen and yachters. The rope was strapped around both ankles and knotted tightly. 'What do you think, Barry?'

'They're not nautical knots,' Barry said. 'They've been tied by someone who doesn't know one end of a boat from another.'

'So, we can rule out seamen.'

'Yes. These knots could be unfastened easily on land but not in the water. They had no chance of escaping the rope once they were in the sea.'

'They had no chance in this weather anyway,' Alan said. 'They're both missing an arm. This one below the elbow and this one at the shoulder.'

'The wounds to the arms are jagged,' Barry said. 'I think they've gone under a boat and been caught in the propeller.' He turned one of them in the water. 'There are more injuries here. This boy suffered before he went in. Look at his back.' Barry pointed to a series of deep wounds that had been cleaned by the seawater.

'Do you think a propeller could do that?' Alan asked.

'Propellers make a real mess, like the arms here' Barry said, shaking his head. 'The wounds to the back are too neat, too symmetrical to be from a boat. If you ask me, they're knife wounds.'

'So, he was tortured, then dropped into the sea?' Alan asked. Barry nodded. He looked at the waves crashing in. 'When did they go in the water?'

'My guess would be yesterday,' Barry said. 'Certainly not much longer than that.'

'If they were spotted at Craig-y-Mor this morning and then floated into the bay, where did they go in?' Alan asked. Barry raised his eyebrows and tilted his head. He scratched his mottled scalp. 'I'm not going to hold you to it. Just give me your best guess.'

'The way the wind has been howling this week, I reckon they were put in on the Holyhead side of North Stack. The tides have brought them around the mountain, by South Stack, and then the rip carried them into the bay,' Barry said.

Alan looked at the man in the red waterproofs. His face was disfigured and bruised. The damage was done before they were put into the sea. It was obvious both men had been tortured before they drowned. They were both dark-haired and well built, probably in their thirties. Kim trotted over and stood next to him.

'They're quite fresh. White European,' Kim said.

'Yes. This one has a lot of tattoos,' Alan said, looking at a full-sleeve. 'Most of his ink are skulls and red rose designs, common in the UK.'

'I can't see any sign of a red dragon or any text in Welsh,' Kim said. 'There's nothing to indicate he's Welsh.'

'I agree,' Alan said. 'What was the call about?'

'We've got another body,' Kim said.

'In the water?' Barry asked.

'No,' Kim said. She seemed distracted by the bodies.

'Where is the body, Kim?' Alan asked.

'On the range near Porth Dafarch Beach,' Kim said. 'It's a male, bound and beaten. Uniform are there and CSI are on the scene already.'

'Three bodies in one day,' Alan said.

'No early dart for you today,' Barry said.

'It doesn't look like it, does it,' Alan agreed. 'Are there any pockets in those waterproofs?' Kim lifted the material to reveal a plastic zip. She undid it and looked inside, pulling out a soggy piece of paper. 'It looks like a receipt of some kind. Can you read it?'

'No. The ink has smudged. I'll bag it.' She pulled a clear plastic bag from her coat and slipped the paper inside. She repeated the process on the other side. A soggy packet of Lambert and Butler tumbled out, along with a disposable lighter. 'Those things will kill you,' she muttered. She pulled the waistband of the waterproofs away from the body. 'Armani underwear. They're not cheap.' Kim moved to the second body and looked inside the wellington boots. 'Look here. They're stamped with the size and where they were distributed.' Alan looked over her shoulder. 'Wylfa Power Station. They're possibly local.'

'I'm not so sure,' Alan said.

'Why not?' Kim asked.

'There are so many subcontractors working on the new site. They're from all over the country,' Alan said. 'Let's see what forensics come up with. We might get lucky.' He checked his watch and walked towards the car. 'We need to take a look at our other victim before the rain destroys everything. Thanks, Barry, and say thanks to the crew.'

'No problem. We'll see the bodies are put into the van.'

Alan ran back to the BMW and climbed in. Kim was a few seconds behind him. He switched the heater onto full blast to clear the windscreen and smiled. Kim blew on her hands.

'Who called this one in?' Alan asked. He pulled out onto the winding road which led to Porth Dafarch. It was a five-minute drive.

'A dog walker,' Kim said. 'Uniform were there quickly and confirmed it's suspicious.'

They were quiet as they drove around the Cliff Bends. The sea was creating a vista that was impossible to ignore. Seaweed and debris littered the road on the lower stretches. As they approached Porth Dafarch, he pulled over onto a grass verge. He could see a white forensic tent about two-hundred yards across a hilly field. It was bending beneath the wind. Rock outcrops dotted the field covered in yellow mosses and spikey gorse. Sheep grazed lethargically, oblivious to the wind. Life on the range carried on as normal. Two police cars were parked further down a steep hill, close to the beach and there was a people carrier parked on the opposite slope near a public toilet block, a CSI van next to it. They climbed out of the BMW and walked towards a stone stile. Alan climbed over and waited for Kim on the other side, helping her down. She managed it with far more grace than he had. His joints were beginning to ache in symphony with each other. The right knee was painful if he walked more than a few yards but he refused to cause a fuss by going to a doctor. They walked into the wind towards the tent. They could hear the waves crashing into the cliffs just a few hundred yards further on and foamy spume floated on the wind. It was all part of living on a rock in the Irish Sea. The smell of the sea was powerful and made him feel like he belonged there. He couldn't imagine living anywhere else. They were greeted by a uniformed officer and ducked into the tent. The odour of the dead engulfed them.

'Afternoon, Inspector,' the CSI greeted him. He hadn't seen her before. She was a redhead with corkscrew curls and white teeth. Her smile was welcoming. 'I'm Pamela Stone,' she said.

'Alan Williams,' he said.

'DS Kim Davies,' Kim said.

'Do we know who this is?' Alan asked.

'This is Kelvin Adams,' Pamela said. 'He's been sprayed with pepper spray, tied up, and beaten around the head and shoulders with a blunt instrument. He's stiff so my estimated time of death is late last night to early hours of this morning.'

'He had ID on him?' Kim asked.

'Yes.'

'Where was it?'

'Uniform found his wallet in the toilet block. His clothes are in the disabled cubicle. It was in the pocket of his trousers, hung on the back of the door. He got undressed for some reason.'

'How did he get here?'

'The people carrier parked on the hill is registered to him at an address in Pensarn.'

'Pensarn?' Alan said. 'That's fifty miles away. It's a long way to come to use a public toilet in the middle of the night.'

'That would depend on what you're using the toilet for,' Pamela said. Alan nodded in agreement. He noticed a wedding ring on his finger. Pamela followed his gaze. 'There's a wife. She's registered on the vehicle insurance along with two teenagers.'

'Have they been informed?' Kim asked.

'No, not yet. Uniform wanted to wait for you to arrive.'

'What do you think the sequence was?' Alan asked.

'He parked up the car and went somewhere. His clothes are soaked. Then he went into the toilets, got partially undressed. He was disabled with pepper spray, tied up, and beaten to death. I think he was forced to walk over the grange. His feet are cut and full of thorns from the gorse, then he was killed here.'

'Is there money in his wallet?' Kim asked.

'Yes. Over a hundred quid and his debit cards are there, along with his driving license,' Pamela said.

'That rules out a robbery gone wrong,' Kim said. 'The level of violence used is unusual. Do you think it could've been personal?'

'You think he knew his killer?'

'Maybe. He was comfortable enough to remove his trousers and hang them up. It's not exactly a fumble in the dark, is it?'

'Where are the rest of his clothes?' Alan asked.

'We haven't found them yet but with this wind, they could be halfway across the Irish Sea. I've asked uniform to search the headland a hundred yards from the victim. I'm sure you'll expand that anyway,' Pamela said. 'His hands are bound with duct tape.'

'The wounds on his head look circular,' Alan said. 'Was it a hammer?'

'I think so,' Pamela said. 'There are two deep penetrating wounds to his shoulder, so I'm thinking it was a claw hammer although we haven't found it yet.'

'That's not the type of tool you carry around in your pocket,' Kim said. 'Or take to a sexual encounter for that matter. The killer came prepared to disable the victim with pepper spray, bind him with duct tape, and beat him with a claw hammer. It was all premeditated.'

'Looking at the bruising here and here,' Pamela said, pointing to the side of the trachea. 'I would say he was strangled too.'

'What with?'

'The attacker's bare hands.'

'So, we're thinking it was a premeditated attack,' Alan said. 'And quite possibly personal. Where's his mobile phone?'

'We haven't found one yet,' Pamela said.

'Is the vehicle open?' Alan asked.

'No. It's locked.'

'Have we found any keys?'

'No.'

'Ask uniform to get an auto-locksmith to open his vehicle and search it. His mobile phone might be in it,' Alan said. Kim nodded and spoke to the officer outside. She ducked back inside a few seconds later. 'Let's hope whoever he arranged to meet here didn't take his phone. Let's find out what network he's on and get a request into his phone provider and see who he was communicating with yesterday.'

'Are you taking him to Bangor?' Alan asked.

'Yes. The rain has removed a lot of our evidence but we may get lucky.'

'I'll have his wife meet us there to identify him. I need to ask her some tricky questions.'

'Rather you than me,' Pamela said. 'Do you want me to expedite the results?'

'Yes, please. I'll clear the cost with head office.'

'Guv,' a voice called. Alan stepped outside. 'We've found a bin bag with waterproof clothing in it. The car keys are in the pocket.'

'Where was the bag?' Alan asked.

'Snagged on a rock over the cliff edge. It looks like someone tossed it off the cliff but couldn't see it had snagged on a rock in the dark,' the officer said.

'Good man,' Alan said. 'Let's have a look inside, shall we?' He turned back to the tent. 'Thanks, Pamela. I'll speak to you later.' She nodded and went back to her investigation.

Alan and Kim walked across the grassy slopes, avoiding the clumps of brambles and nettles, climbed over the stile, and approached the people carrier. It was a dark-blue Ford Galaxy. The lights flashed as it was unlocked.

Alan opened the driver's door and Kim opened the passenger door. The vehicle was spotless and smelled of pine air-freshener. They searched the glove box and the door pockets but found nothing of interest. Alan opened the rear passenger door and closed it just as quickly, then moved onto the rear doors. Kim was next to him as he opened them. The space was packed neatly with fishing equipment. A tackle box, several carbon rods, and a large keepnet. Alan looked at Kim. She shrugged.

'Maybe he didn't come all this way to meet someone,' Kim said. 'Maybe he came here to fish.'

'In this storm?' Alan said. 'There's not much fishing going on tonight. This equipment is bone dry but his waterproofs are soaked.'

'We need to speak to his wife,' Kim said. She was going to add something about women's intuition but didn't need to. Alan nodded that he knew what she meant.

CHAPTER 2

He watched the CSI officers working. They were concentrating their efforts on the body and the toilet block. The vehicle had been removed on a trailer an hour before. He'd watched them finding the bag of clothes and retrieving it from the cliff. That was a mistake. The killer must have thought he'd tossed it hard enough to reach the sea but the wind was so strong it brought it back. Nothing had gone to plan by the look of things. The victim was stronger than he looked and had made it impossible to carry out the original plan. He guessed the intention was to march him to the cliffs, untie him, and throw him off but he'd struggled so hard, he had to be killed there and then. He couldn't carry the body across the grange in the darkness with that wind against him, so he left him where he died. It was a calculated risk. The killer guessed the chances were the police would never connect him to the murder, not in a million years. That's what he thought happened. He might be wrong and it didn't really matter if he was right or not but deconstructing crimes helped him to remain at liberty. Killing someone was easy, getting away with it was not.

As he studied the scene, it occurred to him that his own crimes were far more personal and had more meaning than the one he was analysing. When the urges first appeared, his sense of right and wrong kept them in check for a while. He suppressed them but they became stronger, a constant clamour in his mind. The bloodlust became irresistible and he'd been very careful before indulging in murder and that had been an opportunist moment. Pushing the suicidal man off the cliff had been the first taste. It had given him a high unlike anything he'd experienced before. He was in the right place at the right time. They wouldn't all be that easy. He would have to plan. If he didn't, he would spend his life behind bars.

As time went by, it became clear being too careful would narrow his choice of victims. Not that he spent long picking them; they generally picked themselves. They had fallen into his lap so far. The frequency of his attacks had increased and he was taking more chances but that was normal for all killers. It was to be expected;

the natural evolution of a murderer. Practice makes perfect. Some got caught, most did not.

The urge to kill had completely overwhelmed him. He lived and breathed death. It was all he thought about. The dark desires he had, all but consumed him. It was difficult to function as a normal human being anymore; whatever normal was. Wasn't the urge to kill in all of us but society quelled it? Religion was invented to control our instincts. *Thou shall not kill* etcetera. Maybe he was normal and the rest of the world were sheep waiting to be slaughtered. Maybe.

He took the binoculars from his eyes and blinked to clear his vision. The hammer that was used to kill the man was on the rock, a hundred yards to his left, still caked in blood. They had missed it so far. He imagined touching the cold metal with his fingertips. His heart rate increased and he could feel adrenalin coursing through him. Reliving the attack was a poor substitute for watching the real thing— it was as close as it could be to hearing the screams and smelling the blood. He leaned closer and inhaled the breeze. It smelled of fear and death. They were odours that he craved like heroin to an addict. Although this death wasn't his to claim, it was different, less spontaneous, it was still satisfying.

In his experience, the excitement of stalking a victim and waiting for the perfect time and place to attack were what it was all about. Hearing them plead, listening to them weep was like music to his ear. The rush was more powerful than any drug he'd tried.

His thoughts were disturbed when his email pinged. It was a reply he'd been waiting for. His heartbeat quickened. He ran back to his vehicle and read the reply eagerly, his excitement growing to epic proportions. There was a mobile number tagged at the end of the reply. He punched the number into his phone and dialled it. His breath was trapped in his chest as he waited for an answer.

'Hello.'

'I've got your email.'

'About the knife?'

'Yes.'

'Have you seen the pictures?' the voice asked.

'Yes.'

'Do you have the money?'

'Yes,' he said, his voice quavering. 'How do I know it's the genuine article?'

'Because I'm an expert. I trace these items with due diligence,' the man said, irritated. 'Have you done your homework on the police files?'

'Yes.'

'You've found the evidence files online?'

'Yes.'

'There's a photograph of all the articles taken from his bedroom when he was arrested in ninety-five,' the man said.

'Yes, I've seen that.'

'I've also sent you a photograph of the knife in the evidence cage, four years later in ninety-nine.'

'Yes. I have that too.'

'The last picture was taken today next to a copy of today's *Daily Express*. Do you have that?'

'Yes.' He looked at the photograph and his mouth began to water. His hands were shaking a little. It was the knife. His knife.

'The photographs show the provenance without question.'

He studied the photographs and felt himself grow hard. It was genuine. His mind began to spin. It would bring him so close to him. This was the knife that killed four men in cold-blooded rage. One of his victims was stabbed thirty-six times, just four miles away from where he was sitting now. The weapon was within his grasp. He could almost reach out and touch it. He could smell it and almost taste its evil.

'What's your best price?' he asked.

'Don't mess me about, mate,' the man said. He sounded angry. 'If you are who you say you are, the price shouldn't matter.' There was silence for a moment. 'This is the actual weapon Peter Moore used to attack over forty men. Four of them died on this blade. You know the price is right.'

'There's always room to negotiate.'

'Not on this. Not a chance.' Another angry pause. 'Listen to me, you freak. I've got people queueing up for this. You're first because you've been a decent customer. Do you want it or not?'

'I want it,' he said.

'Final answer?'

'Yes.'

'Good. Ten thousand to the same account as last time. When the money appears in the account, I'll have it couriered, to the same place as last time, first thing in the morning.'

'I'm sending it now,' he said. He pressed send and the money left his account. 'Use the name Henry Roberts.'

'That's sick,' the man chuckled. 'The money is here. Got it. Nice doing business with you,' the man said. 'I'll keep my eyes on the news. I'm interested in what you're going to do with it,' he said, hanging up.

He could feel the blood coursing through his veins. The anticipation of holding his weapon was almost too much to handle. The blade had sliced the skin of over forty men. It had been wielded with lethal force at least four times that the police knew about. It was his Holy Grail. He had so many fantasies about using that weapon. It was difficult to know where to start.

CHAPTER 3

Alan Williams headed back to divisional headquarters at Caernarvon. It was too dark to continue the search in such weather conditions; it would be restarted at daylight. He yawned and stretched his neck, lost in his own thoughts about the case. There were teams of detectives to organise for the following day, which wouldn't take long and then he would be homeward bound—it had been a long shift.

'A penny for your thoughts,' Kim asked. She caught his yawn and turned the heater fan down. Her jeans were warm now but still uncomfortably damp. They would feel like that until she took them off and climbed into a hot bath. She was looking forward to a soak and a glass of pinot; preferably at the same time. She had taken to leaving the bottle in a cooler on the toilet where she could reach it, topping up her glass until the bathwater went tepid and her skin was wrinkly.

'They're not even worth a penny, believe me,' Alan said. 'It's the same old story. We can't pick a direction until the forensic results come in. All we can do is cover all the bases and wait to see what comes back. It's the most frustrating part of the job for me,' he said, glancing at her.

'We don't have a crystal ball.'

'There's a gap in the market for crystal balls.'

'My mind will tick over all night,' Kim said.

'I don't know about you but mine doesn't switch off at night without help.'

'I'm the same. My mind races through all the possible scenarios and suddenly it's four o'clock in the morning. Then I fall asleep and wake up feeling so exhausted, I want to cry.' She laughed. 'My help is a grape called pinot,' she said. 'It works for me.'

'Mine is whisky,' Alan said. 'I can't sleep a wink without it. Especially when there's a new case and no obvious starting points. I wish there was an off switch for my brain but there isn't.'

'There're millions of others all looking for that switch every night,' she said. 'I'm looking forward to mine tonight. My bones are aching with the damp. I need wine, my bath, and my bed.'

'There's something bothering me about the victims in the bay,' Alan said.

'There's plenty bothering me about them,' Kim said. 'You go first.'

'Okay,' Alan said, nodding. 'Why chuck them in the sea knowing they would come up at some point?' he asked. 'There's no doubt they would sink and drown but they would always come up again somewhere unless they weighted them down. They didn't weigh them down. It's almost as if they wanted them to be washed up somewhere.'

'The way I see it, they had two choices,' Kim said. 'Weigh them down so they never come up or at least remove their head and hands and any tattoos to make them difficult to identify. They did neither. Do they want us to identify them, if so, why?'

'To send a message?' Alan said. 'It smacks of a threat to me. *Look what happens if you cross us*, type of threat.'

'I think you're right. I can't see why they didn't weight them down otherwise,' Kim agreed.

'We're on the same page,' Alan said.

'Definitely. It won't stop me thinking about it all night.'

'I have the feeling double measures will be required tonight.'

'Definitely,' Kim agreed.

Alan checked the mirror. The grey-haired man looking back at him was bald on top with a dark-purple growth high on his forehead. It was the size of a small grape and his long-suffering wife had nagged him for years to have it removed. Before she left him, that was. Nowadays, she only nagged him about clearing the mortgage on the bungalow they'd shared for twenty-five years, bringing up their three sons, Kris, Dan, and Jack. It was an interest only mortgage and the property was in negative equity. He didn't see what her problem was. Things would work out. They always did. Not always for the best, granted. Rarely for the best, if he was honest. He sighed and pushed it from his mind.

'What are your thoughts about who they were?' Alan asked.

'I'm not sure.'

'I thought they might be stowaways on a cargo ship. I've heard stories about migrants being discovered aboard ships and dumped at sea. It saves the captain days of paperwork and means he would keep his bonus.'

'They dump them at sea?' Kim asked, shaking her head.

'Yes. They tie them together to make sure they don't stay afloat for long, I guess,' Alan said. 'But our victims are probably from the UK and they've been tortured before they were dumped. What type of people use torture as a deterrent or as a means of information gathering and then dump the bodies in plain sight as a warning to others?'

'Drug dealers,' Kim said.

'That was my answer too.'

'We've got our fair share of them.'

'If we had to pick one. Which of them would be so brutal?'

'Jamie Hollins.'

'My thoughts exactly,' Alan said. 'Have you met him?'

'Yes, a few times. He gives the impression of being harmless but there's another side to him. He's a nice enough guy on the face of it. To talk to him, you wouldn't think he was dangerous.' 'Obviously his record says otherwise.'

'I've interviewed him a few times,' Alan said. 'It's always entertaining, to say the least.'

'Oh, he's a character all right,' Kim said. Alan chuckled and nodded. The word 'character' was an overused term of endearment aimed at people with issues. 'He asked me out on a date, you know?' She laughed dryly.

'I don't believe you,' Alan said, looking sideways at her. 'Jamie Hollins asked you on a date?'

'Yes. It's true. I'd arrested him on a possession charge. We bailed him and thirty-minutes later he called the nick, asked for my direct line, and tried to chat me up. He asked me out on a date and said he wouldn't tell anyone.'

'And?'

'And what?' Kim asked.

'What did you say?'

'What do you think I said?' Kim asked.

'I don't know,' Alan said. He shrugged and kept his face deadpan. 'A lot of women are attracted to muscles and tattoos. It must have been very tempting.'

'Bugger off,' Kim said. 'Actually, I am attracted to muscles and tattoos, just not Jamie Hollins' muscles and tattoos.'

'So, you said no?'

'Of course, I did.'

'Did you want to say yes?'

'Shut up. I'm not having this conversation if you're going to wind me up.'

'So, you did say no?'

'Yes. I said no, you idiot.'

'I bet he was devastated,' Alan said. Kim looked out of the window and ignored him. 'Would you have said yes if he wasn't a criminal?'

'No. Now shut up.'

'Okay. Sorry.'

'Back to the point,' she said. 'He comes over as Mr Nice Guy, always laughing and joking but we both know he's a wrong one. Is he capable of doing that to those men?' She shrugged. 'I'm not sure. He could certainly sanction it. There're a few nutters on his crew who wouldn't think twice. It might be worth having a chat with him, gauge his reaction.'

'Definitely,' Alan said. 'All joking aside, if you feel there's a conflict of interest between you and Jamie, just say and I'll take you off the case.'

'Bugger off,' she said, shaking her head. 'You do know that I don't listen to a word you say, don't you?'

'I'm just looking out for you, sergeant.'

'Don't bother. I can look after myself.'

Alan pulled into the station car park and parked up. He turned to Kim and said, 'I want you to call it a night. I'm going to be half an hour behind you. We'll meet with the team for a briefing at nine.'

'Any news on the team?' Kim asked.

'That's what's going to take me half an hour. I need to speak to the Super and ask him to milk the other divisional headquarters,' Alan said. 'We're going to need to draft in from Colwyn and St Asaph for both cases. I want to keep them separate from the start but I don't want the other DVHQs sending us their deadwood. We need the sharpest tools in the shed.' Kim nodded in agreement. 'Now, go and get some rest. Not too much pinot, mind you.'

'Night, guv,' Kim said. She opened the door and climbed out.

'Night,' Alan said. He made his way to his office and took off his coat. It was time to negotiate for the best detectives he could muster. He opened his filing cabinet and reached inside, taking out a half bottle of Bells and a crystal tumbler. Twisting off the top, he poured two-fingers, and sat at his desk. He took a sip of the warming liquid, savouring the burn in his throat. He dialled the superintendent to glean some support.

'Dafyd Thomas,' the super answered. He sounded weary. Alan pictured him looking at his watch muttering about who would call him at that time of night.

'Dafyd, apologies, it's me,' Alan said. 'Sorry for the call at this time but I'm going to need the A-team on this one.'

'No worries, Alan,' said he replied. 'I was expecting a call from you. Where are we with it?'

'Both cases are complicated and I think we need to keep them separate from day one. I'd like a dedicated team on each murder.'

'There's no chance of a link?'

'I'm ninety-nine per cent certain there isn't,' Alan said. He sipped the whisky. 'I think the Trearddur Bay victims are drug related and I have no idea what the Porth Dafarch incident is, to be honest. We have a confirmed identification and cause of death but no clear motive as yet. Both cases could go one way or the other quickly if we don't get a grip from the start. I don't need any donkeys working on either case, with respect.'

'Alan,' Dafyd said, his tone flat. 'How long have we worked together?'

'Since dinosaurs roamed Benllech.'

'And in all that time, have we ever been stitched up with donkeys sent from the other DVHQs to work on important cases?'

'Yes, sir. More times than I can remember,' Alan said. 'That's why I thought I would mention it. I don't want to be stitched up again.'

'Fair comment,' Dafyd said with a dry chuckle. 'Send me a list of names you definitely don't want and I'll see what we can do.'

'Appreciated.'

'What time's your briefing?'

'Nine o'clock.'

'Leave it with me. I'll do the best I can for tomorrow and the rest will have to slot in as their current caseloads allow.'

'Excellent, thank you.' The call ended and Alan had the feeling Dafyd Thomas would be in his corner. He always was whenever he could. He swallowed the rest of the whisky, pulled on his coat, and headed home.

CHAPTER 4

Alan arrived home in Rhoscolyn at midnight. The bungalow was in darkness, which was odd as his son, Dan had left his car on the drive. He could hear the dogs barking in the living room but couldn't see them. The yellow glare from the single streetlight was enough to turn the patio glass into a mirror. His bungalow was the last in the street, beyond it, there was nothing but miles of undulating farmland that stretched to Silver Bay. There was zero light pollution and the inky black sky was studded with a million twinkling orbs. The plough was clearly visible to the east. He ambled across the driveway to the front door and stopped when he found it open six inches. It was rarely locked but the boys knew better than to leave it open. It wasn't worth the earache they would get from their father. The smell of cannabis drifted to him from inside. He pushed the door open and stepped in, allowing his eyes to adjust to the gloom. The dogs' barking reached a crescendo and they were scratching at the back of the door, excited he was home.

'Dan, are you in?' Alan whispered. There was no answer. He flicked the light switch but nothing happened. Alan swore beneath his breath and walked to the electric cupboard at the end of the hallway and opened the door. The meter glowed yellow in the dark. He pressed the emergency button and the lights came on. The sound of the television blaring came from Dan's bedroom; it startled him. Alan knocked on the door. There was no answer. He knocked again and then opened it. The bed was made but the room was empty. He walked to the television and turned it off. A noise from the second bedroom made him jump. Alan tiptoed along the hallway to the living room and opened the door. Gemma, an Alsatian cross and Henry, a Jack Russell, who thought he was a tiger, exploded from the doorway, circling Alan and jumping up at him before sprinting down the corridor to the bedrooms to investigate. They disappeared into the second bedroom, yapping.

'Get off!' Alan heard his eldest son moaning. Alan followed the dogs and poked his head around the door. He switched the light on. Kris was lying on the floor, covering his eyes with his forearm while the dogs licked his face as if it was covered in Pedigree Chum. 'Get them off, dad. They're doing my head in.'

'What are you doing here?' Alan asked. Kris lived in Holyhead with his wife and two young children. 'Have you had a row again?'

'No, not really. I've been out with the lads and just fancied a smoke before I go home. Get off!' he shouted, pushing the dogs off.

'You just fancied a smoke in my house. Cannabis, I presume?'

'What do you think?'

'You do know I'm a detective inspector, don't you?' Alan said.

'I think you might have mentioned it,' Kris mumbled. 'Will you please get the dogs out of here before I lose my shit.'

'Where's Dan?' Alan asked. 'His car is outside.'

'He went to get some electric. It's on emergency. Fflur took him to Spar,' Kris said.

'Okay,' Alan said. He closed the door and left the dogs mobbing him.

'Dad!' Kris' muffled voice cried. 'Take these bloody dogs with you!'

'You're nearly thirty-two years old with two children,' Alan said. He ignored him and went into the kitchen in search of his off switch. A litre bottle of Tesco's cheapest blended Scotch. He rinsed his glass from the previous night and filled it to halfway. His eyes were tired and he needed some sleep but he knew it wouldn't come without his medicine. He heard the bedroom door open and the dogs scurrying down the hallway. The door slammed closed again.

'This place is a madhouse!' Kris shouted; his voice muffled by the door.

'It is indeed,' Alan said. 'Remind me, why do you keep coming back again?'

Alan opened the patio doors and let the dogs out. They sprinted into the darkness across the fields, Henry's tiny little legs going ten to the dozen to keep up.

'Hiya, Dad,' Dan said from the doorway.

'Hello. Where did you go?'

'I had to go to the Spar to get some electric.'

'I wondered where you were. Thank you for doing that,' Alan said, sipping his whisky.

'You're welcome,' Dan said. 'You owe me twenty-pounds.'

'For what?' Alan asked.

'The electric.'

'Are the lights in your room solar powered?' Alan asked.

'No, they're electric,' Dan said. 'But the last time we had this conversation, you said we should take it in turns to top up the card.'

'And what?'

'And it's been my turn the last three times.'

'I see,' Alan said, nodding. 'Point taken. I haven't got any cash on me but remind me tomorrow.'

'I'll stick a reminder on the fridge next to the other reminders, shall I?' Dan said, pointing to the fridge where a line of reminders hung. 'I don't know why we have to have a prepaid meter in this day and age. It's so embarrassing topping it up in the shop. There's always someone in there I know.'

'You'll have to blame your mum for that.'

'How can it be Mum's fault? She left five years ago.'

'She didn't pay the bill before she buggered off with her fancy man,' Alan said. 'I came home from work one day; she was gone and the meter was there instead. Mind you, the meter doesn't tell me I have to come home from the pub so, it's not all bad.'

'Do you take anything seriously?' Dan asked. Alan shrugged and shook his head. Dan walked into the kitchen and poured a glass of water. 'Kris is in the middle bedroom, stoned off his box. I think he's had a row again.'

'I've seen him. He'll sleep it off,' Alan said. 'He's been smoking weed. Do you think he knows?'

'Knows what, Dad?' Dan asked.

'That I'm a police officer.'

'Sometimes he forgets.'

'When it suits,' Alan smiled.

'Paula doesn't like him smoking it in the house,' Dan said.

'Paula is a very smart lady.' Alan sipped his whisky. 'This might sound like a strange question but who are you buying your weed from nowadays?' Alan asked.

'What makes you think I smoke it?'

'The smell of cannabis and tobacco that permeates from your room and the bag of skunk under your bed,' Alan said. Dan looked offended. 'Do you think your sheets and bedding wash themselves?'

'I forget you're a detective too,' Dan joked.

'Seriously,' Alan said. 'I want to know who is selling the weed in Holyhead nowadays?'

'How come?' Dan asked. 'Are you moving to the drug squad?'

'No. They're way too busy for my liking,' Alan said. 'I'm in the twilight of my career. A couple of murders a day is my limit these days.'

'Why the sudden interest then?'

'I'm working on a hunch. Come on, I'm not asking you for names and addresses.'

'It depends,' Dan said. He blushed. 'There's lots of people selling weed but only two I use.'

'How come?'

'A lot of the stuff for sale is crap. My guy sells quality every time and he never runs out.' He paused, uncomfortable with the conversation.

'How well do you know him?'

'He's a good mate of mine. I've known him since school.'

'And Kris?' Alan asked.

'I get his for him.'

'What about Jack?'

'He buys from my mate, direct.'

'Why direct?'

'He buys a bit extra than he needs himself.'

'Are you telling me my son is selling weed to his friends in Bangor?' Alan asked.

'Calm down. When he moved in with his mates, they were buying it locally and it was crap,' Dan said. 'It's because of the university. The students have money and they'll smoke anything. My mate is cheaper and it's better quality. Jack isn't dealing, he's buying for his friends in the house, that's all.'

'Good,' Alan said. 'Keep it that way.'

'Why all the questions?' Dan asked.

'We pulled a couple of bodies from Trearddur Bay this morning,' Alan said. 'My hunch is it could be drug related.'

'Locals?'

'We don't know yet but I have a feeling that trouble might be brewing in town. If it is, I don't want you three anywhere near it, understand?' Dan nodded.

'We steer clear of the rock stars, don't worry, Dad,' Dan said.

'Rock stars?' Alan asked. 'That's a new one.'

'You know the type. They walk around like they're famous; flash cars, designer gear; sunglasses in November,' Dan said. 'The 'not so discreet' dealers. Don't worry. We don't go near them.' Dan paused in thought. 'But now you've mentioned it, I've heard a few rumours going around.'

'Rumours about what?' Alan asked. He finished his whisky and poured another, his interest fuelled. 'Holyhead is always full of rumours—small towns thrive on them.'

'I've heard that some of the old rivalries are coming back to the surface,' Dan said. 'There's been a lot of threats made on Facebook, apparently.'

'Who's threatening who?'

'Jamie Hollins and Lloyd Jones started it off, but it seems to have spread across town. They're making threats to shoot each other on Facebook, can you believe it?' Dan said. 'I didn't think much of it until now.'

'It might be something and nothing.'

'Do you think your case is connected?'

'Probably not, Dan,' Alan said. 'The type of people who kill their rivals don't shout about it on social media. They get it done, and no one knows who's done it. I've never come across a genuinely dangerous outfit using Facebook. Teenage gangs in London, maybe but serious gangsters, I doubt it very much. Don't mention it to anyone for now. It will be in the press soon enough.'

'Okay, dad,' Dan said. 'I'm going to bed. Goodnight.' He walked over and hugged his dad.

'I'm turning in myself. I'll let the dogs back in first,' Alan said, hugging him. 'Sleep tight.' He emptied the tumbler and refilled it. There was time for another quick one before bedtime.

CHAPTER 5

It was seven o'clock when the courier arrived at the farmhouse outside of Caergeiliog, nearly an hour late. He stopped the van and checked the address twice. Reluctantly, he opened the door and reached inside for the package. The customer waited impatiently at the gate, dressed completely in black. It was the oddest drop he'd made for months. He looked at the derelict structure in awe. It looked like it would disintegrate in a decent breeze. The roof had collapsed into the house years before and thick green foliage, ivy, and saplings sprouted through the rafters. It had been decades since anyone had lived there yet it was the address he'd been given and he had a job to do. Deliver the package to Mr Roberts at the front gate, get a signature, and drive away. It was simple yet looking at the man behind the gate, he knew it was wrong. It was all wrong. Whatever was in the package didn't matter. Whoever the mysterious Mr Roberts was, didn't matter. The fact he was outside a derelict farmhouse didn't matter but it felt like he was party to something morally corrupt. He had never questioned his employer or a customer before, but this job was screaming 'illegal' at the top of its voice.

'You're nearly an hour late,' Mr Roberts said. His eyes were grey and staring. They were unnerving. The courier felt vulnerable and intimidated. He didn't want to be near Mr Roberts any longer than necessary.

'The traffic was bad,' the courier mumbled. 'Sign the screen, please.'

Mr Roberts made a squiggle that was illegible and took the package. The energy from the knife seeped through the bubble-wrap, cardboard, and packing tape and made his skin tingle. He could feel its power travelling through his hand into his veins, saturating his very being with a malignant force. There was evil inside it, cast in the steel. He could feel the courier staring at him as he drove away. Mr Roberts walked away from the gate along a moss-covered path, overgrown with brambles, tearing at the packaging frantically. When he reached the small farmyard where the real Mr Roberts had been found face down with his trousers around his ankles, he could hardly contain himself. He threw the cardboard into the weeds and gripped the handle. There was a swastika engraved on the hilt. The blade glinted in the half light. He ran his tongue along the serrated side of the military knife, drawing blood. He felt the heady rush of adrenalin. He was at the murder scene, holding the weapon used to dispatch Mr Roberts in 1995. The malevolence coursed through him. It was something unholy. He could feel the killer's presence through the handle. The connection between them was finally complete. He could never deny him now, not if he tried. His mother had told the truth all along.

CHAPTER 6

At eight o'clock in the morning, Julie Adams identified her husband, supported by her eldest son. Alan and Kim waited for them to compose themselves. They were shown into an interview room, designed specifically for bereaved families. It was comfortable with settees and no tables or desks. There were no barriers. They had tea and coffee brought in for them and Julie was given a box of tissues and a glass of water. She was obviously distraught.

'I'm very sorry for your loss, Julie,' Alan said. 'Do you mind if I call you Julie?' She shook her head and blew her nose into a white tissue. Her son looked like he was on the edge of breaking down. He appeared to be late teens. 'We want to ask you a few questions about Kelvin and his whereabouts over the last few days, if that's okay?'

'Yes.' She blew her nose and shook her head. 'Kelvin didn't have an enemy in the world. He was such a lovely man. I can't believe anyone would hurt him. I just can't believe he's dead.'

'It must be a terrible shock. Tell me a little about him.'

'I don't know where to start. What do you need to know?'

'Where did he work?' Alan asked.

'He works at the Jaguar plant near Liverpool,' Julie said. 'I mean, he worked. Past tense.' She broke down, her body shaking. Alan waited until she'd calmed. 'I'm sorry.'

'There's no need to apologise. It's only natural you're grieving.' He paused to allow her to compose herself. 'You said he worked at Jaguar. That's in Speke, near Liverpool, yes?'

'Yes.'

'What does he do there?'

'He's an engineer.'

'That must be a good job,' Alan said. 'How long has he been there?'

'Since school. It was Fords then. He completed his degree there and then stayed. It pays well and it's secure, although it's had its moments over the years.'

'Everywhere does,' Alan said. He paused for a moment. 'Did he work shifts or was it a Monday to Friday job?'

'He did shifts when he was an apprentice but for the last twenty years, it's been Monday to Friday. He always finished early on a Friday so we could do something with the boys. My youngest couldn't come. I've had to leave him with my mother. He's heartbroken.'

'I'm sure he is. Are Kelvin's parents alive?'

'No. They both died last year within three months of each other.'

'That's sad. How old were they?'

'Late eighties.'

'A good innings, I suppose,' Alan said. Mrs Adams looked at him, not sure if she was offended or not. Alan sensed how fragile she was. One wrong word could ruin the interview. 'Are you familiar with the area where Kelvin was found?' Alan asked.

'Porth Dafarch. Yes,' she said. 'We stayed in a caravan there when we were courting and we went back every year. He loved it. He went fishing there once a month religiously, no matter what the weather.'

'Once a month?' Alan asked.

'Yes.'

'Was it the same day every month?'

'No. It depended on what we had on at home with the boys. It was usually near the end of the month,' Julie said. She looked at Kim, confused. Kim smiled thinly.

'Did he ever meet anyone else when he went fishing?' Alan asked.

'I don't know what you mean.'

'I mean, was he a member of a club or did he have any fishing pals?'

'Oh, I see. No. He took the boys when they were younger but they grew out of it. He usually went alone.'

'We're a bit confused about the circumstances,' Alan said.

'Oh. Like what?'

'Some of his clothing was found in the toilet block near the beach. We can't explain that,' Alan said. 'Do you know what his routine was when he got there?'

'Were they found in the disabled cubicle?' the son asked.

'Yes.'

'I've been there with him a few times. He used it to change his wet clothes before he drove home,' the son said. 'It's never locked. There are lights in there that always work and a heater. He used it to change his waterproofs before getting into the car.'

'I see,' Alan said, nodding. Julie Adams frowned. 'That makes sense.'

'Why would that be confusing?' she asked.

'I'm sorry,' Alan said. 'We have to be clear.'

'It seems perfectly obvious to me.'

'We have to clarify the sequence of events. What you've told me tells me that he was on his way back to the car when he was attacked,' Alan said.

'As opposed to what?' Julie asked. Her face was like thunder. 'As in why else take off his clothes in a public toilet?'

'There are several possibilities we had to consider,' Alan said. 'It was late at night in a remote spot.'

'You thought he was there to meet other men, didn't you?' she said. Her son glared at Alan. His face darkened in anger.

'Anything is possible. We have to consider all the angles and eliminate them as we collect the answers. It's all part of investigating a murder, I'm afraid.'

'You always see the worst in people, you lot.'

'Obviously, we try not to but we're dealing with a serious crime.'

'Kelvin was a family man, who never put a foot wrong. He wasn't the type of man to look for sex in a public toilet.'

'Is that what you think my dad was doing?' the son asked.

'No, we don't. We have to consider all possibilities in a case like this,' Kim said. 'Things are seldom what they seem but we have to explore all the options. We don't mean to offend you.'

'Well, you have offended us. He's still lying on a slab in there and you're questioning his sexuality and his marriage. How dare you,' the son said. He stood up and grabbed his mum's arm. 'Come on, Mum. Let's go before I punch him in the face.' They stormed out of the room and slammed the door. There was a moment of awkward silence.

'That went well,' Kim said. She looked at Alan, shaking her head. 'You're as tactful as ever. It's a real talent, you know.'

'It was always going to be a difficult conversation,' Alan said with a sigh. He turned to face her. 'I don't mean to sound horrible but I can't think about how offended she is, we had to ask the question and something about this, stinks.'

'Like what?'

'I'm not buying the fishing trip story,' Alan said. 'Not that night.'

'But they said he went every month.'

'Maybe he did but all the equipment in that car was bone dry. Okay, the waterproofs were saturated, and I'll accept that he may well have been getting changed into dry clothes when he was attacked, in which case, where had he been to get soaked?'

'Wave watching, walking, looking for a spot safe to fish in the storm?'

'No. He knew the area well. There's nowhere along that coast where you can fish in a storm like that. It was pitch-black that night, he couldn't see his hand in front of his face, never mind the waves.'

'You have a point,' Kim said. 'Do you want to tell me what you think happened?'

'Nope,' Alan said. 'I haven't got a clue but I know he wasn't fishing.'

* * *

Owen Collins pulled up outside his workshop. He'd worked there as a mechanic since he was ten years old, helping his dad after school and at weekends. By the time he'd reached his teen years, he had stripped and rebuilt an iconic V8 engine, which his father had taken out of a Rover and kept. They worked on it in their spare time and fitted it into a black Capri which his dad drove around for five years. It was the fastest car on the island for a time. He was a natural, feeling his way around an engine with ease. When he left school, he joined his dad in the business and built a reputation as a talented mechanic and a fair businessman. Things went well for twenty years until his father was diagnosed with pancreatic cancer. After six months of traumatic treatment, he succumbed to the disease. Owen was bereft. He'd spent his entire life with his dad at his side. It was as if half of him had died too. Keeping the wheels turning at the workshop had been the only thing stopping him from breaking down. He'd laughed with his wife about being a mechanic having a breakdown. So far, they'd managed to keep it together. Business had taken a downturn with only one pair of hands, but he'd kept his financial issues to himself. He would pull it back. Taking on another mechanic was the solution, but good mechanics were at a premium on the island. The best mechanics usually upped and left for the big money in the cities. There were plenty of poor ones—taking on the wrong person could finish the business. He had to be careful.

Owen opened the shutters and turned on the lights, the radio, and the kettle. He sifted through his worksheets for the day. It was going to be a long shift. A Volkswagen Golf was the priority. He needed to change the starter motor and the oil before lunchtime which was achievable if he had the new starter motor on the shelf. Europarts were supposed to deliver it yesterday but his account was over its limit. He had to clear three-hundred pounds before they would okay any new orders but the three hundred had taken him to his overdraft limit. He was at the end of the road, financially. Cashflow was a killer, everyone knows that. If he could clear all the vehicles waiting to be fixed, he would be liquid again. He wasn't losing money; it was merely a cashflow crisis.

The kettle boiled and he made a brew. It was hot and sweet and the cup warmed his fingers. Nothing worse than cold fingers when you're wrestling a rusty nut with a spanner. A blue van pulled up and he breathed a sigh of relief. It was the starter motor delivery. Today was going to be a good day, he could feel it in his bones. His old dad was up there somewhere looking out for him.

'Morning, Owen,' the delivery driver said. 'Volkswagen starter motor for you, if you could sign here for me, I'll be on my way.'

'Morning, Dai. You're a sight for sore eyes,' Owen said, scribbling on the screen. 'I can crack on now that's here.'

'Hey, while you're here on your own, I've got ten gallons of Castrol Magnatec in the van. It fell off the back of a lorry yesterday,' Di said, lowering his voice. 'I can let you have it for a ton.'

'That's a bargain, Dai but cashflow is a bit tight at the moment,' Owen said. It was an offer too good to refuse even though he wouldn't normally touch anything dodgy. Things were tight and oil was an easy way to make money. He had to drop the oil in the Golf anyway, which would use some of it. 'If you can wait until Friday for the cash, I'll take the lot.'

'Friday it is,' Di said. He shook hands with Owen. 'Where shall I put it?'

'Stick it next to the tyres over there, please mate,' Owen said. He knew it was going to be a good day. 'Do you want a brew?'

'No thanks, Owen,' Di said. 'I've got fifteen drops to make this morning. I'll unload the oil and get off. Someone has to keep the wheels of industry moving.'

'Cheers, Di,' Owen said. They carried the oil in and stored it on a shelf. Di waved and beeped the horn as he drove off.

Owen waved goodbye and walked back to his brew. He finished it off and took the starter motor from the box. The old motor was already removed so fitting the new one would be simple. It was all going to plan. He was fastening the last bolt when a black Range Rover pulled up outside. The windows were blacked out and the booming baseline of gangster-rap vibrated from inside. Owen recognised the vehicle. It was a small island and only one person drove a vehicle like that. The music went off and the front doors opened. Jamie Hollins climbed out of the driver's side, his wingman, Tony John jumped out of the passenger side. Owen had a sinking feeling in his guts. They were trouble with a capital T.

'Owen, my friend,' Jamie shouted. 'How's it going?' Jamie smiled from ear to ear as if Owen was his oldest friend and he hadn't seen him for years. His eyes darted everywhere as if he was nervous, searching for danger. 'Good to see you,' Jamie said, offering his hand. 'Always good to see you,' he repeated.

'Likewise, Jamie,' Owen said, shaking his hand. He was confused and concerned by Jamie's greeting. They barely knew each other. They knew of each other because it was a small town. Owen's father fixed Jamie's father's vehicles over the years but they were hardly old friends. 'What can I do for you, trouble with the Range Rover?'

'No, she's sweet as a nut,' Jamie said. 'I've come to talk business with you.'

'Business?' Owen said, wiping his oily hands on a rag. 'What business would that be?'

'I'm buying a taxi company and I'm going into the motor trade. I'm expanding and I'm going to do you a favour at the same time,' Jamie said.

'And what would that be, Jamie?' Owen asked, his concern deepening. Jamie Hollins didn't do favours for nothing.

'A little birdie tells me that you're experiencing cashflow problems,' Jamie said. 'I'm here to offer you a way out. It's a way to turn your business around and help me out at the same time.'

'I'm not sure where you get your information from but my business is in good shape, thank you,' Owen said. He felt his guts tighten; anger and concern eating him. 'I appreciate the intent but I'm making a living.'

'Let's not bullshit each other. Your credit limit at Europarts is up to the limit, you're over your overdraft with the bank, and a friend at the council offices tells me your business rates are due and they're going up this year,' Jamie said. His smile disappeared. 'You couldn't pay cash for the knock-off oil you just bought.'

'How do you know that?' Owen muttered

'Eyes and ears everywhere, Owen. That's my forte,' Jamie said. 'Your business is floundering at best.' He paused to let the information sink in.

'How do you know all that?' Owen asked again, fuming.

'This is a small town. I have eyes and ears everywhere and a cousin who works at Santander,' Jamie chuckled. 'You're going down the toilet. I can help you to pull it together.'

'I can manage, thank you,' Owen said.

'You might not be able to manage if some of your customers go elsewhere.'

'What are you talking about?'

'You've been servicing Jack Anthony's courier vans since he started, haven't you?'

'Yes,' Owen said.

'He's your best customer. His business is the difference between you folding and trading.'

'What are you trying to say, Jamie?' Owen asked. His face flushed red.

'I'm saying that Jack is considering taking his fleet elsewhere and if he does, it will finish you off.'

'He was here yesterday and he didn't mention being unhappy,' Owen said.

'He doesn't know he's unhappy yet. But if I tell him he is, he will be. Do you see what I mean?'

'Why would you do that?'

'Because I can.' Jamie picked up a wrench and tapped it on a workbench. 'You have something I need and in return, I can help you.'

'What exactly do you want?'

'Like I said, I'm here to help you,' Jamie said. 'You need Jack's business and you need another pair of hands.' Owen was about to protest but Jamie held up his hands. 'Let me finish. I'm going to give you a mechanic. A good one and I'm going to pay his wages for you and I'm going to speak to Jack about keeping his business with you.' Owen opened his mouth to speak but couldn't think of any words to say. 'I'm buying a taxi firm in Bangor and I'll give you all their services and MOT's plus any breakdowns. There's fifteen cars and two minibuses in the fleet. It will turn this place into a little goldmine.'

'What are you talking about?' Owen asked. He shook his head perplexed. 'Why would you do that, Jamie?' Owen put his spanner down and stepped closer to him, incensed. 'Nobody does anything for nothing. What exactly is the catch?'

'No catch. I want to help you. I'm prepared to give you a second pair of hands and extra business,' Jamie said. 'You know Daisy, don't you?'

'Yes, I know him,' Owen said. 'He's a good mechanic.'

'He wants to work for me, here. Except he'll be working for you.'

'Daisy has worked for Peter's garage for years. Why would he want to come here?'

'He's fallen out with the old man and don't underestimate your reputation. He wants to work for someone reputable.'

'It all sounds too good to be true,' Owen said.

'I know what you're thinking. What do I want in return?' Jamie smiled. 'This is how it works. You take two cars a week for me and let Daisy work on them here. You bill me enough to cover the parts and Daisy's labour. The rest of the week, he's your mechanic. That's it.'

'That's it?' Owen said.

'That's it,' Jamie said. 'You keep your business and get a second mechanic. I'll clear your overdraft and your Europarts account as a gesture of goodwill and all you do is let my mechanic work on two cars a week in one of your bays.'

'I'm confused, Jamie,' Owen said. 'You walk in here like my fairy godmother and expect me to just say yes?'

'Have you got mobile banking on your phone?' Jamie asked.

'Yes.'

'Check your account,' Jamie said. Owen took out his phone and logged on. He shook his head suspiciously as he looked at the screen. 'Your overdraft this morning was over fifteen-grand. Now you're in credit. The money was paid in by a haulage company in Llandegfan. No links to me whatsoever.' Owen looked up and shook his head.

'Where's the money from?'

'We took the liberty of buying a Mercedes van from an auction for you last month. Here's the V5 document and here's the seller's slip. They're all in your name,' Jamie said, handing the documents to Owen. 'You sold it to the haulage company yesterday at a considerable profit and the money was paid into your account this morning.'

'This is well dodgy. I don't want anything to do with this,' Owen said. 'I'll transfer the money back.'

'Check the documents, Owen,' Jamie said. 'It's all legitimate. That's your money. No one can trace it back to me.'

Owen studied the papers. Everything looked as it should do. 'Why are you doing this, Jamie?'

'I've told you. I'm buying a taxi firm and I'm going to be buying and selling vehicles. I need somewhere Daisy can work on my motors. Somewhere with a good reputation.'

'What will he be doing to your vehicles, Jamie?' Owen asked. His stomach was churning. The offer to be lifted out from the crushing weight of debt was mouth-watering. Seeing his account in the black was a massive relief but it was all too good to be true.

'I'm going to buy ex-company cars, service them, tart them up a bit, and sell them on. There's nothing to worry about.'

'There's everything to worry about.'

'What is the problem?'

'You. You're the problem.'

'What are you saying to me?'

'You're a drug dealer, Jamie.'

'I'm hurt by that remark.' Jamie touched his heart and frowned.

'Everyone on the island knows you're not just *a* drug dealer, you're *the* drug dealer.'

'Now I'm flattered, thank you.'

'Don't take the piss out of me. You're the top dog in the cocaine business and everyone knows that, so why would you need to venture into motors?' Owen asked. He shrugged. 'The way I see it, you're either laundering money by buying and selling vehicles or you're using the vehicles to traffic coke; stashing your product somewhere in the chassis or the engine blocks. Either way, I'm putting a gun to my head by being complicit. My business might be struggling but I'd rather struggle than be in a prison cell. I have grandchildren on the way.'

'You're a clever man, Owen,' Jamie said, smiling. He patted Owen on the shoulder. 'No one will be able to touch you. You're a legitimate businessman with integrity. No one would look sideways at your workshop. Why would they? Nothing changes on the surface; you fix cars and charge a fair price. No one apart from us three and Daisy will know anything about it.' Jamie shrugged. 'There will be no link back to me that anyone can trace. Not ever.'

'No one else knows?'

'Not a soul.'

'What about your crew?'

'No one but us, Tony, and Daisy. I keep my business close to my chest. You know what this town is like. Everyone knows everybody's business. I have to be careful. I need you to take me up on this deal, Owen. You have my word that there'll be no tangible connection between me and your business.'

'What about the taxi firm in Bangor?' Owen asked.

'My name won't be anywhere on the books for that company. The only person who knows I'm buying it, is you,' Jamie said. 'I've done a lot of preparation to make this work for you.'

'This is a lot to take in, Jamie.'

'Of course, it is. Why don't you sleep on it and we'll talk tomorrow?' Jamie said. 'My advice would be to keep this to yourself. Don't discuss it with the wife.'

'She's the last person I'd be talking to,' Owen said. 'Let me think about it.'

'Tony will drop in tomorrow. No calls or texts between us,' Jamie said, offering his hand. 'This is a no-brainer. Don't pass it up.' They shook hands and Jamie walked back to his Range Rover. Tony climbed into the passenger seat and they drove away. Owen watched them disappear around the bend. He looked up and closed his eyes. The more he thought about it, the more attractive the deal was. He couldn't see any downsides. What could possibly go wrong?

CHAPTER 7

DI Alan Williams was halfway across the island when his phone rang. Snowdonia dominated the skyline in front of him, its peaks covered in snow. The sun was reflecting from it, dazzling him. The radio went off as the Bluetooth connected an incoming call.

'Alan, it's Dafyd.'

'Good morning,' Alan said. 'Is all well?'

'I've just had the most bizarre phone call,' Dafyd said.

'It's too early for bizarre.'

'Bizarre it is, all the same. There's some good news and some bad news.'

'You pick which we do first,' Alan said.

'The good news is both victims from Trearddur are in the system. Their prints hit right away. The bad news is, their information is classified.'

'What?' Alan said. 'Classified. They must be on the informer list.'

'That's what I thought but it's worse than that,' Dafyd said.

'Worse than that?' Alan said. It dawned on him. 'Are they in the job?'

'Yes. I received a call from the Assistant Chief Constable of Merseyside. Both men are officers from their Matrix unit. He said they were working an undercover operation. They were investigating a link to the supply chain of class As to the North Wales area. Until he's spoken to their families and been briefed on exactly what they were onto, they're not to be named.'

'Bloody hell,' Alan said. 'That complicates things. Someone must have blown their cover. It would explain how they ended up in the sea, poor buggers.'

'We're going to have to tread carefully on this,' Dafyd said. 'Are you on your way in?'

'Yes. I'm twenty minutes away.'

'I'll see you at the briefing.'

'Yes. See you there.'

The call ended and the music came back on. Alan turned it down to think. There was something bugging him but he couldn't put his finger on it. He scrolled through his contacts and found the number he wanted. It was probably unethical to make the call but he wasn't going to let that stand in his way. The phone rang three times and answered.

'Major investigation team,' the voice answered.

'Google,' Alan said. 'It's DI Williams from Holyhead.'

'Hello, Alan,' Google said. 'I thought I might get a call from you sooner or later.'

'Really, why's that?' Alan asked.

'I've just heard you pulled two UCs out of the sea. The word is that they're ours, Matrix apparently. It's classified, so it's all over the station. You know how it works.'

'That's what I've been told. Your ACC has put a gag on our investigation until he's been briefed on what they were doing here,' Alan said. 'You wouldn't happen to know anything about it, would you?'

'I'm afraid not, guv,' Google said. 'Matrix are a law unto themselves. Their own senior officers probably don't know the full extent of their UCs' whereabouts. What I can tell you is that there's been a powershift here in the city and I think you're feeling the aftershocks.'

'Sounds interesting,' Alan said.

'Let me put you on hold a minute while I find an office.' Alan waited while Google changed phones. A minute later, the line clicked. 'Hello, are you still there?'

'Yes, I'm here.'

'There're too many ears listening in there. Did you hear about the sentencing for Operation Suzie last week?'

'I read the memos sent around,' Alan said. 'They all got hefty sentences.'

'You're not kidding me. They sentenced thirty-six of them, all tier one, mostly from here and Manchester. They got all the main players off the streets in one sweep and it's left a vacuum.'

'I can imagine it has.'

'We've got foreign outfits from all over the country trying to fill the void and the smaller local crews trying to step up and stay alive. It's like the United Nations of crime out there. They're shooting each other left, right, and centre.'

'I haven't seen much on the news.'

'The press is playing it down so far. They're under the cosh from our top brass but there's a war going on here. I think you're feeling the repercussions of what's happening.'

'It would explain why Matrix were following a supply line down here.'

'Everything has changed,' Google said. 'The drug squad are reporting finds of coke at ninety per cent and some as low as thirteen. The quality is all over the place in the city so by the time it's reached your area, heaven knows what it is. I can see it causing trouble if people think they're being ripped off.'

'That might explain why some fragile truces are breaking down. It makes sense,' Alan said. 'Thanks for the info. Who would I speak to in Matrix to find out who they were investigating here?'

'Paul Johnson,' Google said. 'And I didn't give you that name. If I hear anything relevant to your end, I'll give you a bell.'

'Likewise,' Alan said. 'Thanks, Google.' The line went dead. Alan ran through the main players on the North Wales coast. It takes a special kind of dangerous to abduct, torture, and kill two undercover police officers. That's stepping into the big league in anyone's book. No matter how many times he ran through them, the same name kept floating to the top of the list.

CHAPTER 8

'This is Kelvin Adams from Pensarn,' Alan said. He had a team of thirty detectives gathered in the operations room. He'd intended to start the briefing with the victims pulled from Trearddur Bay but the news of them being UCs had changed the priority. 'His wife claims Kelvin was on a fishing trip when he was attacked. He was pepper-sprayed, forced to walk over the grange, strangled, and beaten to death.' Images of the victim and the crime scene flicked across a bank of digital screens behind him. 'His wife told us that he made this trip every month to fish at Porth Dafarch which was his favourite spot. He was attacked in this public toilet block,' he said, pointing to the screen. 'His son said he always used the disabled cubicle to change out of his waterproofs before driving home in the early hours of the morning. The estimated time of death supports their theory that he was fishing.' Alan took a mouthful of coffee before continuing.

'What we need to clarify is what happened to him,' he said. 'Kelvin said he was going to fish. There were seventy mile an hour winds that night for those of you not familiar with that part Anglesey, Porth Dafarch is twenty-three miles out to sea and the coastline is high cliffs. There are many scrambles down to rocks where fishermen frequent but not when the waves are so high. It would be suicide to climb down there. Nobody was fishing at Porth Dafarch that night. His fishing equipment was packed away in the car and it was bone dry, yet his waterproofs were soaked so, where did he go and what's the motive of the attack?'

'Have we found the weapon he was beaten with?' Dafyd asked.

'Not yet,' Alan said. 'We're sure it's a hammer. The search of the grange will continue this morning. The wind has dropped, and the rain has stopped. In the meantime, I want to know more about Kelvin Adams. Who was he? Talk to his workmates, his bosses, and his subordinates at Jaguar. Simon and Kerry, can you take that please?'

'Yes, guv. I'll call them now and make an appointment.'

'Don't take no for an answer. We need his laptop, work computer, and phone,' Alan added. 'You'll need permission from his wife for his personal stuff and she's not impressed with me at the moment so ask nicely.'

'What did you do wrong, guv,' Simon asked.

'She's pissed off because I insinuated he may have been visiting the toilet block for a more unsavoury reason than getting changed into dry clothes.'

'I can see that not going down well,' Simon said.

'It didn't but I had to ask. He has a teenage son who threatened to punch me in the nose.' The detectives laughed quietly. 'Use kid gloves, I want to build bridges with them. It may well be that Kelvin was just unlucky and in the wrong place at the wrong time but I don't think so.' Alan changed the image. 'Whether it was random or a targeted attack, the killer is a very dangerous individual and we need to lock them up. He went there with pepper spray and duct tape and a hammer. It was premeditated but Kelvin may have been a random victim. If we can work out the motive, we'll be able to narrow down the possible suspects. Alice, I want your team to concentrate on the Kelvin Adams investigation. Call Pamela Stone at forensics and ask her if she can speed up the results on the car. It was spotless when we searched it. Too clean.'

'Yes, guv.'

'I'll need you to coordinate the search at the headland too,' Alan added. 'Keep me in the loop.' He changed the images again. The victims from Trearddur Bay appeared. 'Here's where things get interesting. These two men are undercover officers from the Matrix unit in Liverpool.' A ripple of surprised chatter spread through the gathering. 'We don't know their names yet, but we know they were in the job. Someone blew their cover, abducted them, tortured them, and tossed them into the sea tied together at the feet. I can't think of anything more frightening than having your cover blown by a violent gang. They must have been terrified. We have to assume that whatever they knew, the killers now know. I think that under torture, most people will talk, eventually. If there are more undercover officers in the investigation, then they're clearly in danger. I spoke to an officer from MIT this morning and there's a power struggle going on between organised crime groups across Liverpool and Manchester. It would appear that Matrix were following a supply line into our patch, but someone sussed them as coppers. We don't know who they are yet but that doesn't matter. I want you to show their pictures around on the island. They must have been staying somewhere. Where is their vehicle? Which pubs did they drink in and who were they friendly with? We have to assume their unit won't know exactly where they've been. I want you to split up into teams of two and target the island. One of the victims was wearing wellington boots stamped at Wylfa Power Station. Let's show their pictures to everyone who works on site and speak to the guesthouses and pubs in Cemaes Bay. They may have been working on that side of the island, but my hunch is they were in Holyhead.'

'Why Holyhead?'

'Because that's where all the people involved in drugs are,' Alan said. The room remained quiet. Some of the heads nodded in agreement. 'Keep in touch with your findings. We'll have a debrief at eight o'clock tonight. See you later.'

CHAPTER 9

He watched and waited. It was late afternoon and the sun was fading. The number of cars coming and going had dwindled to the odd one or two. Dog walkers wandered from the woods to their cars, heading home before dark. There were only two vehicles remaining when he climbed out of the car and pulled a black coat from the boot. The temperature was dropping quickly as night approached. He walked towards the paths that threaded through the nature reserve in a long horseshoe shape. They all looped back to where they began; the car park.

Left or right, which one to take? So much in life was impulsive. He paused for a moment and decided to go left. The path became gloomy within a few yards. He put his hands deep into his pockets and walked on. His right hand touched the cold handle of the knife. It weighed heavy in his coat. He wanted a sheath so he could attach it to a belt but couldn't risk buying one online. It would be too easy to trace. No one could know about the knife, not ever.

He slowed down as he went past the pet cemetery. It always fascinated him. He loved reading the names and the inscriptions that people dedicated to their furry friends. They were far more touching than anything he'd seen in a human graveyard. The emotional pain was there to be seen in every line. Humans genuinely loved their pets with all their hearts and of course it was true the love was returned unconditionally, with bells on. Especially dogs. He'd loved his dog Hugo when he was alive. It was heart-breaking taking Hugo to the vet to put him out of his misery. Hugo's hips had gone and he couldn't stand up anymore. He was in constant pain. It was the kindest thing to do.

He saw a woman approaching from the opposite direction. She was walking a chocolate labrador. It was beautiful, but it was a powerful animal too. They weren't aggressive in nature but if you attack a dog's owner, you risk being bitten. Most dogs will defend their owners. It would be noisy and wasn't worth the risk. There would be others. There were always others. He smiled as she approached, and she smiled back. He caught the scent of her perfume and it made him tense. The heady rush of pheromones made his knees weak. He imagined inhaling the perfume from her neck as the knife sliced through her clothes before penetrating her flesh – the look on her face as the light faded from her eyes. Oh God, he wanted to kill her so much. So much it hurt inside, like losing a friend. He had to focus to stop himself from going after her. Focus.

And then she was gone, completely unaware of how close she'd come to a killer. A killer on the Hunt. His pulse was racing as he walked on. He reached the turn in the path and ten minutes later he was next to the sea, heading back to the car park. It was then he saw a man standing just off the path facing the sea. He was looking over to Cable Bay, saw him coming, and turned to say hello. His hand gripped the handle and he felt the static. He slid the knife from his pocket. The man caught a glimpse of it at the last moment, his eyes widened in fear as the blade pierced his abdomen again and again. He opened his mouth to scream but it never came out.

CHAPTER 10

Jamie and Tony parked at the back of the South Stack pub. It was a three-storey building built by the Victorians from red brick with a Welsh slate roof. They walked through the rear beer garden, where a handful of smokers were braving the falling temperatures to get their nicotine hit. The fragrant smell of cannabis floated on the breeze. It was the usual faces in the garden no matter what day of the week it was. They were all locals. It wasn't the type of pub a tourist might wander in to. Some of them were casual acquaintances, some less than that yet most of them would boast they were regulars in Jamie's pub and close personal friends with him. Being associated to him could offer protection, like a forcefield around you. *'Don't touch him, he's one of Jamie's mates.'*

The truth was, they were piss-heads, every one of them, male and female—functioning alcoholics at best. Jamie was polite but he didn't make a habit of befriending his customers as they usually had an agenda; especially as he sold drugs and alcohol, the two substances they desired the most. There were a few people in his employ he could trust but he generally kept himself to himself.

The beer garden locals greeted them with smiles and handshakes. He was cordial but made it as quick as possible. It was like Groundhog Day, same as yesterday and would be the same tomorrow. He was inside the pub in seconds. The dartboard and pool table were in use and there were about a dozen other customers dotted about. They all said hello. Jamie spotted the face he wanted to see and made a beeline for the man.

'Have you paid your tab, Jenks?' Jamie asked. His eyes narrowed; his face taut.

'I was going to ask you for an extension until Friday, mate,' Jenks said, turning white.

'Drink your pint and piss off before I make you eat the glass,' Jamie said. 'If I see your face in here again before it's paid, you'll be drinking your food through a straw for the next six weeks, understand me?'

Jenks swallowed his beer and left like a scalded cat. No one said a word—the show was over. The bar was quite busy, so they walked into the lounge which was quiet. The barmaid brought two pints of Stella and placed them on the bar.

'Thanks, Holly. Has Ronny been in today?' Jamie asked. She shook her head. 'That's three days we haven't seen him. He's never stayed in for three days since he was a baby. Something is wrong.'

'I'll phone Steve and tell him to knock on his door,' Tony said. 'Steve is staying at his mums' a few doors up the street. Ronny never locks the door.' He made the call and instructed Steve to call in on Ronny. 'He'll give him a knock and call me back in ten.'

'Have you been on your Facebook today?' Holly asked.

'No. I don't need to because the first words out of your mouth are whatever bullshit is on there. Who needs to look when I've got you?'

'I like to know what's going on, that's all,' Holly said.

'And what is going on?'

'Lloyd Jones has been shooting his mouth off again. He reckons he offered you a fair fight and you didn't turn up. Called you a chicken shit.'

'Do you know what I have in my car?'

'No, what?' she asked, curious.

'A great big bag of not bothered.'

'Funny, Jamie. You're going to have to shut him up. People are gossiping about you and Lloyd and they're starting to talk about what happened to Paul Critchley.'

'Nothing happened to Paul Critchley,' Jamie said. He gulped from his pint. 'He left town and he's hiding under a rock, the scumbag.'

'Lloyd is a prick. He doesn't know when to be quiet. He isn't going to let it go,' Tony said. 'If you need me to have a word, let me know. I'll shut him up.'

'Someone needs to,' Holly said. She looked at Jamie with disappointment.

'Listen, Holly, don't look at me like that. If I reacted to every dick-head who has a pop at me online, I'd be in jail by now.'

'I'm just trying to help.'

'No, you're not. You're trying to cause trouble. There's a big difference. Wind your neck in and mind your own business.' Holly sloped off towards the bar, offended. 'And stay off my Facebook, you, nosey cow.'

'I was only trying to help,' she protested. She vanished around the corner.

'She means well,' Tony said. 'Even if she's a nosey bitch.'

'She could start a fight in an empty room. I'm trying to keep my head down, but Lloyd Jones is pushing my buttons. I don't need a ruck with him just now. The prick needs to realise Paul Critchley is a grass and he's gone to ground because everyone wants to kick his face in. Why is he so set on winding me up?'

'You know the score,' Tony said. 'Paul is his cousin. You threatened to cut his tongue out and throw him off the mountain the day before he went missing.' Tony shrugged and smiled. 'You can see his point.'

'Whose side are you on?' Jamie said. 'You're supposed to be on mine.' Tony laughed and patted Jamie on the back. His phone rang.

'What? Are you sure?' Tony said. Jamie looked at him confused. 'It's Steve. He's saying he thinks Ronny is dead,' Tony said, quietly. 'He can see him through the kitchen window. He's on the floor in a pool of blood.'

'How does he know he's dead?'

'He said he's grey and the blood has congealed. He's been there a while.'

'Shit,' Jamie said. 'How much of our gear has he got in there?'

'Three kilos and a seventy-thousand in cash.'

'Do you know where he hides it?'

'Yes.'

'He's sure the door is locked?'

'Yes. It's usually never locked.'

'We need to break in, find the stash, and get out. We'll phone the police when we've found it. Tell him not to touch anything until we get there.'

CHAPTER 11

Ronny Green was in his fifties and lived in his family home, left to him when his parents died. He'd been a joiner by trade, a very handsome man with a wicked sense of humour. Everyone loved Ronny. Sadly, in his later years, alcohol got its claws into him and he went downhill quickly. He couldn't hold down his job and spent his days and nights in the pubs. His popularity never waned but he became vulnerable and didn't like to say no. Some people took advantage of his kind nature, but the town's locals looked after him. He was one of those characters that everyone loved.

'Look, he's there,' Steve said. Jamie and Tony peered through the kitchen window. It was dark now but the kitchen light was on. They were in the back yard which had a high wall around it, topped with cement and broken glass. The neighbours couldn't see into the yard. 'I told you, he's long gone. Look at the colour of him.'

'Has he been attacked?'

'I can't tell from here,' Steve said.

'Open the back door, Tony,' Jamie said. His face was like thunder. Ronny was much older but had been a good friend over the years. Jamie had known him since he was a boy and looked up to him when he was in his prime. He'd been a well-mannered man but was as tough as they come. No one messed with Ronny in his heyday. Jamie was gutted to see his friend lying dead on the floor. It felt like a kick in the guts. 'I can't believe he's dead.'

Tony slid a jemmy under the lock and forced it. The doorframe cracked and the hinges creaked as it opened. The trio stepped inside gingerly as if Ronny may jump up and bite them. A stale sour smell hung in the air.

'Don't step in the blood,' Jamie said. 'The last thing we want is the police thinking one of us did this. He's dead as a dodo.' Ronny was grey, his skin taut, his eyes sunken and staring. He had dried blood around his nose and mouth. Jamie studied the body from as close as he dared. 'It looks to me like someone has worked him over. His face is a mess.'

'He doesn't look bad enough to have died from a hiding, Jamie,' Tony said.

'His heart might have given up,' Jamie said. 'He wasn't a well man.'

'Who would hurt Ronny?' Steve asked.

'Someone looking for the stash,' Tony said. 'What other reason could they have?'

'I don't know but I'm going to find out,' Jamie said. 'Let's have a look around. Where did he hide it?'

'There's a freezer in the utility room. It's got a fake bottom,' Tony said. 'He fills it full of ragworms and tripe for fishing.'

'I didn't know he fished,' Steve said.

'He didn't,' Jamie said. 'It was to put the police off if they raided the place. Find it. I want to have a look around upstairs.'

'Okay.'

Tony headed to the rear of the house; Jamie went into the living room. The settee had been slashed to pieces, foam and springs protruded from every tear. The television was cracked, and an armchair had been tipped upside down and the bottom ripped open. He walked into the hallway and climbed the stairs slowly. There was blood smeared on the walls and the handrail. The bedrooms were open and there was a similar scene in each one. The mattresses were cut and ripped open, the drawers opened and tipped onto the floor. It was clear someone knew Ronny was hiding a stash for Jamie. He owned nothing of value himself. It looked like they'd questioned Ronny for the location of the loot and it was obvious he had held out. Jamie wondered how long for.

'Jamie,' Tony called upstairs. 'We've got it. It's all there.'

'Right,' Jamie said. Anger boiled in his guts. It was possible someone had hurt his friend before he died, still withholding the whereabouts of Jamie's stash. He'd stayed loyal right to the end. If someone had hurt him, there would be retribution taken for Ronny. When he found out who had done it, they would wish they'd never been born. Things were coming to the boil and people were overstepping the mark. It was time to put them back in their boxes and teach them a lesson they would never forget. He walked to the top of the stairs.

'Shall we call the cops, now?' Steve asked.

'Yes. I want you to tell them you saw him through the window and broke in the back door to help him but when you got in, you realised he was dead,' Jamie said.

'Can't we just do it anonymously?' Steve said.

'No. The back door has been forced. I don't want that to cloud the investigation. Call them and wait outside for them. They'll ask you a few questions and let you go,' Jamie said. 'I'll see you right for it.'

'Are we going back to the Stack?' Tony asked. 'We need to put this gear away.'

'Not yet,' Jamie said. 'I want you to go and pick up Lloyd Jones. Bring him to the yard. Enough is enough.'

CHAPTER 12

Alan and Kim walked into the Valley Hotel. It was an old coaching house on the A5, with a big restaurant and accommodation above. Outside was a kiddie's play area the size of a football pitch. The drive to Wylfa Power Station was less than twenty minutes from there. It was the ideal place to stay for contractors. He had a hunch that's what the Matrix officers would've posed as; workers from Wylfa or RAF Valley. They walked through the dining room into the bar. There were a handful of locals drinking and watching Sky Sports. One of them was Alan's dentist, a South African man called Johan. He smiled and shook hands.

'Afternoon, Alan,' Johan said. 'Are you having a late lunch?'

'Unfortunately, not. We're here on business. This is my DS, Kim Davies.' Kim shook hands with him and smiled. Johan's eyes lingered on her teeth a little too long. 'Have you ever seen these men in here?' Alan asked. Johan looked at the photograph and shook his head.

'They're not familiar to me,' Johan said. 'Who are they?'

'We don't know yet.'

'I've heard there's been a couple of murders over towards the Bay. Is this anything to do with that?'

'Loosely,' Alan said, being diplomatic. The barman approached. Alan didn't know him. 'A pint of Guinness and a half of smooth, please.' The barman started pouring the beer. 'Have you seen either of these men in here?'

'No, but I only work one day a week,' the young man said. 'You want to ask Harry over there. He knows everyone around here.'

'Thanks,' Alan said. He paid for the drinks and passed Kim the pint of Guinness. She smiled and sipped from the glass. 'Let's go and speak to Harry. Excuse us.' They moved away from the bar and Harry watched them approach. He had slicked back white hair and a Santa beard. Alan recognised him as a herder from the cattle market which had been closed for twenty-years. 'Hello, Harry,' Alan said. 'I think you'll remember my father, Peter Williams, from the cattle auction.' The light of recognition flickered in his eyes. 'I'm his son, Alan.'

'Well, well, well. That was a long time ago. I remember you when you had hair,' Harry said. 'Is your dad still with us?'

'No. He died ten years ago.'

'He was a rogue in that auction,' Harry laughed. 'I remember him buying a Welsh dresser for thirty-pounds and no one could work out who'd bought it. He put the hammer down on his own bid and moved on so quickly, no one noticed.'

'That dresser was still in kitchen when we sold the house last year,' Alan said. 'You have a good memory.'

'Is your mum still here?'

'No. I lost my mum and my sister, Audrey in the space of six months.'

'I'm sorry to hear that. I remember your mum. She was a lovely lady. Very softly spoken. I often teased your dad he was punching above his weight. And he was.'

'He was,' Alan said.

'You haven't come over here to reminisce,' Harry said, putting on his glasses. 'Let's have a look at your photograph. I saw you handing it around at the bar.'

'Thanks, Harry,' Alan said. 'Do you recognise these two men? We think they might have been contractors staying on the island somewhere.'

Harry studied their faces. He shook his head and took off his glasses. 'They haven't been in here,' he said. 'But I've seen them in town having breakfast.'

'When?' Alan said.

'A few times over the last few weeks. They've been eating in the Empire Café near the cinema,' Harry said. 'They're from the Liverpool area. Not Scousers but not far away. The Wirral maybe. I used to deliver that way when I was on the cattle trucks.'

'I remember you driving them,' Alan said. 'Did they say what they were doing here?'

'I can't say they did but I tend to keep myself to myself.'

'Did you see them talking to anyone in particular?'

'It's a friendly little café full of nosey buggers and they were friendly lads, chatted to everyone,' Harry said. 'They spent most of their time chatting to Eric Stott. You must know Eric. He ran the video and DVD shop in town for years.'

'I know him,' Alan said. 'I remember his shop on Williams Street. I can remember renting Betamax videos from him.'

'Betamax?' Harry said. 'Now you're showing your age.'

'I am. That was a long time ago.'

'Speak to him. If anyone knows anything about them, it's Eric. He asks more questions than Parkinson.'

'Now you're showing your age, Harry,' Alan said.

'Who's Parkinson?' Kim asked.

'Drink your Guinness,' Alan said. 'Thanks, Harry. Nice to see you again.' Harry nodded goodbye. Alan checked his watch. 'The café won't be open now but I know where Eric Stott used to live. He might still live there. Let's go and speak to him.' Alan felt his phone vibrating. The screen showed it was the station. 'DI Williams,' he answered.

'Alan, it's Bob Dewhurst.'

'Hiya, Bob,' Alan said. Bob Dewhurst was his opposite number in the uniformed division and a lifelong friend. 'What can I do for you?'

'I thought you'd want to know I've just dispatched a unit to a house on Pump Street. It's a suspected murder victim found in his kitchen by a friend who called around because he hadn't been seen for a few days. It's Ronny Green,' Bob said. 'It looks like the place has been ransacked.'

'Bloody hell. I went to school with Ronny,' Alan said. 'He's connected to Jamie Hollins, isn't he?'

'That's why I called. It's too much of a coincidence, don't you think?'

'Yes. Thanks, Bob. I'm in Valley now. Tell your officers I'll be ten minutes at the most. I want to take a look at this for myself.'

'Will do.'

'A man called Ronny Green has been found dead in his home,' Alan said to Kim. 'He's a well-known guy who fell on hard times. The rumours are he was running errands for Jamie Hollins.'

'Another drug related death,' Kim said, shaking her head. 'It sounds like your friend in Liverpool was right about a power struggle.'

'It does. We need to get a grip on this before things get out of hand again.'

'Again?' Kim asked.

'There was a time in the eighties when the town nearly turned itself inside out. Three small families went to war over the supply chain, mostly cannabis back then. This was way before your average islander could afford cocaine even if they could find any to buy. It took two years to settle down. Not a night went by without someone ending up in casualty. Windows were smashed, cars were trashed, relatives beaten senseless, and then three members of the same family were found in a burnt-out Capri near the quarry.' Alan recalled. 'That was the final straw. The chief constable of the day, a man called Elwyn Hughes called in help from Merseyside and Manchester. They arrested more people in a week than they had in the previous month. The courts were crammed with emergency sessions and twenty-nine people were jailed over two weeks. Things went back to normal for a long time although the underlying grudges are still there, bubbling beneath the surface.' They reached the car and climbed in. 'You might wonder why I'm telling you this, but it could be relevant.'

'Could be relevant why?'

'The three families: the Hollins, the Jones, and the Greens.'

CHAPTER 13

Simon and Kerry were shown into the engineering department and taken to the manager's office through an open workspace—computer terminals were fixed to black desks in rows of thirty or more. Simon counted over a hundred desks with high definition screens on them. Some of the employees hardly paid any attention to the strangers while others speculated who they were in whispers. The section manager looked flustered when he greeted them at the door. He had *'I'm too busy for this shit'* written all over his face. His tie was fastened loosely around an open collar and his sleeves were rolled up. There were sweat patches beneath his arms. His eyes had dark circles beneath them, and his thin lips were pale and turned down at the corners. He had a permanently unhappy expression.

'Barry Trent,' he introduced himself.

'I'm DS Brady,' Simon said.

'DS Leach,' Kerry added.

'I'm Kelvin's boss. Or I was, I should say. Sit down please. How can I help you?'

'We wanted to speak to you and Kelvin's workmates about his general demeanour the last few weeks,' Simon said. 'Did you notice anything out of character?'

'That's a bit vague. I'm not sure what you mean?'

'Did he have any arguments with anyone, did he look stressed or depressed or worried to you?'

'We're always stressed here. The deadlines are unachievable. They'll replace us with robots eventually and they'll probably burn them out too.' Simon smiled but there was no mirth in Barry Trent. His expression didn't change. 'So, to answer your question, no to all the above.'

'He didn't have any disagreements with anyone?' Simon asked.

'No. Kelvin was a model employee, never upset anyone, never caused me any problems at all. He was always on time and never phoned in sick. We got your request for his computer but obviously it contains a lot of patented information so we can't let you take it, I'm afraid. I've taken the liberty of having the hard drive from his computer downloaded onto this,' Barry said. He handed a disc to Kerry. 'Obviously, we've had to remove the classified stuff but his emails, internal and external, are on there. If there's anything else we can do, don't hesitate to ask.'

'Thank you,' Kerry said, taking the disk. 'Who were his friends?'

'He was friendly with everyone,' Barry said.

'Who did he sit next to?' Simon asked.

'Glen Price,' Barry said. 'They worked together on most projects.'

'Can we speak to Glen?'

'No. He's been off sick for a few days,' Barry said. He looked from Simon to Kerry. They exchanged surprised glances.

'When did he go off sick?' Simon asked.

'The day before yesterday.'

'What's wrong with him?' Kerry asked.

'Sickness and diarrhoea his wife said when she called in sick for him,' Barry said. 'I'm sorry. Why are we talking about Glen?'

'Because he sat next to a man who was murdered the same day he called in sick,' Simon said. 'We're going to need his address.'

* * *

Lloyd Jones snorted a line of his own product and closed his eyes to wait for the effect. It was hardly worth waiting for. The gear was shit, again. His sales were down seventy per cent the week before and eighty the week prior to that. The suppliers had stitched him up again. His regular source had just been banged up for ten years and as soon as he was sentenced, his supply chain collapsed. It was like the Wild West now, cowboys everywhere. He'd spent days in Liverpool and Manchester trying to secure a decent supplier. His contacts were running scared from new gangs trying to muscle in on the void caused by Operation Suzie. It was a dangerous time to be unconnected. The samples he'd tried had been reasonable quality, but the end product was garbage. This was the third week with only crap cocaine to sell.

It was better to have no product than to sell shit product. Especially when Jamie Hollins was still selling quality cocaine. He couldn't fathom how that tosser had managed to maintain his supply. Lloyd had spoken to other dealers along the North Wales coast and they were all complaining. All except Hollins; he was a gobshite, full of himself.

He heard an engine running and grabbed his baseball bat before peering through the curtains. There was a taxi outside the house across the road, dropping off the old bint who lived there. She was another gobshite. He couldn't remember the last time he'd seen her sober. You could set your clock by her movements, ten minutes to eleven in the morning, she left to go to Gleesons, a pub on the high street. At half past six, she arrived home with a bottle of wine and a kebab and occasionally, a male victim. One of them had moved in for a few weeks—they didn't have half a dozen teeth between them and the ones they had were black. She saw him looking through the curtains and stuck her middle finger up at him. There was no love lost between them. He flicked a finger back at her and closed the curtains.

Lloyd looked at the packages of cocaine. He'd paid for one kilo and owed for the other. They had given him a line of credit as a gesture of goodwill. He couldn't sell goodwill. They hadn't done him a favour; they'd ripped him off. He wasn't letting anyone get away with that. He picked up his phone, dialling the supplier again. It clicked straight to voicemail. He told them he wasn't paying what he owed them, left a string of expletives in a garbled message, and threatened to shoot them the next time he saw them. The men he'd dealt with were Eastern European, Albanian, or some other godforsaken hellhole. He should have known better, but he was desperate for product. Doing business with Albanians was dangerous; he'd been warned but he hadn't listened. They'd taken him to a rundown pub which stood alone on some waste ground. It was intimidating to say the least. The cocaine was on the table in plain view, not that it mattered—the only people in there were their gang members. There must have been twenty of them, armed to the teeth. Some played pool, some played poker but most of them watched the deal, scowling at Lloyd and his minder, Ron Took. Ron was a giant, but he couldn't stop a bullet. The samples they gave him were quality but the packages he came away with were crap. They promised to deliver the same every two weeks. Securing a regular supply was priceless, so he took the deal not realising the quality was so poor.

If he tried to sell it and pass it off as decent gear, he would lose the customers he had left for good. They would never come back. Most of his customers only came to him because they couldn't buy from Hollins, probably because they owed him money. Their options were limited but they wouldn't buy crap. He had to cut it with something that would give the buyers a buzz, even if it wasn't great and didn't last long. The only thing that would do that was benzocaine. He could buy it online for ten pounds a kilo, cook it with the cocaine, and make 'Brack', similar to crack but cheaper to make and just as addictive. That would triple his money and get him back in the game. Cashflow was king and all his cash was invested in two kilos of shit cocaine. He would have to make the best of a bad lot.

Lloyd sat down with his laptop and searched online for the benzocaine. An hour later he was more frustrated than he had been before he started. Every site that sold the drug was out of stock. It was obvious he wasn't the first dealer to think of the idea. There was so much shit gear being wholesaled, every man and his dog was buying it up and he was at the back of the queue. He googled the other options. Lidocaine had similar properties but was more expensive. It would eat into his profits but he had no choice so he went back through the search process. Lidocaine was sold out too. He stood up and kicked the chair over. It clattered against the wall and landed upside down. It was then he noticed the boots standing in the kitchen doorway. As his eyes moved upwards, he saw the barrels of a sawn-off shotgun pointed at him.

'Are you pissed off, Lloyd?' Tony asked. 'I see you've had a delivery.' Tony gestured to the packages of drugs. 'If it's from Liverpool, it's shite,' he added.

'What do you want?' Lloyd asked, angrily.

'Jamie wants a word with you,' Tony said. 'You've stepped over the line, my friend. I told you to keep your mouth shut last year but you won't listen, will you?'

'I'm not going anywhere with you. If you're going to shoot me, shoot me here,' Lloyd said. 'I know you lot killed Paul. If you think I'll be as easy to kidnap, think again.' Lloyd pulled a flick knife and the blade clicked open.

'You never were very bright,' Tony said. A Taser sent fifty thousand volts through Lloyd's neck and he collapsed onto the carpet. 'Pick him up and stick him in the van,' Tony said to the men who had entered through the front door behind him.

'What about his gear?' one of them asked.

'Leave that where it is,' Tony said. 'We don't move crap like that.'

* * *

Alan and Kim arrived at the house in Pump Street. A marked police car was parked outside. Nearby, a uniformed officer was talking to a man Alan recognised as Steven, although his surname eluded him. They climbed out of the vehicle, struggled into forensic suits from the boot and walked to the front door. The officer left Steven and met them.

'Ronny Green is in the kitchen, guv,' he said. 'I've called CSI. They're on their way. The place has been turned over.'

'Okay. We'll take a look,' Alan said. He pointed to Steven. 'Did he find him?'

'Yes, guv. He hadn't seen him in the pub for a few days. He said the house was locked up, which was unusual. Apparently, Ronny ran an open house. His front door was always open, and people called around all the time. He couldn't get an answer, so he climbed over the back wall and saw Ronny on the floor in the kitchen. He broke in and then called us. The house is as he found it.'

'Is he telling the truth?'

'I think so, guv. I know him, he's not a bad lad. He was good friends with Ronny.'

'Thanks,' Alan said. 'Let's take a look, shall we.'

The front door led straight into the living room. The odour of a ripe dead body hit them. Alan studied the furniture and moved into the kitchen. He knelt next to Ronny. His face was injured, and blood had run from his nose and mouth.

'He's in the foetal position,' Alan said.

'Meaning?'

'A doctor once told me it indicated the victim was in pain. Not external pain but internal,' Alan said. 'It's clear the house has been ransacked but there's no sign of a struggle in here. The witness said he saw the body through the kitchen window. Let's check that.'

They walked out of the kitchen into the yard and looked through the window. The body was in clear view. They went back inside, checked the utility room, and looked in the freezer. Despite being frozen, the tripe and worms were pungent. They scowled and moved away, closing the lid quickly.

'I'm going to have a quick word with Steven outside,' Alan said.

'Is something bothering you?'

'Yes. I don't like being treated like an idiot,' Alan said.

'I'll take a look upstairs,' Kim said, smiling. 'What are you thinking?'

'I'm wondering what they were looking for, whoever they are.'

Alan walked through the living room and out of the front door. The CSI team had arrived. Pamela Stone wasn't with them. He hoped she was busy on his cases. He said hello and walked over to Steven and the uniformed officer.

'You're Steven, aren't you?' Alan asked.

'Steve. Only my old dear calls me Steven.'

'What's your surname, Steve?' Alan asked.

'Dillon,' Steve said.

'That's right,' Alan said. He nodded. 'I remember now.'

'Do I know you?'

'Yes. I nicked you for possession in the nineties. It was in the Angel on a rock night.'

'Sorry. I don't remember the nineties,' Steve said, shuffling his feet. He stared at the floor.

'Funny man,' Alan said. 'It was a long time ago. I'll give you that.' He paused. 'Why did you break in, Steve?' Alan asked. 'If you looked through the kitchen window, it's clear Ronny is dead.'

'I just wanted to make sure,' Steve said. 'He might have needed an ambulance or something.'

'I don't think you thought that, Steve,' Alan said, wagging his forefinger. Steve frowned. He looked nervous. 'You told the officer it was unusual for the house to be locked up.'

'It was. Ronny always left the front door open. I couldn't get in so I jumped over the back. That's when I saw him.'

'Why do you think the door was locked?' Alan asked.

'How would I know?'

'Who searched the house?'

'I don't know that either.'

'Did Ronny hide gear for Jamie Hollins?'

'Jamie who?' Steve asked, squinting. 'I don't know who you mean.'

'You do,' Alan said. 'He was with you when I arrested you in the Angel.'

'Was he?'

'Yes. He was.'

'Like I said, I don't remember the nineties.'

'You did say that,' Alan said. 'If we look at your phone, I reckon there will be a call made to Jamie Hollins or one of his cronies before you called us.'

'Look. I just found the body,' Steve said, feeling the urge to run away. He hadn't deleted the calls. 'That's not a crime is it?'

'No. But breaking in to a crime scene to remove contraband before reporting a crime is,' Alan said.

'I don't know what you're talking about.'

'Did you know Ronny had cameras all around the house?'

'No.'

'They're well hidden. We'll check them and if you're lying to me, you're in trouble.' Steve turned white. He looked like he was going to puke. 'You don't look very well. Are you okay?' Steve nodded. There was an uncomfortable pause. 'I'll let you into a little secret. There are no cameras, but your reaction tells me everything I need to know. We weren't born yesterday, Steve. We'll need to speak to him again.' Alan turned to the uniformed officer. 'Do you have his details?'

'Yes, guv.'

'That's all for now,' Alan said. 'Don't be booking any holidays for a while. We'll need to speak to you again, soon.'

Steve turned and walked away quickly, shoulders hunched, his hands shoved deep into his pockets. 'Knock on some doors,' Alan said to the uniformed officer. 'If people were coming and going all the time, someone may have seen a familiar face leaving through the front door.'

'Yes, guv.'

Alan's phone rang. The screen showed it was the station.

'DI Williams.'

'Alan, it's Dafyd,' the superintendent said. 'Where are you?'

'I'm in Holyhead. We've got another body,' Alan said. 'It's a suspicious death connected to Jamie Hollins.'

'Are CSI on it?'

'They've just arrived.'

'I need you and Kim back here immediately,' Dafyd said. He sounded stressed. 'There's been an important development we need to discuss.'

'I was going to follow up on a lead on our UCs. They were seen eating breakfast in town a few times, so they may have been staying nearby.'

'No. I need to talk to you both immediately. Head back here straightaway.'

The line went dead and Alan looked at the screen, a little bit miffed and very confused.

CHAPTER 14

He watched the docudrama with mixed emotions. Part of him was fascinated, part of him seething with the inaccuracies in the timeline. Peter Moore, the man in black. The story of Wales's only recorded serial killer. Recorded being the operative word. He watched the credits at the end and took it back to the beginning before pressing play again. The knife was resting on his lap. The knife. His knife. It had a life of its own, it whispered to him. When he touched it, images flashed through his mind, the sounds and voices of those it had cut echoed through his consciousness. His fingertips stroked the blade as if it was a loved one. He closed his eyes and relived the recent kill. The man's face, his eyes, the warmth of his blood, the coppery smell, and the sound of his last breath leaving his lungs. He wondered at the ease with which the blade had sliced through him. It was a monumental moment in time. The connection between them was eternal, almost religious. Their souls were entwined for eternity as if they were one person. He checked his watch and wondered how long there was left to watch. There was enough time to watch it through again before he had to go back to work and then he could morph into who he really was. He was changing all the time, becoming more like him by the day. His fate was already mapped out before him. He would become far greater than his predecessors. It was as if he was invisible, walking among them like a ghost, picking and choosing who lived and who dies.

CHAPTER 15

Simon and Kerry pulled up outside a house in Prestatyn. It was on the coast road, detached from its neighbours by a few hundred yards. Ornate wrought-iron gates were fastened to tall brick gateposts, topped with smoked-glass globes. The house was substantial, probably four bedrooms, with a triple garage to the side. It was in total darkness.

'It looks like there's no one home,' Kerry said.

'It does. We'll have to come back another day,' Simon agreed. He put the Ford into first and indicated to move back into the light traffic. A Porsche Cayenne stopped opposite them and indicted to turn into the driveway. The gates opened automatically, and the Porsche pulled across the road. 'I think we're in luck. They're home.' He tucked the Ford behind the Porsche and followed it down the driveway. The driver spotted them and stopped sharply. 'I think we've been spotted.'

The driver's door opened and a tall man with grey hair jumped out. He looked nervous, almost frightened as he approached the Ford. Simon took out his warrant card and opened the window.

'I'm DS Brady and this is DS Leach,' he said, showing his identification. 'Are you Glen Price?'

'Yes. What do you want?'

'We're investigating the murder of your colleague Kelvin Adams and we'd like to have a word with you, Mr Price.'

'I'm very busy at the moment,' Mr Price said.

'It won't take long,' Simon said.

'We're having a family crisis of our own,' Mr Price said. He shook his head and frowned. Simon thought his abruptness was unusual to say the least. 'You'll have to come back another time, I'm afraid.'

'We'll come back in the morning about ten o'clock if that suits,' Simon said. He used a tone that suggested it wasn't a request. 'I have your number; we'll call ahead to make sure you're here.'

'I'm not sure how I can help,' Mr Price said. His eyes darted left to right.

'We just have a few questions, Mr Price, nothing to worry about,' Simon said, finding reverse. 'Enjoy your evening. We'll see you in the morning at ten.'

Mr Price watched them leave, concern etched across his face. Simon watched him in the mirror.

'That was very odd,' Kerry said. 'If anyone has got something to hide, it's Mr Glen Price.'

'There's no doubt about it. He didn't ask anything about the investigation or why we wanted to speak to him,' Simon said. 'Most people would want to help if a friend was murdered. They go out of their way to help, not Mr Price.' Simon pulled onto the coast road and headed back towards the island. 'Mr Price doesn't have sickness and diarrhoea but he does look like a rabbit in the headlights. He's frightened. I'll put money on the fact he knows something about Kelvin Adams we don't.' Simon paused. 'How much does an engineer at Jaguar earn a year?'

'I was thinking the same thing when they pulled in,' Kerry said. 'That Porsche has got to be eighty grand at least, would you think?'

'At least,' Simon said. 'And that house is impressive.'

'I'm looking forward to chatting to Mr Price,' Kerry said.

'Me too.'

CHAPTER 16

Alan and Kim walked into Dafyd's office. There were some familiar faces in the room although he wasn't expecting to see them there. There were some unfamiliar faces too.

'Come in, come in,' Dafyd said. 'This is DI Alan Williams and DS Kim Davies.' The gathering said hello with little enthusiasm. The atmosphere in the room was tense. 'This is DCI Kensington, head of our national Drug Squad and this is Chief Superintendent Hunt from the Matrix unit, Merseyside. Everyone else, you know already.'

'No, hold on a minute,' Alan said. Dafyd blushed. 'I don't know these gentlemen.' He pointed to two men in suits, standing near the window.

'Superintendent Wallace and Inspector Banks, National Crime Agency,' Wallace said, stony-faced. 'We're here in an advisory role only.'

'NCA in Caernarfon, I see why you needed us back so quickly,' Alan said. 'There must be something going on that we don't know about. Would someone like to bring us up to speed?'

'The undercover officers you pulled out of the sea are Mike Jarvis and Patrick McGowan,' Chief Superintendent Hunt said, abruptly. 'Unfortunately, they stumbled into Operation Thor, the biggest joint constabulary investigation ever carried out by our forces.'

'Operation Thor,' Alan said to Kim. He shrugged. 'I've never heard of it.'

'We're in the third year of the investigation,' Hunt said. 'When we close in, we will unequivocally dismantle the supply chain across the North-West and North Wales.'

'Wow, that's a bold statement,' Alan said. 'I don't think that's realistic.' Dafyd shook his head to silence him. Alan ignored his advice. 'Certainly not in the long term.'

'We think it is. We're going to take out every layer of the operation so it will be impossible to build it back up to the level it's at now,' Hunt said.

'You're going to need to break that down for me.'

'We can't go into detail for obvious reasons.'

'You're here telling us there's been an investigation running for three years in our area that we don't know about and now you want us to do what?'

'We have infiltrated over a dozen outfits and we have thousands of hours of audio and video surveillance on the top dealers involved in the supply chain. You can imagine how much time it's taken to get officers established and trusted within the organisations; but it's very fragile.'

'And you're involved in this operation, DCI Kensington?' Alan asked. Despite being part of the Welsh force, he wasn't very familiar with the DCI as Kensington was new to the role.

'Yes. Of course.'

'Okay, what has this got to do with our investigation?'

'You could inadvertently tread on our operation,' Kensington said.

'We can't have that, can we?' Alan said. 'What do you need from us, how can we help you?'

'We need you to tread carefully around the known suppliers in Holyhead,' Hunt said.

'I'm assuming Mike Jarvis and Patrick McGowan were working on something else apart from Thor when they were murdered?' Alan asked.

'Yes.'

'What were they working on?'

'They were working on an Albanian outfit who have been establishing themselves in the North-West for some time now,' Superintendent Wallace spoke.

'Hence your involvement in this?'

'Yes. They're part of a bigger organisation based in London and Amsterdam but lately, their forays up here have been more frequent and violent.'

'Since Operation Suzie?'

'Yes. It caused a power vacuum and the Albanians are set to take over. Jarvis and McGowan were investigating their activities. We think they linked them with your area and followed a lead to the island.'

'The Albanian outfits are heavy hitters,' Alan said. 'Violent in the extreme, I believe?'

'Very,' Wallace said.

'Why would an organisation that big be interested in a small backwater like this?' Alan asked. 'Unless the supply chain is changing direction.' He paused.

'It could be,' Wallace said.

'They're interested in the port, aren't they?'

'We think so,' Wallace said, nodding. 'Things in London are taut. Controlling Liverpool and Holyhead would give them access to two of the busiest ports in the UK.'

'Liverpool is a jungle,' Alan said. 'And Holyhead is a soft target in comparison.'

'Exactly. We think that's what Jarvis and McGowan were following.'

'But you have nothing concrete on them from your investigations here?' Alan asked.

'No. The Albanians haven't come up in any conversations we've listened to,' Hunt said.

'You're talking about your audio surveillance?'

'Yes.'

'You have audio and video surveillance on who exactly?' Alan asked. The hairs on his neck were tingling. He could feel what was coming. The senior officers looked at each other but didn't elaborate. 'Oh, come on. You're monitoring dealers in our area who could be involved in this murder investigation. Are you telling us to avoid certain people?'

'Yes.'

'Jamie Hollins?' Alan asked.

'Especially Jamie Hollins,' Hunt said.

'We need you to give Hollins a wide berth. He's not to be interviewed or questioned, followed or rattled in any way.' Kensington cleared his throat. 'We have his pub, his vehicles, and his other businesses bugged. There are thousands of hours of evidence which could be compromised if you bumble into our investigation. When we arrest him, he will go down for thirty years and his crew will do fifteen each, minimum. We're making an example to every wannabe Welsh Pablo Escobar that drugs don't pay in the long run and we won't tolerate it.'

'I didn't know I bumbled,' Alan said, looking at Dafyd. 'Do I bumble?'

'Sometimes,' Dafyd said, nodding. He intervened before Alan could drop himself in it. 'We can safely say we get the message and the last thing we would want to do is compromise your operation.'

'We're willing to work with you on this,' the chief inspector said. 'Obviously, we want the murders of Jarvis and McGowan investigated to the best of your abilities and the killers strung up by the bollocks, but we need you to leave Hollins alone.'

'That's all very well but what if our investigation leads straight to his front door?' Alan asked.

'We'll have a conversation,' the chief said. His eyes narrowed. 'It's a bridge we can cross when we get there. All we need for now is your assurance that you'll keep our operation in mind. If we keep the lines of communication open, we'll be fine. You can give me daily updates, Dafyd. That way we can avoid any friendly fire.'

'Perfect,' Alan said. He stood up. 'If that's all we need to know, I've got a briefing to update. Obviously, we won't repeat anything you've told us to my team. Do you think your undercover operation could be compromised too?'

'Without sounding callous, Jarvis and McGowan weren't aware of our operation, so they couldn't have named any of our UCs.' The other officers nodded, quietly. 'But the truth is, we don't know for sure.'

'Thanks for the information. We'll keep Dafyd informed all the way,' Alan added on his way out. Kim followed him. They walked towards the operations room, each in their own thoughts. 'What do you think about that?'

'I think we're heading for trouble with Matrix. What do you think?'

'I'm hoping they're wrong about the Albanian crews creeping onto the island. That lot make Jamie Hollins and Lloyd Jones look like boy scouts. They would chew them up and spit them out. I think they would be safer in jail than tackling them.'

CHAPTER 17

Lloyd was stiff and disoriented. His neck felt like it had a steel bar inserted into it. His memory was rebooting. The sequence of events began to slot into place. He remembered being zapped from behind and he began to panic. His limbs wouldn't move. He struggled but his arms and legs were fastened to a metal frame. He opened his eyes and took in the scene through the fog that unconsciousness had left behind. Jamie Hollins was sitting on a workbench surrounded by tools and welding gear. Lloyd guessed where he was. The Hollins family had been welders and farriers for generations before Jamie ventured into narcotics. His brother was a legitimate businessman with a flourishing metal company. They had a yard and workshop on Holy Mountain. It was in an isolated spot and he knew shouting for help was pointless. His voice would be carried out to sea on the wind for no one to hear. The dull sound of the foghorn at North Stack echoed across the mountain. It was a forlorn noise, especially now, he thought, like a harbinger of doom.

'What am I doing here, Hollins?' Lloyd asked, his voice slurred.

'I need to ask you some questions because you're getting on my tits, Lloyd. Did you pay Ronny Green a visit?' Jamie asked.

'Ronny Green?' Lloyd asked, confused. 'I haven't seen Ronny for weeks. He only drinks in your pubs. I heard he's on your payroll now.'

'Pubs?' Jamie said. 'I own the South Stack, that's it.'

'That's what you want people to think but you're not as clever as you think you are,' Lloyd said, a wry smile on his face. 'You own the Ddraigh Goch and the Welsh Fusilier but you think no one knows.'

'Those pubs are dead. Why would I want to own them?'

'It's called money laundering.'

'You listen to some fairy tales, Lloyd. I've heard those rumours too but that's all they are. Back to the original question, Ronny Green was found dead in his house. He's an old friend of mine. Did you call round his house and beat him up?'

'Not guilty,' Lloyd said. 'Ronny Green never did anything to me. My problem is with you, no one else and I don't have a problem saying it to your face either.'

'You don't say it to my face, Lloyd, you paste it all over the Internet like a teenage girl with her knickers in a twist. You're a keyboard warrior, hard as nails when you're sitting in your bedroom but you're nothing. You pissed yourself tonight, tough guy.' Lloyd looked down. He had pissed himself. That was embarrassing to say the least. 'I'm only going to say this once, Lloyd so, listen well.' Jamie stood up and walked over to him. He was holding Lloyd's flick knife. The blade clicked out and Lloyd flinched. Jamie used the blade to free his left hand. 'I'm sick to the back teeth of your threats and ranting about your cousin.' He freed his right hand. Lloyd looked shocked and rubbed his wrists. Jamie cut his ankles free. 'Your cousin, Paul Critchley isn't dead and if he is, I didn't kill him.'

'You threatened to throw him off the mountain and the next day, he disappeared and none of the family have heard from him.' Lloyd moved away from the frame. 'What am I supposed to think?'

'What else happened around that time?' Jamie asked. 'Have a good think about it.' Lloyd frowned. He was clearly shaken and confused at being released. 'Think about who got sent down soon after he went missing.'

'I don't know what your game is, Hollins, bringing me up here with your monkeys glaring at me,' Lloyd said. Four of Jamie's crew looked on. 'There's not one of them would face me one to one.' The men laughed at him and shook their heads.

'You just can't help it, can you?' Jamie said, shaking his head. 'Every single man in this room would destroy you, Lloyd. Your problem is, you think you're Johnny Concrete but the truth is, you're far from it. You get Ron Took to do all your dirty work.' Jamie stared into his eyes so hard Lloyd looked away. He knew he was out of his league. Jamie was a unit, steroid built. He could break people. 'Do yourself a favour and think very carefully about what I'm saying.'

'I'm listening but you're not saying much.'

'Does the surname Hall ring any bells?'

'Hall?'

'They're from Valley.'

'The Hall brothers,' Lloyd said. 'Tom, Matt, and Andy. They're all inside for murder.'

'That's them,' Jamie said. 'How do you think the police knew they were going to Reg Hanney's house that night?' Lloyd looked blank and shrugged. 'I'll tell you how. They were given a tipoff that Hanney was going to be robbed. If the police hadn't been outside, no one would ever have known who'd done it. They would have been in and out. You see, it was an accident Hanney died. They didn't go there to kill him. They were going to take his money and his drugs but he fought back and got knocked down. He banged his head on a table.' He allowed the tale to sink in. 'Did you think the police got lucky and caught them leaving the scene by accident?'

'I've never given it much thought,' Lloyd said.

'Your cousin went missing a week after they were arrested,' Jamie said. 'Do you know why?'

'Because you threw him in the sea with a concrete block tied to him.'

'No, Lloyd. Because people were starting to put two and two together. The police turned up just as they were leaving with the drugs and the money on them and a dead body inside. No one gets that lucky. The only other person who knew about the robbery was Paul because he'd heard them talking when they were planning it. The Halls trusted your cousin. He isn't dead, Lloyd, he's in witness protection. That's why he hasn't contacted your family, he can't. It's part of the deal. They'll give him anonymity as long as he doesn't try to make contact. If he does, the deal is off.'

'You're a liar,' Lloyd said, shaking his head. 'Paul wasn't a grass.'

'Paul was a greedy conniving gobshite,' Jamie said. Lloyd glared angrily but there was doubt in his eyes now. 'He thought if the Halls got nicked, he could step into their boots and run things for a few months while they did their time, make a bit of money, skimming off the top but he hadn't planned on them killing Hanney. It was a big deal at the time. It was the murder of a popular man and people wanted to know how the police happened to be parked around the corner at the right time. It was obvious someone had grassed and once the Halls worked out who it was, Critchley vanished.'

'I don't believe it,' Lloyd said, shaking his head. 'Paul a grass. My uncle Pete would be spinning in his grave.' He looked stunned. 'Why are you telling me this now?' Lloyd said. 'What's this really about?'

'Have you heard about the two men dragged out of the sea in the Bay?'

'Yes, of course,' Lloyd said. 'What has that got to do with anything?'

'A little birdy tells me they're coppers,' Jamie said. 'I know it wasn't us that burned them and I doubt it was your lot.'

'We had nothing to do with that.'

'Things aren't right, Lloyd. Ronny was turned over, he's dead and the town is swamped with shit cocaine. There's a lot of instability at the moment and I'm calling a truce. I don't care what you've said in the past, it's over. I'm not expecting us to be best friends but I'm getting very nervous. My spider-senses are tingling. There's something going on behind the scenes and what I don't need right now is you pecking my head about your scumbag cousin. You see, when you threaten me online, people expect a response. A violent response. When that doesn't happen, people think I'm turning soft. They perceive it as weakness and it's every man for himself at the moment, so I can't be seen to be weak. You know that.'

'So, what are you saying?'

'I'm telling you to you shut your mouth and keep your eyes open,' Jamie said. 'I need to concentrate on business. I'm not wasting any more time on you, do you understand?'

'Fair enough,' Lloyd said, nodding. 'Are you sure they were coppers?'

'As sure as eggs are eggs.'

'And someone here done them in and chucked them in the sea?' Lloyd asked, thoughtfully. 'That's hardcore.'

'It's hardcore all right. It's also a red rag to a bull. The coppers will be swarming all over this island until they put someone away for this. Killing one copper is madness, killing two is off the scale. The thing to remember is whoever did it, is out there and we don't know who they are. You need to keep your head down and eyes open. If you see anything out of the ordinary, get a message to me at the Stack. Likewise, if I hear anything of interest, I'll get a message to you.' Jamie offered his hand. Lloyd hesitated for a moment and then shook it. Jamie folded the knife and handed it back to him. 'Keep that on you, just in case.' Lloyd nodded and tucked it into the back pocket of his jeans. 'Give Lloyd a lift home, please, Tony.'

'No worries,' Tony said.

Jamie watched them leave. He heard the van start and saw the headlights come on. The gates were opened by his men and Tony drove away down the mountain. He flicked the lights off and climbed into his Range Rover. The feeling of being watched was overwhelming. It was with him constantly. He didn't know if it was paranoia caused by too many anabolic steroids or if it was something different. Paranoia was the constant companion of any drug dealer, the good ones anyway. The shit ones didn't care. Most of the small dealers on the island did it to feed their own habit. Jamie didn't touch the shit because that's what it was, shit. It turned people into heroes and overconfident idiots. Most of them wouldn't see danger coming because they were too off their heads to see it. Jamie couldn't see it yet but he could sense it. Danger was close by, very close indeed.

CHAPTER 18

The briefing room was packed. The entire team was back from their investigations. Simon and Kerry had been the last to arrive, their journey the longest. Alan felt a little subdued following his conversation with the senior officers from neighbouring forces. He understood the investment made in a three-year investigation but it threatened to hamper their murder case. It was likely that certain key players would feature in both investigations. Explaining the boundaries to his detectives, without compromising Operation Thor, would be difficult. There were undercover officers placed deep inside the supply chain and they were vulnerable. It was vital Thor was kept a secret for their safety regardless of securing prosecutions. His major concern was the involvement of the NCA. The threat of the Albanian gangs moving to grab power in the area was a real one and that would be very bad news for the island. Anglesey relied on tourism financially and a drug war could have a dramatic effect. Pulling bodies from the sea wasn't conducive to attracting tourists.

'Okay, everyone,' Alan said, calling the room to order. 'I want to wrap this up quickly for today so you can go home, get some sleep, and be fresh for the morning. Once the forensic results start coming in, we'll all need to be on our game.' A murmur of approval rippled around the room. 'Matrix have revealed the identity of our victims. Mike Jarvis and Patrick McGowan were following a lead into the dealings of an Albanian outfit who are moving north from the London area. We don't know what they were investigating or who was involved but they'd been here for a number of weeks so it must have been a solid lead. What we have to take seriously is the mention of an Albanian gang operating along the supply corridor. They're ruthless to say the least. I don't see them having any problems killing police officers if they discovered they were undercovers, so as it stands, they're now top of our list of suspects. It answers a lot of questions as to who would have had the stomach to carry this out and dump the bodies in plain sight. We've got a lead that Jarvis and McGowan may have been staying somewhere in town, Kim and I will follow that up in the morning. Apart from that we've got several sightings across the island which don't amount to much. Keep knocking on doors, there's a vehicle somewhere and their belongings are probably in a hotel room.' He turned to Alice. 'Where are we with Kelvin Adams, Alice?'

'We recovered the murder weapon from the range, guv,' Alice said. 'It's a standard clawhammer, probably from B&Q. There's hair and skin on it. Pamela Stone is rushing it through for prints.'

'Great,' Alan said. 'What about the other DNA results?'

'She's saying tomorrow at the earliest.'

'Good.'

'Simon, what do you find out from the employers?'

'He was a model employee with no axes to grind and we have a copy of his email on his hard drive. Tech are checking through it now.'

'Good. Anything else?'

'Apparently, he sat next to a colleague called Glen Price. They worked together on new projects,' Kerry said. 'Price phoned in sick on the same day Kelvin was murdered. We paid a visit to the Price home on the way back and Mr Price was very evasive, refused to answer any questions at all. We're back there at ten o'clock in the morning and we're going to squeeze him.'

'Excellent,' Alan said. 'There's something about Kelvin Adams we're missing, keep digging and we'll see what comes up. Was there anything else?'

'The Prices live in a substantial property and own expensive cars, guv, and I've asked for financial reports to be pulled,' Simon added.

'Good work, everyone,' Alan said. 'Anything that comes up, I need to know it immediately. Go straight to the island in the morning, we'll meet the same time tomorrow evening for an update.'

CHAPTER 19

Bob Dewhurst was sitting in his armchair sipping a single malt while watching the news. Eileen had gone to bed early with one of her e-readers. She kept misplacing them, buying a new one then finding the old one. Bob reckoned she was the proud owner of at least four Kindles. They kept her entertained and she loved to read. It was her favourite pastime. Whatever made her happy was okay with him. He planned to read more when he retired at fifty-five—two years away but until then, he didn't have the time or concentration span. It only seemed like yesterday when he was a fresh-faced probationer, walking the beat in Holyhead. The high street was thriving back then, the pubs were full and employment was high. That was before joining the Common Market. The EU quotas took the trawler fleet away and the town went into decline. It was like a different town now. Market Street was nothing but charity shops, bookies, and boarded up businesses. He'd lived through its decline and didn't envisage a recovery in his lifetime.

The landline rang, which was unusual at that time of night.

'Hello, the Dewhurst residence,' he joked.

'Sorry to phone you at home, Bob,' sergeant Baker said. 'But I think you'll want to hear this.'

'It's not a problem. What is it, Scott?'

'We had a call from a lady in Valley, Mrs Hindley, reporting her husband Brian, missing. She said he's always home by six-thirty, without fail and he's not rang to say he'd be late and he's not answering his mobile. She said he's a creature of habit and she's very worried. Apparently, he walks around Penrhos nature reserve most days, so I sent a patrol and his car is there but there's no sign of him. They've walked all the paths with torches in case he'd taken ill but they're clear.'

'He could have walked into the sea,' Bob mused. 'I've lost count of how many suicides choose that spot. Are there any mental health issues?'

'I asked if there'd been any problems but she said he's fit and healthy. He's a retired postman with a passion for seabirds. That's why he goes to Penrhos so often.'

'He's not pissed in a pub in town?'

'He doesn't drink.'

'Ah, that puts a different slant on things,' Bob said. 'We can't do anymore tonight if they've searched the paths. It doesn't sound good to me.'

'Nor me, that's why I rang.'

'Who's running the dayshift tomorrow?'

'Sergeant Lee.'

'Send her a message telling her I'll draft in a couple more units to conduct a thorough search. I'll be in for eight. Fingers crossed, he turns up.'

'Fingers crossed, see you tomorrow.'

CHAPTER 20

Alan stopped at Valley Spar on the way home. He bought a pepperoni pizza and a bottle of merlot, conscious that his breath stank of whisky that morning, no matter how many times he brushed his teeth. Chewing gum and mints didn't mask it either—it came from the gut. There were a lot of top brass milling about the corridors of Caernarfon station and since Operation Thor had been revealed, there would be more of them sniffing around. The North Wales force was under the same financial pressure as the English forces and each senior officer jealously studied other department budgets. The cost of Thor would run into the millions and there would be some who would question the return on investment. Detective Chief Inspector Hunt from Matrix had claimed the operation would unequivocally dismantle the drugs supply from the North-West, down the North Wales corridor. Alan thought that was a ridiculous objective, simply because it was unachievable. It would cause a power vacuum and nothing more. Operation Suzie had wiped several crime organisations off the map but had it stopped the supply? Of course not. Nothing could. As long as there were narcotics being manufactured, there would be customers for them. There were many on the force who favoured legalising drug manufacture so that it could be taxed and regulated. Alan was a firm believer that the war on drugs was a war they could never win. There would have to be a paradigm shift in the way it was tackled before anything changed.

He mulled things over as he drove. There were no clear lines of enquiry to follow, only maybes. He arrived home and climbed out of the car. The living room light was on and the dogs were standing on their hindlegs, scratching the glass and barking hello. Dan and Jack were sitting on the settee, laughing at the dogs. He wasn't expecting Jack to be back from Bangor until the weekend. The electric being on was a bonus. He remembered he owed Dan twenty pounds and he mentally kicked himself for not taking some money out of the cashpoint as he'd promised. He opened the front door and the dogs sprinted down the hallway to greet him. Henry grabbed his trouser leg in his teeth and shook it enthusiastically.

'Henry, you nutcase,' Alan said, trying to shake him off. 'Jack, call the dogs in there for a minute while I sort myself out, please. I can't get in the door!' Jack called them but they ignored him and continued to mob Alan. 'One word from you and they do what they want.' He laughed. 'Not exactly the dog whisperer.' He went into the kitchen, opened the wine, and poured a glass. 'What are you doing home?' he called from the kitchen.

'I'm skint,' Jack said. 'I need to eat and wash some clothes. Where else can I go?'

'I don't know,' Alan said, shrugging. 'Don't they have foodbanks in Bangor?'

'My rent is due and I need a sub until the end of the month,' Jack said from the living room.

'The end of the month?' Alan said. 'Which month?' He sipped the wine and let the dogs out of the back door. They bolted across the field and vanished into the inky darkness. A halfmoon glistened so clear it could have been made of silver. The star-studded vista never failed to impress, no matter how many times he looked at it. He absorbed the beauty for a minute or two and then he went into the living room. The boys looked more alike every day. 'There you are. I like you to look me in the eyes when you're robbing me of my hard-earned cash. How much do you need?'

'I owe two hundred, dad,' Jack said.

'I didn't ask what you owe. How much do you need?'

'Two hundred.'

'I thought you'd say that.'

'There's no point in not asking for enough, then asking for more later on.'

'Heaven forbid,' Alan said, analysing his logic. 'I'll transfer it now.'

'While you're at it, can you transfer me the twenty you owe me, please,' Dan said. 'Unless you have cash.'

'No cash,' Alan said. 'I wonder if this will ever end. How old are you all and at what age do you become self-sufficient?'

'Stop moaning and send the cash, please,' Jack said.

'Oh, I'm moaning now. Sorry about that. When are you all leaving home?'

'I have left,' Jack said.

'That's debatable. You might not be here physically every night but you're still a burden on my meagre earnings.'

'It's tough out there, dad,' Jack said. 'I don't think you appreciate how hard it can be.'

'Don't say things like that in front of your brother,' Alan said. 'Or he'll never leave.' He sipped his wine. 'Are you still working at the Octagon?' Alan asked, changing the subject.

'Thursday and Saturday nights,' Jack said. 'I do a set, midnight until four. It's the busiest time. I'm the main event nowadays.'

'Ask for a pay rise then. You'll be able to pay your own rent.'

'That's how I got the sets in the first place. The last guy asked for a pay rise. He didn't work there again.'

'Have you thought about getting a proper job where you work all week, like a Monday to Friday, nine till five type of job?'

'No.'

'Is that your considered reply?'

'Yes. I like working at the club.'

'It's a terrible place. I remember being in uniform and having to do one weekend a month policing outside. There were fights all the way up the high street. It was a pain in the arse.' Alan said. 'It used to be the venue to go to, back then. Is it as busy as it used to be?'

'Nowhere near, dad,' Jack said, shaking his head. 'Most of the pubs on the high street are open until silly o'clock in the morning and there's no entry fee. We charge a tenner on the door. I'm not sure why anyone comes in at all.'

'On a serious note,' Alan asked. 'Have you noticed any changes in the setup lately?'

'What do you mean?'

'I'm not sure. Nothing specific, just changes. Who does the security?'

'Funny you should ask that,' Jack said. He sat up straight as he spoke. 'A couple of weeks back, three of the regular doormen from Bangor didn't turn up and they haven't been back since. They're using agency staff from Liverpool and the manager is pulling his hair out.'

'Why?'

'He's spent twenty years trying to keep the Liverpool security firms out of Bangor—reckons they're bad news and come hand in hand with their own drug dealers and he's not far wrong.'

'What do you mean?' Alan asked, slurping his wine.

'I'm noticing the same faces acting shady, hanging around the toilets and chillout rooms. If I can see it, anyone can but no one is challenging them. The doormen have got to be in on it.'

'What's the manager doing about it?'

'Shitting his pants, basically. He's been staying in the office most of the night. I reckon he's been threatened.'

'What makes you think that?'

'He's an arse but he's always been shit-hot on drugs being sold in the club. He knows the customers are taking coke but he's always made sure it's not inside. The other thing is, I'm hearing a lot of people moaning about how shit the coke is.'

'You're not talking about the liquid type of coke, regular or diet, are you?'

'No, Dad. It's a dance club. People are off their heads on cocaine.' He shrugged. 'I've heard the lads in my digs talking about it too. Apparently, the gear being sold at the moment is crap.'

'I'm hearing the same thing,' Alan said. 'You haven't heard anything about any foreigners trying to muscle in have you?'

'No. I can't see anyone moving the blokes from Liverpool,' Jack said. 'They're all nutters.'

'Unfortunately, I don't think being a nutter will be enough to stop them if they want to move this far north.'

'Are they that bad?'

'Worse, son,' Alan said. 'Much worse than bad. Unless your doormen can stop a bullet.'

CHAPTER 21

The sun was trying to break through stubborn grey clouds as night brightened into day. Seagulls were circling the mudflats, squawking noisily. Bob Dewhurst had gathered thirty uniformed officers to perform an initial sweep of the Penrhos nature reserve. It was a wooded area spotted with duck ponds on the edge of the sea. Brian Hindley's family and friends were gathering on the car park. They'd volunteered to carry out a wider search if the initial sweep failed to find Brian. Bob's fear was that Brian was lying in the undergrowth dead or dying or had stumbled into a pond and was facedown floating in the water. Bob didn't want the wife or daughter stumbling across his corpse. It was frustrating for the family. Being told they couldn't help to look for their loved one was contrary to their instincts but they seemed to understand the police had procedures to follow. Bob had a bad feeling about the search. Men of that age rarely disappear.

The car park was situated between the sea and the wooded area of the nature reserve. That stretch of sea separates Anglesey from Holy Island and it's bridged by a causeway, known locally as the cob. The nature reserve wasn't vast and Bob knew the initial sweep of the paths and bordering areas wouldn't take long. The resident burger van had opened for business and the volunteers were devouring bacon butties and gallons of tea and coffee. It would keep them occupied while the police search was done.

Bob split his officers into two teams of fifteen. One team took the left path and the other team took the right. They moved painstakingly in lines through the trees, scouring the undergrowth and bushes, marking anything of interest. He checked all the ponds himself but there was no sign of anyone floating. The teams met up where the paths met at the closest point to the sea, there was a narrow stretch of rocky mudflats between the path and open water. Bob looked across the sea towards Church Bay. It was a sheltered inlet; picturesque but the tides were deadly. To his right, a narrow tunnel allowed the water to flow under the cob into the 'Inland Sea' when the tide came in and out. The force of the water at that point was frightening and no one could swim against it or away from it. Bob knew if Brian Hindley had wandered too far across the mudflats and been caught out by the turning tide, he could be in the Irish Sea by now. If he'd been sucked through the tunnel into the Inland Sea, they would find his body at low tide. It all depended if the tide was in or out when he went into the water. If he went into the water at all.

'Guv,' a voice disturbed his thoughts. He turned and walked across the path to an oak tree next to the edge of a shingle beach. The sea was no more than twenty-feet away. 'Look there.'

Bob looked down at the rocks and sand between the tree roots. The roots were thick and gnarled and spread for yards before the ground swallowed them up. There was congealed blood on the bark and soaked into the sand.

'That's a lot of blood,' Bob said. He looked around. 'There're a set of footprints in the mud over there.' He walked on the shingle trying to avoid the sand and mud. Parallel marks scored the sand either side of the footprints. 'Someone was dragged to the water here. Give DI Williams a call and get a CSI team in here.' He sighed. 'I'll go and talk to Mrs Hindley and his family. I'll have to explain that we're probably looking for a body.'

CHAPTER 22

He watched the family as they received the news. The wife disintegrated and collapsed onto the tarmac, her family trying to console her and stop her from hurting herself. Other members of the family hugged each other, many in tears, some absolutely hysterical. It was pure ecstasy to listen to. Absolutely heavenly. The sound of their collective grief was more magnificent than any orchestra or opera he'd ever heard. There was such beauty in their pain, such pleasure in their suffering that it brought tears to his eyes. All this anguish created by his own hands. It was poetry in motion. He wished he could film it.

He walked to the burger van and ordered a sausage sandwich and a tea, listening intently to the words of comfort they offered each other. Each one trying to find the most poignant sentence they could muster. Some were fantastic, others sickeningly dramatic. The fact there was no body yet was adding to their agonies. The wife was on her feet now but couldn't support herself. Her jaw was open and saliva dribbled from her chin onto a red windbreaker. A younger version of her, held one arm and an elderly man, who could be her brother, held the other. They were guiding her through the gathering of volunteers towards a white Audi. The passenger door was opened and too many people tried to put her in, all wanting to help but competing with each other to assist. It was the most fabulous thing he'd ever witnessed. The collateral grief was as satisfying as the killing itself. Almost.

'Any sauce, mate?'

'What?' he asked, lost in the euphoria.

'Sauce?'

'Brown please.'

'Tragic, isn't it?'

'Heart breaking,' he said, biting into his sandwich. He swigged the tea and watched the family, silhouetted against the sea. A windfarm nestled on the slopes above Church Bay, adding a striking feature to the scene. The daughter screamed and became hysterical. What a beautiful start to the day. It was simply magical.

CHAPTER 23

Alan and Kim walked into the Empire Café and looked for an empty table. There was one on the far side of the room but Alan didn't want to sit there. It was too out of the way. In the opposite corner, near the window, he noticed Eric Stott sitting with two ladies who were getting up, readying to leave. As they walked towards the counter to pay, Alan approached the table. Eric was sitting on his mobility scooter, wearing his trademark flat cap. He looked up and nodded hello, smiling.

'Hello, inspector,' Eric said. 'Long time, no see.'

'It is a long time,' Alan said. He turned to Kim. 'Eric is responsible for some of the worst videos I've ever seen.' He took a seat opposite him. 'And some of the best. Long before you left school, probably.' Kim sat down next to him. 'This is Kim.'

'Hello, Kim,' Eric said. 'Are you a detective too?'

'I am.'

'What rank are you?'

'Detective sergeant.'

'Well done,' Eric said. 'I like to see people doing well. My daughter went to university, you know. She's head of the child protection unit now.'

'That's a tough job,' Kim said. 'I'm not sure I could do it.'

'I'm very proud of her. Helping kids is a special thing.'

'You should be proud. They do amazing work, day in and day out.'

'You don't mind us joining you?' Alan asked.

'Not at all. My pleasure. I was sorry to hear about Audrey and your mum,' Eric said. 'She was a lovely lady, your mum.'

'Thank you. She was.'

'I don't know how she put up with your dad for all those years. He was a funny bugger, wasn't he?' Eric said.

'He could be stubborn,' Alan agreed.

'No offence.'

'None taken.'

The waitress came and took their order. Alan ordered a bacon toastie and a tea. Kim ordered coffee and toast. Eric had a refill and chatted to the other customers while they ordered.

'What brings you in here?' Eric asked. His eyes sparkled with curiosity. He was a wily man, intelligent but suspicious by nature. 'It's not somewhere you just pop into, so I'm guessing you're here on business.'

'Very perceptive,' Alan said. 'It was you we came to see, actually.'

'Really,' Eric said, slurping his tea. 'Have you come to pay your late video fine? It's been twenty-five years and there's interest to pay.'

'Did I owe a fine?' Alan blushed.

'Probably. Everyone else did,' Eric joked. 'You had a few over the years.'

'I did. I remember not coming for ages because *Rocky* was on a fine and I was skint.'

'Seventy-six that was released,' Eric said.

'Where do the years go?'

'Joking aside, how can I help you good people?'

'There were two men eating breakfast in here last week,' Alan said, showing him the picture. 'Do you recognise them?'

'Yes. Peter and Joseph. They were working for a company testing the level of fibreglass in the marina after the storm,' Eric said.

'What a mess that was.'

'It was. When eighty yachts sink overnight, there's a lot dangerous crap in the water. They were subcontractors working for an insurance company. They said the insurance company was trying not to pay out for the clean-up.'

'Do you know where they were staying?'

'The Caernarfon Castle,' Eric said. 'Just around the corner but you know that. It's five steps from the back of the police station.'

'I thought that place was closed.'

'It was closed for years. They boarded it up but it was bought last year and converted into one of those keyless hotels. You know the type?'

'Yes. You book online and then receive an access code to the front door and a room,' Kim said. 'If you want your bedding changed, you pay more. I stayed in one similar in Chester last year. We didn't see another human all weekend. It had everything you could ask for. Wi-Fi, Netflix, fifty-inch televisions, the works.'

'It's not that good here. There're no televisions and no Wi-Fi. Peter and Joseph said they were the only people staying there but fresh towels were put outside every door every day,' Eric said. 'Things change, not always for the better. I remember when it was a pub, the place being full of police officers at teatime. There was no such thing as drink driving in those days.' He winked at Kim. 'Especially if you had a police helmet in the back window of your car.'

'Why did they put their helmet in the back window?' Kim asked.

'So, the police would know it was another officer driving, usually drunk in those days.'

'I don't know what you mean,' Alan said, shaking his head. 'That's a terrible insinuation.'

'Terrible but true,' Eric said, laughing. His laugh boomed across the café.

'This might seem like an odd question but did you notice what vehicle they drove?' Alan said, steering the conversation.

'Yes. I saw them passing here a few times after they'd eaten breakfast. They have a white van signed up with the company logo. Marine Engineers or something like that. Blue writing.' Eric sipped his tea again. 'They seemed like nice lads; said they would be here for a few months. What have they done, anyway?'

'They're dead, unfortunately,' Alan said, lowering his voice.

Intelligence glimmered in Eric's eyes. He nodded slowly.

'Were they the blokes pulled out of the Bay?'

'Exactly.'

'What did they get themselves mixed up in?' Eric asked.

'We're not sure. Drugs probably.'

'Crying shame, young men like that. Such a waste.'

'It is. Did you notice them talking to anyone else, you know what I mean?'

'I can't say I did but I'm home early these days. I don't venture into the pubs anymore. They mentioned they'd been for a few pints in town.'

'Can you remember where?'

'They mentioned the Chester, the Ddraigh Goch, and the Albert Vaults.' They all looked through the window at the pub across the road. The Vaults was a tiny pub with a decent trade. It was full when other pubs were empty.

'Did they mention anyone they'd met?'

'No. Not that I can recall. I would remember if they'd mentioned anyone local. They would have bumped into all the town's characters in the Vaults. Sorry I can't be more help.'

'Not at all, you've been a great help, Eric,' Alan said. He handed him his card. 'I know you keep your ear to the ground. I need to ask you to do me a favour.'

'You can ask.'

'There's been a lot of arrests away from here but it's going to have a knock-on effect in places like this.'

'Places like this?' Eric frowned.

'I mean coastal towns along the Welsh coast all the way to Liverpool.'

'Knock-on effects like what?'

'There's a power struggle and there will be trouble.'

'And you want me to listen out for information?'

'Don't go out of your way. Just keep an ear open.'

'I can manage that. No problem.'

'We'll leave you in peace,' Alan said. They stood up and shook hands and headed for the door. All eyes in the room were on their backs as they opened the door and walked out. When the door closed, Eric was bombarded with questions. He didn't have to buy another cup of tea all day while the occupants of the café speculated what had happened.

CHAPTER 24

Simon and Kerry pulled up at the home of Mr and Mrs Price. He pressed the buzzer on the gatepost and the gates opened silently. There was no sign of any vehicles as they approached and the upstairs curtains were closed. The initial financial reports had shown Patricia Price had an interior design company registered at companies' house but she hadn't filed any accounts or tax returns for two years. The years prior showed a small profit. They had no credit cards or loans and their vehicles were owned outright. As long as Mr Price earned enough to cover everything, it didn't show anything suspicious so far but if he didn't, questions would be asked.

'Are you ready for this?' Simon asked. He checked his appearance in the mirror and smoothed his dark hair back from his forehead. It was short over the ears and longer on top.

'Absolutely. Bad cop, bad cop,' Kerry said.

'Are there no good cops?'

'Not today. Only bad cop and bad cop.'

'Which one am I?'

'Just pick one and stick with it. I'll do the rest.'

They climbed out and knocked on the door. It was several minutes before Glen Price opened it. He looked frightened, his eyes darted from the gates to the road and around the lawns as if he was expecting someone to be there. Simon couldn't be certain but he thought he was wearing the same clothes as yesterday. He looked tired as if he'd been awake all night.

'Good morning,' Simon said, noting his demeanour. 'Thank you for seeing us.'

'It isn't through choice. I don't know how you think I can help,' Glen said. He was on the defensive immediately. 'Come in. I haven't got long.' He stepped back from the door and let them in, keeping his eyes on the road all the time.

'We won't take up much of your time,' Simon said. The hallway was wide with tall ceilings and a vivid floral carpet. The paintings on the walls were equally vivid. Simon wondered if Mrs Price should be an interior designer at all.

'Good. I'm very busy and this is a waste of my time.'

'How long did you know Kelvin Adams,' Kerry asked, looking at the paintings as if she wasn't interested in the answer.

'Nearly twenty years. We started our degrees together.'

'You must be close if you worked together that long,' Simon said.

'He was a workmate. Nothing more. I don't know anything about what he did after work.'

'After work?' Kerry said, frowning.

'What?'

'We haven't asked you if you did know what he did after work,' Kerry said.

'Well, I'm just saying. This is pointless.'

'You don't appear to want to help with the investigation into your friend's murder, Mr Price.' Glen blushed and looked at him sheepishly, 'I find that very odd.'

'I just don't see how I can help.'

'You can help by chatting to us and answering some questions about Kelvin.'

'I don't know anything about it.'

'About what?'

'What happened to Kelvin. I really don't see how talking to me helps.'

'It helps if you answer our questions and let us decide if it helps or not.'

'It's a waste of time. I don't know anything.'

'We could always do this at the station with a solicitor if you'd be more comfortable?' Simon said. 'We don't want to make you uncomfortable but we do need to talk to you. Would you rather have a solicitor present?'

'No, no, it's fine,' Mr Price said. The colour drained from his face. He appeared to compose himself. 'Come in and sit down.' They followed him into an oblong lounge that ran from front to back of the house. Patio doors led into a huge conservatory to the rear. He pointed to a four-seater settee. 'Please, sit down.'

'We'll stand, thanks, Mr Price,' Kerry said. She pointed to an armchair. 'Take a seat.' It wasn't a request. He sat down on an armchair and looked at the floor. 'Thank you. We can stop this at any time, you understand?' Mr Price nodded that he did. 'When was the last time you spoke to Kelvin Adams?'

'I can't remember, exactly.'

'Did you see him at work the day before you called in sick?' Kerry asked.

'Yes, of course. I was sitting next to him.'

'What time did you finish work that day?'

'About half past five.'

'Was that the last time you saw him?'

'Yes, I suppose it was.'

'Did you talk to him after work?'

'I don't think so.'

'Did you talk to him on the telephone, perhaps?'

'Not that I can remember.'

'We can check your phone records to verify if you did or not,' Simon said.

'You can't do that without my permission.' Mr Price shifted in his seat. He rubbed his hands together, nervously.

'This is a murder investigation. We can and we will check your records.'

'I might have called him,' Mr Price said, nervously. Simon and Kerry looked at each other for a second.

'What about?'

'Pardon?'

'What did you call him about?'

'A project we're working on. Something and nothing really.'

'So, you did call him after work?'

'Yes.'

'You're sure?'

'Yes.'

'It's just that a moment ago, you couldn't remember.'

'I've had a lot on my mind lately. I've been forgetting things.'

'Like what?' Kerry asked. Mr Price didn't answer.

'I hope you don't mind me saying but you look like you're worried, Mr Price,' Simon added. There was no response. 'In fact, I'd go so far as to say you look afraid. Are you afraid of something or someone?'

'No, not at all. I'm tired, that's all. I've not been sleeping very well.'

'Have you seen a doctor?' Kerry asked.

'Yes. She gave me some sleeping tablets but they're not working for me.'

'Where's Mrs Price?'

'She's gone to see a client.'

'A client from her interior design business?' Simon asked.

'Yes.'

'Is she busy?' Kerry asked.

'What?'

'Your wife, is she busy with her work?' Simon pushed.

'She's doing well.'

'We ran your financials last night.' Mr Price looked like he'd seen a ghost. 'You have no mortgage, no loans, or credit cards. It's a nice position to be in. Unusual, but nice.'

'You can't do that,' Mr Price said, mouth open.

'We can,' Kerry said. 'And we have.'

'The cars were bought with cash,' Simon challenged him.

'I don't believe this,' Mr Price said, standing up. He pointed his forefinger. 'We are professional people. I earn good money and my wife does well.'

'Really? Only we noticed she hasn't submitted a tax return for a while,' Simon said.

'How, how, dare you?' Mr Price stammered. 'What has that got to do with anything?'

'Everything,' Kerry said. 'We're investigating a brutal murder. The murder of Kelvin Adams, a man you've worked with for decades. A man you spoke to the night before he was murdered. We need to investigate his family, friends, and anyone who came into contact with him recently and we need to look at every aspect of their lives until we find the killer and lock them up.'

'That's outrageous. I'm not tolerating that kind of scrutiny. We're not criminals.'

'We're not scrutinising you, Mr Price. Not yet, anyway.'

'And what does that mean?'

'Most of the people we've spoken to have been very helpful but you're not cooperating with us. In fact, you're being aggressive and evasive. Why is that, Mr Price?'

'I'm not being aggressive or evasive.'

'You're being both, Mr Price. You're standing up pointing your finger at two detectives who are investigating the murder of a man you've worked with for twenty years.' Simon paused and looked Mr Price in the eyes. 'It's the behaviour of someone who isn't telling us the truth.'

'I've had enough of this. I'm not saying anything else,' Price said. His face was pale and drawn but there was anger in his eyes. 'I don't have to answer your questions. I want you to leave. If you want to speak to me again, contact my solicitor.'

'Okay,' Kerry said, standing up. 'Who is your solicitor?'

'What?'

'Who is your solicitor?' she repeated. 'We'll be contacting them to arrange an interview at Caernarfon Police Station tomorrow morning. You can be as awkward as you like, Mr Price but we're not going away. Who is your solicitor?'

'I can't speak to you tomorrow. I'm busy tomorrow.'

'In which case. We'll get a warrant for your arrest, your choice,' Kerry said.

'Arrest me for what?'

'Wasting police time for a start. There's a reason you're being evasive and we'll find out what that is whether you like it or not. I won't ask again. Who is your solicitor?'

'Tudor Owen, in St Asaph.'

'Fine thank you, Mr Price,' Simon said. His face like stone. 'We'll be in touch with him this morning and we'll speak to you formally tomorrow at Caernarfon station.'

'Caernarfon? Can't we meet at St Asaph?' Price looked close to tears. 'It's much closer for me.'

'Mr Price, we can do it right here and right now without any dramas.'

'I'm not saying any more today.'

'Are you sure? Once we start the process, we can't stop it.'

'I don't understand what you mean. What process?'

'We're chatting to you on an informal basis as a potential witness. If you refuse to answer some basic questions, we'll no longer be looking at you as a potential witness, we'll be looking at you as a potential suspect.' Price stared at his hands. 'Anything to say, Mr Price before we leave?' He shook his head. 'Fine. Good morning to you.'

The detectives walked through the expansive hallway to the front door. Simon opened it and the cold air rushed in to greet them. They marched to their vehicle, both annoyed with Price's obstinate manner. Simon opened the driver's door and glanced at the house. Mrs Price was opening the curtains upstairs. Kerry followed his gaze. They climbed into the vehicle and closed the doors.

'What is he playing at?' Kerry asked. 'Why tell us his wife was working?'

'So, we don't talk to her?'

'That man is driving me round the bend. What do you think he's hiding?'

'I don't know,' Simon said. 'When we spoke to his boss, Barry Trent, he couldn't get us out of there quick enough. He wasn't evasive but he was hardly helpful, was he?'

'Nope. I didn't think much of it until we met Price. His workmates are behaving oddly. Why would that be?'

'I haven't got a clue but I'm convinced they know something we don't. Shall we go back to Jaguar and ask them?'

'Yes,' Kerry said. 'I'll call ahead and ask to speak to everyone he worked with.'

CHAPTER 25

loyd Jones woke up stiff and bruised from his encounter with a Taser. He looked at the empty space next to him and touched the sheet. It was still warm. He could hear the toilet cistern running. The en suite door opened and Zak Edwards stepped out wearing his boxer shorts. Lloyd ran his eyes over him. He was petite and boyish looking for nineteen, almost feminine. His blond hair was bobbed and graduated. Zak was openly gay, which in a small town was very brave. He was a popular lad but there were still intolerant members of the community especially among the older generation. Zak kept himself to himself. He didn't tout himself on social media—he loved Lloyd but Lloyd wouldn't come out. They sneaked around when they could but Zak was tiring of the situation.

He wanted more. He deserved more. It wasn't like he didn't get offers. He did. Some from the most unlikely sources but most of them just wanted sex. If casual sex was all he needed, he would be busy seven days a week, but it wasn't. He had friends on social media who were in same-sex marriages. Some of them had adopted children. They lived normal lives, in love, surrounded by people who didn't judge them. Tolerance wasn't in abundance where he lived. He wanted to be in an ordinary relationship.

That's what he wanted but Lloyd wouldn't so much as acknowledge him in public, especially in front of his friends. Zak often told him they weren't his friends. They hung around with him for the drugs and the money and the kudos it gave them. He'd seen the way they looked at him. Some of them obviously suspected there was a relationship going on. They sneered behind Lloyd's back and some of them teased Zak. They pinched his arse when he walked past and wolf whistled when he walked into the room. Lloyd ignored them as if it wasn't happening. He even laughed at them sometimes. That hurt more than ignoring what was happening. Zak often wondered if Lloyd loved him at all. He thought the fact their relationship was clandestine excited Lloyd. Sneaking around was part of the buzz for him.

'Are you coming back to bed?' Lloyd asked. He pulled back the quilt.

'No. I need to get to work.'

'Oh, come on. I'll be quick.'

'You're always quick,' Zak said, smiling. 'That's why I come back.'

'Take that back right now,' Lloyd said.

'Okay, I take it back but I'm not getting back into bed.'

There was a noise from downstairs. They both looked at each other. The sound of footsteps on the stairs spurred them into action. Zak grabbed a denim shirt, feeling vulnerable in his underwear. Lloyd grabbed a machete from behind the bedside table and stood by the door. The footsteps stopped. Lloyd frowned and waited.

'Lloyd,' a voice said. 'Are you in there?'

'Yes,' he said, opening the door, stepping out, and then closing it behind him. 'What are you doing here, Dad?'

'They've taken your mum,' he said, shaking. His breath was coming in short bursts. He was holding a bloody tissue to his nose.

'Who's taken Mum?'

'I don't know who they were.'

'Tell me what happened.'

'They broke in and dragged her out of bed, punched me unconscious, and took her. I think my nose is broken.'

'We'll get you sorted. Do you feel dizzy?' Lloyd put his hand on his father's shoulder. He shrugged it off and moved away.

'No, I'm not dizzy. Worried sick is what I am. This is your fault.'

'What?' Lloyd asked, confused. 'How can this be my fault?'

'Because they said it's your fault.'

'What are you talking about? How can it be my fault?'

'They said you've been phoning them and making threats. They said you owe them money.'

'I don't owe anyone money,' Lloyd lied.

'They said you threatened to shoot them. You left a message on their phone.'

'Where were they from?' Lloyd asked.

'I don't know. I didn't get the chance to ask them.'

'Were they locals or English?'

'Neither. They were foreign. Your mum was screaming so they gagged her.'

'Did they say where they were taking her?'

'No. They said I was to come here and tell you what's happened and to wait for a phone call.' He wiped a tear from his eye. 'Have you threatened someone?' his dad asked. 'Is this your fault?'

'Go home and wait for me there,' Lloyd said. His dad shook his head. 'Don't argue with me. Go home and I'll follow you there.'

'But they...'

'Go home!' Lloyd shouted, losing his temper.

'Your mum has got a bad heart, you know.'

'I know. Go home.'

'If they hurt her, I'll never forgive you,' his dad said, shaking his head. 'I've kept my mouth shut far too long.'

'Kept your mouth shut about what, exactly?'

'We're ashamed of you. We're ashamed of what you've become, selling drugs to the kids in town. Your customers are our friends' grandchildren. Don't you think what you do has an effect on us? People won't look us in the eyes anymore. You're an embarrassment to your family.'

'I don't need this right now, dad,' Lloyd said. 'Save the lecture for when we get Mum back. I'll sort this out.'

'Who will sort it out?' his dad snapped. 'You and your boyfriend?'

'Go home.'

'Is he in there now?'

'Don't do this, please.'

'Is that why you shut the door so quickly, in case I get a glimpse of him?' he said. Lloyd was speechless for once. 'Do you think we didn't know? Your little boyfriend can't keep his mouth shut. His sister was telling everyone in the Vaults how he wants to marry you and adopt children. Can you imagine how proud I was listening to that?' he asked. 'It made my little heart glow with pride. You make me sick.'

The bedroom door opened and Zak pushed past Lloyd. He was fully dressed. Lloyd tried to stop him but he was adamant he was leaving. He stopped in front of Lloyd's dad. They glared at each other, red-faced.

'Excuse me, please,' Zak said. 'I need to get to work.' Lloyd's dad moved and let him pass. 'Don't bother texting me until you've got the backbone to admit I exist, Lloyd. I've had enough of being a dirty little secret.'

The front door slammed.

'Thanks for that, Dad,' Lloyd said. 'Go home. I'll follow you when I'm dressed.'

'Don't bother.' He turned and walked to the front door. 'I'm going to the police. I should have gone there in the first place.'

'Dad!' Lloyd shouted. 'Do not go to the police. If you want to see her again, leave it to me. I'll sort it out when they ring me. You have to trust me on this.' His father looked sad and confused. 'These are very bad men, Dad. They're dangerous.

When they call me, I'll sort it out with them. It's a misunderstanding, nothing more.'

'You've got two hours,' his dad said. 'If she's not back by then, I'm going to call the police.' He shut the door behind him, leaving Lloyd to contemplate the position. Zak was fuming and hurt. He was stubborn too. It would take some creeping to get him onside again. Coming out wasn't an option. Not now, not ever. The idea of walking through the park holding hands with Zak, pushing a child on a swing didn't rankle with him. He could do that but not here. His dad was a prime example of the antiquated values some clung to. Religion, colour, race, and sexuality were not up for debate with half of the family. The other half didn't have the brains to care. Zak and him in a genuine relationship was a total nonstarter. Any respect he'd built up over the years, trying to get established would be lost in the first wave of gossip. He couldn't think about it seriously. His phone beeped. It was a text message. He opened it and recognised the number. It was his supplier. The Albanians. He wished he hadn't called them and left threatening messages. He opened the message and a video started to run automatically. His legs wobbled and a gasp came from his chest, turning into a whine. He watched tears run from her eyes. There was no sound from her. She was gagged. A man appeared on camera. He was one of the men he'd bought the cocaine from. His eyes were dark, madness in them.

'You said you're not going to pay us and you're going to shoot me the next time you see me,' he said. His voice was monotone, almost bored. 'You'll be sorry you said that.' He turned and put the knife to his mother's throat. Lloyd thought he was going to vomit. 'You have twenty-four hours to pay us what you owe or your mother dies.' The screen went dark, and the message ended with the sound of men laughing.

CHAPTER 26

Owen Collins opened the garage and switched on the lights, the radio, and the kettle. He was a creature of habit, liked a quiet life, and lived for his family. Today was the first day of a new era. An era without the crushing debts he'd accrued by struggling on alone. He hadn't slept well the night before but he'd made up his mind. Taking Jamie's offer was a no-brainer. He was a drowning man clutching a lifeline. If Jamie was true to his word, there were no downsides and he had no reason to believe he wasn't being honest. He didn't agree with what Jamie did for a living but who was he to judge? There was a massive market for cocaine. It was a fact. If Jamie Hollins didn't sell it to them, someone else would. Despite his fearsome reputation, most people on the island respected Jamie. He was a straight-shooter, who had helped a lot of people. Not quite Robin Hood but a decent man with an unusual profession. Owen decided he would take one day at a time and see how the partnership progressed. Waking up knowing his bank account was in the black, had given him a different perspective on life. He felt excited and energised for the first time since his father was diagnosed. The thought of taking the moral high ground by transferring the money back, made him feel sick. His mind was made up.

An hour later, Tony pulled up in a Golf GTI. It was less than twelve months old. Owen felt butterflies in his stomach. This was it. Crunch time. There would be no turning back if he took the deal. He took a deep breath and walked over to the vehicle. Tony climbed out of the driver's door, wearing a Stone Island jacket.

'All right, Owen,' Tony said.

'Tony,' Owen said, shaking his hand. 'Nice jacket.'

'Thanks. Cost over a grand if you want one.'

'I might treat myself to one next year. Too rich for me right now.'

'Did you sleep on our proposal?'

'I did. I'm going to take you up on the offer,' Owen said.

'Good man. You've made the right decision.' Tony took out his mobile and sent a text message. He waited for the reply. His phone beeped. 'Jamie is very happy. To start with, he wants this Golf serviced and the wheels changing.'

'What's wrong with the wheels?' Owen said, walking around the vehicle. 'They're nice alloys. Are they scuffed somewhere?'

'There's nothing wrong with them. He's seen another set he likes better.'

'No problem. Has he got a replacement set?'

'Yes. They'll be delivered by a courier this afternoon.'

'Are they going to take the other set away?'

'No. You can keep the set that's on now. They're nice alloys. Stick them on eBay or sell them to another customer, whatever you like.'

'They're worth a few quid, you know.'

'He hasn't got the time to mess about with a set of alloys. Keep them.'

'Okay, thanks,' Owen said. He had reservations rattling around in his head but this was too good to turn down. 'When does he want it back?'

'Teatime tomorrow, I'll pick it up?'

'That's fine.'

'I'll pay cash. How much will it be?'

'A full service is two hundred and eighty. Call it three hundred in total, swapping the wheels over etcetera.'

'Twenty quid for swapping a set of wheels?' Tony said. 'No wonder you're struggling. Bill us five hundred.'

'Five hundred?'

'Are you here to make money or run a charity?'

'Okay. Five hundred it is.' Owen was shocked.

'About the mechanic we promised you. Daisy will be here eight o'clock Monday morning.'

'Brilliant. I've got a lot on next week; it'll be just in time.'

'Jamie has arranged for the first two vehicles to be dropped off on a transporter. They'll be delivered before lunchtime on Tuesday and we'll take it from there,' Tony said.

'What do you want doing to them?'

'The same as the Golf. Full service and change the wheels. Daisy will know what to do.' Owen nodded but his expression said he wasn't comfortable. 'Don't look so worried. You've just changed your life.'

'I'm not worried. That's all fine with me.'

A taxi pulled up outside and Tony waved to the driver.

'I'll see you tomorrow,' Tony said, walking to the car. 'Don't stress. Enjoy the ride.'

'I will,' Owen said. He waited for the taxi to pull away before punching the air in joy. He thought about his dad looking down on him. 'Today is going to be a good day.' He tried to convince himself that he wasn't worried about the deal but the knot in his guts told him otherwise.

CHAPTER 27

Alan waited for Pamela Stone to finish processing the room before stepping into the Caernarfon Castle, a derelict pub converted into a motel. It was positioned on a steep hill off the high street. The buildings around it were boarded up and in disrepair. Inside was unrecognisable to how he remembered it. There was nothing left of the original footprint. Plasterboard walls and lowered ceilings had transformed the building. A staircase ran up the centre of the building, leading to the first-floor rooms. Laminate flooring and downlighting gave it a fresh, modern feel. He was impressed with the conversion—it had the look of a Travel Lodge type motel. There were eight bedrooms, four on each floor. He walked around each one. They were identical.

'It still smells of paint,' Kim said from the doorway.

'And sawdust,' Alan said. 'Do we know anything about who owns it yet?'

'A limited company based in Guernsey called Mon Holdings. The contact details are a property management company based in Trearddur Bay run by a local guy Will Pinter.'

'I know Will,' Alan said. 'He owned a farm at Llaingoch years ago—he must be in his eighties. We need to speak to him.'

'I've got a mobile number.'

'Good, we'll do it when we're finished here. What did Pamela say her initial thoughts were?'

'She said it looks like two contractors went to work and never came back. There's nothing suspicious in there. Their rooms have got sports bags with spare underwear, some work clothes, and some casual stuff. There're no phones, no iPads, no tablets, or laptops. Either they made a point of staying off social media or their stuff has been stolen.'

'I suppose Matrix officers are likely to be on social media following their targets and finding out who knows who,' Alan said. 'They would have phones. Probably SIM only but they would have them. Where are they?'

'They would have been on them, wouldn't they?'

'I would think so. Has she processed the van?'

'Yes, she's still on it. So far, there's a couple of Hi-vis jackets, some waterproofs, and a bag of tools. Apart from that, it's clean. She's taking prints and DNA swabs but doesn't expect to find anything. It looks like they parked it up, locked it, and then vanished. The kidnappers didn't go near it.'

'If they confessed to being undercover officers, the kidnappers would search their belongings.'

'Maybe.'

'Wouldn't you?'

'What if they didn't talk? They may not have confessed to being police,' Kim said. 'Maybe they didn't know where they were staying. Maybe they didn't tell them anything at all.'

'I'm not convinced. Everyone has a breaking point. I find it odd the van wasn't touched and I don't think their rooms have been searched either,' Alan said. Looking around. 'Do you know what else I find odd?'

'Go on.'

'This place. It's as if it isn't finished.'

'It's basic to say the least.'

'Why spend thousands of pounds converting a building like this and not put in the basics like televisions and Internet access?'

'I thought that. And why pay a laundry service to change the towels for empty rooms?' Kim agreed.

'Who is servicing the place?'

'It's a new company, Cemaes Housekeeping Limited.'

'Where are they based?'

'The address is an industrial unit on the outskirts of Cemaes.'

'Silly question. That makes sense but their operation doesn't. A good businessman wouldn't service empty rooms.'

'Why do it then?'

'The only reason you would do that is if you wanted to make your motel appear to be full every day,' Alan said. 'Google the place and see if it comes up.' Kim typed the motel into her phone.

'Yes. It's here but it's saying it's fully booked.'

'Fully booked my arse,' Alan said. 'How much is a room for the night?'

'Seventy-five pounds per person.'

'That's a hundred and fifty a night, times eight rooms.'

'Twelve-hundred a night is eight-thousand four-hundred pounds a week,' Kim said.

'That's thirty-seven grand a month, over four hundred thousand pounds a year. Add on some extras and room service, alarm calls, Wi-Fi that isn't there, adult films, and you could take that to over half a million a year. It's a different type of laundering we're looking at here,' Alan said.

'I'll get our financials to dig deeper into the Guernsey company.'

'What's the name of the company Will Pinter runs?'

'Sundown property management,' Kim said, reading from her phone. 'I'll give them a call and see how the rooms were booked. It might give us something to follow.'

'It can't hurt to ask,' Alan said. He didn't look convinced.

'You're not telling me what you're thinking.'

'I might be way off the mark.'

'Tell me anyway.'

'Okay. Let's say I've got a lot of cash that needs laundering. I need legitimate businesses to wash the money through, right?'

'Right.'

'I buy a derelict building for a song, convert it into accommodation, and rent all the rooms out every night to fictitious customers who all pay cash. Then I can pay the cash into my motel bank account and suddenly, it's legitimate.'

'But if someone were to investigate, you would have to prove the motel was a functioning business by proving the rooms are serviced and towels and bedding are laundered by a legitimate supplier.'

'Exactly. Now let's say I meet a couple of friendly blokes in a pub, looking for somewhere to stay for a few months. I offer them a couple of rooms and they're seen coming and going, eating and drinking locally. It helps make the place look authentic.'

'But you don't know the friendly blokes are undercover police officers,' Kim said, nodding.

'How could I?'

'You couldn't. No one has searched their rooms and no one has searched their van because no one knows who they were,' Kim said. Alan shook his head. 'What did I say wrong?'

'If I was laundering money through here, that's exactly what I would want you to think. I'd want you to think no one knows because I'd want you away from my empty motel, rapid. I want to know who runs this place and I want to know today. If this is what we think it is, it won't be the only one. Check if the company that owns this place has any other properties on the island. I'm betting on them having a few more dotted about.'

'Okay, I'm on it.' Kim took out her mobile and made a call.

A uniformed officer walked down the hallway.

'Pamela wants a word, guv,' she said. 'She's found something in the van.'

'Thank you, Prita,' Alan said. She was one of a handful of female AHolly officers on the island. 'How are the kids?'

'Noisy and disrespectful,' Prita said, smiling. 'The eldest has decided he wants a gap year before he goes to high school.'

'There's a novelty. Maybe he needs to find himself.'

'He needs to find a hearing aid and listen to what we're telling him,' Prita said.

'They must be a handful. What does Ravi say?'

'He says he wants a DNA test. He doesn't think he's his son.'

'Tell him to look in the mirror, he's his double,' Alan said. Prita laughed. They walked outside into the small car park. Pamela was busy sifting through something in a small evidence bag. 'What have you found?'

'There's a false panel here look,' Pamela said, pointing inside the van.

'How did you find that?' Alan asked, impressed.

'It's standard practice with vans nowadays. We measure the length of the outside against the length inside to the bulkhead. Any deviation indicates a void. It's not rocket science.' Alan smiled. He thought anything she did was amazing. 'When we opened it, we found these. There are hundreds of packets containing all kinds of dubious substances,' she joked, holding a bag of white powder. 'They're all sealed and labelled.'

'How many are there?' Alan asked.

'I haven't got an exact figure yet but it's hundreds, collected over nine months as far as I can see from the dates. They've catalogued what it is, dates and times of purchase, location and the dealers' names in some cases. They were busy boys.'

'They were. Before this goes to the lab, can we have the details of anything they bought on the island, names, location, and what it is. We can collate the dates and times later. That would be a great help.'

'We can do that. Leave it with me.'

'Thanks, Pamela.' Alan glanced over the packets. None of the names stood out to him. 'I'm not seeing anyone jumping out at me here but then I wouldn't expect to.'

'They would've been buying from pub dealers and the foot soldiers not the guys we're after,' Kim agreed. 'But if we get a list of who they are, it will be easy to find out who they work for.'

'My thoughts exactly. How long do you think it will take?' Alan asked.

'Give me an hour and I'll send you a list,' Pamela said.

'Excellent.' He glanced across the road at the back of the concrete monstrosity that was Holyhead Police Station and a thought came to him. The building was no longer occupied by a force. It had been left with a skeleton crew since the island's custody suites were closed and the burden of locking people up was put onto the town of Caernarfon, on the mainland. His forehead wrinkled as he thought.

'What are you thinking?' Kim asked, following his gaze to the station.

'There's an empty police station there, right in the middle of our investigation,' Alan said. 'I'm going to speak to Dafyd about moving our operation here for a few weeks.'

'Logistically it makes sense.'

'I'm not thinking logistics.'

'You're not?'

'No. If fifty detectives land in the middle of a small town like this, it will rattle a lot of cages. People will panic and start talking but they don't know we're already listening. Operation Thor has already got ears here. If the top brass think moving our investigation here will help their cause, they'll give us a green light. It will shake a lot of trees and all we have to do is wait to see what falls out.'

CHAPTER 28

Simon and Kerry were at the Jaguar plant in Liverpool. They took a seat in one of the canteens. It was the nightshift canteen and wouldn't be opened for hours yet. Barry Trent was at a meeting in London and his assistant manager was much more affable. He seemed genuinely upset about Kelvin Adams and was willing to do what he could to help. They spoke to the engineers who sat close to Kelvin, one at a time, and then spoke to those who had been there a long time. There was only one other employee who had been there as long as Glen Price and Kelvin Adams—a Jamaican lady called Geneva Rhodes. She sat down opposite them. Her smile was genuine but there was suspicion in her eyes. She was nervous.

'Thanks for talking to us, Geneva,' Kerry said.

'Everyone calls me Genny.'

'Okay, Genny it is. I'm Kerry and this is Simon.'

'Pleased to meet you both. I was very upset to hear about Kelvin. We started here about the same time and he was always a nice man. He stuck his neck out for me a few times in the early years.'

'Really?' Kerry frowned.

'I was the only black woman in the entire plant,' Genny said. 'You can imagine how that would be for some of our less tolerant employees. If I had to venture onto the factory floor, the air turned blue sometimes. Mostly wolf-whistles and the like but there was a lot of abuse back then too. Kelvin and most of the engineers looked after me. Like I said, he stuck his neck out a few times. He got angry one time with a young mechanic who always took things too far with me—actually punched him on the nose. We were all very young back then.'

'His death must have been a blow to his workmates.'

'It was a huge shock to everyone.'

'How do you get on with Glen Price?' Simon asked. Genny looked disturbed by the question.

'Okay,' Genny said. Her eyes flickered up to the left for a millisecond but Simon caught it. That was a lie. 'Like I said, we've worked together a long time.'

'Did Kelvin and Glen get along?'

'They were very good friends for a long time but not so much in later years.'

'Really?' Kerry said. 'What changed?'

'You'd have to ask them.' Genny shifted uneasily in her chair. 'It's none of my business.'

'Kelvin was murdered, Genny and Glen Price isn't cooperating with us. If there's something you're not telling us?'

'It's personal to them. It's not for me to rake up ancient history.'

'We could do with your help,' Kerry said. 'Whatever you say to us, stays with us. Why did they fall out?'

'It was a long time ago. You can't think it has anything to do with his murder.'

'We don't think anything yet but it's odd that Glen won't talk to us.'

'He's a difficult man sometimes.'

'Talk to us, Genny. When did they fall out?'

'I'm not comfortable talking about it.'

'No one will ever know.'

'It was a long time ago.'

'What was?'

'Okay.' Genny took a deep breath. 'About six years ago, there was an incident. I'm really not comfortable talking about them behind their backs. You could probably find out what happened if you spoke to human resources. It will all be on record.'

'Anything they have will be covered by data protection,' Kerry said. 'They can't let us see their files without a warrant.'

'The police were involved at one point. You can check that, can't you?'

'Yes. Why were the police involved?'

'I'd rather not say,' Genny said, looking around nervously.

'If it's on the record, we'll find out anyway, eventually but it will take us longer,' Kerry said. 'Come on, Genny. Give us something to look for.' Genny folded her hands together and took another deep breath.

'All I know is two men from the factory floor were arrested and they were sacked. We were told they went to prison.'

'Can you remember their names?' Kerry asked.

'I remember one of them. Derek Kio,' Genny said. 'He was the one Kelvin punched in the nose years before. I didn't know the other man. Once we qualified and finished our degrees, we rarely went down to the factory floor but I'll never forget Kio. He was a nasty man, a racist. After that, Glen and Kelvin were never the same. They were lucky to keep their jobs.'

'But what was it all about?' Kerry asked.

Genny shook her head and stood up. 'I've already said too much. It was nice to meet you both. I hope you catch whoever killed Kelvin but I can't say anymore.'

'Thank you, Genny,' Kerry said. 'Nice to meet you.' They watched Genny leave. Her grey business suit was tight around her hips. When she'd gone, Kerry sighed and shook her head. 'What the hell was that all about?'

'I don't know,' Simon said. 'I think we should check the PNC to see what Kio's conviction was for before we make a decision.'

'I'll call the station,' Kerry said.

'There's a local station around the corner in Halewood,' Simon said. 'They would be the first on site if anything happened here. It might be worth calling in for a cup of tea and a chat with the desk sergeant. If you want to know anything about anything, ask the desk sergeant.'

'Good idea,' Kerry said. Her call connected. 'I need a PNC check on a Derek Kio. He's from the Merseyside area.' There was a pause. 'He's doing a fifteen-year stint for armed robbery,' she whispered to Simon. 'Go back six years for me and see what else is on his record.' She waited, anticipation building. 'He got four and a half years for possession with intent. Cocaine.'

'That changes the slant of things. No wonder Barry Trent didn't want us digging around. That must have been embarrassing for the company,' Simon said. 'Let's call at the local nick and see if anyone remembers what happened.'

CHAPTER 29

Bob Dewhurst sipped his tea next to the burger van at Penrhos. Divers were checking around the inlet to the Inland Sea, avoiding the deadly current that roared through the inlet itself. Another team were scouring the coves and reeds of the Inland Sea in rigid hulled inflatable boats—the sound of their outboard motors carried across the cob. The Inland Sea was calm and shallow and would give up a body, eventually. If Brian Hindley was in there, they would find him. Further out to the west, a coast guard launch was trawling in a grid pattern between Holy Island and the lighthouse at the Skerries. It was like looking for a needle in a mountain of needles. Some of Brian Hindley's family and friends refused to go home until he was found. It was almost academic if he was alive or dead, they wanted to be there. He could understand that. It was easier to watch the search operation than to sit at home not knowing what was going on. The press and thirty or so ghouls were gathered along the cob like vultures on a telegraph wire, waiting for the sight of a dead body being lifted from the water. Part of him hoped Brian Hindley wouldn't be found in daylight so the press couldn't get their morbid photographs. The family were suffering enough without seeing pictures of his body posted on the Internet. Bob spotted Alan's BMW being stopped by uniformed officers at the cordon near the main road.

'How long are you holding the public back at the road?' the burger van owner asked. 'I've got a living to make, you know.'

'Are you kidding me, Jim?' Bob said.

'No. I'm not kidding. It's not every day we get a crowd like that here,' Jim said.

'Listen to me, Jim. You've never sold so many cups of tea in a month as you have today. Half the North Wales force is here. You'll be up all night counting your money.'

'I could be taking a lot more if you let the public in,' Jim said. His moustache overhung his top lip like the bristles of a yard brush. 'I'm missing an opportunity. A man has to make a living, you know.'

'We've got a job to do here. How many punters do you think are going to come here to wander around the woods when there's a killer on the loose at Penrhos?'

Jim stopped smiling and shook his head. 'Not many.'

'You didn't think of that, did you?'

'Not really.'

'We've got a job to do, so let us get on with it and while we're here, we'll keep drinking your tea and buying your bacon. Look, more customers,' Bob said, pointing.

Jim walked away sulkily to serve another uniformed police officer. Alan had parked up and was approaching with Kim.

'How's it going?' Alan asked.

'Nothing to report yet,' Bob said. 'Do you want a brew and I'll show you where we think he went into the water.'

'A tea and a coffee, please,' Kim said. 'No sugar.'

'Coming up,' Jim said.

'What are the chances of finding him?' Alan asked.

'It all depends when he went into the water. If the tide took him through the inlet to the Inland Sea, we'll find him, eventually. But if he went out into the bay, there's probably no chance.'

'Let's hope he's inland. On a different subject, I've had a call about Ronny Green's death,' Alan said.

'That was quick. What killed him?'

'A perforated peptic ulcer. He probably didn't know he had an ulcer until it burst. The doctor said he would have gone down quickly and gone down hard, banging his face on the floor. It explains the blood around his nose and mouth.'

'So, he wasn't attacked.'

'No. Somebody must have called around and found him dead and chanced their arm at finding a stash in the house. They gave up when they couldn't find it, then locked the door when they left.'

'You're assuming he had a stash,' Bob said, sarcastically.

'They weren't looking for his coin collection,' Alan said. 'I'm guessing he was hiding gear for Jamie Hollins but it's all conjecture now. It doesn't matter anymore. He's gone too soon and it's very sad.'

'Poor bugger,' Bob said, passing them their drinks. 'When your number is up, it's up.'

'Isn't that the truth,' Alan agreed.

'Come on, I'll show you where we found the blood. This way.'

'Is that guy in the burger van Jimmy Fish?' Alan asked, looking back at the burger van as they walked away.

'It is. You've got a good memory.'

'That's not his real name,' Alan said to Kim.

'I gathered that.'

'He used to sell fresh fish on the market when he was younger. The name stuck.'

'As they do around here,' she said, watching the coast guard in the distance. 'What do we know about Brian Hindley?'

'He's a retired postman with nothing remarkable to note.'

'What's the family background?' she asked.

'They're all local. No one with any form,' Bob said.

'Anyone with an axe to grind with him?' she asked.

'Nothing obvious so far.'

'Have the ponds been searched?' Alan asked.

'Once the divers have checked the inlet, they'll check the ponds. They're silted up and very shallow. If he was in there, we'd have seen a body but we might get a murder weapon if there is one.'

They took the right-hand path and stopped near the pet cemetery. Alan hadn't been there for many years. He tried to remember the last time he'd walked around the nature reserve. Probably when he was first dating Kath. They took the dogs there in the early days of their relationship before kids and the job got in the way. It was a world away. The dogs they walked that day were dead, Kath was gone, and life had carried on regardless. It carried on regardless, full-stop.

They reached the shingle beach and ducked beneath the crime scene tape. The area was deserted. Uniformed officers and the CSI had finished their investigations.

'The blood is there; spatter on the tree trunk and the roots. A trail runs across the shingle towards the sea.'

'You think he was stabbed here and then dragged into the water?'

'Yes. The drag marks are clear. Unfortunately, the tide has taken everything beyond the mudflats,' Bob said. 'It drops away quickly there. The killer didn't have to drag the body far. You can see the marks clearly here.'

'I agree. The drag marks can't be explained away,' Alan said. 'It's feasible someone committing suicide could cut their wrists and walk into the sea but the drag marks say someone was attacked here and taken to the sea to be disposed of.' He turned to Bob. 'I agree we're looking for a victim and a killer.' He looked at the footprints again. 'Kim, put Alice's team on this. Put an appeal on Mon Radio and we need a sign and some posters next to the burger van. We need to talk to witnesses who were here yesterday afternoon after four o'clock.'

'What about the *Chronicle*?'

'It came out today,' Alan said. 'Let's call them later. Call the radio first.'

'What do you think is going on?' Bob asked.

'I think there's something in the tap water,' Alan said. 'The world has gone mad and I need some more detectives.'

CHAPTER 30

The sun was fading when he arrived home and he unlocked the front door and switched the lights on. It was warm inside—the heating was on permanently. It cost him a fortune but she couldn't tolerate the cold. She could sense the slightest drop in temperature. Her tongue was as sharp as his knife and one day, he wished the two would meet. He could slice her nasty tongue from her fat head and that would make her think twice about criticising him. Criticism was her art. She could slay him with a sentence. From being a boy, he remembered her negative comments. He wasn't clever enough; tall enough; handsome enough; fast enough; helpful or polite enough. She seemed to resent him being there at all. She was suffering now and he could end her suffering without blinking but then why should he? He enjoyed watching her suffer. It would become too much and one day he would put her out of her misery but not today. He would plod on as usual and play the dutiful son.

The situation at home suited him. It had all the trappings of normality and was like camouflage. No one could see the monster in their midst. On the face of it, he was the mild-mannered bachelor who worked hard and cared for his ailing mother. She was bedbound most of the time. It was rare she moved from her bedroom and when she did, it was only as far as the bathroom. He got help from the local authorities. The council were brilliant with the elderly on the island. Carers came in to bathe her and manage her toilet needs. He couldn't do that. Not ever. The thought of seeing her naked or wiping her backside made him sick. If they ever took her support workers away, they would have to put her in a home. The problem was, homes were ridiculously expensive and his wages wouldn't touch the cost of fulltime care. The care she received now was expensive. They had to contribute to the cost. She had some money put away but he'd watched it dwindle from a decent sized nest egg to a pittance. If she took a turn for the worse, it wouldn't cover six months care. Then it would be time to slip something in her tea or smother her with a cushion. That might be fun.

He crept into the hallway and took his boots off, quietly. Her television was blaring. It was always blaring as her hearing was poor but she wouldn't wear her hearing aids. They gave her a headache, she said. It was all right for everyone around her to have a headache as long as she was all right, nothing else mattered. On the bright side, her deafness covered a multitude of sins. She never knew when he was in or out unless he popped his head around the door. He told her work kept asking him to do overtime, which lately, was true. Every couple of days, he would sit with her for a few hours. They would drink tea, eat eclairs, and watch a film together although she rarely saw them to halfway through. Her medication made her drift in and out of consciousness and her concept of time was warped. She told the carers and the odd visitor that he was the most caring son in the world and that he sat with her every night after work. The days blurred into one for her. She was deteriorating fast and her lifeforce was almost exhausted. He wondered if she knew. He wondered if she'd ever really known what she was doing. Her ability to point out his mistakes was unquestionable yet she seemed to be clueless about her own. Becoming friends with Peter Moore had been a classic.

The serial killer, Peter Moore was twenty years her senior when they met in the early nineties. She'd worked for him at the cinema in Holyhead, selling choc ices and sweets during the intervals and clearing up the litter and cleaning the toilets when the public had gone home. They became friendly and he offered her some vodka in his office one night. That's when he'd raped her. Right there, on the desk. At least, that was what she'd told everyone when it eventually came out. She would never have told a soul if it hadn't come out the way it did. When he was growing up, he had no idea who his father was. His mother told him she'd met his dad on a night out in Blackpool and remembered his name was John something and he might have been in the RAF. She couldn't remember anything else. Of course, he wondered who his father was and what he did for a living in the airforce. He dreamed his father was a fighter pilot and he would come and find him some time in the future, any child would.

It was purely by chance he'd found out the truth. A local girl of eleven had been raped. It was a particularly brutal attack and the case went viral. The police made an appeal for local men to come forward and have their DNA tested to eliminate hundreds from the enquiry. Obviously, he was one of the first to volunteer. His DNA was a hit on the database but not in that particular case. It was another case. A historic case. The DNA match identified him as a close relation to someone in the system linked to a different crime but they didn't say who. He was interviewed by local detectives, one of whom lived on the island. When they interviewed him, the questions were confusing and ambiguous. The officers appeared to be as baffled as he was by the line of questioning and even at the end of the interview, he didn't have a clue what it had been about. Months later, one of the detectives had a drunken discussion with some of his friends in a pub. It was overheard by some of the locals and repeated. It spread like wildfire and eventually reached Holyhead. He remembered the day he found out like it was yesterday.

'I heard about you being interviewed after we had that DNA test. That must have been a massive shock,' a workmate said. They were having a pint after their shift. 'What did your mum say about it?'

'What are you talking about?'

'Finding out your dad was a nutter serial killer. Wales' only serial killer.'

'What the hell are you talking about?'

'I heard your dad is Peter Moore...'

He'd swallowed his pint and left without a word. He was the only one who hadn't heard the rumours. It all clicked into place. The DNA test and the odd questions when he was interviewed. He knew his DNA matched a possible relation but he had no idea who or what the relationship was. The police daren't divulge that. It was a drunken faux pas that opened Pandora's box but the information answered a lot of questions. The secrets, the silence, the shadows around his conception. The night out in Blackpool and the one-night stand with the mysterious John-something, was bullshit. He drove home in a rage and confronted his mother. She didn't deny it. When she told him, his father had raped her in the cinema and that his father was a serial killer, he couldn't have been any happier. It was a joyful epiphany. He knew there was something inside him, something different, something evil. Finding out who his father was, answered a myriad of questions. Now he understood what he was.

CHAPTER 31

Simon and Kerry called ahead and were given the code for the police station car park. They were greeted at the front desk by a ruddy faced sergeant, who looked like he was way past his retirement date. He gestured to a side room, and they went in and sat down. The room smelled of disinfectant and air-freshener. Someone had scratched 'PIG STY' into the wall. It had been painted over but was still visible. They were offered tea by a civilian officer and they chatted quietly until the uniformed sergeant entered. He brought a waft of Old Spice aftershave with him. It reminded Kerry of her dad.

'I'm Eddie,' the sergeant said, introducing himself.

'Simon and Kerry,' Kerry said. They all shook hands.

'So, you're from Anglesey?' the sergeant asked.

'We are,' Simon said.

'Come to the big city for a day out?'

'Something like that.'

'We've got a caravan in Benllech.'

'Nice part of the island,' Kerry said.

'I gather you have some questions about an incident down the road at Fords,' he said.

'Jaguar, Land Rover,' Kerry said.

'Sorry. It was Fords for so long, that's what us old timers call the place. The place is better now than it was. We used to have a lot of problems with that place. Theft was rife for years. We were there every day. Anyway, I digress. How can I help?'

'We wanted to know about an incident which resulted in a man called Derek Kio being sent down with another man. About six years ago.'

'Ah, Degsy Kio,' Eddie said with a wry smile. 'Now there's a man who couldn't stay out of trouble if he was locked in an empty room and chained to the floor.' Eddie chuckled to himself. 'He would steal the shirt off your back and come back the next day for your vest. I don't know who checked the references on his application form. How he got a job there, I'll never know. Someone turned a blind eye, if you ask me. In those days, it wasn't what you know but who you know that counted. Everyone in this city wanted to work there. It was a good job and well paid and the perks were good. Do you remember when every job had its perks?'

Simon laughed. Kerry looked confused.

'So, you do remember him,' Kerry said.

'You couldn't forget a man like Degsy Kio. He was one in a million.'

'Can you remember what happened?' Simon asked.

'I remember bits and pieces although the chronology might be askew.' Eddie thought for a moment. 'The factory used to be much bigger back then and the production line ran twenty-four hours a day. It only shut down on one Sunday a month for maintenance. There were three, eight-hour shifts; mornings, afternoons, and nights but then the company made cuts and redundancies and it was taken to two, twelve-hour shifts. Day shifts and night shifts. Twelve-hour night shifts are hard graft and they mess with your sleep pattern. A lot of the workforce used certain drugs to get them through the week.'

'Cocaine?'

'Got it in one. There were thousands employed there back then, a lot of them had worked for Ford before they started building Jaguars and Land Rovers. Selling cocaine on the nightshift was rife. You can imagine it was a lucrative trade to be in. Thousands of customers and no police force as such. Some of the dealers made thousands of pounds a month.'

'Didn't they have security?'

'Of course, they did, but most of them were on the dealers' payrolls. They turned a blind eye and pulled the odd employee who was stealing tyres and the like.'

'That would have been a lucrative business to be in,' Simon said.

'There were frequent turf wars over the factory. People were paid to recruit certain other people. People like Degsy Kio. The management tried a crackdown and one of the directors was run off the road. He crashed into a motorway stanchion and never walked again. They never caught anyone. About the same time, another man was assaulted in the stores. They fractured his skull with a wrench. He was lucky to survive. Of course, no one saw anything or heard anything. There was a wall of silence. No one liked a grass. Eventually, the management asked us for help and we descended on the place with sniffer dogs. You've never seen so many men running for the toilets in your life. The dustbins were literally full of little white packets of powder. I'll never forget it. Degsy Kio was found with a substantial amount of coke in his locker. He claimed he'd been set up by some of his customers from the offices upstairs but the management closed ranks and his accusations didn't fly.'

'He said the drugs had been planted in his locker?' Simon asked.

'That was the gist of it from what I can remember. I did think it was odd leaving his stash in an unlocked locker,' Eddie said. 'But then, Degsy was an arrogant man and arrogant men make mistakes. I wouldn't put it past him to think no one would dare go into his locker. At the end of the day, the drugs were in his locker and he was arrested. He was bound to deny they were his. Degsy and his sidekick were sent down for possession with intent to supply.'

'How much did he have?' Kerry asked.

'Two kilos sealed and wrapped ready to sell,' Eddie said. Simon made a whistling sound. 'After that raid, the company employed a security company that had drug dogs and introduced random drug tests and it all settled down.'

'Can you remember the names of the other men involved?' Kerry asked.

'I might be able to if I could dig out the investigation files to jog my memory but they'll have been archived on the system. I can ask if they can be recovered.'

'Does the name Kelvin Adams ring a bell?'

'No, can't say it does. Should it?'

'He worked here at the time. He was the man who was murdered.'

'I see.'

'What about Glen Price?' Kerry asked.

'No. I don't remember him but I do remember one name who was interviewed. It made me laugh because it rhymed with David Brent from *The Office* and he was an arse like him. Barry Trent. He was interviewed by the drug squad a few times.'

'Can you remember what his involvement was?' Simon asked.

'Kio said Trent was high up the food chain and, financed the product coming into the factory but it was never proven. He managed the engineering department, if I remember rightly.'

'He still does.'

'If he's still in the same position six years on, it must have affected his career.'

'He does have a certain paranoia about him.' Kerry said.

'That's been really helpful, thank you,' Simon said. 'Thanks for the tea.'

'You're very welcome. Leave me a number and if I can locate the interview list, I'll give you a call.'

CHAPTER 32

Alan decided to call in to the farm where Will Pinter lived. Kim had tried calling the number on the website and she'd asked for Will by name. The woman on the other end said he wasn't available. When Kim pressed, she said Will was taking a sabbatical. Alan said Will didn't know how to spell sabbatical never mind know what one was. He'd been a farmer all his life and only dabbled with property letting when he'd built some holiday lodges on his farm. That was years ago. Something about it rankled with him. Kim had gone to Cemaes Bay to find the laundry company that serviced the Caernarvon Castle motel as they weren't answering the phone. They decided to split up and catch up on the telephone later before the evening debriefing.

When he got to the farm, he was surprised at how well it looked compared to the last time he'd been there. The farmhouse had new windows and doors fitted to it. Will wouldn't entertain double-glazing. He was from the generation who wore more clothes if it was cold, even inside the house. The gates to the fields were galvanised metal as opposed to the old wooden five-bar gates Will built and maintained by hand. There were two new barns, new equipment, and a new Land Rover in front of the farmhouse. He could see other polycarbonate sheds across the fields. The farmyard used to be a mud bath full of geese; now it was concrete and clean. If Will Pinter was still living there, he'd had a personality bypass. Alan parked up and walked to the door. He knocked on it and waited. A shadow loomed at the end of the hallway and grew as it approached the door.

'Hello,' the large man, who opened the door said. He looked irritated at the intrusion.

Alan showed him his warrant card. 'I'm detective inspector Williams. I'm looking to speak to Will Pinter.'

'You'll struggle with that,' the man said. 'My uncle Will has been in Fairways for three years. He had a stroke in twenty fifteen. It was a bad one. He doesn't know what day it is anymore, doesn't recognise us when we visit. What do you need to talk to him about?'

'He's listed as the director of a property letting company called Sundown and we need to talk to whoever runs it.'

'I've lost count of the number of phone calls I've made to them. He's nothing to do with it anymore. That's the name he used when he was renting out the lodges to tourists but that was years ago. People send brochures for all kinds of stuff addressed to Uncle Will. Someone has nicked the name of the company and are using his identity. Probably avoiding paying tax. If you find out who it is, lock them up, will you.'

'I'm sorry to have bothered you. I didn't get your name,' Alan said. He thought the reason for using Sundown as a front was far more sinister than avoiding the taxman.

'Gar,' the man said.

'Thanks for your time, Gar.'

'No problem,' Gar said, closing the door.

Alan walked back to the BMW and checked his phone. The screen was clear. He climbed in and drove towards town, dialling Dafyd Thomas on the way.

'Hello, Alan,' Dafyd said. 'What are you up to?'

'I'm chasing shadows.'

'Are you catching any?'

'Do you remember a farmer called Will Pinter?' Alan asked. 'He farmed at Caer Rhos, at the bottom of the mountain in Llaingoch.'

'Yes. I remember him, why?'

'Something isn't right at the Caernarvon Castle motel. I think it's a front for money laundering and the company maintaining the place is listed as Sundown Property Management, owned by Will Pinter.'

'He'll be getting on now, won't he?'

'He's in Fairways, has been for three years.'

'And you think it's connected to our UCs being killed?'

'They were staying there. It's too much of a coincidence for it not to be. Jarvis and McGowan were professionals, highly skilled operatives. Staying there may have been their downfall. They inadvertently walked into the hornet's nest. We'll keep digging until we find who's behind it.' He paused for thought. 'I think you need to speak to Hunt about it. We might be treading on Operation Thor.'

'I'll fill him in when he calls. If they'd known about the Caernarvon Castle, they would have told us to leave it alone. Carry on as normal unless we hear otherwise,' Dafyd said. 'How's the search at Penrhos going?'

'The divers are searching and the coast guard are helping out. Officially he's still missing, unofficially we're looking for a body.'

'You're positive?'

'Absolutely no doubt about it. There's a lot of blood. Someone was dragged from the path into the sea. The evidence is clear.'

'Another murder. It's like living in Midsomer. What the hell is going on this week?'

'There's something in the water,' Alan said. 'Better to stay off the island for a while.' Dafyd agreed. Alan thought about his next words carefully. 'I want to move our investigation to Holyhead Station.'

'Why?'

'The impact of fifty detectives landing in town will rattle a few cages. I think it will create chatter that might help us. It will certainly help Operation Thor if people start to get nervous. I bet their audio surveillance will be interesting to listen to if we set up there.'

'It would certainly put the cat among the pigeons. Logistically it makes sense.'

'All we'll need is a new kettle. Everything else is there. It makes perfect sense to me. You know what Holyhead is like; it will be the talk of the town in every shop, pub, club, and bookies.'

'Alan,' Dafyd tried to get a word in.

'It will also give the public some confidence that we're reacting to the recent murders quickly and efficiently. People will be frightened in their own homes. We need to show a presence and I think it would benefit the public and the investigation.'

'Have you finished?' Dafyd said. 'Only I can't get a word in edgeways.'

'Sorry. I've been thinking about it a lot.'

'I can tell. It's a good idea for all the reasons you've mentioned. When are you thinking of switching?'

'Tomorrow.'

'I'll have a word with Bob Dewhurst and get him to shift some of the desks into the operations room. Anything else you need, let me know.'

'Thanks, Dafyd,' Alan said. 'I've asked Kim to contact Mon Radio and set up an appeal to anyone who was at Penrhos after four o'clock. I know you've been on Mon FM a few times. Is there any chance you could pull some strings?'

'Kim has already called me. I've made a few calls and they're going to make an appeal every half an hour with the news and weather.'

'Perfect. Thank you.'

'No problem. Any progress on the Jarvis and McGowan investigation?'

'Yes. We've recovered a quantity of staged buys from their van. They were very thorough at cataloguing who they bought from and where. Pamela is putting a list together. It will give us the name of every dealer they bought from while they were on the island. I think it will point us towards whoever fingered them as undercovers. It will certainly narrow it down.'

'Good work. That's a breakthrough. Are you heading back?'

'I'm on my way. We've got an update briefing at eight.'

'I'll see you there.'

CHAPTER 33

Kim turned onto an industrial park on the outskirts of Cemaes Bay. The satnav told her she'd reached her destination but she couldn't see the building she was looking for. She checked the unit number and drove on. Most of the units were abandoned, used tyres and rusty oil drums spotted the empty car parks. A static caravan business was thriving on the biggest unit, like an oasis in a desert of decay. Caravans of all shapes and sizes were stacked three high. Next door, a mechanic was busy fixing motorbikes. He looked up and stared at her as she drove past. The last unit on the left was the one she was looking for. A 'To Let' sign was fixed above the roller shutters. She parked on the forecourt and climbed out, leaving the engine running. There was no one around to steal her car. She walked up to the reception and tried the door. It was locked and the lights were turned off. A poster in the window advertised industrial laundry services, washing, ironing, and delivery. She peered through the window and looked inside. The reception desk was unmanned. There was a diary and a pot of pens on it. She took out her mobile and dialled the number on the poster. It rang and switched to voicemail, instructing her to leave a name and number, which she did, leaving out the fact she was a police officer. She had a feeling it might put off the owners of the business from calling her back.

Kim looked inside again but couldn't see what was in the storage area beyond the office. The adjoining door was ajar but not enough for her to see inside. She walked across the forecourt to the roller shutters and tried to peer between the slats but it was too dark inside to see anything. A noise came from around the corner. It was the sound of breaking glass. Kim walked towards it. The land adjacent to the unit was overgrown. The brambles were chest height. She stepped over a large tractor tyre and followed the noise. Another smash made her jump. It was coming from the rear of the building. She tiptoed to the corner and looked around, trying to step lightly. The source of the noise became clear immediately.

'Hey!' Kim shouted. The kids froze and looked at her. They had a milk crate full of bottles and they were systematically smashing them with bricks. 'You shouldn't be doing that here.'

'Who says?' one of the kids said.

Kim showed her warrant card. 'I do. Bugger off home.'

The kids ran, weaving through the brambles with practised ease. She noticed a small window in the back wall and looked inside. It was a small kitchenette with a water heater on the wall above a sink. There were two mugs on the draining board. It looked clean and well maintained but told her nothing about what went on inside. Kim made her way around the unit to her car. She sighed as she climbed in and decided to go back to the motorcycle mechanic and ask him a few questions. He was tinkering with the seat of a Harley Davidson when she pulled up. She turned the engine off and climbed out.

'Hello, officer,' the mechanic said, as she approached.

'Is it that obvious?' Kim asked.

'I've always been able to spot you lot a mile away,' he said, laughing. His tattooed hands were black with oil. A hand-rolled cigarette hung from the corner of his mouth, where his grey beard was stained brown with tar. 'Before I started fixing bikes, I used to steal them. That's a long time ago, though.'

'How long have you been trading here?'

'Fifteen years. I had a place in Benllech for ten years but the rent kept going up. This place is empty, as you can see. The council don't charge us any business rates as an incentive to stay trading here. I saw you nosing around the laundry. What's the interest with that place?'

'I need to speak to the owners,' Kerry said. 'Do you know them?'

'Nope. I've seen a woman coming and going in a little red van. I don't think they have much business yet. It's early days, I suppose.'

'How long have they been there?'

'A couple of months.'

'This might seem like an odd question but have you actually seen any laundry, you know, being delivered?'

'There were a few deliveries when they first moved in. I saw machines being fitted and bales of linen and towels being delivered.'

'Washing machines?'

'I'm not an expert but it looked like a big washing machine and a drier, industrial stuff. But there hasn't been much activity there since.'

'Thanks for your help,' Kim said. 'Much appreciated.'

'You're welcome.'

Kerry drove to Caernarfon, frustrated but not surprised. She was none the wiser as to whether the laundry was in fact a commercial laundry or part of an elaborate money laundering operation. Laundering the cash was a simple theory, which would have gone unnoticed had it not been for the murder of the motel guests. Proving it was a front for something more sinister, was not as simple as it seemed. The owners were hiding behind legitimate looking facades and they needed to dig deeper to find out who they were.

She reached the station and walked into the briefing with fifteen minutes to spare.

'We're all here, so let's crack on,' Alan said, bringing the room to attention. 'What's the latest from Penrhos?'

'Still no body, guv. The coast guard and divers have stopped searching until sun-up tomorrow. CSI have identified a size-ten boot print on the mudflats and another near the tree. They're saying it's a generic sole used by a variety of manufacturers. Tracking it is virtually impossible. If we get something to match it to, we can use it,' one of the team said. 'They also confirmed the blood is Brian Hindley's—it matches DNA samples taken from Mr Hindley's home.'

'Okay. Have any witnesses come forward?'

'Four people so far, all there after four o'clock but none of them saw anything untoward. Two of them remember a woman walking a chocolate Labrador in the woods. We've got another three to follow up on.'

'Okay good work. Simon, what have you and Kerry been up to?'

'We've got a very unwilling workmate coming in tomorrow morning with his solicitor. We went back to the Jaguar plant and spoke to his workmates. There was an incident six years ago which resulted in two men being sent down for possession with intent. Kelvin Adams, his colleague Glen Price, and his boss Barry Trent were all interviewed in connection with conspiracy. We spoke to a sergeant at the local nick who remembers it happening. He's going to locate the interview notes if he can and let us have them. They might help. We can't tell if it has anything to do with the Adam's murder until we get Price to open up. He's acting very squirrely.'

'Possession with intent,' Alan said, thinking. 'Mrs Adams didn't mention that. Alice. Speak to Pamela Stone. Ask her to retest Kelvin Adam's vehicle, specifically for cocaine.'

'Yes, guv.'

'Retest the body too,' he added.

'Guv?' Alice looked confused.

'How do people carry drugs on their person?' Alan said.

'Internally,' Alice said.

'Exactly right. Adams was found naked and we recovered his clothes from a toilet block. He may have been removing drugs from his backside. We might be way off but now we have a link to drugs we have to test everything again.'

'Do you think he was a courier?' Alice asked.

'I don't think anything for sure but it's possible. He made the journey every month regardless of the weather. It may have been a delivery run.'

'Are we linking the murders, guv?' Simon asked.

'Not yet, but we can keep an open mind. We have no motive for Adam's murder except that he bumped into a random killer. What's more likely?'

'We've got the initial findings back for McGowan and Jarvis,' Kim said. 'The cause of death was drowning. Their shoulders were dislocated, indicating that they were hung from something, arms above their head. They both suffered broken bones and multiple stab wounds—their feet were badly burned, probably with a blowtorch.'

'Jarvis and McGowan were staying at the Caernarfon Castle, which those of you who worked at Holyhead will remember fondly as the pub at the back of the station,' Alan said. 'It's been converted into a motel. They were the only two guests yet the other rooms were serviced daily. There're no televisions and no Internet. At first glance, it looks like a genuine motel but it's nothing more than a façade. I'm sure of it.'

'Money laundering?' Alice asked.

'We think so. The company who owns it are registered in Guernsey and the management company here is listed as Sundown, run by a man who has been in a nursing home for three years. He can't speak let alone run a business.'

'And I checked out the laundry company who services the motel and it doesn't appear to be a functioning commercial laundry. One of the local traders on the estate said a woman turns up occasionally in a red van. We need the registration of the van and we need to speak to her. I'll look into getting the utility bills for the unit to see if they're using electric and water at the rate a legitimate laundry would.'

'Pamela Stone recovered some staged buys in the UCs' van and they were very thorough in cataloguing who they bought from. Shortly, we'll have a list of everyone they bought drugs from while they've been on the island. I want every single one of them brought in and rattled. We need to know who they work for, how long they have worked for them and what they remember about McGowan and Jarvis being in Holyhead.' A murmur of excitement rippled through the room. 'Very importantly, we're going to relocate the investigation to Holyhead nick so we can round up the dealers with ease, bring them in, lock them up, and sit on them until they give us something. Word will spread around town very quickly and people will start talking. When they do, we'll be listening. If whoever killed the Matrix officers is in town, we'll flush them out. In the meantime, I'm going to ask Dafyd to go public on the drug find. We want them to know we're coming. They'll panic and make mistakes. I want you to squeeze as much information out of them as you can.'

'When are we starting in Holyhead, guv?'

'Tomorrow. We'll meet at eight o'clock tomorrow morning and share out the names on Pamela's lists. It will be a busy day so go home and get some rest.'

* * *

He stood and watched his mother sleeping. Her breathing irritated him. No, it was more than irritation, it was anger. Her breathing angered him. He wondered how long it would continue. In and out, in and out. The air rasped in her throat. A muscle in her cheek twitched, making her mouth turn up at the corner. He wondered what dreams she had. She never spoke of her dreams, never had—and she'd never asked him about his, not even as a child. It was probably better that she hadn't. If she had known the truth of what went through his mind, she might have smothered him in his bed as a child. The darkness inside him had always been there and had grown with him, festering and poisoning his soul.

He remembered the first time he felt the urge to kill. It was on the breakwater when he was just twelve-years old. His friend Callum was fishing with an orange handline while he watched the yachts bobbing in the marina. They were sitting on the edge, their legs dangling. There was a fifteen-feet drop from the lower level of the breakwater into the marina which was flat and calm. On the other side, it was a much longer drop into the sea, which was rough that day. Occasionally, a wave crashed over the top and they had to keep moving to avoid being soaked. Wave dodging was all part of the adventure. Callum was sticking bacon onto his hook to attract the crabs and conger eels and he remembered wanting to hit him with a rock. He wanted to hit him over the head with a rock and push him into the water to watch him drown. There was nowhere to climb out, even if you could and he yearned to watch him tire and sink beneath the surface. He remembered the desire like it was yesterday; it was almost erotic. Callum had no idea what he was doing when he wandered off to find a rock suitable for the job, nor did he realise that catching an eel had saved his life. A second later and the rock would have cracked his skull but he hooked it at just the right time. He pulled the eel from the marina and it wriggled and squirmed desperate to be free of the hook. It was a big eel, as thick as the boy's wrists at least and its jaws snapped open and closed, razor-sharp teeth exposed. Callum landed it but the eel wriggled towards him, almost biting his bare legs. He dropped the handline and ran as fast as his legs would carry him and ran straight into a wave. Callum was saturated and stood with water dripping from his chin. The eel wriggled over the edge and dropped into the water, diving deep to freedom and the boys laughed so hard, he thought he would pee in his pants. When the laughter subsided, the urge to kill his friend had gone and he tossed the rock into the harbour. It was the strangest feeling. The anticipation he'd felt as he approached with the rock in his hand, had felt like nothing he'd felt before. It was an awakening within him and he knew without a shadow of a doubt that it would return. He wanted it to return and when it did, he welcomed it like an old friend.

He turned out the light and closed the door, heading down the stairs to the front door. His coat was hanging on a hook. He picked it up and struggled into it, feeling the weight of his knife. His knife. *The* knife. He'd made a slit in the lining so that he could carry it comfortably and access it when he had the urge. He felt its energy travel up his fingers, through his bones, and into his bloodstream. It was a rush but it was weaker than it had been at first. His heartbeat quickened. There was a hunger in his soul and he had to feed it.

CHAPTER 34

Alan arrived home to a full house. The dogs performed their usual chaotic greeting before he let them out of the back doors. He could tell they hadn't been out all day from the way they sprinted across the field, bumping into one another as they ran. Henry's little legs were a blur as he struggled to keep up with Gemma. After a hundred yards, he gave up on the race to cock his leg on a tree. It made Alan chuckle.

'Poor little bugger,' Alan said to himself. 'He must have been desperate. Don't worry, boys, I've let the dogs out.' No one replied. 'Am I the only one who knows we've got two dogs?' he said, filling their bowls with fresh water.

'They're your dogs,' Kris said.

'They're your mother's dogs, actually. She left them and you lot here and took the antiques because they're valuable and don't need feeding.' Silence was the reply. 'Have they been fed?'

'I fed them this morning,' Dan said, from the living room. Alan opened his bottle of shiraz while he watched Henry race off into the darkness, trying to catch up. The lads were unusually quiet and remained in the living room. He thought that was odd.

'What are you three up to?' he called out. They didn't answer. He walked into the living room. 'No one has asked me for money, yet.' Jack and Dan were sitting on the settee, Kris was in the armchair. They all had a bottle of Tiger beer and there were three empties on the coffee table. 'You're all very quiet. What's going on?'

'Apparently you've been seen in town, searching the Caernarvon Castle and asking questions.' Dan said.

'I'm a detective inspector. I have to search places and ask questions.'

'Funny.'

'I'm not trying to be funny. It's sort of what I do. It's compulsory really,' Alan said. 'If I didn't ask questions, they'd sack me.' His sons stared at him, unimpressed. 'I haven't seen you so quiet since your grandad enforced a television and pocket money ban. He knew where to hit you the hardest.'

'It's not funny, Dad,' Dan said. 'We have to live here.'

'I live here too,' Alan said. 'I've lived here a lot longer than you have and no one has had a problem with me being a policeman. I've got a job to do, so either tell me what the problem is or stop sulking.' None of the boys spoke. 'Come on, spit it out. What exactly is the problem?'

'I went to buy some weed from my mate tonight,' Dan said. 'He won't sell it to me.'

'How is that my fault?'

'Because you're my dad.'

'Tell them you're adopted.'

'You're so annoying. Everyone in town is talking about you being at the Caernarfon Castle, tossing the place, and everyone knows you're my dad. My mate who sells to us is crapping himself that you'll arrest him.'

'I haven't just started being related to you. I've always been your dad and I haven't arrested him yet.'

'You aren't listening. He's panicking and won't sell me anything.'

'I see. This is an emergency,' Alan said. 'The presence of police officers in town has sent a shockwave through Holyhead's underworld. Crime will grind to a halt and my sons can't buy cannabis. Someone, call the cops.' The boys looked at him stony-faced. 'Hold on a minute, I am a cop. Panic over.'

'It's not funny, Dad,' Dan said.

'Are you serious?'

'Very. It's not funny.'

'You've got a face like a smacked arse because you've run out of cannabis and that's my fault?'

'It's not just Dan. I've texted my mate to see if he has any to sell us and he told me not to go anywhere near his house until it's all over,' Kris moaned. 'Because of you, we've been excommunicated.'

'I don't think you can be excommunicated from a cannabis supply but that's terrible. I'm so sorry. I can't apologise enough,' Alan said. He wiped an imaginary tear from the corner of his eye. 'I never would have gone there if I'd realised the impact it would have on your lives.'

'Be serious for once, Dad,' Jack said.

'Okay. I'll be serious. You need to grow up, all three of you.'

'That's very useful,' Jack said. 'Thanks.'

'Listen to me. I'm investigating four murders.' He held up four fingers. 'Not one, not two, not three but four murders. Two of the victims are police officers. The victims had wives and children and grandchildren and the killers are still out there.'

He shrugged. 'Silly me for not thinking how the investigation might affect your cannabis supply. I must be losing my marbles. How inconsiderate of me.'

'We know you have a job to do.'

'Thanks for that but it was inconsiderate of me. Not exactly *Dad of the Year* material.' He shook his head and sighed.

'Sarcasm isn't helping the situation.'

'What would you like me to do, stop the investigation?'

'Don't be silly.'

'Wait. I could steal some cannabis from the evidence room for you.'

'Not helpful.'

'I could throw myself off the breakwater?' The boys looked at each other. Dan looked a little embarrassed. 'Come on, boys. Four families are traumatised, their lives devastated, and you're worried about buying dope.' Alan shook his head. 'Do me a favour and grow up.'

'Sorry,' Dan said. 'I didn't mean to sound flippant about what you do. I didn't think of it like that. Everyone's talking about it.'

'Good. I hope they are. It's a small town. News travels fast. Things in Holyhead are about to get uncomfortable for anyone dealing, no matter what they're selling, weed or otherwise.'

'What do you mean?' Dan asked.

'We've recovered hundreds of staged buys that are catalogued with dates and the names of the dealers who sold it. We'll be investigating them. Every one of them.'

'Are they from town?'

'Not just town; all over the island.'

'Why are you telling us that?' Jack asked. 'Shouldn't that be secret?'

'It will be all over the news tomorrow,' Alan said. 'We're sending a message that we're coming for them.'

'Why would you warn them you're coming?'

'They'll panic. People will start turning on each other very quickly. Just you wait and see.' The boys looked at each other nervously. 'You'd better hope your friend isn't on that list but if he is, he'll be charged.' Alan sipped his wine and looked at them in the eyes one at a time. 'You three think it's a joke smoking weed every night and I get that. It's no big deal. It doesn't make you Pablo Escobar but what you fail to realise is that selling the stuff is a crime.'

'It's just cannabis. They're selling it in Holland and Barret.'

'That's different and you know it. As far as we're concerned, drugs are drugs are drugs and two undercover police officers have been abducted, tortured, and murdered by someone in the drug trade. They strung them up and burned their feet with a blowtorch and then tied them together and tossed them in the sea to drown. Can you imagine how frightened they must have been?'

'I've said sorry,' Dan said. 'There's no need to go on about it.'

'I think there is every need to go on about it,' Alan said. 'I've been thinking about what you said the other night.'

'Oh, for God's sake. What did I say?'

'You said, your supplier never runs out and his cannabis is always good quality.'

'It's true. What's wrong with that? That's why we use him.'

'It's just a bit of weed, Dad,' Kris said. 'Don't make a big thing out of it.'

'Is it just a bit of weed?' Alan asked. The boys frowned. 'You said it's always good. You're thinking quality, I'm thinking quantity. I'm thinking supply chain,' Alan said.

'What are you talking about?'

'I'm detecting. I'm a detective. That's what I do, detect.'

'I don't know what you're talking about.'

'If your friend never runs out and the quality is consistently good, he either grows it himself, buys it by the ton, or he's very close to the grower. Whichever it is, he's likely to be a serious player.' The boys looked at their bottles of beer. 'So, in his case, it isn't just a bit of weed, is it?'

'Never thought of it like that,' Jack said.

'It's not just "a bit of weed, dad",' Alan said. 'It's probably a shitload of weed. He could be growing warehouses full of the stuff. Your friend doesn't just buy the odd batch from here and there, if he did, he would run out and the quality would vary. Possession of a bit of weed for your own use is very different to cultivating with intent to supply. About ten years difference. If he's in that league, he's in trouble.'

'I never thought of where he gets it from,' Dan said.

'No, you didn't. And let me tell you another thing. If your friends have cut you off because I've been seen in town in a forensic suit, they've got more to worry about than selling a bit of weed. My experience is people who scare quickly have got a lot to be scared of.' He drained the glass and went back into the kitchen to refill it. The dogs had returned and were lapping thirstily at the water, tails wagging. Alan opened two tins of food and emptied them into their bowls, adding multicoloured biscuits to it. Gemma was drooling when he put it down. He walked back into the living room and the boys stopped talking immediately. 'If I was in your shoes, I'd stay away from the dealers in Holyhead for a while.' The boys nodded that they understood. He sat down and sipped his wine. 'Now I want to turn my brain off. What time's the football on?'

CHAPTER 35

Lloyd Jones drove through the tall gates, pulled up outside the boatyard and turned off the engine. They used the old workshops as a base for their operation. He grabbed the cocaine from under the driver's seat and opened the boot latch. Ron Took came out of the workshop and closed the gates.

'Leave them open, Ron,' Lloyd said. 'The others will be here soon.'

Ron opened them again. He walked to the car and opened the boot and rummaged in the tyre well. The vehicle rocked beneath his considerable weight. He lifted out the spare and opened a hatch beneath it, removing what was stored there. Ron was six-feet six and twenty stone. His hands made a pint glass look like a half. He was Lloyd's cousin. They walked into the workshop in silence. Ron didn't know what to say. He couldn't find the words. They closed the doors and Ron put three handguns on the bench. Lloyd picked up a Glock seventeen and checked the magazine was full. He placed the magazine on the bench and blew down the barrel.

'Are you a hundred per cent sure you want to do this?'

'Your Auntie Nina has been kidnapped, Ron,' Lloyd said. 'What do you want me to do?' He lowered his weapon and took out his phone. He replayed the video message.

'I can't believe this,' Ron said. 'They did this because you wouldn't pay for a kilo?'

'I paid for one and owed for another but it was shit. I told them I wasn't paying for shit. What was I supposed to do?' Lloyd protested. 'I didn't think they would kidnap my mother. The Albanians don't play by the rules. They ripped me off with cut cocaine and then start kidnapping people when I complained. Who does that?'

'Albanian drug dealers,' Ron said.

'Exactly.'

'You said, you threatened them?'

'I left a couple of poorly worded voicemails.'

'Uncle Keith said you threatened to shoot them.'

'I didn't mean it literally.'

'They took it seriously.'

'I know that, Ron. You're not helping,' Lloyd said. 'Whatever I said, they've crossed the line. I'm going after the bastards. Are you in?'

'Of course, I am. How are you going to find them?'

'You don't need to worry about that,' a voice said. 'We've found you.' They heard the sound of weapons being cocked. Ron looked around and held up his hands. Lloyd looked at the magazine and calculated if he could reach it, load and shoot before they shot him. 'You could try to load that gun but then your mother would lose her head before you reach it. Put the gun on the bench, kneel down, and put your hands behind your head.' The two men did as they were told. 'Cuff them and get them in the van.'

CHAPTER 36

Jamie was standing in the window overlooking the harbour. The Irish Ferries ship, *Ulysses* had docked at the Salt Island berth and a seemingly never-ending stream of articulated lorries rolled off. He watched through binoculars as a car transporter appeared; it weaved along the dock and reached the customs area. Uniformed officers intercepted it and ordered the driver to take it into the customs shed. Jamie focused the glasses on Skinner's monument, which towered above the town on a clifftop across the harbour. Next to the monument, three men watched the same vehicle from the darkness. They looked agitated that it had been stopped for inspection. Jamie wasn't in the least bit worried. He paid a lot of money every month to make sure his shipments came through. Most of the dealers from the North-West relied on the big outfits in the cities for their supply but Jamie had quietly moved away from them years before. He didn't need a supplier; he was the supplier.

His phone vibrated. He looked at the screen and shook his head.

Customs have stopped the truck

What part of, no communication until the transporter is clear of the harbour, did they not understand? He texted back.

Everything is fine. Carry on.

He watched the men across the harbour. They were smoking. He was certain they wouldn't take their cigarette butts when they left. They were stupid and left a DNA trail behind them everywhere they went. Stupid. Brutal but stupid.

'Why are we showing them where the gear comes in?' Tony asked.

'I don't like dealing with them any more than you do but their money is as good as anybody's.'

'Are you not worried they'll try to take us out and secure the supply line for themselves.'

'All they know is we use the port. Nothing more. They're stretched up here. London is their stronghold. They bring Afghan heroin in by the ton. High grade cocaine isn't their speciality until now.'

'If they've got London stitched up, why are they dabbling with coke up here?'

'They're buying quality gear from us, cutting it to shit and selling it on to the dealers in the city. Lloyd Jones went to Manchester and bought crap from them, that started off here. People will get sick of buying crap and a few weeks down the line they'll stop cutting it and sell high quality gear and they'll clean up. They'll cut the legs from under the smaller dealers and take over. That's how they operate. They can't be trusted.'

'So, they'll need us for now.'

'Yes, for now. Taking us out now would be like killing the golden goose but at some point, they'll try.'

'Of course, we won't let it happen.'

'They're too far from home to be a threat to this operation, Albanian or not. The outfits in the cities will rally. It might take a while but they'll send them back to London with a kick up the arse. In the meantime, we'll sell them as much as they want.'

Jamie played down the Albanian threat. The biggest threat he had was the police were moving in, he knew that but their focus was on the flow of drugs out of the cities and into Wales, not the other way around. They were running around bragging about the damage they'd caused to the supply chain through Operation Suzie but they fixated on the myth that the cities were the epicentre of supply and that was a fallacy. He brought more uncut cocaine into the country in a week than they moved in a month and he was distanced from it all. With Owen Collins on board, that took the number of garages working for him to eight, spread from the island along the coastline. His acquisition of a third taxi firm gave him more vehicles and more drivers. The month before, he bought two courier firms and three car dealerships. More vehicles he could use to give the appearance of legitimacy. Vehicles need cleaning, so he had set up six car washes to valet his vehicles. There would be no record of how many times each vehicle would be cleaned each week. Some of the vehicles would simply drive from one carwash to another. There would be an unlimited number of opportunities to process cash with impunity.

Cash was the biggest problem all dealers encountered. Every business in the country, sole trader or massive conglomerate had to prove where every penny came from. Any movement over £8800 had to be flagged by the banks and verified. Money laundering was the key to every organisation. Get it wrong and your house of cards will crumble. The only other option was to hoard cash but it could only be spent in small amounts. Hoarding large amounts of cash was problematic and vulnerable to theft. He couldn't trust anyone. Not with cash. He was constantly looking for opportunities to wash cash through a business and deposit it cleanly into a bank, where it could be moved abroad into the obscurity of offshore cyberspace. He had a two-year plan before he closed up shop and moved abroad with more money than he could spend in ten lifetimes. Keeping one step ahead of the law until then was his focus. Activity across the harbour caught his attention.

The Albanians were on the move as soon as the transporter cleared the customs shed. He didn't want them there but they insisted on watching every time a shipment landed. They were very suspicious. For them, messing up a deal carried a death sentence. There was no room for failure in their organisation. Jamie watched a second car transporter exit the ferry. This was the real mule, the first just a decoy for the benefit of the Albanians. They didn't need to know everything. He kept his cards close to his chest for obvious reasons. He checked the transporter through the glasses. There were eight vehicles on the transporter all carrying five kilos of coke. Forty kilos in one shipment and it would all be off the island within forty-eight hours, which equated to a quarter of a million pounds in notes, which had to be washed clean. It was a headache—a headache that could cost him twenty-five years if he wasn't very careful. When the second transporter cleared, he made a call on his mobile.

'It's cleared, Mike.'

'Where are they being unloaded?' Mike asked. Jamie didn't tell anyone where a shipment would be taken until it was cleared through customs.

'Take the decoy to Pentraeth Motors and the mule to the dealership in Llangefni.'

'How much are our foreign friends taking this time?'

'Half.' Suddenly, Jamie felt uneasy. 'Where's the handover?'

'Under the old bridge. They're taking it across the Straits to the mainland in a rib.'

'Okay. Double your security,' Jamie said. 'I've got a feeling in my bones.'

'Don't worry. It'll go like clockwork,' Mike said, hanging up.

CHAPTER 37

Zak walked along the Newry promenade with a bottle of cider in his hand. Streetlights bathed the grassed areas with a yellow tinge. A road ran along the promenade, broken by speed-bumps and mini-roundabouts. The pinging noise of yacht rigging echoed across the marina and he could hear the waves crashing over the breakwater. Behind him, an Irish ferry was docked at Salt Island, its lights reflecting from the sea. Any other time, it would be romantic to walk there, even alone. He didn't need a partner to appreciate the romance of a situation. But he didn't feel romantic. He felt numb. Heartbroken. But most of all, he felt betrayed. Lloyd was an idiot sometimes but he loved him. It was that simple.

There was a problem; the problem was Lloyd. He checked his phone again but his screen was blank. Lloyd wasn't going to message and Zak was too stubborn to make the first approach. He thought about phoning and telling him everything would be okay and they could go back to a secret relationship but deep inside, he knew it wouldn't be okay. Not now, not never. Enough was enough; he had to walk away. It would hurt for a while but in the long term, it had to be done. If he wanted to be happy then he had to cut him loose and start again. It wasn't even fun anymore. Lloyd had become brooding and morose. Life before Lloyd had been fun. Less intense but fun. Stumbling into a relationship had changed everything. Lloyd refused to recognise their relationship yet became intensely jealous if he so much as spoke to another man. Zak was an outgoing fun-loving character and Lloyd stifled him. He needed a partner to appreciate him for who he was not hide him away.

A car went by, the headlights blinded him for a second. The driver stared at him. He looked vaguely familiar. They nodded hello to each other. Zak didn't think much of it. His head was elsewhere tonight. He reached the end of the promenade and decided to walk down the quarry road towards the boatyard, where Lloyd ran a small business buying and selling boats. Lloyd went there late at night sometimes, doing his dodgy deals. Why else would anyone go there at night? He never spoke to him about his business and Zak never asked, despite the fact he knew what he was involved in. It wasn't his place to quiz him. Zak's mother and sister had warned him about getting involved with Lloyd. They said he was trouble, a drug dealer and not a very good one. His sister said his gear was crap. Everyone in town knew what he did but Zak didn't listen. He'd been smitten.

The top road to the quarry was the old railway line which had carried stone. It was straight but unlit. Holy Mountain loomed above, a black mass against the backdrop of stars. The sky was clear of clouds and a million stars twinkled above him. The full moon cast silvery light over everything. The moon cast enough light for him to walk safely. He saw headlights coming the other way and stepped off the road onto the grass verge. A van roared past at a reckless speed followed by a minibus. He could make out the outlines of men inside. Zak thought it odd at that time of night although lots of fishermen fished off the breakwater at night. Night time brought the big conger eels closer to shore. The noise of the waves crashing over the breakwater told him fishing wouldn't be much fun tonight—in fact, it would be very dangerous.

Zak didn't care. He finished his cider and tossed the bottle into a bush, wishing he'd bought another one. As he neared the fork in the road, which led to the boatyard, he stopped and looked towards it. The lights were on. Lloyd might be there alone. They could talk things over and maybe sort things out. The prospect made him question all his doubts about the relationship. There were too many doubts to ignore. It was doomed until Lloyd acknowledged it existed, which would be never. He made up his mind not to walk there. It defeated the object of trying to make a clean break. He took three steps in the opposite direction and then stopped. It couldn't hurt to talk, even if it was to agree it was over. He turned around and set off towards the boatyard. The gates were open and Lloyd's car was there. He headed for the workshop and was surprised to find the door was wide open. Taking a deep breath, he stepped inside. There was no one there.

'Lloyd,' he called. 'Are you in here?'

He took a quick look around but the workshop was empty. Whoever had been there, had left in a hurry. It had an abandoned feel. Zak sighed and left, closing the door behind him. Lloyd must have gone somewhere in another vehicle, probably with Ron. They were always together, not that it bothered Zak. He took the quarry road and kept walking until the glint of headlights behind him made him turn around. The lights cast a long shadow in front of him and he waved his hands to make his shadow dance. It made him laugh. The vehicle was travelling slowly and Zak stood still until it drew level. The driver's window went down. He looked inside and smiled.

'Fancy meeting you here,' Zak said. He remembered a series of encounters. It was before Lloyd, when things were simple.

'What are you doing here at this time of night?'

'Just walking. I'm going to the quarry and then I'll go back along the Rocky Coast.'

'Do you want a lift?'

'Why not. I've got nothing better to do.' Zak walked around the car and climbed in. The driver pulled off and headed towards the darkness of the quarry.

CHAPTER 38

Tony had overseen the vehicles being stripped of their cargo. It took less than five minutes for their teams to remove the alloys, replace them with normal wheels, and load them back onto the transporter. They'd distributed what needed to be moved and taken the rest to Porthaethwy, a small community under the Menai Bridge, on the Straits. He positioned men on both sides of the water in case the handover went wrong. They were hidden from view and ready for their Albanian customers to arrive. He watched the inky waters running right to left. It was almost silent. Only the sound of the odd vehicle crossing the Britannia bridge, further down the Straits, broke the calm. The sound of an engine drifted to him. He watched as a van approached. It slowed down and stopped and the headlights flashed twice. Tony returned the signal. Almost immediately, an inflatable rib approached the slipway beneath the bridge, which towered above them. The Albanians climbed out of the van and bundled two men towards the rib. They were bound, gagged, and blindfolded. One of them fell and was dragged up roughly. Tony recognised the bulking figure of Ron Took. He was taken aback to see them there, especially tied up.

'What's going on?' Tony asked himself. 'That's Lloyd Jones and his sidekick, Ron Took.'

'What are they doing here?' Mike asked.

'I have no idea.'

'Where do you think they're taking them?'

'Who knows? They've obviously pissed off the Albanians. They don't look like they're here by choice.'

'Shall we take the gear to them?' Mike asked.

'No. Let's wait and see what they're up to.'

Ron and Lloyd were forced into the rib and made to sit on the edge. Two of the Albanian men climbed in, shouting orders to the pilot, leaving just two of them on the slipway. One of them gestured to Tony to bring the goods to them. Tony thought about it for a second and then gave the order.

'Drive over.'

'We're supposed to carry it over,' Mike said.

'I said drive over.'

Mike put the vehicle in gear and edged towards the slipway. He stopped ten yards from the Albanians on the dock. Tony slipped a Glock 17 into his waistband and opened the door. Mike followed suit. He grabbed two canvas bags; Mike grabbed another. They walked to the slipway and put them down. The Albanians approached. One of them opened a sports bag and showed them their money. Tony took two bundles out and checked the notes in the centre of the stack to make sure they weren't fakes. He nodded they were fine and Mike took the bag back to the car.

'What's going on with them?' Tony asked.

'Do you know them?' the Albanian asked.

'This is a small island.'

'They owe us money. We want it.'

'Fair enough.' Tony walked away. 'Nice doing business with you.'

Tony took a last look at the two men and shook his head. He felt sorry for their families. Lloyd's dad had been friendly with his father when they were younger. Part of him wanted to help them but he knew he couldn't. He had men hidden, so would they. They couldn't risk a shootout, there was too much money at stake and besides that, the Albanians were nutters. Upset them and they'll go for your family and they won't stop until they're all dead. Whatever Lloyd Jones had done, he would have to pay for it himself. Tony had tried to give him some advice years before but he'd ignored it. Lloyd always thought he knew better. He'd tried to step up to the big league and the big league had a different approach to rules. There were no rules.

CHAPTER 39

Alan walked into the operations room at Holyhead Station. It looked like it had years before when the station was fully operational. He felt like he'd come home. Most of his team were gathered and already distributing the list of names, compiled by Pamela Stone. There were over seventy buys from fifteen dealers across the island. They had targeted names that appeared on the list more than three times. Four of the people on the list were inside and one of them was dead.

'We've whittled it down to ten names, eight males, two females. They've all got form,' a detective said. Alan couldn't remember his name but he knew he was from St Asaph.

'The rest are unknown, even to officers from the island,' another added.

'Let me have a look over them again,' Alan said, leaning over the screen. He shook his head. 'I don't recognise them. The names on here are the next generation of dealers. Concentrate on the ten names for now. We can always expand the search later.' He took off his coat and hung it on the back of a chair. 'Has anyone ordered breakfast?'

'Breakfast?' Kim said. 'What do you mean?'

'You know. The stuff you eat in a morning.'

'I know what it is. I didn't know you wanted me to organise breakfast for the team.'

'My mistake,' Alan said. 'You didn't know because I haven't asked you yet. How many officers have we got here right now?'

'Forty-five, including you.'

'Let's order bacon or sausage sandwiches for everyone. Call the Empire Café, Dave,' Alan said. 'We want everyone to know we're here. Ordering forty-five butties to be delivered to the police station, should get the tongues wagging. Everyone in town will know we're here by lunchtime.'

'Will do. Shall I order half and half.'

'Yep. That's fine.'

'Brown or red sauce?'

'Pervert,' Alan said. 'Brown sauce is for breakfast. Red is for chips only. And don't let me hear you talking like that again.'

'Yes guv. Sorry guv.'

'Okay, everyone,' Alan said, calling the team to heel. 'Developments overnight please, Kim.'

'The search for Brian Hindley has restarted, two teams of divers and a coast guard launch but there's nothing new to report as yet.'

'How many people have come forward from the radio appeal?'

'Dozens but most of them aren't in the time frame we're looking for. We've narrowed it down to eight credible witnesses.'

'How many have mentioned the woman with the chocolate Labrador?'

'Four.'

'But no one knows who she is?'

'No.'

'Put an appeal on Facebook and Twitter for owners of chocolate labs. Someone knows a neighbour or family member with that type of dog.'

'Shall we focus on the island?'

'She may have been a tourist. Widen it. We need to speak to that lady.'

'Will do.'

'Is anything back from forensics?'

'The rope used to tie the UCs has been identified as a brand imported from China. It's sold in chandlers and widely used in the fishing industry across Europe,' Andy said. He was in charge of the evidence log. 'The wellington boots are from a batch ordered by Wylfa Power Station from an online company called Welly-king. Apparently, they over estimated what they needed and a few dozen pairs ended up on the island's car boot sales. Pamela said she would have some more results back this morning.'

'Good.'

'What time are Simon and Kerry interviewing Glen Price?'

'Ten o'clock. They got his phone records late on last night. Kerry said she was going to stay up and go through them.'

'Good timing. Chase up the interview notes from Halewood. They'll make interesting reading. We might find a motive.'

Forty-minutes later, a phone rang. Kim picked it up.

'It's the reception desk. Breakfast has arrived.'

'Grab a sandwich everyone and then let's track down those dealers. We'll debrief at seven tonight.' Alan's mobile rang. He looked at the screen. 'Morning, Bob,' he said. 'Give me some good news please.'

'I'm afraid I haven't got any good news,' Bob said. The tone of his voice reinforced that it wasn't. 'We've got another body.'

'Bloody hell,' Alan muttered. 'Where?'

'In the quarry. A dog walker spotted it floating in the pit this morning. We've pulled him out. He's a local lad, Zak Edwards. He's been stabbed multiple times.'

'Jesus,' Alan muttered. A cardboard box full of sandwiches was being distributed. Kim put a bacon in front of him. He shook his head and she swapped it for sausage. 'Are CSI there?'

'Yes. Pamela Stone is processing the body now. She's saying it was a frenzied attack.'

'Bob, don't let his name leak out until we're ready. I don't want his family turning up at the scene.'

'Only me, you, and the officers at the scene know who he is.'

'Okay. We'll be there in the time it takes me to eat a sausage brechdan,' Alan said. 'Although I've suddenly lost my appetite.'

'Sorry to be the bearer of bad news,' Bob said. 'Enjoy your breakfast.'

CHAPTER 40

Simon and Kerry opened the door to the interview room at Caernarfon station. Glen Price was sitting next to his solicitor, Tudor Owen, a handsome man with a taste for Hugo Boss suits and Gucci shoes. His aftershave was choking. Simon had had dealings with him on a few cases. He was a decent criminal lawyer with a menagerie of crooked clients. His practice made most of its money from the drudgery of insurance claims, conveyancing, and probate. He wondered why an engineer from Jaguar had ever engaged the services of a lawyer like Tudor. Glen Price looked nervous. Tudor looked serious; he took off his glasses and shook Simon's hand.

'Detective Brady, always a pleasure,' Tudor said, revealing new veneers.

'Likewise, Tudor. This is Sergeant Leach,' Simon said.

'Call me Kerry.' She shook his hand and noticed the lack of a wedding ring.

'Nice to meet you, Kerry.' Tudor shook her hand a little too long and then put his glasses on. His serious face returned. 'Is my client under caution?'

'Not yet,' Simon said. 'Mr Price wouldn't cooperate with us so we thought it would be simpler to continue here in case we need to caution him.'

'I see,' Tudor said, glancing at his client. He wasn't sure why his client was so nervous. He'd seen enough guilty clients to be able to gauge their stress levels. Nervous clients were a liability. 'I think we should start at the beginning. Wipe the slate clean and see where we end up, shall we?'

'That's fine,' Simon said. He turned his attention to Glen Price. 'Are you okay, Glen?'

'Yes.'

'Do you mind if we call you Glen?'

'No.'

'Good. I want to clarify something, Glen. When we spoke to you yesterday, you told us that you talked to Kelvin Adams after work on the night he died.'

'Yes.'

'What did you call him about?' Glen blushed red and looked at his hands. He couldn't maintain eye contact. 'Glen?'

'I can't remember, exactly.'

'Come on, Glen,' Simon pushed. 'Your friend of twenty years was murdered, you spoke to him hours before, and you can't remember what you spoke to him about. I don't believe you.'

'I mean I can't remember the exact conversation. I'd had a few glasses of wine. It was something to do with work.'

'What about work?'

'Nothing you would understand. A technical issue.'

'We wouldn't understand. Really?' Simon said, shaking his head.

'My client answered your question,' Tudor said. 'I think we should move on.'

'Okay. Do you know a man called Derek Kio?' Simon asked. 'He worked at Jaguar and was known as Degsy.'

'No. The name doesn't ring a bell.' Glen look very uncomfortable.

'Here is a picture of him,' Kerry said. Glen glanced at it. He shook his head but it was obvious the image had an impact on him. 'You must remember him. There was a drug raid at the factory and he was caught with cocaine in his locker.' Glen looked blankly at the photograph. 'It was a lot of cocaine. Two kilos. He was selling it to the nightshifts. That type of thing doesn't happen every day.'

'I don't remember the name or recognise him. There were thousands employed there.'

'You must remember the drug raid. It was six years ago.'

'No. I don't recall it.'

'You were interviewed about it and that's something people don't forget in a hurry.'

'I vaguely remember. That's a long time ago,' Glen said. He looked like he'd been given an electric shock.

'This man, Derek Kio, was sentenced to four and a half years for possession with intent to supply. That doesn't happen every day. Are you sure it doesn't ring any bells?'

'No. I can't say it does, sorry.'

'Derek Kio worked on the production line when he was arrested,' Kerry said. 'You, Barry Trent, and Kelvin Adams were all interviewed by the detectives investigating.' She waited for an answer. Tudor looked perplexed. 'I assume your client hasn't mentioned this to you.'

'What my client has discussed with me is our business. Why are we focused on this Derek Kio character?'

'It will become clear,' Simon said.

'Can I ask where you're going with this line of questioning?'

'We're not going anywhere. We just want Glen to tell us why he called Kelvin just hours before his murder. I don't think we're asking too much, do you?' Simon asked.

'He's told you. It was a technical issue at work. Now, move on please.'

'Okay, we'll accept your explanation for the night of the murder but you called him after work eight times this week,' Kerry said. Glen looked stunned.

'How the hell do you know that? Have you looked at my phone records?'

'Of course, we have,' Kerry said.

'They can't do that,' Glen said.

'We can,' Simon said. 'And I told you we would be accessing your records.'

'They can,' Tudor said. 'And they obviously have. Do you need a break to talk to me?'

'No. I'm all right. I haven't done anything wrong.'

'No one is saying you've done anything wrong, Glen,' Simon said. 'We're trying to map out the last days of Kelvin's life. You spent a lot of time with him at work and called him eight times this week after work. Surely, you can see why we're asking you about it.'

'Not really. I think you're wasting my time and your own.'

'You worked with him all day. So, why call him eight times in three days after work?' Kerry asked. 'It's a simple question.'

'Tell us what's going on, Glen. Your friend was bludgeoned to death with a hammer.'

'Nothing is going on. I'm sorry Kelvin is dead but it's nothing to do with me.'

'Why all the calls after work?'

'I told you. Technical stuff.'

'Why not wait until the next day to discuss it?'

'I was working late at home.'

'Do you recognise this number?' Kerry asked, showing him her screen. Glen shook his head. 'It's a prepaid number and it called you twenty times in the last seven days. Who does this number belong to?'

'I don't know.'

'You don't know who called you? You spoke to them, Glen,' Kerry said. Glen blushed. 'You answered the calls from this number six times last week and you spoke to the caller for over an hour in total. Then you stopped answering the calls but they never left a voicemail.'

'I don't know who it was.'

'I find that odd,' Kerry said.

'It's not odd, he's lying,' Simon said.

'You spoke to them for an hour, Glen, and then when you came off the phone, you made two calls within minutes. Can you remember who you called?'

'I'm not sure.'

'I'll remind you. One was to Kelvin Adams and the other was to Barry Trent.' Kerry waited for an answer. Glen wrung his hands and avoided eye contact. 'I find it a huge coincidence that the three of you were calling each other each time this number called you.'

'Who does this number belong to?' Simon asked.

'Glen, if you know who that number belongs to, I suggest you tell them,' Tudor said.

'Listen to your brief, Glen,' Kerry said. 'Who did you speak to for over an hour and why did you call Kelvin Adams and Barry Trent straight afterwards?'

'Okay, that's enough for now. My client is obviously stressed. We'd like to take a break, please.'

'That's because he's lying.'

'I need a break to speak to my client,' Tudor said. 'Can we have ten minutes and some tea, please?'

'No problem,' Simon said, standing up. 'Any sugar?'

'No thanks,' Tudor said. He looked at Glen who just shook his head. Simon had seen many suspects in his time and Glen Price looked more like a suspect than a witness every time he spoke to him. There was a haunted look in his eyes. He'd been backed into a corner and he couldn't talk his way out of it. Whatever he was hiding, there was no doubt in his mind it had something to do with the murder of Kelvin Adams.

CHAPTER 41

The drive to the quarry was hampered by vehicles blocking the narrow road. It was a popular spot for dog walking in the mornings. The railway banking was still there, flanking the road on both sides, so there was nowhere to turn around. A traffic police car was trying to reverse the jam up the narrow track but it was a slow process. Half an hour later, when the bottleneck was cleared, they drove to the quarry and parked up next to a CSI van. Two uniformed officers guarded the entrance to a path which led to the waterfilled pits. Crime scene tape had been strung across. There were two pits, both square, both very deep and bitterly cold. A human couldn't survive in the dark waters for more than a few minutes, not that it had mattered to Zak Edwards.

Alan climbed out of the BMW and looked around. It looked different to the last time he'd been there. In happier times, his ex-wife had kept her horses nearby. Holy Mountain towered above them, sheer cliffs climbed up to gentler grassy slopes higher up. The quarry buildings had been renovated and cleaned and the tall chimney rebuilt and made safe. Most of the buildings were shells but one had been turned into a café—the site attracted a lot of visitors, locals and tourists. The grounds were landscaped and new paths had been built. Alan was impressed and made a note to bring the dogs there sometime. They headed towards the path and a uniformed sergeant met them.

'Morning, guv,' he said, lifting the tape. He looked visibly shocked. 'He's down here.'

They followed the path between tall blackthorn bushes in silence until they reached the first pit. Pamela Stone was kneeling next to a line of yellow evidence flags that were stuck in the ground. The body was covered. It was close to the water's edge. Pamela looked up as they approached.

'Morning, Pamela,' Alan said.

'Hello,' she replied.

'We really need to stop meeting like this,' Alan said.

'It's becoming a habit.'

'What have you got so far?'

'This is Zak Edwards. He's nineteen years old.' She removed the plastic sheet which covered his body. 'He was found in the water topless and his jeans had been pulled down to his knees. There are multiple stab wounds to the back, buttocks, and legs. I'm not sure exactly how many but there're over thirty.' She covered him again.

'Any signs of a struggle?'

'No. If you follow me over here.' She walked to a nearby bench. The commemorative plaque was to a man who'd been mayor of the town for a while and the biggest crook on the island, Alan remembered. 'See the blood pooled here and the body shape in the middle?' she said. Alan nodded. 'I think he was stabbed in the back here and he fell forward onto his face and then the killer followed him down and kept on stabbing him. He bled out here and was then moved and put into the water later. Much later. I think he was here for a while, a few hours at least. He wasn't robbed. His wallet is still in his pocket, his watch is on his wrist, and there's a gold chain around his neck.'

'It's not a robbery,' Alan agreed. 'I don't know what it is for certain but I hope it isn't what I think it is.'

'What do you think it is?'

'Familiar.'

'You think there's something familiar about the way he was killed?' She looked at Alan and waited for a response, unwilling to go any further. He nodded but didn't speak.

'I can see by the look on your face that there's something else on your mind,' Alan said. He looked at Kim, who'd been quiet so far. 'What do you think?' he asked Kim.

'The way the victim was killed is familiar,' Kim said. 'Trousers down and a frenzied knife attack from behind. The same as Henry Roberts, Peter Moore's first victim.'

'Exactly,' Pamela said. 'I haven't examined the wounds in detail but first impressions are it's a hunting knife of some type with a jagged edge on one side, blade on the other.'

'Which is similar to the weapon Moore used,' Alan said.

'Correct. I've not confirmed the number of injuries yet but I'm betting there will be thirty-six stab wounds,' Pamela said.

'I wasn't going to say anything until you did,' Alan said. 'They're too similar to be anything but a copycat. And I don't want that repeated in the newspapers,' he said looking around. 'We've got enough going on without the world's press descending on the island too. That's all we need.'

'It's going to happen,' Kim said. 'This makes Brian Hindley's disappearance look completely different too. They were both stabbed and dragged into the water. The press will say it's the same killer or worse, we've got a serial.'

'What about Kelvin Adams?' Pamela asked. 'People will link all three, even though the MO is different.'

'We can't stop people speculating, especially online. It's going to happen whether we like it or not.' Alan sighed. 'Have we found his clothes?'

'A T-shirt and jacket,' Pamela said. 'I've had them rushed to the lab.'

'Thank you,' Alan said. 'Had they been in the water?'

'No. They were folded on the bench.'

'We need to find Brian Hindley's body and we need to get lucky with Kelvin Adams, so we can separate the cases before the press pick it up.'

'Are you sure they're separate?' Kim asked.

'I'm ninety per cent,' Alan said.

'I'm ninety-five,' Pamela said.

'Me too,' Kim said.

'We need to go and speak to the Edwards family,' Alan said. 'He doesn't look like he was dragged here. What do you think?'

'There are no defence wounds, his face isn't marked. I think he was brought here of his own volition, lulled into a false sense of security, and attacked from behind. The first blow may have incapacitated him instantly but I won't know until we get him to the lab.'

'What's the address on his identification?' Kerry asked.

'Nine Porth-y-felin Road,' Pamela said, reading her notes.

'Do you know it?' Kerry asked.

'Yes,' Alan said. 'It's next to the Vic. I knew the landlord there for years. John Green his name was. He's dead now.'

'We'll go and see the family before they find out from Facebook,' Alan said, pointing to people on the mountain. They were a long way away but they were filming the scene. 'There won't be a signal up there so we've got a head start. Come on,' he said to Kim. 'I'll let you do all the talking. I don't want to upset another family this week.'

CHAPTER 42

The house on Porth-y-felin was built on a steep hill, at the end of a terrace. The quarry road crossed above it less than a few hundred yards down the hill where there was an old railway bridge. Through the archway was the dry dock for the marina and a pub called the Boathouse. The dry dock was like a graveyard of old boats rotting away—the toys of the rich that had become bored with the novelty of owning a boat. Alan knew Zak must have known the area very well. When Alan and Kim arrived, Zak's family were eating breakfast; the smell of bacon hung in the air. They broke the news as sympathetically as they could, keeping the details to a minimum. Explaining their theory, Zac had been murdered in the same manner as a victim, murdered by a serial killer twenty-three years prior, wouldn't help the family to cope. The family was very close. His mother, sister, and stepfather were devastated by the news. It was chilling to watch them breakdown. Within twenty minutes of being told, the house was packed with grieving family and friends. The sound of wailing could be heard down the street.

Despite the pandemonium, Alan asked to see Zak's room and his sister took him up to the third floor, where the loft had been converted into a fourth bedroom. His room was very tidy. Tidier than any bedroom his own sons had slept in. The walls were decorated with black and white photographs of the island, mostly coastal shots. They were good photographs. Zak obviously had an eye for a picture. On his bedside table was a picture of himself and his sister, Leyla.

'Zak was a keen photographer?' Alan asked.

'He was always out walking along the coast to the quarry. The mountain was his favourite place,' Leyla said. 'I can't believe someone has killed him.' Her bottom lip quivered, and the tears spilled over. 'He was such a gentle boy, with a beautiful soul.'

'Did he often go to the quarry at night?'

'He went there any time he fancied, no matter the time or weather. His boyfriend has a boatyard down there,' Leyla said, sobbing. 'Have you spoken to him yet?' Her eyes narrowed.

'No, we haven't spoken to a boyfriend. I didn't know he was gay,' Alan said. 'Now you've told me, we will.'

'You must be the only one in town who doesn't know,' she sniffled. 'They call him Zak gay, like there's loads of other Zaks to identify him from. My mum knew he was gay before he did.'

'What's his boyfriend's name?'

'Lloyd Jones,' she said. She was holding back. The name rang alarm bells in his head. Her expression changed. The light in her eyes darkened.

'You don't like him, do you?'

'That's an understatement. I can't stand the creep.'

'Why is that?'

'Lloyd is all about Lloyd. He doesn't acknowledge Zak in public. He's ashamed of who he is. I've told Zak a thousand times to get rid him.'

'There must be more to it than that.'

'He's dangerous.'

'What makes you say that?'

'What he does for a living.'

'Which is?'

'He's a dealer. And a shit one at that.'

'What makes you say he's shit?'

'His gear is crap. Everyone says it is.'

'Really?' Alan feigned surprise. 'Do you think he would ever hurt Zak?'

'I wouldn't put it past him. They were always arguing, splitting up, fighting about something or another. He gave Zak a black eye last year. My family were livid. Zak insisted it wasn't Lloyd but we all knew it was. Lloyd was nearly lynched.'

'Really? What, did they argue about?'

'They could argue about what colour the sky is,' she said. The tears flowed again as she sat on the bed and picked up their picture. 'Lloyd wouldn't come out. That was the main thing, and he was jealous, very jealous. Zak couldn't talk to anyone. He made him come off Facebook, Twitter, and Instagram. Zak loved Instagram. He had thousands of followers. His photographs are amazing. Zak told me there'd been argument yesterday.'

'Between him and Lloyd?'

'And Lloyd's father.'

'What about?'

'Lloyds father is a retarded bigot.' She shrugged. 'He didn't hear it all but it was something about Lloyd's mum. His dad said something nasty about Zak. He's a total homophobic knobhead. Zak said he left and told Lloyd not to ring him again until he was prepared to come out. He was very upset.'

'I can imagine he was. Whereabouts is Lloyd's boatyard?'

'Along the quarry road, turn right at the fork towards Soldier's Point. You can see it a bit further down on the left-hand side. I don't know why he bought it. He doesn't know anything about boats. The last one he sold, sank in the harbour after a week.'

'Something else he's shit at?' Alan said.

'Yes.' Leyla smiled through her tears. 'Something else he's shit at. Are you going to speak to him?'

'Yes. We speak to a victim's partner as a matter of course. So, he'll be top of our list.'

'Can we see Zak?'

'Yes. We can arrange that.'

'What are you looking for in here?' Leyla asked.

'Answers,' Alan said. 'Sometimes the answers are right under our noses and other times we never find them.'

'Did he suffer?' Leyla asked, clutching the photograph. A knock on the door interrupted them.

'Can I have a word, guv?' Kim asked from the doorway. He nodded, relief flooding through him.

'We'll speak again soon, take care of your mum,' Alan said. Leyla laid down on Zak's bed and sobbed.

CHAPTER 43

Alan drove down Porth-y-felin, under the bridge and onto the Newry. He took the quarry road again, this time taking the right fork. The boatyard was on their left. They stopped outside the gates. He could see the breakwater at the end of the track. It stretched a mile and a half out to sea, protecting the coastline and creating the calm for the marina. A passenger ferry was navigating its course around the lighthouse on its way to Dublin, seagulls floated above the scene, their cries as much a part of the coast as the sea itself.

Alan saw an Audi parked in the yard. He called the station and had the number plate run. It came back as belonging to Lloyd Jones.

'That's his vehicle,' Alan said, opening the door. 'Let's go and have a chat with Mr Jones.'

'Zak's mother can't stand the man,' Kim said.

'She's his mother and no one will ever be good enough, although his sister feels the same. Lloyd Jones is not what I'd call a popular man. I've never met him but his name has been coming up quite often. I think he's been trying to establish himself as a rival to Hollins.'

They checked around the Audi. The doors were unlocked. Alan had the urge to open the boot but didn't. He knocked on the workshop door and waited. There was no reply. He peered through the window and noticed the lights were on. There was no one inside. He went back to the door and tried the handle. It opened with a creak. They stepped inside and looked around. It appeared to be a functioning workshop. The tools were new and the benches tidy and in good condition. Alan spotted something that had no right to be there. He pointed to it.

'That is a Glock 17 magazine and it appears to be full,' he said. 'It would be a schoolboy error to take your gun and leave the bullets behind.'

'Maybe it's a spare.'

'Maybe. Why leave it in plain sight with the lights on and the door open?'

'Good question. Why have the lights on at all unless he left when it was dark?'

'And why leave his car in the yard unlocked?' Alan said. 'Unless he left in a hurry.'

'Or maybe he panicked after stabbing his boyfriend to death.'

'Maybe but why leave the car?'

'Because we'd be looking for it.'

'Let's get CSI in here. Make it part of the Zak Edwards' crime scene.'

'Okay. I'll make a call,' Kim said. She stepped outside into the yard and called the station. A noise from the Audi made her tense. She cut off the call and walked to the back of the car. The noise came again. It was a sniffling sound coming from the boot. 'Guv, come and look at this.' Alan stepped out and approached the vehicle. The sniffling sound came again. He looked at Kim. 'I think someone's in there.'

'So, do I,' Alan agreed. He opened the driver's door and clicked the boot lock. It sprung open. They looked at the elderly woman, bound and gagged inside. Her eyes were open and she looked terrified. The sunlight was dazzling after being in the dark so long. Alan removed the gag and she sucked in air greedily. She was panicking. 'It's okay, you're safe. We're police officers. What's your name?'

'Wendy,' she said.

'Wendy what?'

'Wendy Jones.'

'Are you Lloyd's mother?' Alan asked.

'Yes. Are you going to get me out of this car, or not?' They undid the ropes and helped her sit up. She put her legs over the edge and Alan pulled her out. 'Where am I?' she asked. Her hands were shaking and her knees looked weak.

'You're at your son's boatyard,' Kim said. 'Who put you in the boot of this car, Wendy?'

'I don't know but they were talking a foreign language. They took me from home. I was in a van, I think. Then they dragged me out of the van and dumped me in here. Is my husband here?' she asked, looking around. 'Did he report me missing?'

'We're not sure but we'll ask him. When did this happen?'

'Last night, I think. I'm a bit confused about what's happened.'

'Are you hurt anywhere?' Alan asked.

'No. I don't think so. Where's my Lloyd?'

'We don't know, I'm afraid,' Alan said. 'But we'll help you to find him. Now, we need to get you to hospital to make sure nothing is broken.'

CHAPTER 44

Simon Brady and Kerry Leach went back into the interview room. Glen Price was pale and drawn. He looked like he was terrified. Tudor wasn't happy either. He didn't want to be there, that much was obvious. The dynamic between him and his client had changed. Simon sensed the mood darken.

'Are you ready to begin?' Kerry asked.

'I've advised my client not say anything else to you,' Tudor said.

'In which case, we'll be arresting him,' Simon said.

'You said they won't arrest me,' Glen said, panicking. He turned ninety degrees in his chair. 'He's just said they're going to arrest me.'

'You need to listen to me, not them. They won't arrest you.'

'We will arrest you, Glen,' Kerry said, adding to the pressure.

'I'm not being arrested. It was Derek Kio,' Glen said. The room fell silent. Tudor shook his head in despair. 'The number that kept ringing me. It was Derek Kio.'

'Derek Kio is inside for armed robbery,' Simon said.

'That didn't stop him from ringing me all the time, making threats and accusations,' Glen said. 'You should be interrogating him, not me. He's the criminal. I couldn't believe it the first time. I couldn't even remember who he was. Then he started making accusations.'

'Accusations about what, exactly?' Simon asked.

'About what happened at the plant,' Glen mumbled. 'He said the cocaine was planted in his locker and he said he knew it was one of us who did it. I told him I didn't know what the hell he was talking about but he kept on ringing. He said he was going to kill me and my wife.'

'I don't understand,' Kerry said, shaking her head.

'What don't you understand?'

'Why he is threatening to kill you.'

'Because he thinks we planted cocaine in his locker.'

'Did you?'

'No, I bloody well didn't!'

'Why does he think you did?' Simon asked. Glen hesitated.

'I don't know.'

'He must have told you why he thinks you set him up,' Simon said. 'Didn't you ask him why?'

'I might have. I can't remember. I was flustered.'

'When did you last see Derek Kio?' Kerry asked.

'Years ago,' Glen said.

'When he was arrested and jailed or since then?'

'I don't remember.'

'Try to remember. Have you seen Derek Kio since he was jailed for possession with intent, or not?' Kerry said.

'Not.'

'So, out of the blue, six years later, he rings you from prison and says he's going to kill you?'

'Yes, and my wife.'

'He was going to kill you unless you did what?' Kerry asked.

'We give him money, of course.'

'He's trying to extort money from you?'

'Yes.'

'For what?'

'Compensation, he said, for the time he spent inside.'

'How much did he ask for?'

'Sixty grand.'

'That's very specific,' Kerry said.

'What?'

'Sixty thousand is a very specific number. Why not seventy or a hundred?'

'I don't know. Ask him.'

'Do you owe him sixty thousand pounds?' Kerry pushed.

'No.'

'Why did you call Barry Trent and Kelvin Adams so soon after speaking to Kio?' Simon asked.

'Because he said to. They were involved at the time. He thinks we set him up.'

'Kio thinks they're involved in what?' Kerry asked.

'You know what. When the factory was raided. We were all spoken to about it. I said at the time, it was nothing to do with me.'

'Why does Kio think any of you are to blame for planting cocaine in his locker?' Simon pushed.

'I don't know. The man's a thug. He always was a thug.'

'And why does he think you owe him sixty thousand pounds?'

'Because he's a nutcase.'

'Did he threaten Kelvin Adams?' Kerry said.

'He threatened all of us. He said to get the money together or we'd all be in for it.'

'If I had been arrested for possession and put in jail, I would hold up my hands and say, 'fair cop'. If you can't do the time, don't do the crime. However, if I'd been arrested for possession of cocaine that didn't belong to me, I would be pissed off. I would be very pissed off indeed.' Simon tapped his fingers on the desk. 'It sounds to me like Derek Kio is very pissed off. So, why would he randomly pick three names out of a hat and blame them for sending him to jail?'

'Why are we wading through ancient history?' Tudor said. 'I don't see the relevance.'

'Glen and Barry and Kelvin have been threatened by a known criminal and Kelvin Adams has had his head bashed in with a hammer. It's as relevant as it gets,' Simon said. 'Glen was one of the last people to speak to Kelvin on the night he died. I'm going to ask you again. What did you speak about, Glen?'

'I told you. A technical issue with work.'

'Bullshit.'

'Did you agree to pay Kio?' Kerry asked, changing tack.

'No. Of course not.'

'Why didn't you go to the police?' she asked.

'I was going to but Barry told me not to.'

'Why?'

'He said he didn't want it all raking up again at work.'

'What about when Kelvin was murdered?' Kerry said. 'Surely, you must have thought Kio could have something to do with it?'

'Why would I think that?' Glen asked. He shifted uneasily in his seat. 'I had nothing to do with Derek Kio and I had nothing to do with Kelvin being murdered so why would I link the two together.' He looked at Tudor. 'Are you going to say anything today?'

'You're going around in circles here. I think my client has been very helpful,' Tudor said. 'If there's anything else you want to ask him, do it now, we've had enough.'

'Are you kidding me, Tudor?' Simon said. 'Your client has been withholding information which could become vital to a murder investigation. He's not going anywhere until we've ruled him out.'

'Wait a minute. Ruled me out of what?' Glen said.

'Ruled you out of the investigation,' Simon said. 'Because of your reluctance to tell the truth, we have been focused on Kelvin being murdered by a random stranger. There was no clear motive until now.'

'I'm not convinced anything my client has said has actually changed your investigation,' Tudor said.

'Then you haven't been listening to a word he said,' Kerry said. She looked at him and held his gaze, daring him to argue. 'Three men questioned in a conspiracy to supply case are being threatened by a career criminal who accused them of being involved at the time. Now, one of them has been murdered.' She shrugged. 'Your client has given us a clear motive for murder.'

'My client has spoken openly and honestly about a historic incident where, a man with a criminal record for distributing cocaine, was caught red-handed with cocaine. It's hardly ground-breaking police work, is it? What on earth has this to do with my client?' Tudor said. 'If Derek Kio made accusations at the time of his arrest, I'm sure your colleagues would have investigated them, wouldn't they?'

'Of course, they would,' Kerry said.

'Then why are you pertaining to know better that the officers who worked the case at the time?' Tudor asked. 'You're on a fishing trip at best. You have a tricky murder case with no obvious motive and you're reaching into the mire of the past to find something. Forget it. That's not happening today.' He paused. Kerry and Simon listened. 'If Mr Kio has made threats, then they need to be investigated too. My client needs to be protected, not harassed. He could have no knowledge of what Derek Kio has done from prison. Your connection of the past and the present is spurious at best, ridiculous in fact. Do we actually know where Mr Kio is?'

'No, but we can find out with a phone call,' Kerry said. 'If Glen had been honest from the beginning, we would know and we'd have spoken to him by now.'

'We can't change the past. You know everything he does now,' Tudor said. 'Charge him or let him go. He's not saying another word today.' He waited a second and then stood up. 'Come on, Glen, we're leaving. They're not going to charge you.'

CHAPTER 45

He watched from the bridge that spanned the Inland Sea at Four Mile Bridge. It linked Anglesey to Holy Island. There were about twenty people there, some relatives of Brian Hindley, others just curious onlookers who happened to be there at the time and decided to stay and watch. The remainder were ghouls and press photographers who'd got wind of the find online. A canoeist had spotted a body floating in the reeds close to the Holy Island coastline. The coastguard boats couldn't access the Inland Sea, so the lifeboat station sent a small rib and a crew, from Trearddur Bay on a trailer. A helicopter was launched from RAF Valley to guide them to the body from above. The activity at Four Mile Bridge drew attention away from Penrhos nature reserve. More people were arriving in cars, parking up, and running to get a decent view.

It was what he'd planned. He knew the body would float that way when he put him in the water. The tide was being sucked through the inlet like water down a plughole. It was obvious the victim would head into the inland waters. The last thing he wanted was it floating out to sea and never being found. That would be no fun at all. Watching the distress of the family on the bridge made it all worthwhile. This was what it was all about. It was almost as good as killing him again. Almost.

The lifeboat crew signalled that they'd located the body and the helicopter turned and headed back to base, its job done. They strapped the corpse to the raft used to recover bodies. It kept the victim in one piece. He listened to the chatter from the crowd. People speculated it was Brian Hindley. The family were stuck in limbo, hoping it wasn't because then they had to accept, he was dead, but wanting an end to the uncertainty. The uncertainty was like torture. They could grieve the disappearance but not the death—there was no closure. Loss without confirmation of death left the door open for hope. Hope is a dangerous thing for a grieving family. Their expressions were priceless; masks of anguish. It was so moving, he felt tears in his eyes. Tears of joy not pain. He wanted to laugh aloud, take out his phone and photograph them. There was incredible beauty in their pain. He felt he could reach out and touch their despair. It was mesmerising. His eyes moved from one to the next, soaking up the images of grief like blotting paper in ink. He breathed in deeply, tasting the agony in the air. It was a heady mix.

He heard a car door closing and then another one a few seconds later. The vehicle was an Audi. A white one. His heart began to pound. It was the wife, oh joy of all joys. This was better than he could ever imagine. Mrs Hindley being there was the icing on the cake. The blood was thumping through his brain. He couldn't have planned it better if he had tried. Her legs looked weak as she ran across the road to the bridge, threatening to collapse beneath her. People turned to see who it was making all the noise. She was whining like a dog pining for its owners to come home. A sort of high-pitched intake of breath. Not quite a scream but almost. Her brother was trying hard to keep pace with her. The family members already there parted to let her have the space closest to the wall. Oh, this couldn't be any better. It was too good to be true. He edged along the bridge until he was only yards away. He could smell her perfume. It was a brand his mother once wore. White Linen. He'd often wondered if it was that scent which attracted her rapist, his father. The perfume excited him. It was a coincidence beyond his wildest dreams. She had her hand over her mouth as the lifeboat left the reeds and motored out to deeper water. It weaved slowly towards the bridge; the pilot an expert on the rocks and shallows beneath. There was a flutter of activity on the boat. He knew it would happen. They'd realised the number of people on the stone bridge and had been told over the radio the family were there. The boat stopped and they covered the corpse with a tarp. He inhaled her perfume and watched her tears running down her cheeks. They glinted in the sun like liquid diamonds. Her eyes showed the agony within. As the boat neared, she caught sight of his shoes and recognised them as her husband's. The scream that came from deep inside was the sweetest sound he'd ever heard. Her knees gave way and she folded to the pavement. He reached her and squeezed her arm around the bicep, stopping her falling further. She looked into his eyes. *I killed him.* His eyes tried to communicate to her. *I killed him.* She seemed to sense the evil in him and tried to free her arm but he held her tight. His knuckles were touching her breast. *I killed him, stabbed him and took his eyes.* It was such an erotic moment, he nearly ejaculated. Her distress was driving him demented. He wanted to kiss her on the mouth, hard and then choke her to death. It was so intense the moment seemed to last for hours.

'You can let go. We've got her, thank you,' the brother said, lifting her. She pulled away from him. The crowd swallowed her. He waited until she'd gone from view and then moved away. As the lifeboatmen put the body into the hospital van, the tarp fell from the body. A dozen cameras captured the eyeless corpse. It was the image that would be on the front page of every red-top the next day. His emotions had never been so deep. This experience had been pure rapture. It was the best day of his life so far.

CHAPTER 46

O wen was pleased. Daisy had slotted right in as he knew he would. He was a good mechanic. There was no messing around with him. He got on with the job and had a nice manner about him. He was fun to be around too. With the extra pair of hands, he could take on the extra business and make a decent margin, especially as the new mechanic was being paid for. His mood had changed for the better, even the wife and kids had noticed.

Tony had been to pick up the Golf and Owen had already lined up a buyer for the alloys who was happy to pay eight hundred for them. That was more than he'd earned the month before after all his outgoings. He could see pound signs flashing before his eyes. This was a situation he had to milk for as long as it lasted. There had been no mention of Jamie Hollins. Daisy didn't mention him or the arrangement, which suited Owen.

Later in the afternoon, two sets of wheels were delivered by courier, ready to be swapped. He stacked them on racks next to the ramp where Daisy had set himself up to work. They were nice alloys and he couldn't see anything shady about them. He decided to stop worrying about it. It had been a long time since he could think about taking his wife and kids out for a meal and he was going to surprise them this Sunday. If things went to plan, he wouldn't have to think about being able to spoil them again. Wasn't that what running your own business was all about? Of course, it was.

The phone rang. Owen answered it. It was the business manager of the taxi company in Bangor. He wanted to project his profit and loss accounts for the next twelve months and booked the entire fleet in for servicing, staggering the bookings over the year. Owen made a quick mental note that it would equate to about three-grand a month with a fifty-per cent profit margin. He wanted to jump up and down and punch the air but resisted the temptation. So far, Jamie had delivered on his promises. Maybe getting into bed with a drug dealer wasn't such a bad thing.

CHAPTER 47

Simon Brady and Kerry Leach walked to their vehicle in silence. They both felt completely deflated. Tudor Owen had called their bluff and they'd been forced to fold their hand. Glen Price was up to his neck in something which linked them all to an incident six years prior but without evidence, they were speculating. Any good solicitor could run rings around speculation. They were stuffed without something solid to challenge him with. As they reached the car, Simon tossed Kerry the keys.

'You can drive,' he said. 'I want to make a few calls on the way back to the island. We need a chat with Derek Kio. I think he'll be more forthcoming than Price about what happened at the factory, especially as he thinks he was stitched up. If he thinks he can shift the blame or tarnish their squeaky-clean reputations, he will spill his guts.'

'What about Barry Trent? Do you think he'll talk to us?'

'I don't see why not. He might relish the chance to tell us his version of what happened.'

Kerry opened the Nissan and climbed inside. She glanced in the mirror and saw a tired face looking back at her. Her roots needed dying. She had the dye in the bathroom cabinet but simply hadn't had the time to do it. Work and sleep always took her time. The knot in her stomach told her she wouldn't be doing it anytime soon. Her roots were bottom of the priority list. Simon made a series of calls. There was a lot of effing and blinding going on, before, during, and after each call. It sounded like he was getting the run-around and he was losing his temper. Kerry had enquired about Kio herself only days before and was informed he was doing a long stint for armed robbery. Simon came off the phone and banged his fist on the dashboard.

'What is it?' Kerry asked. She glanced sideways. His face was like thunder. 'Come on, don't keep it to yourself.'

'That makes us look like bloody idiots,' he muttered.

'What does?'

'Kio was released from HMP Wakefield ten days ago,' Simon said.

'What?' Kerry sighed. 'Are you kidding me?'

'Nope.'

'He was doing a long stretch for armed robbery. How has he managed that?'

'His case fell to bits on appeal. Two of the key witnesses failed to show up and another one changed their statement. He walked free from the court.'

'So, he was out when the calls were made to Price and more to the point, when Kelvin Adams was murdered.'

'Yes. That changes things dramatically. We've gone from having nothing to having a motive and a suspect.'

'What's the next step?' Kerry asked.

'We let Glen Price sweat and track down Derek Kio. We need to bring Barry Trent in and rattle his cage, see what he's got to say. That will be interesting. At least we've got something to go at. The DI will be made up.'

'Are you going to ring him and tell him?'

'No. We'll be there in half an hour if you put your foot down,' he said, looking out of the window. Kerry glanced at him and accelerated. At last she felt like they were getting somewhere.

CHAPTER 48

Alan Williams was listening to Pamela Stone updating him on the forensic results which had been returned. He had her on speaker phone. Kim and a bunch of other detectives were sitting in a semicircle around his desk, listening intently.

'The interesting results are from his hands,' she said. 'Kelvin Adams had traces of soil and moss beneath his fingernails. More than you would expect there to be if he had crawled away from the killer at some point.'

'What does that tell you?' Alan asked.

'On its own, not much but he had a wood splinter in the palm of his right hand. The wood was polished and treated on one side, rough on the other. I think it's from a spade handle. When you combine the two things, I think he'd been digging.'

'Digging?' Kim asked. 'Digging what?'

'I can't tell you that, unfortunately but I can tell you that this particular type of moss only grows on rock and it needs salt to survive. It doesn't grow anywhere inland. I've researched it and it's rarely found more than twenty meters from the sea. Whatever he was digging, it's close to the cliffs.'

'It explains what he was doing on the range and why his waterproofs were soaked but what was he digging for?' Alan asked.

'I might be able to shed some light on that too,' Pamela said.

'Go on.'

'When I swabbed the palms of his hand, I found traces of urea, lactate, and acidic residue.'

'Which is what?' Alan asked frowning.

'It's what I would expect to find on a twenty-pound note,' Pamela said. 'I think he'd been handling money. A lot of it. It was engrained in his skin.'

'So, Kelvin Adams was digging and handled money,' Kim said. 'Was he burying money or digging it up?'

'He goes to the same place every month,' Alan said.

'They could have a stash there which they access monthly to avoid having to answer any embarrassing questions about where their cash has come from?' Kim speculated.

'I agree. He's digging it up. We need to search the range along the cliff line,' Alan said. 'I know St Asaph have ground penetrating radar equipment and officers trained to use it. Get on the blower and ask them if we can borrow their search team.' A detective moved away to organise the search. 'What else have we got, Pamela?'

'His body and his car were clean for drugs. All the tests were negative.' Simon and Kerry entered the incident room. Alan beckoned them over. 'My initial look at Brian Hindley tells us he was stabbed with a long weapon, sharp one side, jagged the other. There are four wounds to the abdomen, three to the back, and the eyes were removed. His lungs are full of water, so he was alive when he was put into the sea.'

'Does the weapon match the Zak Edwards murder?' Alan asked the question everyone wanted to ask.

'Yes. My initial findings make them a match.'

'How far would go?' Alan said. 'Was it the same weapon?'

'I would say yes.' Pamela paused. She seemed reluctant to continue.

'Is there something else?'

'Yes. The stab pattern matches Peter Moore's fourth victim.'

'Jesus Christ,' Alan muttered. 'Is there anything on his body that will help us?'

'He's been in the water a long time but we've recovered trace beneath his nails and black fibres on his fingers. It's too early for me to say what they are at this stage. If, anything else comes in, I'll ring you.'

'Thanks, Pamela,' Alan said, ending the call. The team remained quiet, mulling over the information. 'First things first. If Kelvin Adams was digging up money, that's our motive to murder. What we need to work out, is who knew he was going there to dig it up?'

'I think we might know the answer to that question, guv,' Kerry said.

'Good,' Alan said. 'Let's hear it.'

'Glen Price received a number of calls last week from a man who worked at the factory at the same time as Adams, Price, and Brent. He's a convicted villain we thought was doing a fifteen year stretch for armed robbery,' Kerry explained. 'It turns out, his case was overturned on appeal and he was freed, ten days ago.'

'And who is he?'

'His name is Derek Kio. He worked at the car factory six years ago when the place was raided for drugs. He was found with two kilos in his locker and was sent down for four years but he always claimed the drugs had been planted on him. He implicated Barry Trent as the financer. Trent, Adams, and Price were all interviewed several times but there was no further action against them.'

'So, Kio has form for violence?' Kim asked.

'Yes. Price told us Kio phoned him and threatened to kill him and his wife unless they came up with sixty thousand pounds.'

'That's an odd amount,' Alan said, frowning.

'We thought the same. Price's phone records show a flurry of calls he made after each call from Kio. He called Adams and Brent immediately afterwards.'

'To sum it up, we've got four men implicated in possession to supply. Brent was evasive. Adams is dead, Price isn't talking, and Kio is free and making threats,' Simon said.

'My money is on Kio following Adams, seeing him digging up cash and taking the opportunity to rob him,' Kim said. Simon frowned. 'Sorry, you didn't hear the forensics earlier. Pamela Stone called before you walked in. She thinks Adams had been digging near the cliffs and that he'd been handling money.'

'Okay. Let's get a warrant for Price and Brent. We'll interview them under caution. Find out where Derek Kio is now. Merseyside will have a handle on him. Ask them to pick him up and we'll transport him to St Asaph,' Alan said.

'On what charge?' Kerry asked.

'Suspicion of murder,' Alan said. 'There's no point in beating around the bush. Good work you two,' he said to Simon and Kerry. 'I'll let you arrange the arrests and run with the interviews. Once we pick up Kio, let me know.' He sat back in his chair and sighed. 'Okay. You've all had chance to think about what Pamela told us about Brian Hindley. What are your thoughts?'

'We've got a nutcase running around the island who thinks he's Peter Moore,' Kim said. She shrugged. 'If we keep the facts that the stab patterns are the same as Moore's victims quiet, maybe the press won't make the link.'

'We need to keep a lid on it for as long as possible. At least we can legitimately separate the cases now. If Kerry and Simon concentrate on the Adams case, Alice's team can focus on this.' Alan stood up and leaned on his chair. The phone rang and Kim answered it. She chatted to the caller, excitedly, picked up a pen and scribbled some notes on her pad. Alan waited for her to hang up. 'You look like that was good news,' he said.

'That was the owner of a chocolate Labrador. She saw the appeal on Facebook.'

'Was she at Penrhos?'

'Yes. She's the woman the other witnesses mentioned. She said there was one car parked there when she left and the last person she saw entering the nature reserve was a tall man dressed in black. She thought he might have been in uniform. He's early thirties, has dark hair, shiny black shoes, and a long black overcoat. He said hello to her. She doesn't know why but she had the impression he was a policeman.'

* * *

Derek Kio downed his vodka and sipped his pint. He'd been drinking chasers since opening time. Being released from prison had been an unexpected bonus although, on this occasion, freedom came with a whole raft of danger. He couldn't be sure, but he had a feeling the prosecution witnesses had been tampered with by someone on the outside. It certainly wasn't his doing. Derek didn't have the reach to threaten anyone from inside. He'd been a small fish in a big pond on the outside, on the inside, he was a tadpole. It had come as a shock how fragile his position was when he'd been arrested with two kilos in his locker. The support he'd been promised from his associates was non-existent. They ran for the hills at the first sign of a policeman and pretended they hardly knew him. He had less importance than the dirt on the factory floor. They'd cut him loose and let him hang for it. Not one single member of the outfit tried to communicate with him or help him in any way, shape, or form. Not even a text message. When he went down, he thought they would support him inside and look after his family on the outside but they did nothing. His wife struggled to feed their kids and pay the bills. Her family helped out, reluctantly and they revelled in telling her, 'we told you so', at every opportunity. After years of struggle, the strain was too much and she buggered off with another man, taking his kids with her. He had no idea where she was or how his kids were.

That was down to Barry Trent, Kelvin Adams, and that snake, Glen Price. Price had always looked down his nose at him, even when he was selling thousands of pounds worth of gear for them. He pretended he didn't even recognise Derek on the odd occasion he ventured onto the shop floor. The bloke was a first class tosser. Derek never trusted him. The other two had seemed okay but he'd misread them all. Backstabbing bastards, the lot of them. They would pay him what was owed to him, every penny. He vowed when he got out, they would pay and he meant to fulfil that promise.

The problem was, he'd been the go between. He was the man at the coalface, grafting, taking the risk, selling kilos of white powder to the workforce. They bankrolled it all. He sourced the cocaine and maintained the supply, which was harder than it sounds. Maintaining a quality product was difficult. Dealers came and went like the wind. It was a dangerous career and a short one for many of them. The threat of being arrested or worse, succumbing to rivals was ever present. One month, the coke was perfect, the next it was cut to nothing.

It was Derek who had taken all the risks and it was Derek who had taken the fall and it would be Derek who squared things off. It was time to straighten things out. Price had stopped answering his calls but he couldn't avoid him forever. He needed to keep a low profile but he would knock on his door if he had to. They owed him and he was going to collect. Derek ordered another double and knocked it back in one gulp. It nearly came back up. He gagged and covered his mouth with his hand.

'I hope you're not going to be sick, mate,' the barman said. He was a brute with a nose that looked like he'd been hit in the face with a spade. 'I think you've had enough, don't you?'

'I'll tell you when I've had enough,' Derek said. He glared at the barman, projecting the image of a tough guy. He was far from it but most people avoided conflict if possible. 'I'll have another double vodka.'

'Leave while you've got the chance to walk out,' the barman said, smiling. 'Or we'll carry you out.'

The men drinking at the bar put their pints down and stared at him. Derek realised he was in a local pub full of regular drinkers. Even if he could fight, he wouldn't win this one. He finished his pint and put the glass down, then turned for the door. Someone at the bar called him a wanker but he ignored the jibe. He pushed the door open and stepped out onto the pavement. The sun was shining, and the sky was blue. He breathed in deeply, enjoying his freedom. He felt a thump in his chest. It was like being hit by a sledgehammer. Gunshots rang out and he felt three more bullets slamming into his body. His eyes widened as he realised what was happening. A fifth bullet took off the side of his skull, spraying the pub window with pinkish goo. Derek was dead before he hit the pavement.

CHAPTER 49

Jamie Hollins was sitting in the lounge bar of the South Stack pub. The lounge was closed to the public when he was using it. He couldn't be bothered with the local piss-heads mithering him with their inane bullshit. He was waiting for Tony to return from a fact-finding mission. Rumours of a massive team of detectives crawling all over town were rife. Holly was hovering between the lounge and the bar, trying to keep the punters happy. Most of them were pissed and trying to get into her pants but none of them had a chance. She was far too sharp to let any of the locals within touching distance of her. Jamie respected her for that. She was a diamond despite her being a nuisance sometimes. She caught him staring at her and stuck her tongue out.

'What are you looking at?' she asked, head cocked to the side. She wasn't flirting. He'd never seen her flirting with anyone. She was friendly enough but if anyone took her the wrong way, she put them straight very quickly.

'I'm wondering if you've had your lips done again,' Jamie said.

'My lips have never been done and they never will be done, cheeky bollocks,' she said. She was disparaging about the young girls in the pub, walking around with a permanent pout. Fish-faced-empty-heads, she called them. 'I can barely afford lipstick on what you pay me, never mind fillers. They're not exactly the best tippers in here, either. I'm stuck with what I've got. What you see is what you get. I'll never be able to lift or tuck anything working here.'

'No. That's true but it's warm and dry, I let you have crisps at cost, and the conversation is electrifying,' Jamie said, straight faced. 'There's nowhere else in town where you could be as intellectually stimulated as you are here. There're pros and cons to every job. You don't know how lucky you are.'

'If it's stimulation you need, I'm your man,' a local known as Paddy said. He was a greasy looking scruff with long hair and a beer belly that hung over his dirty jeans. He stroked a stringy ginger beard with nicotine-stained fingers.

'Not while I've got breath in my body, Paddy,' she said. Holly looked at him and rolled her eyes to the ceiling. 'Your wife will be in when she finishes work. I'll mention your offer to her and see what she thinks, shall I?' Paddy flushed red and turned away. 'What's the matter, have you changed your mind?'

Paddy emptied his glass and walked towards the door. Jamie laughed and shook his head.

'I think he's changed his mind,' Jamie said. He watched Paddy open the door and step out onto the pavement. Tony walked in with a concerned look on his face. 'See what I mean? Where, else would you get offers like that?'

'I'm glowing with pride,' Holly said, clasping her chest. 'Thank you for giving me the opportunity, boss.'

'Don't overdo it, Holly.' Jamie joked. 'Can you do me another pint and pull one for Tony too, please. I'll be over there.' He sat in the corner in their usual seats. Holly poured the drinks and carried them over. Tony sat down and waited for her to be out of earshot. 'Why the long face?' Jamie asked.

'There's a team of Dibbles stationed in the old nick. Mags, from the Empire Café, told me they ordered breakfast for over forty of them. The word is they're arresting anyone selling and taking them to the cells to be questioned.'

'Questioning them about what?'

'Who sold drugs to the coppers they pulled out of the bay and who works for who. They're trying to work out the hierarchy on the island.'

'No. I don't think so,' Jamie said.

'What?'

'They already know that, Tony. Never underestimate the Dibbles. They're not as daft as they look. I'm not sure what they're looking for but we'll find out soon enough.'

'This is really bad, mate. They're all over town. Maybe you should lie low for a while. It's only a matter of time before they come in your direction.'

'They already know who is involved, Tony,' Jamie said. 'Knowing is very different to being able to prove anything. They're trying to get people to give evidence. That's a different kettle of fish.'

'What do we do?'

'Point them in the right direction.'

CHAPTER 50

The sun was fading when he got home. He could hear the carers upstairs banging about like a pair of clumsy elephants. They chatted to his mother without expecting an answer. He reckoned they asked the same questions of everyone they cared for, while they changed sheets, emptied bedpans, redressed bedsores, and bathed them. It was a well-rehearsed act played out many times each day. They were like blue-clothed whirlwinds, in and out in a flash, yet without them, he would be scuppered. He heard his mother's voice, rasping. She was asking for water. It was a heartrending moment. A moment of realisation that his mother was no longer capable of looking after her basic needs. His heart flipped for a moment and he felt a deep sadness. There were moments of intense emotion in his heart, especially when he thought about her struggling to take a drink herself but they were like the flash of a camera bulb. They only lasted a fraction of a second and then they were gone and the numbness returned. It was like a shroud of ice around his soul which melted for a millisecond, then refroze again. He knew that wasn't normal, whatever normal was. One thing was certain, he would kill her one day and then all her problems would be gone. He wanted to wait for his father to die in prison first, so that he could be there on the other side to greet her when she passed over. Imagine her horror when she saw him again after all those years. He was approaching eighty. The bastard couldn't have long to go, surely not. When his father died, it would be all over the news. *Serial killer, Peter Moore was pronounced dead today, blah blah blah.* When it happened, he would wait a little while and then send her to him. He would tell her what he was doing and why and he would leave her alone for a while to prepare herself for the transition. That would be fun. He was looking forward to it.

'Hello there,' a voice made him jump. He was away with his thoughts. The carers were standing in the hallway. Their rotund physiques were squashed inside pale blue uniforms, which bulged at the seams. He wondered how the stitching held beneath the strain. 'I didn't hear you come in. Have you just finished work?'

'Yes.'

'Have you been keeping everyone inline?'

'As usual.'

'We've finished with your mum for today, we'll be back first thing in the morning. Will you keep an eye on her water jug?'

'Yes. Of course.' He knew she was struggling to pour a drink but she would drink everything he gave her if she had the chance and then she would be peeing all night long. 'Is she saying she's been thirsty?'

'No. She seems happy in herself but her jug was empty when we got here and she guzzled two glasses of water while we were changing her so she must have been thirsty. We've changed her, and she's had a wee so she'll be fine.'

'Okay. Thank you very much. See you tomorrow.'

'Are you here tomorrow morning?'

'No. I'm on an early shift. These murders have meant we're being pulled in for overtime. I won't be back until late tomorrow night.'

'Okay. Well, if you think of anything we need to know, put it in the book.'

'Will do,' he said. She tried a smile but he didn't return it. He wondered what she would look like if he stuck the knife into her guts and twisted the blade. His imagination changed her facial expression into a mask of agony. He could feel her blood; it was warm on his hand. She opened her mouth in a silent scream and he leaned forward and bit off her tongue. It wriggled in his mouth.

'Are you okay?' she asked, frowning. She took a step back.

'Sorry. I was daydreaming,' he said. 'I'm tired. It's been a very long day.'

'We'd better be off then,' she said. She scurried for the front door, eager to be away from him, her sidekick on her shoulder. He wasn't sure what she'd felt when she stared into his eyes but he knew she'd felt something. His energy was growing, becoming something else. It was beginning to seep from his body and lesser mortals could sense the evil. The front door closed behind her and her colleague and the house was quiet once more.

'Yes. You're right. You'd better be off,' he said to the empty room. 'It's not safe here.'

CHAPTER 51

Kim Davies walked into the Stanley Arms and approached the bar. There were two men sitting on stools drinking pints of dark beer. They stopped their conversation to look at her backside. Her jeans hugged her hips where they should. She pretended not to be offended by their attention. It wasn't the first time she'd used her sex appeal to break the ice with potential witnesses. The barmaid walked in from the kitchen. She was ginger and attractive. Freckles dotted her cheeks and nose. Kim ordered a pint of Guinness and took it to a seat near the window. The men watched her in silence. They turned back to the bar when she sat down facing them. She could see the barmaid shrugging and shaking her head. The men had obviously made enquiries about her but they didn't know each other. She took out her phone and scrolled through her emails, pretending to be distracted. A door opened at the rear of the pub and a wiry man in camouflage trousers and flip-flops, stepped out of the toilets. His hair was woven into grey dreadlocks. He eyed her suspiciously but her smile melted his concern. He made his way over and sat down next to her.

'Hello,' he said. 'I haven't seen you in here before. I'm Lee. They call me Lee Punk.'

'Lee Punk?'

'Yes. It's my nickname.'

'Is that because you have dreadlocks?' Kim asked.

'Sort of.'

'Shouldn't it be Lee Rasta?'

'I had the nickname before the hairstyle,' he said laughing. 'I was a punk as a teenager. The name stuck with me.'

'I've noticed that around here,' Kim said.

'Where are you from?' Lee asked. He took out a tobacco tin and took off the lid while they chatted. It was full of skunk. The scent was powerful. He took a cigarette paper and began rolling a joint.

'I've been based in Caernarfon,' Kim said. 'But I'm working here for a few months.'

'Really?' Lee asked. 'What do you do?'

'I'm a detective sergeant with the North Wales MIT.' She took out her warrant card. Lee Punk looked like he was going to cry. He put the tin back in his pocket quickly.

'It's for my own personal use,' he mumbled.

'I'll decide that.' She showed him a picture of Mike Jarvis and Patrick McGowan. 'Do you recognise these two men?' His eyes betrayed him. He recognised them but he shook his head. 'Before you say no, I know you know them because they were undercover drug officers and you sold cannabis to them on six different occasions. They are recorded in evidence for a major investigation. It was high quality skunk, just like what's in your tin.'

'I don't remember them.'

'I don't care if you remember selling drugs to them or not because we have proof you did. Six times. What you remember is irrelevant. If you help us, this goes away.'

'Am I under arrest?' Lee asked.

'That depends.'

'On what?'

'Your next answer,' Kim said.

Lee put his head in his hands. 'I'm not a grass.'

'Calm down. The barmaid and the men at the bar are watching us, so I suggest we go out the back into the smoking area to talk.'

'I've got nothing to say to the police. This is a small town. Everyone knows everyone.'

'I can take you out of the front door in handcuffs if you like and then everyone will know you've been arrested and spoken to. Make your mind up, Lee.'

'Okay,' he said.

'After you,' Kim said, gesturing to the door. They walked out of the beer garden door and up a set of stone steps which led to a patio area and a car park. She could see the police station to her right and the Caernarfon Castle in front of her. Crime scene tape sealed the doorway. Alan Williams was sitting at a table, waiting for them. 'This is Detective Inspector Alan Williams. He's the senior investigating officer on this case.'

'What case?' Lee asked. He fiddled with a dreadlock, nervously. 'What is all this about?'

'Sit down,' Alan said, ignoring his question. 'My sergeant has informed you we have documented evidence of you selling cannabis to undercover officers on six occasions?'

'Yes. She has. You're a bunch of sneaky bastards.'

'I'll ignore that for now. We need to know where and more importantly, who your drugs come from.'

'Are you high?' Lee snorted. 'I can't tell you that. You'll have me strung up from a tree. No one in this town is going to rat on their suppliers. Not a chance.'

'Someone kidnapped those officers, interrogated them, and threw them into the sea to drown. They were murdered,' Alan said. Lee shuffled uncomfortably in his seat. 'We don't think they were killed by someone at your level. Killing police officers is another mindset completely from someone like yourself. I bet you just sell to regulars in a couple of pubs, make a bit of money and smoke for free, right?' Lee shrugged. 'I bet you're on benefits too. It beats getting out of bed every morning and working for a living, doesn't it?'

'I've got chronic fatigue actually,' Lee said. His face blushed red. 'I can't work full time and there's no part time work around here.'

'I don't care,' Alan said. 'Your quiet life could be turned on its head by tomorrow morning, or you could give me a name, anonymously of course, and carry on as if we never met.'

'I'm not a grass,' Lee said, shaking his head.

'These officers had wives and children,' Alan said. 'No one deserves to die like that. All we need is a name. No one will know where it came from.'

'I'm saying nothing.'

'Okay. Your choice.' Alan waved to two uniformed officers, who were waiting in an unmarked car. They approached the table. Lee watched them with interest.

'Arrest him and lock him up next door,' Alan said. He stood up and walked away. Kim followed him. 'We'll keep him overnight and talk to him in the morning. He might have a different outlook on it tomorrow.'

'Where are you going? Wait a minute!' Lee protested. He struggled against the uniformed officers as they cuffed him. 'I've got a wife and kids at home. She'll go off her rocker if I don't go home. What do you want to know?'

'Like I said, we'll talk to you in the morning.' Alan walked down the steps into the pub. Lee bombarded him with a tirade of abuse, mostly questioning if his parents were married. He ignored the abuse and turned to Kim. 'They need to know we're not messing around. We ask them once and if they lie or refuse, they go into a cell until the next day. Sooner or later, one of them will talk.' His mobile rang and he checked the screen. 'Hello, Bob,' he answered.

'How's it going?' Bob Dewhurst asked.

'We've made progress on the Adam's murder. Did you find anything for us from your schedules?'

'No. I'm sorry. We had no patrols at Penrhos anytime that day. I've double checked the overtime rotas too. Whoever your witness saw, isn't one of our officers.'

'Thanks, Bob. That's a relief. It was worth a look,' Alan said. He was secretly disappointed. The uniformed man was a good lead. 'I'll call you if anything else comes in.'

'Hold on,' Bob said. 'Don't rush off. I've got the details of your red van from the laundry unit in Cemaes bay.'

'Great,' Alan said. 'That's good news.'

'The van is registered to Will Pinter, Sundown Property Management, Trearddur Bay. It's on a company insurance policy.'

'Someone is taking the piss,' Alan said.

'That's what I thought.'

'Leave it with me,' Alan said. 'We need to get that company unravelled to see who's behind it. Someone is going to a lot of trouble to stay anonymous. I'll call back later.'

'Thanks, Alan,' Bob said, hanging up.

'What did he say?' Kim asked.

'He said he's checked the rotas and there were no uniformed officers at the nature reserve that day,' Alan said. 'The witness was very credible. She seemed certain the man was in some kind of uniform. What other types of uniforms are seen on the island?'

'Community support officers,' Kim said. 'But they'll be on Bob's schedule.' She thought for a moment. 'Traffic wardens, maybe?'

'Maybe. What about those arseholes from Kingdom Security?'

'The litter police?' Kim said. 'They do wear black uniforms and I wouldn't trust any of them. They're bullies and thugs.'

'Get onto them. They give out fixed penalty notices to people who drop litter, people who drop cigarette butts, dog walkers who don't pick up their crap; they give them out for fun. See if they had any employees on Holy Island that day or if any notices were issued on this side of the island.'

'Okay.'

'While you're on to them, see if they have any employees living here.'

'They've been hostile to anything we've asked for before,' Kim said. 'But I'll try.'

'If they give you any nonsense, call Dafyd straightaway and get a warrant for their records. The sighting of a uniformed man is key. It's all we have to go on. I've got a feeling our witness has seen someone who was on their way to work or on their way home. Either way, we'll find him.'

CHAPTER 52

Simon checked all the warrants were correct. Glen Price was to be arrested by Flintshire and taken to St Asaph, where he would be held until MIT were ready to interrogate him. Ideally, they would have interviewed Barry Trent and Derek Kio first. They could then challenge Price with the information gleaned from the others. It was all straightforward enough in theory, but it wasn't going to plan. Simon was on the telephone, desperate for information.

'I'm waiting for confirmation of Glen Price's shifts this week.'

'Hold the line,' the voice said. The line went quiet. Simon waited impatiently for two long minutes. It clicked into life again. 'Can I ask who's calling?'

'I've already explained this to two of your colleagues. I'm Detective Sergeant Brady, North Wales Police. We need to know when Barry Trent will be working next, please.'

'I see. Please hold the line.' The line clicked and Adele began singing one of her mournful ballads. He knew the words and had all her albums but he didn't want to listen to her right now. She was nearing the end of the song when the line clicked on again. 'I'm afraid he's off sick at the moment.'

'Sick?'

'Yes. I'm afraid so.'

'When did he say he would be back?' Simon asked.

'I'm afraid we can't tell you that. It's confidential.'

'This is a murder investigation. Unless you want twenty detectives crawling through your files, I suggest you answer the question,' he said, trying to remain calm and professional. 'When did he say he would be back?'

'Yesterday.'

'Did he call in to say he wouldn't be back?'

'No.'

'Thank you. That wasn't hard, was it?'

'Can I ask why North Wales Police are calling here about Barry?' the HR officer asked.

'I'm afraid we can't tell you that, it's confidential,' Simon said, hanging up. It was childish but made him feel slightly better. Dealing with jobsworths was a nightmare. Kerry was on the other line talking to the Merseyside force. She didn't look happy either. He leaned closer to her and lowered his voice. 'Barry Trent called in sick for work yesterday. Have you got any good news?'

'No. Merseyside went to execute the warrant at his home address. Barry Trent isn't at home. The car is on the driveway, but the lights are off and there doesn't appear to be anyone home. Do you think he's done a runner?'

'God knows,' Simon said.

'What about Kio?' she asked.

'Merseyside are tracing his last known address. There're no probation reports as he was freed on all charges. He can go where he likes. They said they'll call me back. We need to speak to them both before we have another crack at Price. How difficult should this be, bloody typical!'

The phone rang and Kerry answered it. A few sentences were exchanged. She shook her head and then thanked the caller. The look on her face said it all. It was more bad news. 'What is wrong?' Simon asked although he didn't want to hear the answer.

'That was the station at Coppice Hill, Liverpool city centre,' Kerry said. 'Derek Kio was shot dead coming out of a pub last night. Four shots to the chest, one to the head. There're no witnesses. They're pulling CCTV in the area and said they would call back if there's any progress.'

'That sounds like a hit to me,' Simon said. 'That can't be a coincidence,'

'Who would take him out like that? Form an orderly queue, springs to mind. Where the hell is Barry Trent? If Price gets a sniff of this, he might clam up completely. We need to tell the boss.'

* * *

Barry Trent was sitting on a plastic chair in a very dark damp cellar which had an unsavoury smell to it. The stench clung to the flesh at the back of his throat, making him gag. His wife, Rosemary, was sitting back to back on another chair. He could feel her body quivering against the cold. She was sobbing uncontrollably. They were bound with duct tape, blindfolded, and gagged. He could hear water dripping in the corner to his right and the scurrying sound of rats all around. He wanted to be able to reassure Rosemary but he couldn't. It was physically impossible. Even if he could speak, she wouldn't believe a word he said anymore. She would leave him this time.

There was no doubt about it.

The first time he'd been questioned at the plant, her father had insisted she leave him and come home to live with her parents. He was a circuit judge and a lifelong member of the Masonic community, as were the officers who'd investigated the raid. They were convinced he was involved in the supply chain but couldn't prove it. Barry Trent was never good enough for his daughter, never in a million years. She had her bags packed ready to go but the police released him and told him there would be no further action. They were happy to nail Derek Kio to the wall for possession. There was no point in muddying the waters. A jury wanted simple evidence of guilt. Exploring the possibility of a wider conspiracy would only throw in the element of doubt. Beyond all reasonable doubt. That was the key to a conviction. They had the drugs and they had their suspect, red-handed. There was no need to embark on a fishing trip and complicate things.

Barry convinced her the entire thing was a sham and it was all contrived by a criminal desperate to implicate management in his conspiracy. It was sour grapes and nothing more. She listened to him and she stayed, although he could always see the shadows of doubt in her eyes. Her father didn't speak to him again, which made life difficult, especially at Christmas and on birthdays. He knew the investigating officers from the Masonic lodge, and he knew they were straight. They had told him the facts about the Kio case and they told him the truth about why Barry Trent hadn't been investigated further. Luckily, Rosemary didn't believe their version of events. The fact they didn't charge him was enough for her to believe Barry was innocent. If he'd been guilty, they would have charged him. It had been a crossroads in their marriage and although they stayed together, she never looked at him in the same way as she had.

This was a different situation altogether. There could be no explanation why she was tied to a chair in a cellar, bound and gagged. Whatever happened next, this was the end.

Everything had been swept under the carpet until that retard Kio got out of prison and started shooting his mouth off. This was on him. He always was a liability. The cellar door opened with a creak and he heard footsteps on wooden stairs. Four sets, maybe five. The voices were male and gruff, smokers and drinkers for sure. One of them laughed and it sounded like he had sandpaper in his windpipe. They removed his blindfold and gag and stood around him in a semicircle. He could smell cigarettes, whisky, and cheap aftershave. He blinked against the light. A single bare light bulb hung from the rafters. There were five men dressed in jeans and leather jackets. One man wore a parka with a fur hood. They had dark hair and olive complexions. Their eyes were full of contempt.

Barry looked around. His eyes settled on two big oil drums in the corner. They were set on wheels so they could be moved easily. Something in the air was making his eyes water, something caustic.

'Hello, Barry Trent,' the man in the centre said. His jeans were faded. A black leather jacket hung from wide shoulders. He had an angry scar on his right cheek, which ran from below the eye to his jaw. His right hand was tattooed with an emblem he didn't recognise. 'Let me introduce myself. My name is Agon and these are my associates. We're Albanian businessmen.' His men laughed. 'Do you know why you're here?'

'No,' Barry said. A heavy punch to the side of his face rocked his brain like a marble in a jam jar. He hadn't seen it coming and it stunned him.

'Don't lie to me, Barry Trent,' Agon said. 'Every time you lie, we hurt you.'

'I won't lie to you. Don't hit me.'

'Okay. Let's see how we go, shall we?' Agon said. 'Do you know Derek Kio?'

'Yes. We worked at the same factory some years ago.'

'Good. That's the truth but not quite the entire truth. You were in business with Derek Kio, yes?' Barry wanted to say no but didn't want another blow to the head. 'I asked you a question. Were you in business with Kio or not?' He delayed his answer too long. Another punch sent streaks of white lightening through his brain. 'Do you like being hit in the face, Barry?'

'Okay, okay,' Barry said. A tear ran from his eye. It was a tear of helpless frustration. 'Yes. I worked at Halewood with him, but it was a long time ago.'

'You didn't just work with him. You were in business with him.' Barry shook his head. 'He's not understanding the rules so we'll change them. Every time he lies, punch his wife in the face,' Agon said. Rosemary panicked and was squealing. She began fighting against her bonds.

'No, no! Don't. Don't hurt her,' Barry said, his voice panicked and garbled. 'Okay, Agon. I was in business with him for a while. Then he was sent to jail.'

'Good. That's better. Let's put all the cards on the table.' Agon grabbed a chair and sat opposite Barry. He looked into his eyes. 'Derek Kio bought a lot of cocaine from us. He always showed up on time and he always paid cash. After a while, we began to trust him. His customer base was growing, so we gave him some product on credit. Then he was arrested and put in jail.'

'I didn't know anything about any product on credit,' Barry said. 'We always gave him the cash to buy it outright. I swear I didn't know anything about this.'

'Whether you knew or not, the facts are the facts. Are you questioning what I'm telling you?' Agon said, frowning. Anger flashed in his eyes.

'No. Of course not. I'm just saying I didn't know.'

'This is the problem with this business. There is a lot of money to be made. You all made a lot of money in a short space of time, but people get greedy. You can't trust anyone in this game. This happens all the time. Your best friend will double-cross you for the right amount of money.'

'I know that but what is it you want from me?' Barry asked.

'We want our money, that's all. Just what we're owed, nothing more.'

'What money?' Barry asked. 'I don't understand.'

'Let me explain it for you. I'm not being clear enough.' Agon sat back and took a deep breath. 'Derek Kio never told us about you and your two friends. Kelvin Adams and Glen Price, right?' Barry nodded. 'When he was arrested, the police took two kilos of our drugs, which is all part of the gamble we take when we give credit. I accept that but we didn't know he had partners. We decided we would wait to seek compensation from him when he got out. And we did wait, but he said he didn't have any money. Of course, that wasn't acceptable. We persuaded him to try to get it, so he tried an armed robbery and ended up back in jail. That was when we ran out of patience.'

'I don't understand,' Barry said. 'What has this got to do with me?'

'Derek Kio owes us for four kilos of cocaine plus interest. In today's market, that's about three-hundred thousand pounds. Some of our colleagues put pressure on him in jail and that's when he told us about you and your friends. He told us that you have the money that he owed us, and he thought you would give him his share when he finished his sentence. We pulled some strings and sprung him from prison, but he still couldn't get us the money he owes.'

'I still don't see what this has to do with me,' Barry said. The side of his face was swollen now, turning blue and deep red.

'Derek Kio is dead. We shot him on the street, blew his brains all over the wall,' Agon said. Barry could feel Rosemary shaking violently. 'His debt is now your debt. He worked for you and you kept the money you made and hid it from the police when Kio was arrested. Where is it?'

'I have no idea what you're talking about. Once Derek was arrested, we all went our separate ways and barely spoke again. We thought Derek had the cash hidden somewhere.' Barry shrugged. He shook his head. 'Honestly, I don't know where he put it.' Another punch to the jaw knocked him off balance. The chair tipped over and he cried out like a scalded cat. 'Please,' he shouted. 'I don't know where he put the money. Kio must have had it because we didn't. All we had was a small pot of money we kept for expenses. We all got a few grand each and never talked about it again. Kio must have kept your money.'

'If Derek Kio had the money, he would have paid us what he owed, trust me. When he said he didn't have it, I believed him. Pick him up.' Two of the men dragged the chair to its feet. Barry couldn't hold his mouth closed. He thought his jaw had been broken. Blood and saliva dribbled from his mouth, drooling down his chin. 'Listen to me, Barry Trent. Listen very carefully. Derek Kio is dead. That's my bad.

Your friend, Kelvin Adams was murdered. It might be an unfortunate coincidence, but I doubt it. Your friend Glen Price has a big house and a new Porsche, now, you can call me suspicious natured if you like but someone isn't telling everyone the truth.'

'I am telling you the truth,' Barry said. 'I really am. We don't have a big house or new cars. We do okay but we're not rolling in it. If I knew where the money is, I would tell you.'

'You would?'

'Yes. You have my wife bound and gagged behind me. I don't know where it is or if it even exists. Honestly, I don't know anything about it.'

'Do you know what?' Agon said, nodding. 'I believe you.'

'You do?' Barry said. He sighed with relief.

'Yes. I do. I believe you don't know where our money is.' Agon stood up. 'Kill both of them. Put them in the acid barrels.'

'What?' Barry muttered.

'Put Mrs Trent in first and let him watch. Wait until they're dissolved before you move them and pour them into the river. Make sure they're never found.'

CHAPTER 53

He scrolled proudly through the news sites, BBC, Sky, ITV, Google, and the online newspapers. They were all carrying the images of Brian Hindley being recovered from the Inland Sea. Some had blurred the face to obscure the fact his eyes were missing, others enhanced it. The image had gone viral on Instagram and Twitter. It was such an enormous buzz. Every comment, good or bad, pumped more adrenalin into his veins. It was sheer ecstasy. He couldn't remember being prouder of anything he'd done. This was the pinnacle of his achievements in life so far but there was so much more to come. He hadn't really started yet. The possibilities were endless, and he wanted to explore them all. He watched footage of Mrs Hindley collapsing and there he was, grabbing her arm. Touching her breast with the back of his hand, looking into her eyes and seeing her pain. He paused the image and stared at it. When he looked at his watch, an hour had passed but he had no recollection of it. He let the images run at normal speed. It was all so surreal. Beautifully played out for the world to embrace, and they would embrace it. People loved killers. They would love him. He meant to be remembered for generations to come. People still talked about Jack the Ripper one-hundred and thirty years later. He would make the Ripper look like a choirboy. He would make his own father pale into insignificance and historical obscurity. People remembered the bizarre, the sick, the twisted, and the pure evil killers. They were the ones who time wouldn't forget and he would be among them. He would walk through history like a God.

The one thing that was spoiling it all was the fact the press hadn't connected his work with his father's legacy. Not yet. There was no mention of the similarities in the murders, yet he had mirrored two of his father's crimes. They were almost identical. The position and number of stab wounds was the same. Surely, they would see it couldn't be a coincidence. How could they miss that? He read on through the breaking news sites and thought about it. The conclusion he came to was that the police hadn't released the facts. They didn't want the press to connect the murders at all, let alone tie it to a serial killer from the nineties. It was a public image disaster. Senior officers would be inundated with enquiries from the public, the press, and their hierarchy. They had hidden the evidence and it wasn't acceptable in any way. He looked at pictures of the SIO. A man called Alan Williams and his detective sergeant, Kim Davies. They were responsible for catching him and locking him away for the rest of his life. He wasn't ready to be caught yet. There was so much to do. The police weren't being honest with the public and dishonesty riled him. He'd been lied to all his life but he would right that wrong. Many wrongs would be avenged before he was done.

He went back to the BBC site and found the journalist who had written the article, then did the same for the *Daily Mirror, Express,* and *Mail.* Their contact details were simple to find. He typed out a two-page email, detailing the similarities between the Anglesey murders and Peter Moore's murders. He used an untraceable email provider and pressed send. That would do it. You can't hide what was happening from the public, he thought. They have a right to know. His artistry needed to be shared with the world, to be admired and talked about. He would be written about for decades, like all serial killers before him. They became legendary. Books about him would be read, films about him watched, documentaries would be made. Millions of people would be in awe of his evil doing. They would be fascinated, captivated, and repulsed by his brutality but they would remember his name. He closed his eyes and imagined his father in his prison cell, watching the news in the morning. He would choke on his breakfast. It was a touching moment, father and son so connected across the miles. Their cosmic energy would merge and become more powerful. He would be so proud of his son for the first time. The news of a copycat would spread around the prison like wildfire. His father had revelled in the notoriety during the trial, waving for the cameras and smiling like a sportsman on a victory lap. He was giving him that notoriety back. It was his gift—the first of many. His next gift would be something so special, the world would never forget it.

* * *

On the range, uniformed officers were scouring the cliff edges, looking for signs of disturbed earth. The spongy soil was deep and dark, covered in thick grasses and moss. Officers from St Asaph were using GPR on any area flagged as a possible burial site. It was a thankless task but most of the ground was rock or shallow earth—they managed to cover a mile of headlands before dinnertime. Alice was losing the will to live when she heard officers calling to her. She could see three of them waving their arms. They were a few hundred yards away, gathered around a rocky outcrop. The grass around it was deep. It was nearly waist height. One of the officers was using a spade to lift something. The GPR unit were moving their machine in a grid pattern.

'What have you got?' Alice asked. Her hands were deep in her pockets, protected from the wind.

'There's a board here covered in grass and moss. We're going to lift it,' an officer said.

'We've got another one,' a GPR unit sergeant called from about ten yards away.

'Let's see what's there,' Alice said.

Four officers used spades to prise the corners away from what looked like a metal box, buried in the earth. The lid moved easily and they laid it to one side. There were bales wrapped in black plastic. One of them was open. An officer lifted the corner to reveal bundles of twenty-pound notes.

'That's a lot of money,' Alice said. 'Let's get it out of there and to the lab.' She walked to the next site. The four officers repeated the process but the lid was stuck. One of them cleared some earth away to reveal bolts, which were rusted solid. 'It's been sealed. Get a grinder on those bolts.'

Fifteen minutes later, the irritating noise of metal grinding metal filled the air. Sparks flew from the wheel. It started to rain again, and the wind picked up. Alice felt uneasy about what was in the second dig. The bolts were cut free and they tried to prise the lid again. It came free with a sucking sound. Alice looked inside. The decomposed body of a woman was curled up in a few feet of water. The decomp was advanced. Next to her was a handbag. One of the officers lifted the bag with a spade and placed it on the grass. Alice pulled on a pair of gloves and poked around inside. She spotted the pink colour of a driving license and looked at the degraded text.

'This is Patricia Price, Glen Price's wife. Simon and Kerry said they saw her in the bedroom window of their home. Whoever they saw, it wasn't Patricia,' Alice said. 'Now, that puts a different slant on things. Better get the boss on the phone.'

CHAPTER 54

Alan arrived home after ten o'clock. The lights were on, which was a bonus. He wanted a hot shower. His bones were aching. The dogs were performing their usual rowdy greeting and he could see Dan sitting on the settee with Fflur. He climbed out of the BMW and grabbed his shopping. Two bottles of whisky and a tuna and sweetcorn sandwich from the whoopsie aisle. His prize item of the day was a black cherry trifle for one, which was half price. He was looking forward to it so much, he was willing to leave the sandwich in the fridge for the next day. His appetite was crap at the best of times but at the end of a long day with a large scotch in his hand, it was virtually non-existent. He had to discipline himself to eat something, even if it was trifle. It might not be on the most nutritious list but it was better than nothing. Man cannot live on tea and whisky alone although he had tried.

He opened the front door which was on the latch as usual. Dan let the dogs out of the living room and they sprinted down the hallway, a noisy melee of fur and teeth. They jumped and circled him as he edged his way into the kitchen with Henry clinging to his trouser leg. He opened the patio doors and the dogs forgot him and bolted across the field into the darkness. Alan put his sandwich and the trifle into the fridge and poured an inch of whisky into a crystal tumbler. He swallowed it in one gulp and poured another two inches. He was enjoying the burning liquid when his phone buzzed.

'Hello, Alice,' he answered.

'Pamela Stone has confirmed the body is Patricia Price. She's been there for years rather than months.'

'No wonder Glen Price was so squirrelly. Have they found him yet?'

'Simon and Kerry are over there now. The local plod are going to breach tonight but they're convinced the place is empty and his Porsche is missing.'

'What about the money?'

'They're still counting it.'

'Good work, Alice. Get some sleep and we'll catch up tomorrow.'

'Okay, guv. See you tomorrow.' She ended the call, and he felt tired, worn down by it all. He sighed and filled up his glass.

'Hiya, Dad,' Dan said from behind him. 'How's the investigation going?'

'I'm not sure I'm the right man to ask, I'm only in charge of it. If you want to know how it's going, you'll have to ask the BBC.'

'It's not going well then?'

'It's going as well as it can be without someone walking into the station and confessing to everything. It's just the way these things go. It's complicated,' Alan said, filling the dog's water bowl. 'We're making progress slowly. Have you lost any more friends today because I've been out and about detecting things?'

'No. Look, I'm sorry about that. We were being selfish. I've felt bad all day.'

'So, you should,' Alan said. 'You're a selfish brat. Who do you think you are, buying the electric all the time and making sure I've got milk in the fridge for my coffee in the morning?' He handed Dan two twenty-pound notes. 'Here's the forty pounds towards what I owe you. Sorry it's late. I called at the shop on the way home and took it out of the cash machine. That was all it would give me. Jack's got more money than me and I'm a grown up.' Dan took the money and hugged his dad. 'How's your day been at the university?'

'Crap. It's always the same this time of year. The students' rents are due for their final term but they've spent all their money on beer. I spend most of my time explaining to the parents the reason why their child is going to be evicted from their halls of residence is because they can't pay the rent. The standard answer is, *"they gave them the money for the rent already"*, and I have to explain that their child didn't give it to us. They drank it.'

'Funny. I'm glad my kids haven't cost me any money,' Alan said sipping the whisky. He frowned and Dan smiled. 'Well, that's a lie but you know what I mean.'

'So, did you do what you said you were going to do?'

'What did I say I was going to do?'

'You said you were going to arrest the dealers in town today?'

'Some of them. Some of them used their brain and answered our questions and we let them go. The ones who didn't answer are in the cells, sweating about being interviewed tomorrow.'

'Who did you lock up?' Dan asked. He shifted his weight from foot to foot, nervously. 'Anyone we'd know?'

'Probably. Everyone knows everyone.' Dan looked worried. 'Why don't you tell me who you're worried about and I'll tell you if I've heard their name on the list?'

'I don't know many of them. Only my friend who sells us weed.'

'What's his name?'

'His wife is flapping because he hasn't gone home. She thinks he might have had an accident or something,' Dan said, dodging the question. 'I didn't have the heart to tell her he might be banged up.'

'If you don't tell me his name, I can't help you, can I?'

'Lee,' Dan said.

'Lee Punk?' Alan asked. Dan nodded. 'Text his wife and tell her he's safely locked up in the cells and he'll be home before lunchtime tomorrow.'

'Thanks, Dad,' Dan said. He took out his phone and sent a text. 'How are you getting on with the other murders?'

'That's a different conversation. One I don't want to have tonight,' Alan said. 'In fact, I don't want to think about it at all.' He emptied the glass and refilled it before walking into the living room. Fflur had gone to bed, he assumed as she wasn't on the settee which was good as he wanted to sprawl. He sat down with a sigh and put his feet up on the table. It wasn't long before his exhausted mind switched off, his eyes closed, and he fell asleep.

CHAPTER 55

Kim checked her email. There was a reply from Kingdom Security. Two of their employees were on the island when Brian Hindley was murdered but they were handing out on the spot fines in Beaumaris and Red Wharf Bay at the time. The paperwork would back that up if necessary. They also confirmed that they had no employees currently residing in Holyhead or on Anglesey. Data protection made it impossible for them to be more specific about past employees. She folded the laptop away and went into the kitchen. It was time to relax.

He watched as Kim poured a glass of red wine. She sipped from the glass and then licked her lips. Her hair was pulled on top of her head into a bun, still wet from her shower. The dressing gown she was wearing was open to her chest, revealing her cleavage. She was doing it on purpose to tease him. There was no doubt about it. Her skin had a sheen. She'd applied some kind of lotion to it. He wondered what she smelled like, how her skin would feel to his touch, and how she would react when his hands were on her. Would she struggle against him or panic and freeze? It would be a true voyage of discovery when the time came. The clock was ticking and it wouldn't be long now. It had taken time to plan. It wouldn't be a random opportunity snatched at, grasped and taken gratefully like the others—it wouldn't be like them at all. She would be so special. So very special. He wanted to have time with her not because she was attractive and he desired her, but because she was the opposition and she must be destroyed. He would enjoy that. It was a battle of wits between the detectives and him. A battle that he would win. He would win because he had no boundaries and they wouldn't expect him to come for them. There were no constraints on the way he played the game but she had to play by the rules. That was her weakness, the chink in her armour. Without her detective sergeant badge, she was just a woman. He was bigger and stronger; he had a knife and he was mentally unstable. Some might think that was a disadvantage but they would be wrong. Although he had a plan, it was unlikely he would stick to it when the time came, but that was okay. Sometimes he slipped into a frenzy without knowing. He couldn't help it. Whatever course it took, it would be a scintillating voyage of discovery, exploring her body, smelling her, penetrating her, tasting her, eating her and then dismantling her body bit by bit. That was the plan and it was a beautiful plan, so beautiful it brought tears to his eyes. He couldn't wait but he would have to. There were things to be done first and then she would be his. His forever.

She closed the blinds and his view of her was gone. He felt robbed. There was a glow inside him which had been extinguished suddenly and now he felt barren. The vivid thoughts he was having had turned to black and white and then vanished. Anger replaced them and began to grow inside him. She was a prick tease and he would punish her for that. The anger increased. He knew it would fester until it was released through the knife. All the anger and frustration filtered through him, into the steel and into the victim. They would feel the hatred as they bled. He checked his watch. It was past midnight. He walked back to his vehicle and climbed inside. There was somewhere he needed to be.

CHAPTER 56

Tony pulled into the car park at South Stack lighthouse. It serviced the café at the top of the mountain and was popular with walkers and climbers. Ellin's Tower glowed white in the moonlight. Hundreds of feet below, the sea glimmered and the beam from the lighthouse turned relentlessly. It was late and there was no one around. Even the star gazers and sexual deviants had gone home to bed. There were three cars and a motorbike parked at the far end of the car park. The cars were full, windows down, cannabis smoke spiralling upwards towards the stars. No one cared about the police coming. There was one road up the mountain and one road down and headlights could be seen from miles away. Ancient tribes had lived there because of its panoramic viewpoint. No one could approach without being seen. It made the perfect place for a secret powwow.

He pulled over and parked up next to the vehicles. The men stopped chatting and got out of their respective vehicles. He knew all the faces, some were friendly, some enemies but they all had something common tonight. Old rivalries were put to one side while they fought a common enemy—the police. It was a gathering of the island's more notorious players—the men who didn't work nine to five jobs and made a living on the edge but were not far enough up the ladder to be driving a Porsche or wear a Rolex. They were held together by a fragile peace, a peace which was threatened by the investigation. He approached them and shook hands with each one in turn. There were fourteen of them from all over the island. It was enough people to make sure the word was passed on to as many people as possible. Bad news travelled fast on the island.

'You all know what's going on in town?' Tony asked. The men nodded.

'Dibble are everywhere, man.' Someone moaned. 'It's bad for business.'

'I've heard they're lifting anyone who's so much as smoked a spliff?' another said.

'I heard it's something to do with the dead coppers they pulled out of the bay.'

'It is,' Tony said. 'It's not random. They're working through a list of drug buys the undercover coppers made before they were snuffed. I've heard they made a lot while they were here. Chances are, we'll all be pulled in at some point. The Dibble are asking questions about the supply line. They're looking for whoever killed the undercover cops and they're assuming it was someone at the top of the tree.'

'Your boss must be shitting his pants,' a man from across the island said. Tony felt like slapping him down but this wasn't the time for butting horns.

'That's why we're all here,' another said. 'He wants us to cover his arse for him.'

'Listen to me,' Tony said. 'They think they know who is who and who is responsible but they can't prove it yet. The Dibble are going nowhere until they catch the killers. They could be here for months arresting people, ruining your businesses. If that's what you want, then get in your cars and go now.' No one moved. 'If we all stick to the same line, we'll be fine. You've all had the text from Jamie's burner phone?' Everyone nodded. 'Okay. Delete it. Stick to that and the Dibble will be gone in a week.'

'You think it will be that simple?'

'No. Jamie has a plan.'

'What's the plan?'

'I don't know but it doesn't matter. You do your part and we'll do the rest.'

'He'd better remember this when it's all over.'

'He will. Are we all agreed?' Tony asked. The gathering nodded they were, some more reluctantly than others. 'Good, thanks for coming. Any problems, you know how to get hold of me.'

Tony walked back to his car and watched as the others started their engines and drove out of the car park. It was a mile down the mountain to the bottom. At the end the mountain road, they turned in different directions and drove off into the night. Tony wasn't sure what would happen but the next few days would tell.

* * *

Jamie checked the mirror. They were there again, following him. The vehicle was a long way back, but it was there. He knew they were tracking him. They'd been tracking him for years. They thought he didn't know but he did. He'd known after a tipoff on day one. It paid to have men on the force. The operation into his network was advanced and detailed but all they had was mundane day-to-day chitchat. He was sure there were audio devices planted here and there, so he made sure nothing was discussed indoors. They swept their vehicles and the pub for electronic bugging devices every few months so as not to raise suspicion. It was standard practice in his business. So far, they'd found four. The search was all part of the dance with the authorities. If they swept for devices too often, the Dibble would be panicked into acting, not enough and they would be sure they were onto them.

He slowed down enough to make them think he was stopping and then sped up around the corner and closed the gap on a vehicle ahead of him. The surveillance team would just see the headlights and think it was him. Turning into a field, he killed the lights. A few minutes later, the surveillance vehicle drove past the entrance and carried on around the bends ahead following the wrong vehicle. The road was too narrow to turn a car around. They would have to drive miles before they realised it wasn't his car and that he'd slipped their tail.

Jamie reversed onto the road and drove a few hundred yards before hiding the Range Rover in a copse of trees. He climbed out and went to the boot, opening it, he reached in and removed a spade and some bin bags. The contents of the bags were light, and he set off through the trees. The wind blew and made the branches sway, creaking noises surrounded him. He stopped and looked around to make sure no one was following him. If he screwed this up, he would go to jail for life. The wind dropped and the noises subsided. His eyes adjusted to the darkness and he was sure he was alone. He set off again into the night, unable to use the torch on his phone. It was too risky. His sense of direction was good, and he'd been along this path before. It was fifteen minutes before he reached the building. He could hear the hum of electricity and the smell of cannabis tainted the air. This was an insurance policy he'd taken out years before and now it was time to make a claim. It wouldn't take long to do what he needed to do and then he could go home and sleep tightly. He made a call on his mobile and then started digging.

CHAPTER 57

He watched the toilet block for hours just as his father had years before. Peter Moore had attacked over twenty men on Pensarn Beach, stabbing many of them, sexually assaulting some, eventually killing four of them. If the assaults, sexual or otherwise had been reported to the police, his father would have been caught much sooner. It was his fourth victim; this last murder led to his arrest. He left blood at the scene, a schoolboy error if there was one. His entire killing spree had been reckless and unplanned. It was little wonder he only managed to kill four before he was caught. How could he have been so stupid to leave DNA at a murder scene? Had he panicked, been disturbed, or did he not know he was bleeding? This was one of the problems of choosing such a public place to commit such a heinous crime. That was the big difference between him and his father. He wouldn't make such basic errors of judgement, that was a certainty. It was obvious that he was far more intelligent than his father or his mother. If they combined their IQ's they wouldn't be as clever as he was. His intellectual prowess was far superior to theirs. It was as clear as day that they were as thick as mince. He often wondered how they'd managed to produce a child with such intellect. The other thing he wondered about was his father's sexuality.

His father had targeted men, mostly cruising for casual sex. That was quite common with serial killers. So, had Dennis Nilsen and Jeffery Dahmer, who killed twenty-nine men between them. They trawled gay bars for their victims. He had to respect them. To get into double figures without being caught was an achievement in itself. He also had massive admiration for John Wayne Gacy, who sexually assaulted and killed thirty-three young men, but they were tricked into going back to his house rather than lured there for sex. He had a trick he did with a pair of handcuffs, putting them on himself, then escaping from them. He would then trick his victims by putting the cuffs on them and telling them he would teach them how to escape them. Once they were cuffed, he would pounce. Most of his victims were raped. Did that mean his father was gay or bisexual or was he into men sexually because they were more promiscuous and made easy targets? If things went wrong during an attack, his victims were unlikely to report an assault to the police or their families because they weren't out of the closet. Reporting any type of sexual assault or a visit to the casualty department would beg the question, where were you and why were you there in the first place?

The toilet block was the bait which attracted like-minded men like moths to a flame. Little did they know there was psychopath stalking the place and many of them had their wings burnt. He had spent many hours wondering what his father was, and he'd concluded that there was no specific category to label him with. There was no box the stick him in. He was a sexual predator who escalated to murder and enjoyed it. He thought about his father and mother and their encounters. His existence was proof that his father also had sex with women. If you could call rape sex and he wasn't sure you could. It appeared to him, his father wanted violent sex with either male or female as long as he was the assailant.

He wasn't like his father in that respect, not exactly. Sex with females had been far more satisfying although rare. His awkwardness socially made it difficult for him to attract women. They rarely hung around long enough to get to the stage where they would consider having sex with him. On the occasions he went with men, they'd been effeminate and compliant. If he closed his eyes, they could have been female until they wanted him to touch them. That was when he knew he preferred women. It was all academic anyway but the differences between him and his father were clear.

Yet here he was at Pensarn Beach, watching men cruising in the toilet block, just like his father had all those years ago. He was going to replay his father's final murder for the world to see but he would improve on it. It would be like comparing a painting of 'our house' by a five-year old to a masterpiece by Da Vinci. Once this was done, the mimicking would cease. He'd paid homage to his father enough and he would step up to a level his father could never have dreamed of, let alone achieved. He would show him what could be done with thought and planning and intelligence. It was the natural progression of the next generation. He would move on and move up. His next murders would be epic. They would be on an unimaginable scale and would reach television screens the world over. They would launch him into immortality.

A vehicle approaching the toilet block slowly caught his eye. This was the one.

CHAPTER 58

Alan woke up with a thick head and a sore throat. Gemma was curled up on his feet and Henry was on the pillow next to him. Henry sensed he was awake and licked his face.

'Henry!' Alan moaned, pushing him off the pillow. Henry righted himself and scurried back onto the pillow, launching a second offensive. 'How the bloody hell did life come to this, Henry?' Alan said stroking his head. 'What did I do to deserve you? The first thing I see in the morning is your ugly mug.'

He pushed off the quilt and swung his legs out of the bed. Gemma jumped down and stretched, her tail wagging furiously. 'Who wants to go out?' Alan asked, climbing into a pair of grey joggers. He pulled a hoodie on and padded towards the kitchen, flicking the lights on as he went. Dan was in the living room watching the news, eating a bowl of cereal. Alan poked his head around the door.

'Morning,' he said.

'Have you seen this, Dad?' Alan rubbed his eyes and squinted at the screen. His eyes were still bleary. It was *BBC Breakfast* news.

'What is it?' he asked. The image of Peter Moore appeared on the screen, followed by an image of Zak Edwards and Henry Roberts. It answered his question. His heart pounded in his chest. He felt his stomach churn. 'Oh, for God's sake, how the hell have they got that already?'

'I'm guessing you didn't release this?' Dan said, slurping his tea.

'No, I did not but when I find out who did, they're going to get a kick up the arse.'

'Why. Was it leaked?'

'Yes, probably. It would have got there eventually but we wanted a bit of breathing room before it did. This is going to bring attention from way upon high. I'll have the top brass breathing down my neck at every turn and they'll be second guessing every decision I make. On top of that, every journalist within a thousand miles will be mithering for an exclusive.'

'Give them one and make a few quid,' Dan said, shovelling granola into his mouth. 'Or tell me what to say and I'll do it and split the money with you.'

'Thank you very much,' Alan said, heading into the kitchen. He opened the patio doors and let the dogs out and then switched the kettle on. His mobile began to vibrate. He took it out of his hoodie pocket and looked at the screen. It was Dafyd. 'Morning, Dafyd.'

'Have you seen the news?'

'Yes.'

'How the hell did they get hold of this?'

'I don't know. It could have come from anyone actively working the case, the technical staff, the uniformed division, you know how these things go,' Alan said, yawning. He grabbed a mug and plonked a teabag into it. 'I'm certain none of the detectives would want to attract this kind of attention.'

'I don't like to think it but it would be worth a lot of money to someone.'

'It's all right to think it just don't say it aloud. The other option is the killer told them what the similarities are between his murders and Peter Moore. The fact we were keeping the stab patterns under wraps for now must have been pissing him off. He will want that splashed across the Internet.'

'Do you think that's likely?'

'It's more likely than one of my detectives doing it.'

'I suppose so but I'm not sure the ACC will see it that way. He'll be pointing his finger at everyone within earshot of the case. You know what a trusting soul he is.'

'He'll see it for what it is, a media shitstorm heading in his direction. His natural reaction will be to duck so it hits someone else in the face. If he starts giving you grief, tell him to lean on the press to tell us where they received the information. If it's an anonymous tipoff, they'll be open and tell him it was but if they paid an informant for it, they won't confirm or deny anything. Then we'll know where it came from.'

'Do you think he wants the attention that much?'

'Yes. Our killer has a fascination with Moore and he also likes the limelight. He's seeking notoriety and the best way to get that is to expose what he's trying to achieve. I don't suppose we'll know his exact reasoning until we catch him.'

'I'll have to call you back, Alan,' Dafyd said. He sounded stressed. 'The ACC is on the other phone.'

'Good luck with that,' Alan said, putting the phone down. He made his cup of tea and walked to the patio doors, looking out over the fields to Snowdonia. The sun was coming up, chasing the stars from the sky. It was a peaceful vista. He soaked it in, and it calmed him. The calm before the storm. His phone vibrated. It was Dafyd again. 'That was quick.'

'Not quick enough. I've just had my ears bashed. Apparently, it's my responsibility to keep a lid on the press and make them print balanced articles rather than sensationalist ones about serial killers from the nineties.'

'How do you do that?' Alan asked, sipping tea.

'I should have asked for instructions. Bloody idiot.'

'You didn't call him that, did you?'

'No not yet. I'm to contact our press office and ask them to find out where the information came from.'

'Like I said, good luck with that.' The line went quiet. Dafyd was talking to someone. Their voices were muffled. He could hear Dafyd swearing under his breath. He waited for him to come back. 'Are you still there?'

'Yes. We're going to need more than luck, Alan,' Dafyd said.

'What now?' Alan asked, not wanting to know the answer.

'A body was found this morning, stabbed to death in Pensarn. He's a thirty-two-year-old father of three from Abergele.'

'Not in the toilet block on the beach?'

'Unfortunately, yes.'

'Jesus Christ! This guy is completely off the scale.'

'How do you want to play this one?'

'Who's on the case?'

'Detectives from St Asaph, until you get there.'

'Tell them I'll be an hour and tell them to keep the press as far away as they possibly can. It won't take long for them to make the connection.'

'As you said before, good luck with that. I'll ring you later.'

The line went dead, and Alan sipped his tea. He stared at the mountains and breathed deeply. The dogs came into view, racing back across the field. He put food and water in their bowls and went back into the living room. The news was still focused on the possibility of a copycat serial killer in North Wales and they were interviewing a profiler who had worked with the Metropolitan force ten years before. It was a tenuous link at best. All they needed now was a medium and a criminal psychologist and they had the full serial killer interview kit. He sighed and shook his head.

'This will turn it into a circus.'

'This is great. It's going to be sick,' Dan said. 'You'll be famous.'

'And you'll have no friends left.'

'You're joking, aren't you?' Dan said, standing up. He finished his tea and looked at his phone. 'I've had texts this morning from people I haven't spoken to since school. Everyone is buzzing about this and you're Johnny on the spot. I think I'll start a vlog. People make a fortune from vlogs.'

'Oh, good. At least we can take some positives from it,' Alan said, rolling his eyes. 'It amazes me what excites people. There's a nutter out there who's killing men because he has a fixation with a murderer from nearly thirty years ago and people are reaching out to you to see if you know anything they don't.'

'Pretty much, yes,' Dan said. 'I'll be flavour of the month at work. Don't worry, I won't tell anyone anything you've said about it.'

'I haven't said anything about it,' Alan said.

'I can make stuff up, just to impress them.'

'Please don't make stuff up. Let the press do that themselves.'

'I'm joking, Dad,' Dan said hugging him. 'I'm off to work. I'll see you later. I won't say have a good day at work because it looks like it will be shit.'

CHAPTER 59

Bob Dewhurst was listening to the radio. The news was well and truly focused on the Anglesey murders and the possibility of a copycat killer. Copycat killer. It rolls off the tongue, he thought. The only upside was it took the focus away from the painfully overreported issues with Europe. If anyone mentioned Brexit again, he would arrest them. As the news reports drifted from one angle to the next, the complexity of the story became clear. This would be big. Very big indeed. It would attract the interest of the average person and it would be big news. It was going to get very crowded on the island. Every film crew, their production teams, and their dog would be jostling for hotel rooms and a parking space. The hotels, cafés, and bars would do well out of it, if nothing else. An active serial killer was always good for the local economy.

He was considering handing in his retirement papers early when a call came in from the station. A concerned local had phoned the non-emergency line in the early hours of the morning and reported a man staggering drunkenly on an isolated stretch of road near the base of the mountain. He'd last been seen climbing a gate into a field. The station was under pressure, so he decided to look into himself. He had to drive that way on his way to work.

He slowed down when he reached the area the caller described. There was a ditch alongside the road, then a barbed wire fence. Beyond the fence was a narrow line of trees and then open grazing land. A few hundred yards across the field was a farm building made from corrugated polycarbonate, green in colour. It was low and Bob didn't recall it being built. He didn't recall who the land beyond the fence belonged to either. It would be one of the local farmers. When he reached the five-bar gate the caller had mentioned, he stopped the car and climbed out. He walked to the gate and looked into the trees. If someone had climbed over, looking for shelter against a bitterly cold night and driving rain, they could be injured somewhere in the long grass beyond. He swore beneath his breath and climbed over the gate. The metal was cold and wet. He landed with a bump on the other side, his knees reminding him they were over fifty. There was flattened grass ahead of him leading to the trees. The pattern indicated someone had walked there recently. Probably as recently as last night. Bob fastened his jacket and followed the trail.

The footprints led through the grass, beneath the trees, and across the field towards the green building. The grass was too long to see a human lying down. He decided to carry on, just in case someone had fallen asleep drunk. They would die from hypothermia before they sobered up. Bob kept walking in a zigzag pattern to cover as much ground as possible. As he did, he noticed the whiff of cannabis on the breeze. It was subtle but it was there. He scanned the horizon for someone smoking but there was no one in sight. There was a difference to the odour. It didn't smell burnt. It smelled fresh, like the plant. As he neared the building, he heard the hum of electricity—the type of sound you would hear from an electric substation. The hairs on the back of his neck bristled. He looked around for signs of life but couldn't see anything but the green building. There was cannabis being grown nearby, probably inside. He was certain and decided to get closer to investigate. It was then another smell drifted to him. It was the unmistakable stink of human decay.

CHAPTER 60

Alan arrived at the scene and parked on the sand. Pensarn Beach was wide and seemed to go on forever in both directions. Dafyd had done a good job of keeping this one from the press so far. There were a handful of onlookers further up the beach, taking pictures on their phones. The toilet block had been cordoned off and two CSI vans were parked nearby. He walked across the sand and ducked beneath the tape. Two detectives from St Asaph were standing in the doorway of the gents. They saw him approaching and greeted him. Alan was familiar with their faces but couldn't remember their names. He shook hands with them and went inside. The stench of urine made his eyes water. Graffiti covered the walls and the frosted glass windows were cracked. Pamela Stone was kneeling on the tiles, recovering something she thought was relevant. Alan was certain that taking DNA swabs and trace evidence from a public toilet was probably every CSI's worst nightmare. Pamela looked up and smiled thinly. Her eyes weren't as bright as they usually were and her expression showed that her work was taking a toll today.

'He's in that cubicle here and he's in that cubicle there,' she said, pointing to the only two cubicles. 'His ID is there. Philip Trotter from Abergele, aged thirty-three.'

Alan frowned. That didn't sound good. He looked into the first cubicle. Philip Trotter's body was kneeling on the floor, the torso leaning over the bowl as if he was being sick. His hands were tied behind his back. He looked into the second cubicle. The seat had been put down and Trotter's head was placed on it facing the door for impact, eyes wide and staring, tongue protruding in a silent scream.

'He's escalating,' Pamela said. 'Removing the head is not his MO.'

'This one hasn't developed his MO yet,' Alan said. 'He was mimicking Moore from the outset but he's a showman, hence the escalation. Everything he does is to attract attention to his crimes. First, he mimics a serial killer to get a shock reaction when we realise what he's doing, then he goes one better and removes the head. God knows what's next. This was Moore's last murder. He was arrested shortly afterwards. There's nothing to copy now, so what's he going to do next?'

'He's going to develop his own MO from here on,' Pamela said. 'Whatever he metamorphoses into, it's not going to be pretty.'

CHAPTER 61

Kim drove through Llaingoch until she reached a cluster of police vehicles and CSI vans. A uniformed officer with a yellow hi-vis waistcoat waved traffic away, making drivers turn around and use alternative routes to wherever they were heading. Thankfully, there was no media scrum clogging up the narrow access road. She pulled onto the grass verge, as close to the ditch as she dared. It had been raining and the water was flowing quickly. She left the vehicle and walked to the gate where Bob Dewhurst was waiting. He saw her approaching and waved hello.

'Hello, Kim.'

'Bob,' she said. 'How are you?'

'Bloody awful, to be honest.' Bob gestured to the path beneath the trees. 'I'm thinking of packing this in and getting a proper job.'

'At your age? It's way too late for that,' she said. 'They don't have lollipop men anymore.'

'Cheeky bugger. It's a few hundred yards past the edge of the tree line. I'll walk you over there.'

'Is there any vehicle access?' she asked.

'No. You'll see why when we get there.' They walked through the trees and across the meadow. 'Whoever owns this doesn't want anyone driving too close to it.'

'How did you find him?'

'A concerned citizen called in and said they'd seen a man staggering down the road drunk and were concerned he might end up being knocked over or fall in the ditch. I came this way to work and checked it out. There was a trail leading to the farm. I could smell cannabis and hear electric transformers, so I carried on, thinking I'd stumbled on a cannabis farm. That's when I saw the body. I smelled it first and followed my nose,' Bob explained. 'The right arm and hand were protruding through the soil. It looked like it had been disturbed recently.'

'Disturbed by an animal, fox or a badger, maybe?'

'I'm not sure. I'll let you decide.'

They reached the rear of the building and Kim could smell everything Bob had described. Cannabis and decomposition. As they turned the corner, she saw three CSIs working on recovering the body. The stench was overpowering.

'He's been there a while,' Kim said.

'Probably since he disappeared,' Bob agreed.

'Has anyone told the family?'

'Not yet. I thought it would be better to have him removed before we say anything.'

'Good call.'

They watched the CSIs bagging evidence and placing it into plastic boxes. She knew one of them as Victor; he stopped working and approached them.

'Hello, sergeant,' he said.

'Is it definitely him?'

'We think so. The ID in his wallet belongs to Paul Critchley. There's a driving license and a debit card,' Victor said. 'And there's a silver St Christopher around his neck. It was on the list of personal items his family gave to the police at the time of his disappearance. There're tattoos on the arms and legs but the decomp is too far gone to distinguish if they're definitely Critchley's. The fact they're there at all, with the ID and the chain tells me it's him.'

'What state is the body in?'

'He was busted up. His legs and jaw are broken and there's a couple of fingers and toes missing but I can't tell if they were stolen by creatures until we get him back to the lab.'

'And what's in the secondary site?' Kim asked.

'Three bin bags with various items of clothing, two jackets, a baseball cap, two T-shirts, a denim shirt, and a jumper. There's also half a dozen cigarette butts, which we should be able to take DNA from.' He picked up an evidence bag. 'This is the motherload. Two wallets. One belonging to Mike Jarvis and the other Patrick McGowan. I'm making an educated guess that the DNA on the clothing will belong to your murdered UCs.'

'All this evidence drops into our lap from an anonymous phone call?' Kim said, shaking her head. 'I think someone pointed us in the right direction, when it's clearly the wrong direction.'

'It did cross my mind,' Bob said. 'I'm never this lucky. Do you want to look inside?'

'Yes. That's good enough for me for now. Let's take a look.'

They walked the perimeter of the building until they reached a narrow door. It was wedged open and the smell of skunk was heavy on the air. Inside was a cannabis farm on an industrial scale. Rows of plants were bathed in LED lights, irrigation tubes ran from the ceiling, providing water. Extractor fans were humming, maintaining a stable temperature. There were thousands of plants standing six-feet tall and a nursery for germinating young plants.

'Now that's what you call a cannabis farm,' Kim said. She looked from one end of the building to the other, trying to count the number of plants. It was in the thousands. 'This is a multimillion-pound operation. Anyone threatening this is going to wind up dead.'

'Like Jarvis and McGowan. Absolutely. Do you know who owns it, yet?' Bob asked.

'Not yet. There's an umbrella company but we're digging deeper.'

'Whoever it is, is going to be proper pissed off that they've lost this.'

'And some,' Kim added.

CHAPTER 62

Simon and Kerry were conducting the search of Glen Price's home. The front door was breached, and armed response swept the building before the search could begin properly. It appeared the occupants had left in a hurry. Cupboard doors had been left open and there were clothes dotted about on the floor. There were pictures of Glen abroad, posing alone but none of him and his wife. Patricia Price had been erased from the house. It appeared that Glen Price had buried his wife and then carried on as if nothing had changed. He'd masked her departure well—apart from not submitting her tax returns. That was an oversight.

'So, Patricia had no family in the area?' Simon asked.

'Her brother lives in Australia, but her phone records show no contact between them. No one noticed she was dead. Price knew that no one would miss her. No wonder he bottled it when we turned up, asking questions. His cosy little life would be put under the spotlight and his wife's absence would have been exposed. He panicked.'

'Where do you think the money we found came from?'

'At Porth Dafarch?'

'Yes.'

'They made a lot of money selling drugs at the factory until Kio was jailed, the other three were implicated and questioned so one of them hid their stash of money and Adams returned to it every month and took enough to keep them happy without having to explain any large amounts going into their bank accounts. Everything was rosy until Kio came out of jail and demanded his share of the profits. They say no, so he follows Adams, kills him, and spoils everything.'

'What about Patricia Price?'

'Who knows? She wound up dead during a domestic, Glen panics and asks for help. They hid her near the money because they knew it was safe there. Safer than putting her body in the sea. They always come up eventually.'

'It's all speculation, I suppose. The poor woman. Imagine being married to a bastard like that and ending up in a hole in the ground and no one even knows you've gone,' Kerry said. 'It's so sad.'

She walked into the bedroom where Price slept. The quilt was pulled back and unmade. One of the wardrobe doors was open and half the contents were missing. The remaining garments were women's clothes, belonging to someone under thirty-ish, at a guess. She picked through them. They were winter clothes.

'She took all her summer stuff,' Kerry said. 'They've gone somewhere hot.'

An open door led to an en suite. Kerry searched the bathroom and checked the medicine cabinet. She found three bottles of lithium with Patricia's name on them.

'She was bipolar,' Kerry said. 'The last date on the prescription was three years ago.' She closed the cabinet and opened the washing basket. There was a pair of jeans, which were muddy around the legs. She pulled them out. 'Look at these jeans. They're very muddy.'

'Bag them.'

Kerry put them into an evidence bag and peered into the basket. Underneath the jeans, she found a mustard coloured sweatshirt. 'Look at this,' she said, removing it from the basket. 'This looks like blood on the sleeves and the cuffs and there's splatter on the chest here.'

'Messy,' Simon said. 'What you'd expect from a hammer attack don't you think?' He shrugged. 'I had Kio down as the killer but I might be wrong.'

'It looks like it. The blood on this takes some explanation.'

'So does his vanishing trick.'

'Definitely. We thought the killer was taking Adams to the cliffs to throw him off but maybe Price wasn't taking him to the sea. Maybe he was taking him up onto the range because Adams was the only one of them who knew where the money was hidden.'

'That makes sense. So, where is Price now?'

'I'd be on a beach counting my money. We need to check the airports.'

CHAPTER 63

Alan called a briefing to bring the team up to speed. Events were happening fast and everyone needed to know where they were. The press had descended on the island talking to anyone who would speak to them. There were plenty of takers, most of them talking crap and speculating or repeating gossip they'd overheard in a pub. The discovery of Patricia Price and an undisclosed stash of money at Porth Dafarch had fuelled speculation of a connection to organised crime and the murder of two undercover officers. The press was linking the deaths and without the facts, who wouldn't? On the face of it, Alan would have done the same. Not that it mattered. Even with the facts, the press would make what they wanted to of the story. One of the redtops had run with the headline, 'Unholy Island'. Alan couldn't argue with that.

'Okay everyone,' Alan said. The gathering settled down to listen. 'Glen Price's Porsche has been found at Manchester airport. He took a flight to Bangkok with a thirty-year-old woman called Stephanie Mortimer.' The image of Stephanie appeared on the screen. She was an attractive brunette with mischief in her eyes. 'She's a widow. It appears they've been an item since about the time Patricia disappeared. I want one of you to look into how her husband died, please. We're trying to track them down but it's unlikely we'll be able to extradite.' He turned from the screen. 'Anything from the lab, Kim?'

'The blood on the sweatshirt taken from Price's house is a match for Adams' blood type, but it's too soon for DNA results to confirm it's his, yet. The mud on the jeans has an unusually high salt content, consistent with being from the Porth Dafarch area. Pamela said she'll be able to say if it's definitely from there when she's run some comparisons.'

'Glen Price was at the murder scene and he's covered in the victim's blood,' Alan said. 'Okay. So, we're working on the assumption Kio, Trent, Adams, and Price were working together selling cocaine at the car factory, until Kio was arrested. The others were interviewed and clearly spooked. They hid their money and then when things settled down and Kio was sent down, they filtered it out bit by bit over the years but only Kelvin Adams knew where it is. At some point, Price kills his wife and asks Adams to help him dispose of her, which he does because he knows a remote place where he's hidden stuff before. So, she ends up next to the money. Kio comes out of prison, making threats to kill Price if he doesn't give him money. He bottles it and contacts Trent and Adams and tells them Kio is demanding money from them. They say no but Price wants to pay him off, so he follows Kelvin Adams to Porth Dafarch. He waits until Adams has recovered some of the money, hijacks him in the toilets when he's getting changed, and tries to force him back onto the range to show him where the money is stashed. Adams puts up a fight and Price kills him. He takes the money he'd recovered and buggers off to the Far East. Adams is dead. Derek Kio is dead. That leaves Barry Trent.' He clicked the remote. The images of Barry Trent and his wife appeared. 'The Trents are missing but their car is at their home. There are signs of a break in and signs of a struggle inside.' He replaced their image with an image of Derek Kio, dead on the street. 'Kio was assassinated in broad daylight.' He tapped the screen. 'If Glen Price is our mastermind in this case, we have to assume that an engineer from a Jaguar factory is capable of kidnapping the Trents and shooting Derek Kio outside a pub in the middle of the afternoon before fleeing the country.' He looked around the room. 'Simon, Kerry, you interviewed him several times, was Price capable of this?'

'Not a chance,' Simon said.

'Was he capable of hitting Adams over the head, possibly. The evidence says he did. If he was being threatened by Kio, it would have made him act irrationally. He may have panicked and asked Adams for the money to pay off Kio, but Adams said no so, he decided to take it for himself. I can see that happening but was he capable of kidnap and assassination in daylight, in a public place, not a chance.'

'I agree,' Alan said. 'The question we need to answer now is if Price isn't behind this, who is?' No one offered the answer. 'Who is at the top of the tree? Simon, Kerry, you stay on this please. Speak to the Merseyside Drug Squad and the Matrix unit. Ask them if they have any historical information on who they were likely to be buying their cocaine from. I would focus on Derek Kio. If he was putting the pressure on Price, someone may have been putting the pressure on him. Someone will have an idea who they were buying from so let's find out.'

'Yes, guv.'

'Sorry to interrupt, guv,' Kim said. 'We've got a name for the owners of the land in Llaingoch.'

'Surprise me?'

'Sundown Property Management, owned and operated by, Will Pinter.'

'Will Pinter is bedbound with dementia. The farm has been in the family since it was built. I think we might be missing a trick here. Let's piece all this together,' Alan said. 'The dealers we've questioned so far are all pointing their fingers at Lloyd Jones.'

'Conveniently, he's done one,' Kim said.

'Exactly. Some of the dealers we interviewed have gone a step further and told us the good cannabis sold locally is coming from a character known as Worzel Gummidge. What do we know about him or her?'

'We've got a profile on Facebook but not much else.'

'I've been told in confidence that the best quality cannabis with a regular supply comes from a guy called Lee Punk,' Alan said. A murmur passed through the gathering. 'You're familiar with him as he was questioned this morning. We need to watch Lee and sooner or later, he'll lead us to his supplier. I'm guessing it's this character Worzel.'

'What about the farm Will Pinter owned, guv?' Kerry said. 'We're dismissing Pinter as a cover for fraud yet everything we look at leads us to this company, Sundown Property.'

'Okay. What are you thinking?' Alan said.

'He did trade under this name, didn't he?'

'Yes. For twenty-years.'

'Isn't feasible someone involved with his farm is still running the company in his name. They could be running the money laundering at the Caernarvon Castle, the laundry, and the cannabis farm as a single business.'

'Yes, it's feasible.'

'Anyone growing cannabis on that scale needs to be able to hide the money, so they set up the perfect operation to do that, but we stumbled across it by chance, investigating another case.'

'When I went to see Will Pinter, his nephew answered the door. His name is Gar, which I assume is short for Gareth. The farm looked like a lot of money has been spent on it. I thought the farm was doing well but it could be dirty money,' Alan said. 'Get a warrant for the farm, the house, the buildings, everything. Bring him in and let's see what he's got to say.'

'What about Operation Thor, guv?' Kim asked.

'What about them?'

'Paul Critchley,' she said. 'Jamie Hollins threatened to kill him and throw him off the mountain the day before he disappeared.'

'In an ideal world, we should arrest him and check we're not treading on their toes,' Alan said. 'But we're not so, we won't. Get in touch with DCI Kensington and tell him that if they don't move on Hollins today, we will. He's in a position to vanish. We need to interview him about Critchley but ultimately, he's their catch.'

'I'll speak to him, guv.'

He changed the image to the toilet block at Abergele. The room fell deathly silent.

'Phillip Trotter was murdered here in the early hours of this morning. He was a thirty-three-year-old father of three. You all know the history of this place. Peter Moore killed his last victim, Tony Davies, here in December ninety-five. The murder is identical, except our copycat upped the ante and removed the victim's head.' The gathering listened intently. 'This is our man again, no doubt about it. He's exhausted the Moore killings, so now he's going to have to develop his own MO. Alice, I want your team to concentrate on this now.'

'Guv. Where do you want us to start?'

'We have one sighting of him shortly before Brian Hindley was murdered. The man at Penrhos wearing a black uniform. We know he's not one of ours and we know he's not an employee of Kingdom Security.'

'Could be a transport copper off the railway?'

'Maybe. It could be a customs officer from the port. Look into both.'

'Yes, guv.'

'Watch this footage,' Alan said. The screen showed a clip from *Sky News*. The camera panned from the cob, across the sea to Church Bay, zoomed in on the Skerries lighthouse, before focusing on the car park at Penrhos nature reserve. The Hindley family were gathered there. 'There were a lot of cameras on the cob while we were looking for Brian Hindley and there were cameras on the mountain when we found Zak Edwards. Our killer is a showman. He craves attention and wants to create the news. My hunch is he wants to be there too. I think our killer will be on some of these images and I want your team to gather as many images of this case as you can. Use Instagram, use Facebook, use the online news reports and look for a man in a dark uniform. I think he's there for us to find because he can't help himself.'

'Okay, guv.'

'You all know what needs to be done. We'll meet here tomorrow morning at nine-thirty. Any developments, keep me in the loop.'

CHAPTER 64

The BBC was running an extended report on breakfast news. They were using clips from the Peter Moore documentary, the *Man in Black*. There was his father, smiling and laughing for the camera as if he was being filmed for a comedy. He was fascinated by the article and had to sit down to watch it. There were things to do but they could wait for a few minutes. The reporters who worked on the article had been to the island. One of them was filmed at Penrhos, the sea emerald green behind him. They explored the life of Brian Hindley and Zak Edwards and debated how the killer picked his victims and why. The pattern of knife wounds was discussed and one of their criminology experts said the killer was a psychopath obsessed with Peter Moore. No shit, Sherlock. He wondered how long the man had studied for his degree to come up with absolute nuggets of deduction like that. It was almost genius to work that out. He thought about cutting out his tongue and then asking him how psychotic he thought that was on a scale of one to ten. If that was the best he could come up with, he really needed to change career. The piece touched on the latest murder but they had no details. Footage of Pensarn Beach from the eighties had been tagged into the article in an effort to be the first channel to cover it in any detail. It was magnificent. They had weaved images of his victims into a story alongside images of his father's crimes. Father and son engrained in serial killer history forever. It was a milestone. There would be more. They would be talked about in the same breath forever.

He watched until it finished and they switched to the weather and then he sniffed the cushions one at a time. One of them was lower than the others—the place she favoured when she watched the television in the evenings. He pushed his face deep into the material. Her perfume was heady, like Poison, or Alien. They were easy to identify because they were so potent. They didn't suit everyone, but they would suit her. He turned the television off and walked into the kitchen. The fridge was a vision of a health-conscious adult. Juices, smoothies, and yogurts. No wonder she was so lean. Her muscles looked toned. He was looking forward to feeling them, squeezing them, and biting into them until the skin broke and her blood filled his mouth. That would be beautiful. He opened the cupboards, one at a time and then closed them again before opening the next. Clean and tidy. Well organised and functional. She was all those things and so much more. His fascination with her was growing. The closer it came, the more intense the emotions. His heart was pounding as he left the kitchen and climbed the stairs.

The bathroom was still warm from the shower she'd taken. There was condensation on the tiles above the bath. The toilet seat was down. She'd put bleach around the bowl. The smell was powerful. He breathed in deeply through his nose. Her deodorant hung in the air. He closed his eyes and walked along the landing into her bedroom. The door was open. He stopped in the doorway and sniffed. This was going to be so erotic. He put his hand on the knife and felt his fingers tingle before he stepped inside. She wouldn't be back for hours and hours, but he was more than happy to wait. He took out the knife, a roll of duct tape, and some handcuffs and put them onto the dressing table. He fastened the handcuffs to the headboard and imagined her there, thrashing and twisting, fighting against him until she became exhausted and succumbed to his greater strength. It would be painful; so very painful, yet it would be exquisite. He stood in front of her wardrobe, pulled down his trousers, and looked at himself in the mirror.

CHAPTER 65

When Alan arrived at Caer Rhos farm, Gareth Pinter was being pulled out of his Land Rover by armed police. His wife was in the passenger seat, screaming and shouting. Uniformed officers opened her door and tried to get her out. She was flailing about like a lunatic, and one of her shoes flew across the yard. Her language turned the air blue. Spittle shot from the corner of her mouth as she struggled against the officers. Gareth was the opposite. He didn't struggle at all. His expression was that of a condemned man on the way to the gallows.

'I don't think I've heard a woman swear like that,' Kim said, shaking her head. She opened her door and climbed out. 'I've certainly never heard so many c-words in one sentence.'

'She's a Holyhead girl,' Alan said. 'You don't mess about with Holyhead girls. They've got hearts of gold until you cross them.'

'Are you talking from experience?'

'Yes. When I was a young man growing up here, most of my girlfriends were far tougher than me and much better fighters.'

Alan looked at Kim and smiled. He could see cases in the boot of the Land Rover.

'Looks like Gareth and Mrs Pinter were off somewhere,' Kim said. 'And I don't mean Tesco.'

'Let's hope there's something here we can use,' Alan said.

They walked over to the first barn. Officers forced the lock and slid the doors open. Inside was a huge green tractor with a wooden trailer attached to the rear. Next to it was a little red van. They walked over to it. Alan opened the door and took out a clipboard. It was a laundry list and an invoice for the Caernarfon Castle.

'This is our red van from the laundry.'

'And they've left hard copies of invoices for us,' Kim said. 'I think most of it will be done online. Have they got any tablets or laptops with them?' she asked, turning to the uniformed officers behind her. One of them nodded and held up a computer bag. 'Give it to the CSI and asked them to rush it through.'

'Okay, guv.'

Alan looked around and couldn't see anything else relevant. Most of it was agricultural equipment that looked to be in mint condition. So good, it probably hadn't been used. He walked to the next barn. Officers opened the locks and pulled up the roller shutters noisily. Inside were three quad bikes. They were huge. Not the type people ride on the road.

'That's a beast,' Alan said. He looked at the engine capacity. 'A thousand cc. These machines would carry a house.' At the back, he spotted they were fitted with tow-bars. 'How far do you reckon it is from here to the cannabis farm?'

'About five miles to the west,' Kim said. 'It's grazing land all the way. You could tow everything you need to build it behind these things without ever going near a road. It's so remote, no one would notice.'

'No one did,' Alan agreed.

'When we came in, did you notice the other polycarbonate buildings across the fields?'

'I did,' Alan said. 'I think we should have a look, don't you?' he said, climbing onto one of the quads.

'Get another officer and follow us please, sergeant,' Kim said to a uniformed officer. She climbed onto a second machine and they started their engines. The uniformed officers climbed onto the third machine. 'We're going to look at the other buildings across the fields,' she shouted over the noise. The officers nodded and followed as they pulled out in convoy.

The quads made easy work of reaching the other buildings and Alan decided he wanted one for himself although he had no idea where he would go on it. As they neared the structures, the polycarbonate sheds were bigger than they looked, and they were deceivingly long. When he turned the engine off, the hum of electricity became audible and the smell of cannabis was wafting on the breeze. Kim smelled it too and looked at him. Then she looked towards the bottom of the mountain and pointed to more sheds.

'There are three more over there,' she said. 'Let's make sure these are what we think they are then we can drive over and look at them.'

'Okay,' Alan said. He climbed off the quad and they approached the first building. The door was padlocked. 'There's a toolbox on the back of that quad.' A uniformed officer opened the toolbox and routed through, coming out with a pair of bolt cutters. He snapped off the padlock and opened the door. 'You might as well open them all, please,' Alan said. He stepped inside and put his hand over his nose. 'This is skunk. It stinks.'

'This is as big as the one we found yesterday,' Kim said. 'And there's another five. No wonder they were trying to launder the money. I bet they couldn't get rid of it fast enough.'

They walked down the main aisle that ran between the plants. The plants ranged in size. Tallest at the back, almost ready to harvest, younger at the front. It was an impressive set up.

'How many people would you imagine it takes to tend these plants?' Alan asked. 'Imagine when it comes to harvesting the buds. It must take five or six people. There are seven sheds and thousands of plants so who works here?'

'I imagine it's done at night and they harvest continually, which would negate the need to have lots of people working here. I don't think they'll harvest all the ripe plants at the same time. They do it daily and keep a steady production going. If you did it that way, you could do it with three, maybe four people. The irrigation is automated, the lights are on timers. It's low maintenance.'

'Let's get CSI in here. They might find some prints and tell us who works here.'

He walked to the rear of the building but there was nothing to see but plants, plants, and more plants. The smell was making him queasy. Alan made his way to the front door and then walked into the second building. It was the mirror of the first, as was the third.

'Why bury Critchley on your own land?' he asked, Kim.

'Critchley was an informer. He might have threatened to expose this. Although I wouldn't have buried him on my own land.'

'You wouldn't, but not everyone is as savvy as you,' she said. 'No one would have found these farms if it wasn't for Jarvis and McGowan. Maybe they genuinely believed he would never be found. Critchley's body has been there a long time. It wasn't planted recently to incriminate Pinter.'

'I can't help but be sceptical about how we found this. It was as if we were led to it.'

'Guv,' one of the uniformed officers interrupted them. 'You should see this.'

Alan and Kim walked behind him until they reached another door at the side of the building. The lock had been snapped open. They looked inside. A rusted metal bar ran from one side of the room to the other, just below the ceiling. It was bolted in at each end. Two pairs of handcuffs hung from the bar; the bracelets stained dark brown with dried blood.

'Jesus,' Alan said. He imagined Jarvis and McGowan hanging from them. A grid was fixed to the floor at the centre of the room and a hosepipe was attached to the wall. 'They've hosed the place down.'

'I think Pamela Stone will confirm this is where they were interrogated, do you?'

'I don't need her to confirm it but I'm sure she will. We'll nail the bastards with this. They'll go away for life.'

'Who are they, guv?'

'I've got a good idea who works here, and you can't work here and not know what's going on.'

CHAPTER 66

Detective Chief Inspector Kensington wasn't happy. He felt like they'd been forced to pull the trigger prematurely on Operation Thor. DI Alan Williams had run roughshod over their entire case. He'd driven a coach and horses through the lower echelons of the organised networks to find his cop-killers. His strategy had worked. He put pressure on the minor players at the bottom and the house of cards collapsed. The arrests at Caer Rhos appeared to be going well. The killers of Mike Jarvis and Patrick McGowan were cannabis producers on an epic scale. The Matrix officers must have got too close, so they were questioned to see what the police had and then murdered. He was glad DI Williams had captured them but during the investigation, the body of Paul Critchley was found. It was recovered from the same farmer's property, but it incriminated Jamie Hollins for murder. Alan Williams wanted to arrest him as part of their investigation but gave Operation Thor the option to arrest him first. It meant they had to act quickly. Whoever killed Paul Critchley was almost a secondary priority.

'We're all in place, sir,' the coordinating officer said over the radio.

'Go, go, go,' Kensington said. He was anxious. It was the culmination of years of undercover work and millions of pounds of public funding for which he would either get a kick up the arse or a pat on the back.

* * *

Jamie was looking out of the window of his flat, above the South Stack pub. He wasn't surprised to see the arrival of the police in great numbers. Armed police entered the building through the front and rear entrances, followed by uniformed officers and detectives. Three evidence vans pulled up on the car park next to pub, and a CSI team parked across the road. He sipped his tea as the armed officers moved noisily through the pub. He heard heavy footprints on the stairs. There was only a minute or so to act. He took out his phone and texted Tony John although he had a feeling Tony would be handcuffed in a police car already. They would take all his employees in first, squeeze them for information and offer them a deal to squeal on their boss. He didn't think anyone would take a deal, no one would dare. Getting a shorter sentence wouldn't help if they were dead. It was better to say nothing, take your punishment and live. Prison was a dangerous place, especially for a grass. They didn't live very long. The door burst open and the storm troopers charged in, screaming at him to kneel and put his hands up. Jamie sipped his tea first and smiled, then he kneeled. The officers were shouting at the top of their volume.

'Can you stop shouting, please?' Jamie asked. 'I can hear what you're saying and you're giving me a headache.'

'You'll have more than a headache if you give us any of your shite, Hollins,' the lead officer said. Another officer was reading him his rights. 'We've been waiting for this for a long time. You're going down, sunshine.'

'I'd like to make my phone call, please, officer,' Jamie said. 'I need to call my solicitor. I'm afraid I won't be saying anything until I've spoken to him.'

'You're going to need more than a solicitor to help you. You'll need a magician.'

'I don't need a magician, but I will need to speak to Superintendent Wallace from the National Crime Agency. He's the only one I'll speak to.'

'What are you talking about, Hollins? He's nothing to do with this investigation. You'll be interviewed by the officers in charge of this operation. You're not in charge anymore, sunshine.'

'Neither, are you. I'm afraid, I won't be saying a word until Superintendent Wallace has heard what I have to say. There're higher powers than North Wales Police.'

'Oh, really?'

'Yes. The National Crime Agency are.'

'You're a smart arse, Hollins, but you don't know what you're talking about.'

'The NCA are calling all the shots these days, you boys are just the plod to them. Dibbles with a big stick and a big mouth but you control nothing.'

'Shut up.'

'I won't be shutting up anytime soon. So, I suggest you speak to your superior; that will be Detective Inspector Kensington and tell him you'll need to get in touch with Superintendent Wallace as a matter of urgency.' Jamie smiled. 'You've only got twenty-four hours to hold me and the clock is ticking, tick-tock, tick-tock, tick-tock.'

* * *

Owen Evans was trying to change the oil in a Renault. The drain plug was rusted solid and he was trying every trick in the book to shift it. Drilling it out was the last resort but it wasn't what he wanted to do. Daisy was working on two of Jamie's cars in the other bay. The radio was on, the kettle was on, and it was warming up outside. Summer was on the way and summer made everything better. He could spend time with the wife and kids, making the most of the beaches and coastal paths. Just when it seemed life was taking a turn for the better, three police cars and two vans screeched to a halt outside. Owen stood open-mouthed as armed police officers exited their vehicles and trained their weapons on the two mechanics. He was confused at first until he looked at Daisy, but Daisy was texting like a maniac. This was Jamie Hollins' fault. There was no doubt about it. He'd never done anything illegal in his life and yet policemen were pointing nine-millimetre pistols at his head. What else could it be? The police officers were screaming at him to put down the wrench and kneel. He closed his eyes and wished he was somewhere else and then did as they said.

'Owen,' Daisy shouted over the melee.

'What?'

'Don't worry,' Daisy said, smiling. 'They won't find a thing.'

CHAPTER 67

Lee Punk was peddling his bike as fast as he could. His missus wasn't talking to him again but there was nothing new there. She hated what he did for a living but he didn't hear her moaning when she was in the supermarket with a trolley full of food and drink or buying shoes on eBay. Bringing up children was an expensive hobby and where else could he earn a living? He was forty-something with a nose ring, tattoos, and dreadlocks. His benefits covered the rent and electric and not much more. To eat and clothe themselves and their kids he needed to work, and his profession was acquiring good quality weed and selling it to his regular customers at a profit. It was illegal but it was honest. He didn't rip anyone off, and he didn't steal from people or hurt anyone. There were plenty of traditional careers that were far more unsavoury than what he did. Politicians for one; bunch of dishonest lying toe-rags. At least he didn't lie to anyone, except the police of course, and the missus. Sometimes, she wound him up and got above herself. He was a good man trying to do the best by his family. She needed to show a bit of appreciation.

He checked his watch and swore beneath his breath. There was a lot to do today. He'd promised Gareth he'd harvest sheds two and three. They were ready to be cut. He liked harvest days. Gareth would weigh what they harvested and pay him, never thinking Lee had kilos of skunk in the lining of his coat and his bike frame stuffed full of cannabis leaves and stalks. Some people loved smoking them. Gareth classed it as waste that he pulped and threw away, so Lee would rescue whatever he could sell.

As he cycled past Llaingoch Primary School, he noticed the first police car in the distance. Then he saw a second and a third. He turned off the road and took a footpath which skirted the farm on its way to Rocky Coast. The path led to an asphalt road, which climbed to a knoll where he could see over the farm. He stopped and felt sick. His heart sunk to his feet. The farm was crawling with police and CSI teams. Plants were being dragged from the sheds and thrown into the back of trucks like rubbish. They had no idea of the care which had gone into nurturing those plants or what their value was. Idiots. He was watching his livelihood go down the toilet. It was sickening. He wondered if Gareth had been arrested or if he'd managed to skip before they were raided. He had a few of the uniformed boys on the books to warn him of any raids, not that he could do much apart from vanish. They couldn't move the volume of plants they had. If they were raided, they ran, simple as that. It was always the gamble. They'd had fifteen years without a single blip and not a sniff of the police suspecting anything. Gareth's uncle Will had started it all off, all those years ago when he started renting out lodges on the farm. One of the tourists, who came regularly, was a cannabis grower from Manchester. They became friendly and he educated Will in setting up a grow. It was so remote, they built up the farm shed by shed until it was producing tons. Over the years, Will had buyers all over the country and they made money.

Everything was fine until Will started to decline. Gareth took over but wasn't as bright as his uncle. He knew how to propagate cannabis plants like no one else he'd ever met. He had green fingers which could grow plants higher and bushier than anyone else. It was a skill which had made them millions of pounds and kept Lee Punk and his family in a fashion no other employer could have done legitimately. It looked like the Pinter dynasty had come to its final chapter. Lee thought about hanging around until the police were finished, then he could scavenge the sheds and barns to see if there was anything of value left. It was tempting but too dangerous. There was nothing to link him to the operation but if he got caught on the site, he would be part of the conspiracy to cultivate and distribute cannabis on a commercial scale. That was big time in prison and his missus wouldn't put up with him doing time. She'd always been clear about her position on him being arrested and jailed. She wouldn't wear it and she wouldn't wait for him, nor would he see his kids until they were old enough to make their own minds up. The consequences of being caught on the farm were far too great. It was the end of an era and he would have to sit down and plan a future. He had the knowledge and skill to grow weed, if he could find an empty premises where there were no prying eyes. They would be few and far between, but it was a preferable option to getting a job. Lee took a last look at his livelihood being dismantled and turned his bike around.

'Hello, Lee,' Alan said. 'We thought you might show up here. Did you work for Gareth Pinter?'

'No comment,' Lee said.

'Okay. Arrest him. We'll let Gareth know we have you in custody. He'll be worried you'll give evidence against him.'

'He knows I won't say nothing.'

'You need to have a good think about that, Lee. You're not just looking at conspiracy charges. You're looking at three conspiracy to murder charges,' Alan said. Lee frowned and looked confused.

'I don't know what you're talking about.'

'Really?' Alan said, scratching his chin.

'Yes. I don't have a clue.'

'Paul Critchley?' Alan said. 'You know him, don't you?'

'He left town ages ago. People said he was a grass.'

'He was a grass and he ended up buried in a hole in the top field but don't pretend you don't know that,' Alan said.

'I don't know anything about that.'

'How many kids have you got?' Alan asked. He paused. 'They'll be dads themselves by the time you get out. You'll become a granddad in a prison cell.'

'I don't know anything.'

'You can't kidnap and string up police officers and throw them into the sea to drown.'

'Police officers?' Lee said. 'You mean the ones pulled out of the bay?'

'Yes.'

Lee looked stunned but he didn't reply. Alan watched his reaction. His words had the desired effect. The best thing to do was plant the seed and then let him stew in his own juice. He might not have been actively involved in the kidnap, but he may have seen something out of the ordinary. Something that didn't mean anything at the time but becomes clear with the gift of hindsight. Staring down the barrel of some serious charges tended to add clarity and loosen the tongue. Kim put his arms behind his back and Alan saw a tattoo on his forearm. It was a portrait of the scarecrow character from the late seventies and early eighties, Worzel Gummidge. That made sense. The detectives who had been tasked with following him took him to their car and put him in the back seat.

CHAPTER 68

Alan and the team were sitting in the operations room at Holyhead Station. Pamela Stone had just arrived to talk through the evidence before Gareth Pinter, Jamie Hollins, and their crews were interviewed. The sound of chatter filled the air as the team swapped information. Alan ended a telephone call with Dafyd Thomas and sighed. There was a lot to think about.

'What did Dafyd have to say?' Kim asked. She wiped her nose with a tissue. Alan could see she wasn't well but she would soldier on. She was a tough one although he didn't want the whole team coming down with a virus. He would keep an eye on her.

'They've taken Jamie Hollins and his cohorts to St Asaph,' he said. 'Hollins is playing games.'

'What's he doing?'

'He's refusing to say anything to anyone except Director of Operations Wallace.'

'He's National Crime Agency, isn't he?' a detective asked.

'Yes,' Alan said. 'At the top of the tree.'

'Why would he do that?'

'Wallace is the direct link to Interpol and Europol. Hollins might have something he can use to soften the blow.'

'He's clever if he's bypassing DCI Kensington. That will piss him off. What does that mean for Operation Thor?' Kim asked. She shrugged. 'The wheels could come off the entire operation.'

'That's what happens when people underestimate the value of communicating with the local force. They've been arrogant and that might bite them on the arse.' Alan sipped his tea. 'Anyway, Hollins isn't my concern for now.' He turned to Pamela. 'Thanks for coming in. Where are we?'

'That depends where you want me to start,' she said.

'Wherever you like.'

'Let's begin with the Adams evidence.' She flicked a curl behind her ear. 'The blood on the sweatshirt taken from the Price home is from Kelvin Adams and the mud on Price's jeans matches samples from Porth Dafarch.'

'Yes!' A cheer rippled through the gathering. Some of them shook hands. Pamela waited for them to calm down.

'We've also found trace in the Price's vehicle recovered from the airport. There's blood on the driver's seat matching Adams and grass and pollen common to the range.'

'So, we're in no doubt, Glen Price killed Adams,' Alan said. 'His motive is the money the group made selling cocaine at the car plant. What information did you get from Merseyside about Derek Kio?' he asked Simon.

'We spoke to an officer who was in the Matrix unit for ten years. He remembered Derek Kio, and he said Kio bought his coke from an Albanian outfit based in Manchester. They were making a play to get a hold in Liverpool and Kio was a good customer. He said they were investigating a senior police officer who was orchestrating the deals for the Albanians at the time, but nothing came to fruition. Professional Standards Department looked into him but couldn't nail him.'

'Did we get any names?' Kim asked.

'Not on the internal investigation, obviously. The Albanian outfit was run by Agon Domi,' Simon said, checking his notes. 'Apparently, he was forced out of Tirana by his own bosses for being too brutal. They sent him here to oversee operations in the UK to get him out of the way.'

'Too brutal for the Albanians?' Kim asked.

'Yes. He had a thing for disposing of people in barrels of acid, usually still alive. Apparently, he disposed of a judge and sent the photographs to his colleagues. It upset the status quo so they moved the problem here.'

'Check with DCI Kensington and see if the name is connected to the outfit we're looking at,' Alan said. 'They might not be the same. If they are, it doesn't look good for the Trents. I hope Barry Trent and his wife are on a beach somewhere although, I doubt it. Let's hope Agon Domi and his crew didn't get hold of them.' He slurped his tea and emptied the cup. 'Is there anything back from the Caer Rhos farm yet, Pamela?'

'Yes. I've got the initial report on Paul Critchley. He was beaten badly and then his throat was cut. Judging by the amount of blood taken from the soil, he was buried there soon after he died. Probably immediately after his throat was cut. The angle of the cut suggests he was kneeling down next to the grave, the killer standing over him at his back. Then he was cut and pushed into the grave to bleed out.'

'So, we need to work out who put him there and why,' Alan said. 'There're are no shortage of suspects. We know Critchley informed on a robbery that was planned by three brothers, Andy, Mathew, and Thomas Hall. A dealer called Hanney was killed during the robbery and the brothers were arrested at the scene. Critchley vanished a week later. We know where he ended up but who put him there?'

'The brothers were popular. They worked in the pubs in Trearddur Bay and Valley. Thomas and Andy were chefs in the Bull and the Driftwood and Mathew was the bar manager at the Beach Motel. They had a big family and a lot of friends,' Kim said. 'There would be a long line of people wanting revenge.'

'But would any of their friends have the knowledge and knowhow to take Critchley and bury him on the Pinter farm?' Alan asked. Kim shook her head. 'Probably not. I think whoever killed Critchley, did it because he was an informer, not because of the Hall brothers. That narrows it down somewhat. Who had the most to lose? Hollins? Gareth Pinter?'

'The DNA recovered from the belongings found near Critchley, all match Jarvis and McGowan as does the blood found on the handcuffs in the shed and the trace we recovered from the drain,' Pamela said. 'We recovered some cigarette butts too. There's DNA on them but no match in the system. Get me someone to match them to and we can put them there.'

'So, they were definitely tortured on that farm?' Kim asked.

'Yes. And it can't be a coincidence that the UCs' belongings were buried so close to Critchley. The chances of that happening by chance would be in the millions-to-one. We'd have to assume whoever buried Critchley, buried their belongings in the same spot too,' Pamela said.

'Why do that?' Alan asked. 'Why put all the evidence against you in one place?'

'Unless you want it all to be found at the same time,' Kim said.

'Exactly. If you wanted to make us look in the wrong direction, you would figure out a way to make us stumble across Critchley's body. Suddenly, the focus is on Gareth Pinter.' Alan studied the faces in the room. Most of them agreed with the possibility that their find was too good to be true. 'What about the cannabis taken from the farm?' Alan asked.

'It's the same strain as the samples Jarvis and McGowan bought in town.'

'Okay. Do we have anything that can put Gareth Pinter or Lee Punk in the room where the UCs were held?' Alan asked.

'No, not yet but we're still working on the trace.' Pamela shook her head. 'They did a good job of washing the place down.'

'Thanks, Pamela,' Alan said. 'We've got enough to have a first run at Pinter. Let us know as soon as you get anything else, please.'

'I will,' she said, standing. She put her laptop away and put on a long black bubble-coat. 'Good luck.'

As she was leaving, Kim called after her, 'Pamela, what's been found at Jamie Hollins' property?'

'Absolutely nothing,' she said. 'The pub and his flat were totally clean. DCI Kensington had a warrant drafted for a garage owned by a guy called, Owen Evans but that was clean too.'

'Owen Evans?' Alan said. 'I've known him since he was a teenager. His dad fixed all my cars when I was a lad. Why would anyone link him to Hollins?'

'The information was that Hollins was using it to launder money but there's no money trail and no evidence at the garage. They searched it with the drug dogs and money dogs and found zilch.'

'Where did the information come from?'

'I believe it came from an informer. Turned out to be a wild goose chase,' Pamela said. 'I'll call if we get anything else.'

* * *

Eric Stott was reading the newspaper and drinking tea from a pint mug in the Empire Café. He always took his own mug and a newspaper in with him. The news was full of the copycat murders and the reign of terror imposed by Peter Moore in the nineties and by his modern day protégé. He remembered Moore being arrested as if it was yesterday. It was a long time ago but that's how life goes by. Blink your eyes and suddenly you're fifty, wondering where it all went. The murders were in late 1995— he was jailed after killing four men in as many months. It was big news in Holyhead back then. The small port town could lay claim that Wales' only recorded serial killer owned and operated the local cinema. Everyone talked about buying a ticket for a film, a choc ice or a bag of Maltesers from the murderer, even if they hadn't been there for years. There was a macabre excitement about having been close to him and some people milked it for all it was worth. Lots of people said they had known there was something not right about Moore. He was creepy and odd looking and so on and so on. Eric remembered *Toy Story* was released that November because he had bought a couple of pirate copies for his video shop and they were rented out for the following six weeks. He remembered Moore too, with his Nazi moustache and piercing eyes. It was always in the eyes.

Moore had been a freak of nature, but this copycat was far more twisted. What made someone wake up and want to copy that? There had to be something intrinsically wrong with the way their brain was wired. Were they born that way or did life twist them into something unholy? What turned them into monsters? Something germinated in his mind. It was an echo from the past; it prickled his conscience. There was a voice saying, what if...

CHAPTER 69

Gareth Pinter looked devastated. He looked like a rat in a trap, eyes frightened and darting here and there. Alan and Kim sat opposite him and his brief. Her name was Gilly Something, from a practice in Liverpool and she smelled like the perfume counter at Boots. There didn't seem to be any single scent; it was a mingle of sweet and spice. Alan introduced themselves for the tape and then took off his jacket. He undid the top button of his shirt and loosened his tie. Gilly Something was scribbling in her notebook. He wondered if she was reminding herself that her client was one of the biggest cannabis cultivators Wales had ever encountered and that she should put her hourly rate up. He could clearly afford to pay top dollar.

'Okay, Gareth,' Alan said. 'I think we should put our cards on the table and let you see how much trouble you're in.' Gareth shrugged but didn't speak. 'The charges for commercial cultivation of cannabis will be significant and I'm right in saying you don't deny growing it?' He shrugged again. 'I need you to speak for the tape, please. Do you deny growing cannabis on your farm at Caer Rhos?'

'No.'

'Good. Everything at the farm, including the buildings and contents will be seized while the investigation continues.'

'Have you locked the house up?'

'There are fifty police officers there,' Alan said. 'Your property will be secured when the search is completed.'

'Make sure they do,' Gareth said. 'I'll sue you if anything is broken.'

'I think you're underestimating how long you're going to be locked up for, Gareth,' Alan said, calmly. 'There's a dead body buried in your field. Can you tell me how Paul Critchley ended up buried on your land behind shed four?'

'I don't know,' Gareth said. He became agitated. 'That's nothing to do with me. I haven't killed anyone.'

'He was beaten and tortured and then his throat was cut, and he was buried in your field.'

'Not by me, he wasn't.'

'Did you know him?'

'I knew of him.'

'Did you know he was an informer?'

'Everyone in town knew he was a grass,' Gareth said. 'That doesn't mean they all wanted to kill him. He was no threat to me.'

'You had more reason than most to remove a police informer.'

'How do you work that one out?'

'You had a huge operation. People like Critchley get people like you put inside.'

'Critchley wasn't Sherlock Holmes. He was a retard. He only ever repeated what he'd heard from someone else. Nobody trusted him. He would never have had a Scooby Doo about me or the farm.'

'You seem to know a lot about him, suddenly.'

'You hear bits and pieces. It's a small town. I didn't know the man.'

'How did he end up on your farm then, coincidence?'

'I don't know. You're the detective, work it out.'

'Let's say we believe you for a moment. Who else works on your farm?'

'No comment.' Gareth grinned. Behind the sarcastic grin was a frightened man, Alan could feel the fear and uncertainty oozing from every pore.

'Lee Punk works for you. Roberts is his real name, right?'

'No comment.'

'Anyway, we've got Lee Roberts in custody. We'll be interviewing him this afternoon. He looks very nervous indeed.'

'I've never heard of him.'

'Come on, Gareth. Do you think we were born yesterday?' Alan asked. He sat back in his chair. 'If you lie to us, the courts will throw away the key.'

'No comment.'

'Tell us what happened to Mike Jarvis and Patrick McGowan in the washroom?'

'Who?' Gareth frowned. He looked confused.

'They were undercover Matrix officers from Merseyside. They were hung up from a bar by handcuffs and tortured at your farm.'

'I have no idea what you're talking about,' Gareth said. 'I grow weed. I don't kill coppers. Do you think I would bring coppers to my own farm if I was going to kill them?'

'Where else would you take them?' Alan said. 'It's remote there. There're no nosy neighbours to see or hear anything. You've been getting away with murder there for years, pardon the pun.'

'Why would I want to kill policemen?' Gareth asked. He blushed red, getting angry. 'They've legalised the stuff I grow. It's only a matter of time before the government are building farms like mine. I had nothing to do with their murders.'

'I think you realised they were staying at your hotel, which is a front, and you panicked.'

'No comment.'

'You thought your money laundering operation was about to be uncovered so you kidnapped them, questioned them, and then threw them in the sea.'

'I have no idea what you're talking about.'

'Your uncle set up a company, Sundown Property Management, which is registered at Caer Rhos farm.'

'That's not a crime, is it?'

'That company owns the Caernarfon Castle and Cemaes Laundry Services. Jarvis and McGowan got too close, probably by mistake. So, you removed them from the picture,' Alan said. Gareth looked at his hands. 'Tell me you don't launder your money through the company.' Gareth looked at Gilly Someone. She whispered in his ear.

'No comment.'

'Making a no comment interview now won't do you any favours in court,' Alan said. 'If you didn't kill them who did?'

'No comment.'

'Okay. We'll leave it that for now,' Alan said. 'Interview terminated. Let's have a word with Lee Punk Roberts, shall we?'

Gareth smiled and yawned, stretching his arms above his head. Alan felt like punching him in the face but resisted the temptation. It was all front. Underneath the bluster, he was shitting his pants.

* * *

Alan and Kim were waiting in the interview room when Lee Roberts was brought in. Lee was a bundle of nerves. His brief was a local duty solicitor who looked way out of his depth. Kim was taking the lead on his interview but a sniffle had turned into a full-blown head cold. She wasn't feeling one-hundred per cent. Lee was chewing his nails when he sat down. Alan introduced everyone for the tape and nodded to Kim.

'Are you nervous, Lee?' she asked. He looked at her as if she was an alien. 'There's no need. Just be honest with us and you'll be fine.'

'Wouldn't you be nervous?' he said. His hands were shaking. 'This is the second time you've locked me up and I've not done anything.'

'That's not strictly true, is it?' she said, sniffling. She wiped her nose with a tissue. 'You've been cultivating tons of cannabis and selling some of it in the pubs in town.'

'That's all I've done. I water some plants and make sure they're growing properly. Do I look like I'm making millions out of it?' he moaned. 'I ride a push bike for God's sake. I admit selling a bit of weed here and there but I haven't done anything else. I'm just a working bloke trying to make a living.'

'Okay, Lee. We take your point. How long have you worked for Gareth Pinter?'

'I worked for Will before he got sick,' he said. 'Gareth's uncle. He was a top bloke. I worked for him. He took me on about fifteen years ago when no one else would give me a job. I worked the farm. He had sheep and cattle back then.'

'When did they start growing cannabis?'

'About the same time. That's why he took me on, you see. I was growing a couple of plants in my loft and my weed had a good reputation in town. Will approached me one night in the George and told me he was going to plant a grow. A big one. He reckoned he had a customer in Manchester who would buy as much as he could grow. And he said he needed someone who knew what they were doing with the plants. He said he'd been asking around and people were saying my weed was the best. So, I said yes, obviously.'

'Obviously,' Alan said, nodding.

'It's all right for you,' Lee said. 'Your parents had money, and they made sure you went to school.' He pointed his finger. 'I remember you. And I know your sons, too. You had a good education, I left school with nothing. I did what I did to feed my family, so don't sit there judging me.'

'I'm not judging anyone,' Alan said. 'I was being quite genuine. If I'd been in your position, I probably would have done the same. A job is a job and you had a talent for it.'

'Are you taking the piss?' Lee asked.

'No.'

'He isn't taking the piss, Lee,' Kim said. 'So, fifteen years ago, you started tending the plants for Will Pinter and selling some of it in town?'

'Yes. It was good stuff and I had a steady supply. Will sold it to me at cost. But it wasn't much. I only ever sold enough to pay the bills and keep the wife happy. I just want a quiet life.'

'Tell me about why they call you Worzel,' Alan said.

'What?'

'The tattoo on your arm. And the nickname.'

'I was a punk when I was young. So, I was a bit scruffy in the eighties. My mates used to call me Worzel. You know what it's like here. The name stuck. But I preferred Punk, so it wore off over the years.'

'We interviewed a lot of the cannabis sellers in town. They all gave your name,' Kim said. 'They all said you supply them.'

'So, what? I've not denied selling it. They will say my name because most of them buy from me, including your lads,' Lee said, shrugging. Alan nodded and smiled. Lee didn't understand his reaction. 'Your lads buy weed from me.'

'I'm aware of that,' Alan said. 'Buying it to smoke in a cigarette is different to growing it in sheds as big as a football pitch, Lee.' Lee looked frustrated. 'What we're asking you about is the big league. You and your boss are at the top of the tree.'

'I'm not at the top of anything,' Lee said, shaking his head.

'I think you're underestimating yourself,' Alan said. 'Our investigation identifies you as the main supplier of cannabis in Holyhead. You're the hub between the farm and the smaller dealers.'

'What does that mean?' Lee asked. He looked defeated.

'Don't worry about that for now. You sold cannabis to Mike Jarvis and Patrick McGowan on six occasions,' Kim said. 'We have them recorded in evidence.'

'So what?' Lee shrugged again. 'I've admitted selling weed. They approached me in a pub and asked me for weed, so I sold it to them. I didn't know they were Dibble.'

'You are the link between them and your boss, Gareth Pinter,' Alan said.

'What are you talking about?' Lee blushed.

'You sold dope to undercover officers.'

'Yes. I've admitted that.'

'Did you get suspicious of them and tell your boss about them?'

'No,' Lee said. He shook his head. 'I didn't give them a second thought.'

'You're lying,' Kim said. 'I think you saw them snooping about town, going from pub to pub buying from different people and you realised what they were up to. So, you told Gareth.'

'Bollocks,' Lee snapped. 'I didn't say nothing to Gareth. I never say anything about selling weed to Gareth because he gets funny about it. He's paranoid that I'm telling everyone where I get it. I tell everyone it comes from Liverpool. I've never talked to Gareth about it. We hardly talk at all, to be honest. He's an odd bloke but he leaves me alone to do my job. He pays me on time and doesn't give me any shit but that doesn't mean we're mates or anything. I tell him nothing.'

'Someone did,' Alan said.

'Well, it wasn't me.'

'Did you notice them around town, apart from when they bought weed from you?' Alan asked.

'Notice them, like what?'

'You know. Town is a small place, most of the pubs are locals, used by the same people, week in and week out. You'd notice new faces, especially faces who had bought cannabis from you.' Lee shook his head. 'Especially people from away. The pubs are empty nowadays, you would notice them, wouldn't you?'

'I noticed them around a few times. So what?'

'You noticed more than that,' Alan said. 'You noticed them buying from other people, didn't you?'

'I might have. So what?'

'People rarely buy from lots of different dealers, it's too risky. You thought it was odd and became suspicious, didn't you?'

'I didn't think about it, to be honest. I don't care what anyone else does.'

'You did think about it,' Kim said. 'You did notice, and you told someone what you'd seen. You discussed them with someone.' Lee didn't answer but he blushed again. 'You feel guilty, Lee, don't you?'

'Guilty about what? I haven't done anything.'

'You feel guilty because you said something to someone that got those men killed.' She let it sink in for a few seconds. Lee started to sweat. 'They were hung up and tortured on the farm where you work, Lee. It won't take much for a jury to agree you're involved in their deaths. You're an accomplice in three murders.'

'Are you mad?' Lee asked. 'I didn't kill anyone. I wouldn't do anything like that. I'm not a bad man.'

'Maybe not. You don't come across as a killer,' Kim said. 'Someone else did the actual killing so, tell us who you talked to about them?'

'I didn't talk to anyone about them.' Lee was panicking. It was obvious he was frightened. 'I didn't say anything to anyone.'

'We don't have time to waste, Lee. This is your last chance,' Alan said. 'You noticed them about a lot and you noticed them buying different drugs from different people. You were suspicious, so you told someone about it. Who did you talk to about them?'

'I didn't.'

'You're going to go down for murder, Lee,' Alan pushed. 'Do you want to see your kids growing up through prison bars when they visit you?'

'Jamie Hollins,' Lee said. He was wringing his hands. His bottom lip was quivering. 'I talked to Jamie. I didn't mean anything by it. I just said they were odd.'

'What did Jamie say?' Kim asked.

'Nothing. He told me not to worry about it.'

'Did you ever talk to Jamie about the farm?' Alan asked.

'Yes. Sometimes. I trusted Jamie. He never told anyone anything I said.'

'Did he ever come to the farm?'

'A couple of times when Gareth and his missus were on holiday. He said he was thinking about setting up a farm on the mainland. I showed him around a couple of times and showed him the setup, how the lights and irrigation work,' Lee said. His eyes filled with tears. 'I'm sorry those men were killed but I had nothing to do with it. I didn't know that would happen, honestly.'

'Interview terminated,' Alan said. 'That's enough for now. Thank you.' They stood up and left the room. Lee looked distraught—his solicitor looked bamboozled. They walked down the corridor and up the stairs in silence. Alan believed Lee had nothing to do with the murders, even if he'd inadvertently fingered the undercover officers. It was one of the hazards of the job. Staying undercover in a small town was impossible.

'How are you feeling?' Alan asked.

'I feel like shit.'

'You look like shit.'

'Thanks.'

'You're very welcome.' He patted her on the back. 'Go home, have a hot toddy and get some sleep.'

'I'm all right.'

'You're not all right.'

'I believe he didn't tell Gareth Pinter, do you?' she said, changing the subject.

'Yes. I do.'

'Alan,' a voice shouted from behind them.

'Yes,' he replied, turning around. A uniformed sergeant beckoned him.

'There's an Eric Stott on the telephone, says it's urgent.'

Alan thought about saying he was busy. It wasn't a lie. He was busy but as he said earlier, it was arrogance to ignore local knowledge. 'I'll be there now,' he said. 'I'll follow you in a minute. Finish up and go home and get some rest.' Kim nodded and walked on. Alan went to the reception desk and picked up the landline. He could hear Eric's booming laugh on the other end.

'Hello,' Alan said.

'Hello,' Eric said. 'Let me go somewhere quieter.'

'Okay, no rush.' He heard his electric scooter whirring.

'That's better,' Eric said. 'I've been following the Peter Moore copycat story in the news.'

'There's plenty of it to follow,' Alan said. 'I'm not sure how much of it is true but there's plenty of it. How can I help you, Eric?'

'You might think I've lost my marbles, but an old rumour came back to me this morning. It might be nothing but I just felt I needed to tell you,' Eric said, lowering his voice in a conspiratorial tone. 'Do you remember the Trudie Watkins case?'

'Yes. A young girl raped and murdered. The killer was an Iraqi illegal with mental health issues. You're going back a bit there, Eric. Why are asking me about that?'

'Because they asked for all males between seventeen and sixty to volunteer their DNA. Do you remember?'

'Yes. I remember that.'

'Did you work the case?'

'No. I was seconded to the Met for four years. The wife wanted to try living in the big city.'

'How did that work out?'

'Just another nail in the coffin,' Alan said. A twinge of sadness touched him. 'Tell me about this rumour.'

'Okay. There was a rumour going around at the time that a security guard from the Road King truck stop had a hit on the database,' Eric said. 'But it wasn't the killer's DNA. Not that killer anyway.'

'I'm not following you.'

'The rumour was, his DNA matched as a close relative to another killer.' He paused. 'But not just any killer—a serial killer. Peter Moore.'

'He was his son?'

'That was what they were saying. His mother said Moore raped her.'

'How true was this rumour?' Alan asked. On the face of it, it didn't mean a jot but the skin on the back of his neck began to crawl. Something rankled. 'Where did it come from?'

'It came from a detective sergeant who lived in Rhosneiger. He's dead now. I checked.'

'How did you check, Eric?'

'Facebook,' Eric said.

'Have you mentioned this to anyone else?'

'Not yet.'

'Please don't, Eric. Not until I say it's okay.'

'Okay.'

'What was the man's name?'

'Trevor Young. He lived with his mother on Newry Street for years. I think he still does.'

'And he's a security guard at the truck stop?' Alan asked. He knew they wore dark uniforms, not unlike the police.

'Yes. He's worked there for years. Proper little Hitler by all counts. He's not very well-liked—not many friends, if you know what I mean.'

'Thanks for the information, Eric,' Alan said. He felt his pulse quickening. 'It's very important this doesn't leak out. I know I can trust you to keep this quiet for now, can't I?'

'Of course, you can.'

'Thanks again,' Alan said. He hung up and thought about the news. Being related to someone didn't mean anything yet all the alarms in his head were ringing.

CHAPTER 70

Alan walked into the operations room, a puzzled expression on his face. Kim spotted him and made him a cup of tea, taking it to his desk. She went back to the kettle and made herself a lemon drink laced with paracetamol. He thanked her and sipped it. She stirred her lemon and waited for him to settle before speaking.

'What was so urgent?' she asked.

'I'm not sure,' Alan replied. He turned to face her. 'You look awful, go home.'

'I'll drink this and see how I feel. Tell me what Eric said.'

'He was reading the newspaper this morning, when he remembered a rumour from years ago.'

'I love a good rumour,' Kim said. Alan told her what Eric had remembered.

'You're joking?'

'No. He was a direct hit to Peter Moore. Trevor Young is his son.'

'Our Peter Moore has a son?' she asked, taking it in. 'I wouldn't have thought women were his thing. I had him down as a homosexual with mental issues.'

'Maybe he was. The mother claimed she was raped. In the cinema, where she worked for him.'

'That fits with his profile,' Kim said. 'Rape would be right in his psyche.'

'She kept it a secret for years. Trevor Young didn't know who his father was until the DNA test hit and he was interviewed by detectives. The detective who interviewed him was from Rhosneiger but I don't remember him. I was in London back then. Anyway, he blabbed and the rumour spread but it was years ago and it died off just as quick as it started.'

'Look him up on the PNC.'

'I will. You look him up on social media and see if we can get an image. If we can, give it to Alice's team and tell them to doublecheck all the images they've collected to see if he's on any of them,' Alan said.

'Okay.' Kim checked Facebook. 'He has a profile but it's inactive. I've got a picture though.'

'He looks like Moore without the shit moustache,' Alan said.

'Why is it shit?' Kim asked. She frowned. 'Have you ever had a moustache?'

'I have,' Alan said. 'My brother-in-law, Tim, used to call me, Alan-half-tash.'

'Why did he call you that?'

'I have absolutely no idea.'

'I'll send this to Alice. You do know we're getting excited about a very creepy coincidence, don't you?'

'Yes. That's what I thought. It has no bearing on our case, yet I think we should speak to him, just for peace of mind.'

'We most definitely should,' Kim agreed. 'Do you have an address?'

'No. Somewhere up Newry Street.'

'Newry Street,' she said, surprised. 'My car is parked on Newry Street.'

'That's probably how she got the job at the cinema. It's a hundred yards up the road.'

'I'll get the number,' Kim said, searching the Internet. 'We should go there right now.'

'I think so too,' Alan said. 'I'm not sure if it's not just morbid curiosity but something is niggling at me. We don't have anything to get a warrant, we'll just have to wing it. Get Bob to send a uniformed patrol to park in the street, just in case.'

CHAPTER 71

Alan knocked on number fifty-five Newry Street. Kim was standing to his right and an unmarked police car was across the road with three uniformed officers inside. Another was positioned at the rear, just in case. He didn't expect any fireworks but he had no warrant and needed to bend the rules slightly. There was no answer. He knocked again and looked through the letter box. There was movement upstairs. He saw thick calves at the top of the stairs and closed the flap before they could see him spying. The door opened and a ruddy faced carer looked at them, annoyed at being interrupted.

'Yes. What do you want?'

'I'm Detective Inspector Alan Williams, this is Detective Sergeant Davies. Can we speak to Trevor Young?'

'No. He's at work.'

'Is his mother here?' Alan asked.

'His mother is three-sheets to the wind,' the carer said. Alan frowned, confused as the what that meant. 'She has dementia. Advanced dementia. She doesn't know who Trevor is, most of the time. What is this about?'

'No need to worry about it,' Alan said. 'We're just trying to talk to everyone who works in a security role on the island. He still works at Road King, doesn't he?'

'Yes. He's been there since it opened. I'll tell him you called.'

The door slammed closed and Alan sighed. He looked at Kim and shrugged. They walked away from number fifty-five to his BMW. She coughed and wiped her mouth with a tissue.

'We're going to the truck stop, aren't we?' she said. Alan shook his head.

'We're not going anywhere,' he said. 'Get in your car and go home. I need you on your game tomorrow. Get some sleep and I'll see you in the morning.' She tried to protest but he refused to listen. 'Go home and that's an order.'

'Okay, okay. I'll tell uniform to follow you there.'

'I'll be fine. It's a busy place. I just want to look into his eyes. I'll call you later. Get some sleep.'

CHAPTER 72

Kim called at the supermarket and picked up some paracetamol, wine, and a cottage pie. She had veg in the cupboard although cooking wasn't top of mind. It had been a long week and her cold had wiped her out. Her reflection in the mirror looked ten years older than it should do. She was probably rundown by the long hours she'd been working. The case had taken a toll on her. Her eyes were sore, her throat was sore, and her head was aching. Alan was right, she looked like shit. Her bed was calling to her, telling her to climb in and sleep, like a siren calling a ship onto the rocks. She knew if she closed her eyes, she wouldn't wake up until the following day.

When she pulled up outside her terraced house, the windows seemed darker. The sun was fading quickly, casting shadows from the trees. A movement in the downstairs window caught her eye but when she focused on it, the shadows shifted as the boughs of the trees swayed on the breeze. The twigs curled and uncurled like skeletal hands waving a warning. A shiver ran down her spine and she felt uneasy. It was her cold giving her the shivers, what else could it be?

Kim turned the engine off and opened the door. A cold breeze blew through her clothes, touching her skin with icy fingers. She grabbed her handbag and the shopping and walked to the front door. The houses either side were empty, holiday homes rented out through the summer. She welcomed the tourists when they came, and she welcomed the peace and silence when they went home. She craved the proximity of other humans in the dead of night. It was during the long dark hours that her fear of the dark came to fore. She'd been scared of the dark since being a child but had hidden it well as an adult. It was different when there were tourists next door. She felt safer despite there being a brick wall between them. Knowing someone was close by was a comfort. Sleeping alone had its downsides, especially if she woke up in the middle of the night when her mind was racing. Every creak and crack was an approaching predator or worse still, a ghost or phantom or zombie. The fear was completely irrational yet it was a fear and it was real. She was a seasoned detective in the daylight hours, a five-year-old girl at the dead of night.

The door opened and she closed it behind her, dumping her handbag on the stairs. She carried the shopping into the kitchen and plonked it on the worktop. It was dark and gloomy. She switched on the lights and felt a chill. The central heating was on a timer but she'd narrowed the hours of operation to save money. She opened the boiler cupboard. Something sprang towards her and she jumped back. Her mop fell out and landed on her feet, making her gasp. She muttered beneath her breath, cursing herself for being such a wimp. Her heart was beating faster than it should. She couldn't understand her anxiety. Was it working on the Anglesey murders or the copycat killer, or something else? She flicked on the boiler and turned up the temperature. It came on with a whoosh. She heard a bump upstairs and looked at the ceiling as if her eyes could penetrate it. It was silent again. There was nothing but the hum of the boiler.

Kim emptied her shopping bag and opened the wine. It was merlot tonight. She poured a large glass and sipped it. It was nice but she could barely taste it because her nose was blocked. She filled up the kettle and switched it on. She was going to take a hot lemon drink and a glass of wine to the bathroom, shower and then crash on the bed and watch a movie for as long as her eyes would stay open. The kettle boiled and she ripped open a sachet of lemon powder and added it to a cup, pouring hot water onto it. It would be too hot to sip for a long time. She put her cottage pie in the fridge, resigned to not eating tonight. Food was not the priority. Sleep was.

She reached the bottom of the stairs and switched on the light. Nothing happened. The bulb remained off. She swore and tried the switch again. Nothing. Upstairs was in darkness. Kim swigged her wine and stormed up the stairs. Her pulse was racing as she climbed into the darkness. She didn't like it one bit. As she reached the landing her foot caught the top step and she tripped, trying hard not to spill her drinks. She lost her footing for a moment and only maintained her balance when her shoulder hit the bedroom doorframe.

Kim used her elbow to switch on the bedroom light. She was going to step in when the urge to pee interrupted proceedings. The bathroom was to her left. She stepped inside and put the light on, putting her drinks down on the side of the bath. A smear on the mirror caught her attention and a sour smell tainted the air. She couldn't wait—pulled her pants and knickers down and sat on the loo. The seat felt warm. Too warm. Much warmer than it should have been in an empty house. The smell was excrement. Someone had taken a dump on her toilet, recently. Very recently.

There was someone in her house. She reached for her trouser pocket and felt for her mobile. It wasn't there. She racked her brains but didn't recall taking it from the cradle in the car. Adrenalin coursed through her veins and she prayed for her pee to stop. She listened intently but couldn't hear anything. Was this just a case of her nerves on edge because she didn't feel well? Her nerves didn't warm the toilet seat or smell of shit. Burglars did that. She wiped herself and pulled up her clothes, moving slowly and listening, her senses on overdrive. A creaking floorboard made her freeze. She held her breath, frightened to let it out. The bathroom door was wide open. She could lock it and wait it out, hoping the burglar would flee in panic but something told her he wouldn't. The window wasn't wide enough to escape through and she would be trapped. Her sense of dread was immense. She felt sick. Her mind raced, looking for a plan.

She reached over the bath and switched on the shower. It was four big steps to the top of the stairs and then she could bolt for the front door. She took a breath and closed her eyes. One, two, three, she counted in her mind and then she ran. She reached the top steps and cleared three without thinking, instinct driving her on. She was halfway down, then her heart stopped in her chest. Her mouth opened wide—a scream lodged inside. A man was standing at the bottom of the stairs, smiling. The smile was that of a mad man. It was Trevor Young. He was holding a large hunting knife in his right hand. She stopped dead in her tracks and turned to run back up the stairs. The sound of his footsteps behind her struck terror into her brain. She screamed although no one could hear her. He was only three steps behind her.

CHAPTER 73

Alan pulled into the car park at the truck stop. Across the road, a huge Premier Inn had just opened. The surrounding fields were full of sheep grazing and dotted with ancient standing stones. The truck park itself had about forty trucks on it. The barriers were manned by security guards. Two of them were chatting near the entrance. Alan approached them and they eyed him suspiciously. He flashed his warrant card and they relaxed.

'I'm looking for Trevor Young,' Alan said. The men looked at each other. A silent communication passed between them.

'He swapped his shift today,' one of them said.

'When is he back in?'

'You'll have to ask Rosie. She's the gaffer.'

'Rosie Lyons?' Alan asked. 'Is she still here?'

'Yep. She's the boss.'

'Where can I find her?'

'She'll be inside running the show. If not, she'll be in the office. Ask for her at the counter.'

'Thanks,' Alan said. He was tempted to ask about Young. But he had no grounds to ask and he didn't want to spark off speculation among his colleagues. That wasn't fair. The fact his father was a bad man didn't mean he was. He walked inside the cavernous café. There was a pool table near the door. Two truck drivers were playing and drinking pints of beer. There were thirty or so diners and the place still looked empty. He approached the counter and spotted Rosie. He hadn't seen her for a while but she looked the same—but older. Everyone looked older nowadays, he thought. She spotted him and her face lit up with a smile. 'Hello, stranger,' Alan said.

'Hello, Alan,' Rosie said. She came around the counter to speak to him. They hugged briefly and she kissed him on the cheek. 'How many years has it been?'

'Too many.'

'I haven't seen you in here before,' she said. 'Is this business or pleasure?'

'Business. I'm looking for Trevor Young.' He was purposely vague.

'He swapped his shift. He's been struggling lately with his mum being so poorly.'

'When is he back at work?'

'Is he in trouble?'

'No. I just want to talk to him.'

'Monday,' Rosie said. 'He's got some holidays to take so I told him to take them. He's got a new woman so I'm being nice. Do you want a coffee or something?'

'I'll have a tea,' Alan said.

'Sit down over there,' she said, pointing to a quiet area. Alan went to the window and looked out. Rosie came over and put two cups on the table. 'So, what's the gossip?' she said, smiling. She had an infectious smile.

'Gossip? Some things never change, Rosie.' He laughed.

'You can't beat a good jangle,' she said.

'You said Trevor has a new woman,' Alan said.

'Yes. Her name is Kim something or other. He's been prattling on about her all week.' She put her hand over her mouth and whispered. 'I can't remember the last time he mentioned a woman. I think he's a virgin,' she chuckled. 'I suspected he didn't like women for a while but then he asked me out, the cheeky bugger.'

'I bet you were in there like a shot, not many virgins around here.'

'I'm not that desperate, yet, cheeky bugger!'

'Seriously though, I bet that was awkward,' Alan said. The name Kim was echoing around his head. 'What's he like, between you and me?'

'Odd,' she said. 'Very odd indeed. He's polite enough and very reliable, just odd.'

'Odd how?'

'I thought he wasn't in trouble,' Rosie said. 'Are you telling me fibs?'

'No. He's not in trouble. His name came up in something we're investigating. I just need to chat to him. It's nothing serious.'

'Excuse me, Rosie,' a waitress said, nervously.

'What's up?'

'Chef says if he doesn't get a break soon, he's going to die of exhaustion.'

'Tell chef to stop being dramatic. I'll get him covered in a minute.' She turned back to Alan. 'Sorry. I'll have to get back, lovely to see you again. Call in and we'll have a catchup.'

'That would be great,' Alan said. He stood up and headed for the door. Alan felt anxious. He didn't know why. He dialled Kim's number but she didn't answer. She might be in the bath or asleep. Alan couldn't accept either explanation. Trevor

Young had been talking about a woman called Kim. It didn't sit right. He got into the BMW and head towards town.

CHAPTER 74

Kim cleared the top of the stairs and sprinted for the bathroom. Young was seconds behind. She ran through the door and slammed it closed behind her, trying to lock it. Young barged the door with his shoulder and it opened six inches. The knife hand came around the door, slashing and stabbing at thin air. She screamed and tried to shut the door on his wrist, but he was too strong. She felt the pressure lift for a second and then he barged the door again. This time, it opened further. The knife was coming dangerously close to cutting her. She looked around for inspiration. He pushed the door hard and knocked her backwards. She staggered and fell into the bath, cracking her skull on the tiles. Blood flowed and lights exploded in her mind. The shower was still running, making everything slippery. She couldn't get out. He was on her in a flash. The knife sliced the top of her right arm; burning pain seared her brain. Blood ran in the water towards the plughole. He stabbed again, this time the tip pierced her stomach above her hip. The pain was intense and she squealed. His weight crushing down on her was sapping her strength. She would die here, if she did nothing. Her hand grasped at nothing, desperate to find something to use as a weapon. She found her cup and she flung the hot lemon into his face. He cried out as the liquid scalded his face and he fell backwards, banging the back of his head on the toilet cistern. Blood trickled down the porcelain.

Kim struggled out of the bath, arms and legs flailing wildly. She could hardly catch her breath. Young was stunned. He was on his back on the floor. His eyes were closed. Kim grabbed the wine glass and threw it at him. It caught him under the eye, causing a gash. He didn't move. Kim looked for a second and ran for the door. She looked back. His eyes blinked open and focused on her. He smiled like a lunatic and jumped to his feet. Kim was at the top of the stairs when she heard him behind her. He roared in frustration. She used the handrails to support her as she sprinted down the stairs, taking them two at a time. The front door was in sight. Freedom was just a few yards away. She could outrun him and reach the street.

Young stopped at the top of the stairs and grabbed the blade end of the knife. He threw it hard. It spun through the air and hit Kim between the shoulder blades. The blade penetrated deep into the muscle, between her ribs, and punctured her left lung. It felt like she'd been hit with a sledgehammer. Her knees buckled and she collapsed in a bloody heap against the front door. She reached behind her and tugged at the blade, pulling it from the wound. White hot pain zipped through her nervous system like lightening through a conductor. She felt blood flowing down her back.

Young was on her like an animal, punching, kicking, and biting. He scratched her cheek with his nails. She felt his teeth on her neck. They pierced the skin and ruptured muscle. Kim screamed and pulled away, but he was frenzied and he was strong. He grabbed her hair and smashed her head against the door. There was a dull thud and she felt her brain bouncing off the inside of her skull. The pain was blinding. She screamed for help as he cracked her skull on the floor tiles. A deep gash opened up and blood ran into her eyes. He pulled her head up once more, higher this time. This time would crush her skull for sure. She twisted but couldn't break free. He bit her ear and she could feel the gristle cracking. She lashed out and stuck the knife into his throat, under the chin. His eyes widened in shock. His muscles failed and he toppled forward, his own weight forcing the blade deeper, through his tongue and up into his brain. His body went limp and his eyes dulled. He stared at her accusingly. Kim felt her blood leaking from her wounds. She was weak. Her strength was completely sapped. She felt her grip on the knife loosen. Her eyes were heavy. She tried to move him but she couldn't. Darkness descended and she lost consciousness.

CHAPTER 75

Jamie Hollins was brought from his cell into an interview room. Director of Investigations Harry Wallace from the National Crime Agency was sitting across the table. He was in deep conversation with another suit. Jamie nodded hello to his brief, an organised crime specialist called Ralph Gladstone. Gladstone's client list read like a who's who of regional gangsters. He sat down and shook hands with him.

'Who is this?' Jamie asked, gesturing to the suit.

'Rupert Biggins from the Home Office,' the man said. He looked down his nose at Jamie.

'I want to make it clear, we're not here to make deals or break any rules,' Wallace said. 'Anything you tell us today, will be considered and we will inform the judge you were cooperative at sentencing.'

'You can stick consideration right up your ring-piece, Mr Wallace,' Jamie said. 'What I'm about to tell you will blow your head off and get you promoted so we either do this or we don't.' The sinews in his thick neck twitched like wire beneath the skin. 'You can verify anything I say and if I'm lying, lock me up and throw away the key. If it's the truth, I walk away from here and you'll never hear from me again.'

Wallace looked at Biggins. Biggins nodded.

'You've got a major problem with our Albanian friends,' Jamie said. 'Agon Domi is the main man.'

'We know that,' Wallace said, deflated.

'I should hope you do,' Jamie said. 'But do you know he's been paying a senior police officer a percentage of their take for over ten years?'

Wallace and Biggins looked on stony-faced. 'I assume you have a name or is this a fishing trip?' Wallace said.

'Detective Chief Inspector Kensington, head of North Wales Drug Squad,' Jamie said. 'He was part of the north west's Regional Organised Crime Unit and a senior officer for Titan. He's been protecting them for a cut of their profits. I can give you bank account details, telephone numbers, dates, times, and associates.'

'How have you acquired this information?' Biggins asked.

'Because I like to know what's going on around me and make sure that I know everything about my enemies, Mr Biggins. I do my homework. You should do yours. Mr Gladstone has a memory stick in his possession which contains everything I have on DCI Kensington. Obviously, I have copies which I can leak to the press if at any time you try to shaft me. Are we clear?'

'Let's see what you have,' Wallace said.

Ralph Gladstone reached into his pocket and handed over a memory stick. Wallace took it and opened the door. He was gone for ten minutes before he returned. He closed the door and sat down.

'It appears to be genuine,' he said.

'It is genuine,' Jamie said. 'Now, about the Albanians. Agon Domi has an industrial unit in Irlam, Manchester. You will find him and most of his associates there. They store automatic weapons and grenades in a void beneath the fridge in the kitchen. Their drugs are stored in a wall-space behind a shelving unit next to a desk he uses for paperwork. Their money is in a safe behind the desk. Only Agon has the code.'

'How do you know all this?'

'Reconnaissance. I do my reconnaissance. I pay people to give me information. Here's a beauty for you,' Jamie said, smiling. 'Agon Domi took Jarvis and McGowan to Pinter's farm, tortured them, and chucked them in the sea. And he killed Paul Critchley.'

'What?'

'You'll find text messages from him to this number on his phone records,' Jamie said, writing the number down. 'Check the number. It was one of the phones Critchley used.' Jamie sat back in his seat. 'I'm not a detective but I would say whoever buried your undercover officer's gear where you found it, also buried Critchley, wouldn't you?'

'It's likely,' Wallace agreed.

'Mr Gladstone told me you recovered DNA from cigarette butts buried with their belongings,' Jamie said. Wallace shifted uncomfortably in his seat. 'Okay. You didn't know that, did you?' Wallace shook his head. 'It doesn't match anyone in the system because they're not in it. Kensington had their details removed. Test Agon and his cronies, and you'll put them at the scene.'

'Are you sure about this?'

'Positive. I'm giving you the proof. On top of that, I'm prepared to state Agon Domi told me in confidence that he did those officers.'

'And you'd testify to that?'

'Not in open court but if my identity is hidden, yes.'

'Why are you giving him up?' Wallace asked.

'Simple, I don't like the bastard.' Jamie leaned forward. 'There's a workshop there. Underneath a workbench near the window is a hatch which leads to the basement. Agon has a thing about dissolving people in barrels of acid. If you're really lucky, there might be a couple of his latest victims in there. Lloyd Jones and Ron Took are still missing. They're probably still alive because Lloyd owes him money. If they are, they'll be in that basement. I guarantee it.'

'That will take a few hours to organise,' Wallace said. 'I'll need an address and an idea of the opposition we'll encounter.'

'No problem,' Jamie said. 'Take your time. I'm not going anywhere.'

CHAPTER 76

SIX WEEKS LATER

Alan parked on the driveway and turned off the engine. The dogs were going ballistic against the glass. Kim walked into the living room and waved through the window. She had an apron on, which made him laugh. Her attempts at cooking tea had been apocalyptic. She cooked lamb chops on one side, leaving the other side raw and bloody and her beef curry was like spicy charcoal. He had been polite and tried it, then ordered a takeaway. She was trying because she was bored. Being on sick leave was driving her insane. He walked to the front door and she met him in the hallway and wrapped her arms around him. She kissed him on the lips and it felt nice. More than nice, it felt right. It felt like something he'd missed for a long time and he glowed inside. Nearly losing her had been the catalyst to tell her how he felt about her. He loved her, simple as that.

'Have you had a good day at the office?' Kim asked. He laughed and squeezed her. 'Ow!' she cried. He let her go quickly. 'I've been stabbed you, clumsy bugger.'

'Sorry, I forgot,' Alan said grimacing.

'You forgot I was stabbed?'

'No. I forgot it still hurts.'

'Don't forget again,' she said, kissing him.

'Will you two get a room,' Dan said, coming out of his room.

'I have got a room,' Alan said. 'It's next to the bathroom but I actually pay for mine. It's called a mortgage. You should get one.'

'I've just got one, actually,' Dan said. He hugged his dad and walked into the kitchen.

'Did he just say he's got a mortgage?' Alan asked Kim.

'Yes. He told me earlier,' she said.

'Bloody hell,' Alan said. 'Where is he going?'

'Go and ask him.'

Alan walked into the kitchen. Kim followed him and poured two glasses of red wine. His consumption of whisky had stopped when Kim came out of hospital. He had done it himself without any prompting from her and he felt better for it. She said staying at his house was temporary so Alan could look after her while she recovered but she was still there.

'Where are you going to?' Alan asked.

'I've bought a house on Holbern Road,' Dan said. 'It's a five-bedroom at the top of the street.'

'One of the old guest houses?' Alan said.

'Yes. When Jesus was still alive.'

'Five bedrooms. At least you can put your brothers up when they fall out with their girlfriends,' Alan said. 'Kris will be made up.'

'I'm hoping to be there in a month or so. You can help me paint it, if you like.'

'I'm busy that day,' Alan said.

'Funny,' Dan said. He emptied a tin of beans onto a plate and stuck it into the microwave. 'I heard from Lee Punk today,' he said.

'Oh really. How is he coping?' Alan asked, sipping his wine. He felt a twinge of guilt, which was odd. Locking up your son's friends wasn't pleasant.

'Okay. He said his missus has been to see him and she's said she's not leaving him, so he was buzzing. And he got to see the kids.'

'What has his solicitor said?'

'He's looking at five years, probably be out in two. Gareth is looking at twelve depending on the DTO. How does that work, Dad?'

'They estimate how much money was made from crime and ask for it back. If they can't or won't pay, they convert it into jailtime and add it to their sentence. Trouble is, there's no parole on DTO time.'

'We won't see him anytime soon,' Dan said. His beans dinged and he took them out. 'Lee said Jamie Hollins is looking at twenty-years. Is that right?'

'I haven't heard anything about Operation Thor since the SIO was arrested.'

'Has Kensington been charged yet?' Kim asked.

'They've charged him with everything they can think of and some more. His arrest has thrown every conviction he's ever been involved in, into question. There will be appeals left, right, and centre going back decades.' Alan sipped the wine again. 'It brings the entire operation into question. I'll be surprised if everyone arrested in Thor isn't released on appeal.'

'Even Jamie Hollins?' Dan asked.

'They've seized his properties and gone through the motions, but we'll have to wait and see. Apparently, it was his information which led to GMP arresting the Albanian mob for killing the UCs and recovering Lloyd Jones and Ron Took. Who knows what will happen?' Kim looked at him and shook her head. He knew exactly what she was thinking. Hollins had been very smart. Very smart indeed. 'What is that smell?' Alan asked. 'Something is burning.'

'Oh shit,' Kim said. She opened the oven and a cloud of black smoke spiralled skywards. Alan and Dan laughed. She took out a charred lump of smoking substance. 'Steak and kidney pie, anyone.'

'Where's the takeaway menu?' Alan said.

EPILOGUE

Holly Jones was watching the news and eating scrambled eggs and bacon. The item was covering the murder of a couple in Cambodia. Glen Price, a British man and his Thai girlfriend were found stabbed to death in a beach hut in Sihanoukville—a beach resort in the south. According to the reporter, Price had left the country with his long-term girlfriend, Stephanie Mortimer, but she'd been homesick and left him after a few months. They played an interview with Stephanie as the one who got away. She came over as a nice lady, very smart. They were pitching the story as a mystery as Price had been wanted by the police for the murder of his wife and a colleague and he'd allegedly stolen money from an Albanian organised crime gang. She thought it sounded like he was a sleaze bag who got what was coming to him. Everything comes out in the wash, it always does. She took another forkful of breakfast and chewed it, washing it down with a mouthful of coffee. Her phone rang and the screen showed a withheld number.

'Hello,' she answered.

'Holly. It's Jamie.'

'Wow,' she said. 'How are you?'

'I'm fine.'

'Where are you?'

'I can't tell you that.'

'Okay. I've been watching your Facebook to see if you post anything. I thought you might get a mobile smuggled inside.'

'I'm not in jail Holly but I can't tell you where I am because you're a grass.'

'What are you talking about?'

'You're an informer.'

'Don't be stupid. You know me.'

'I thought I did.'

'I don't know why you're saying that.'

'Because I told you I was storing gear with Owen Collins at his garage.'

'So what? You told me lots of stuff.'

'But I wasn't storing gear there. It was a test, you see?'

'No.'

'I needed to know who was leaking information to them. The Dibble raided the place and searched high and low, but they didn't find anything because there was nothing there. There never was.'

'I don't know what you mean, Jamie.'

'You were the only one who knew. You told the police. You're a plant.'

'I'm not.'

'You know what happens to a grass, Holly.'

'I'm going to hang up now and if you call me again, I'll call the police.'

'Call them,' Jamie said. 'I've got away with murder before, I'll do it again. See you soon, Holly.'

THE END

AUTHOR NOTES

In the early 80s, Alan John Williams started dating my sister, Kath. They were married and brought up 3 sons, Kris, Dan and Jack, who have grown into men, that I'm proud to know. Alan quickly became a close friend to myself and my brother Tim and was more like a brother than an in-law. Alan died in 2018 and we all miss him. Writing, The Anglesey Murders is my way of keeping him around for a while. It makes me feel closer to his memory. I've kept his character as close to his as I can and I think he would smile if he read it.

We've lost some good friends along the way. Tony Doutch is one of them. He was my best friend as a teenager and he's often in my memories. Reading through the edits, he's weaved into the story without me realising it. That happens sometimes when you're in a creative bubble. Fiction and reality merge into the ages. I miss Tony so it's okay he's in there. Any likeness to anyone else is purely coincidence.

To read the 2nd book, A Visit from the Devil;
https://www.amazon.co.uk/gp/product/B07YN3TVDK

or to read the entire boxset for less than £6.00;

https://www.amazon.co.uk/dp/B08122Z9RQ

Printed in Poland
by Amazon Fulfillment
Poland Sp. z o.o., Wrocław

63619106R00155